The German Mother

BOOKS BY DEBBIE RIX

The German Mother

Debbie Rix

Bookouture

Published by Bookouture in 2023

An imprint of Storyfire Ltd.
Carmelite House
50 Victoria Embankment
London EC4Y 0DZ
United Kingdom

www.bookouture.com

ISBN: 978-1-83790-190-6
eBook ISBN: 978-1-83790-189-0

For my mother

Particular attention should be paid to the Press... with ruthless determination the State must keep control of this instrument of education and place it at the service of the State and the Nation.

ADOLF HITLER, *MEIN KAMPF*

PROLOGUE

The authorities had given the child a new name soon after she arrived. She had lost track of how long she had been there but knew she had been nearly ten years old when they had first brought her here, because she had been looking forward to her tenth birthday party. Her mother had promised cake and games. Here, no one celebrated their birthday. No one made a cake or bought anyone a present. As a result, ages, like names, became unimportant. Survival was all that mattered. 'You've been lucky,' they told her, but she didn't feel lucky.

Her duties were simple but relentless. At five she rose, washed her face and hands, and put on her uniform – grey serge with a grey cotton apron. Once dressed, she went to the dining hall – an echoing white room with a high ceiling and a polished floor. Its windows had been bricked up, so the time of day, or of year, had no meaning. The only light came from overhead metal light fixtures. Breakfast was laid out on a steel trolley and consisted of a small piece of bread and glass of milk. The child ate alone at a long refectory table.

After breakfast she worked down in the subterranean

laundry in the basement until bedtime. Here she boiled sheets, pulling them out of the scalding water with tongs as long as her arm. After that she pushed them through a mangle, turning a large wooden handle to squeeze out the water, and hung them to air on the overhead rails. Once dry, they were ironed, folded and stored. Storing was her favourite part of the day, for she was allowed out of the steaming basement, to wander the shabby corridors, pushing a trolley of folded linen, delivering it to the wards and staff bedrooms.

The child had learned to avoid the eyes of the other inmates. Most of them were troubled; many wailed or screamed as if in pain. All were painfully thin. It upset her to see them suffering so, particularly the other children. Most swiftly disappeared. The little Jewish girl with nut-brown eyes, who had cried herself to sleep, was gone within days. She was told the child had died suddenly and had been buried in the hospital cemetery.

And so, she learned to close her mind to the suffering of others. Survival was all that mattered. She had shown herself to be willing and able, and in the end, they had let her live because 'she was one of the lucky ones'.

At night, her subconscious took her to places that frightened her – recurrent dreams in which she was being driven through the night, and of children screaming. These nightmares always ended the same way – with her waking in the half-light, a fine sweat on her brow.

One day, something happened that reawakened some small part of her memory. She had been placing piles of folded sheets onto the shelves of the wide cupboard on the upstairs landing when through the window she had noticed a woman with golden hair standing outside the hospital, staring up at the building and weeping. The woman seemed familiar – the cast of her profile, the curl of her hair. The child placed a hand on the glass, and called out; but the woman neither heard, nor saw her. Instead, she turned away, climbed into her car, started the engine and drove off. For a moment, the child felt a rush of sadness and loss that almost overwhelmed her. But her natural sense of optimism rose to the surface. Everything would be all right, she told herself, because *she* would survive.

PART ONE
THE PROPAGANDA WAR

1920–1933

Anyone who spreads his ideology by terror and brutality against all force will one day gain power and thereby also the right to bring down the state.

JOSEPH GOEBBELS, 1926

1

MUNICH

Minki Sommer stood in the grand entrance hall to Munich's Ludwig-Maximillian University, and inhaled the faint scent of furniture polish overlaid with male sweat. For a girl who had been brought up an only child, and had attended an all-girls school, her arrival at this bastion of education was both exhilarating and nerve-wracking.

Born and brought up in Augsburg, Minki was the only child of Greta and Gunther Sommer. Gunther owned a steel factory supplying raw materials for the armaments industry, and his fortunes took an upturn when Germany went to war in 1914. But tragedy had struck a year later when Minki's mother died of cancer. Her father had buried his grief in his work and sent Minki away to a convent school.

When the war was over in 1918, Gunther was gloomy about Germany's financial stability. 'Our economy is totally destroyed,' he often told his daughter. 'If I wasn't in steel, I don't think I'd have survived the last four years. As it is, my business is booming.'

As was the custom at the time, Gunther expected his only daughter to care for him and their house when she left school, but Minki had other ideas.

'I really must finish my education, Papa. I want to go to university and study English.'

'Go to university! What a ridiculous idea. You're a lady, and will one day marry. Until that time you should be at home looking after me.'

'And I *will* look after you, Papa, I promise – as soon as I get my degree. After all, it's what Mother wanted.'

Minki's mother had been a great beauty, and the love of her father's life. The invocation of her name had the desired effect on her father – as it often did.

'I wasn't aware Greta had ever expressed a view about these things,' he replied, looking puzzled.

'Oh yes,' Minki insisted, 'Mutti often said she hoped I'd go to university.' It was not true, of course, but Minki hoped this small lie would be swiftly forgotten. A good Catholic, she would go to confession that evening and ask for forgiveness.

Her father capitulated, but only with the proviso that she lodge with a respectable professor of his acquaintance. And so Minki had got her way – the first of many such successes, as it turned out – and found herself on the verge of a new independent life away from her controlling father's influence.

Minki's first term at university set the course for the rest of her student life. She worked hard, and quickly rose to the top of the class. Her fellow students were mostly men and, far from resenting her academic supremacy, they were soon under the spell of the tall, willowy blonde with turquoise eyes, and a pale, almost ethereal complexion. Although inexperienced with members of the opposite sex, Minki soon discovered she could use her looks to get her own way. Men seemed powerless to resist her. But it was her sense of humour – and especially an ability to laugh at herself – that made her irresistible to the only other female in the class.

Leila Hoffman was shorter than Minki by a head. She had long wavy dark-brown hair, worn in an untidy bun on top of her head, and kind brown eyes. No one would have described her as beautiful, but she was pretty, with a neat symmetrical face and delicate bone structure. As the two girls grew to know one another, Leila – who still lived at home with her parents – became intrigued by Minki's upbringing, which was so different from her own.

'How old were you when your mother died?' Leila asked one day, as they walked through the city centre after a lecture.

'Thirteen. It's a bad age to lose one's mother,' replied Minki matter-of-factly.

'I'm so sorry,' said Leila, taking Minki's arm. 'I can't imagine the pain of losing your mother at that age. I almost feel guilty that both my parents are still alive.'

'Don't be silly,' said Minki. 'I didn't tell you the story to get your sympathy – it's just part of who I am.'

Their route had taken them past Café Luitpold – a smart establishment in the centre of town, which served coffee and cakes to the well-heeled citizens of Munich.

'Shall we have coffee?' Minki asked.

'I shouldn't really,' said Leila, glancing at her watch. 'I promised my mother I wouldn't be late... besides, isn't it rather expensive?'

'Oh, don't worry about that – I'll pay,' replied Minki, pulling her inside. 'Besides, the food at the house where I live is simply appalling. If I don't have something to eat here, I'll be starving by bed-time.'

They sat at a table in the window and, as she sipped her milky coffee, Minki continued the story of her upbringing.

'I was a late developer in some ways. I had no brothers or

sisters – and so no one with whom to compare myself. Oddly, before my mother died I hadn't seen myself as a young woman, if you understand me. Until that time, I'd just been a "person" – running wild in the countryside, climbing trees... spoiling my clothes. What was wonderful about my mother was that she just accepted this behaviour – she never tried to change me, or complain about the torn blouses and skirts. Instead, she taught me to sew. "If you're going to rip your clothes," she told me one day, "you should at least know how to mend them."'

'After she'd gone...' Minki paused, gazing out of the café window, tears welling up in her eyes, '...I felt utterly bereft. The day she passed away, my father insisted I say my farewells. There she was, lying on the bed, dressed in her best nightgown, as a priest said prayers over her. She looked so peaceful – as if she were just asleep. Instinctively, I leaned over to kiss her, but as soon as my lips touched her cheek I reeled back in shock. Her skin was so cold and clammy and nothing like the soft warm cheek I was used to. I was so upset I ran back to my room and lay on my bed, sobbing for hours. When I got up, there was blood all over my skirt and the eiderdown – my period had started, you see. I was utterly bewildered... lost and frightened. My mother had never discussed these things with me. I suppose she presumed she would be there to explain it all when it happened. Anyway, I changed my clothes and ran down the corridor to ask my mother what to do, but of course she couldn't answer. That's when it really hit me – she was gone forever.'

'How awful for you,' said Leila, reaching across the table, and squeezing Minki's hand.

'My father, of course, was no help. He didn't know the first thing about girls. If it hadn't been for the housekeeper, I'm not sure how I'd have managed. Anyway, as soon as my mother was buried, my father sent me away to a convent. In many ways it was the worst thing he could have done. I felt totally abandoned, and somehow the surroundings – with mass every day, and nuns everywhere – made it worse. I'd prayed for my mother constantly throughout her illness, and when she died I felt God had turned his back on me. What little faith I had left was destroyed at that school.' She paused for a moment, before adding: 'Do you believe in God?'

Minki had observed that Leila never replied to anything without giving it serious thought. Now, her friend screwed up her eyes as she concentrated on her answer: 'I'm not sure,' Leila said at last. 'I was born into the Jewish faith and therefore I am unequivocally Jewish, but whether I'm a "Jew" is a harder question to answer. I believe in spirituality – perhaps in a higher being if you like – but what that has to do with formal religion, I don't know. In the end, as long as you're kind and thoughtful to those around you – nothing else really matters, don't you think?'

'I think,' said Minki, leaning across the table, and kissing her friend's cheek, 'that you are one of the sweetest, wisest people I've ever met.'

Towards the end of their first term the pair joined the university newspaper. They outperformed their male colleagues, in terms of both output and scoops. Each developed their own individual areas of interest. Leila concentrated on the serious issues of the day, writing about politics and economics – searing polemics, often critical of government policy. Minki, meanwhile, focussed on the lighter side of life, writing lively diary pieces, together with articles on the arts.

This early success crystallised an ambition that she had been nursing for some time, and as the long summer holidays approached Minki announced that she intended to become a journalist when she left university.

'I thought you said your father expected you to move back home,' Leila pointed out.

'What he expects and what I will do are entirely different

things. I'm never going home again. After university, I'm going to become an independent woman.'

Leila was impressed. Although her own future was undecided, Minki's certainty that her life would amount to something was inspirational.

At the end of her first year, Minki informed her father that she would stay in Munich over the summer to continue her studies. In fact, she had decided to spend the holiday looking for new, more convivial lodgings.

One afternoon, after a walk in the verdant Englischer Garten, she found herself in a district of Munich called Schwabing. As she delved into the little cafés and shops, she observed how the inhabitants were of a more 'artistic' bent than the normally staid residents of Munich, with their dirndls and polite conversation. Walking down Theresienstrasse, she passed a restaurant called Café Stephanie, and noticed a woman with tumbling auburn curls, who wore a feather boa and fur coat, accosting men in the street. As Minki got closer she was able to hear their conversation. The woman was offering her body in return for money. Although initially shocked by this spectacle, Minki was fascinated. She stopped a few metres further on and lurked in a shop doorway, from where she could watch the woman at work. She seemed so confident and cheerful – laughing with the men, accepting their cigarettes. Most of her potential 'customers' made their excuses and left, but one took her up on her offer, and the pair disappeared inside the café. Fifteen minutes later she saw them emerging back onto the street. As the man slipped away, the woman suddenly called out in Minki's direction. 'Hey, you there, what are you staring at?'

Minki, mortified at being noticed, shrank back into the shadows. 'Nothing,' she muttered, 'I'm so sorry.'

'What's the matter, never seen a woman chatting up a man before?'

'Well, not like that,' replied Minki, more boldly.

The woman threw her head back and laughed. 'Come and show me how you'd do it then?'

'Oh, no,' said Minki hurriedly, 'I really couldn't. Anyway, I have to get home.'

'Don't be such a bore. Come inside and have a drink with me – I won't bite.'

The woman led the way into the café and, in spite of her reservations, Minki followed. There was something intriguing about this auburn-haired creature, with her glamorous clothes and lively manner. The woman settled herself at a table by the window. 'Bring two glasses of port, Gerhard, there's a good chap,' she said to the man behind the bar.

As Minki sat down opposite her, she noticed the woman's green eyes, fine porcelain skin and high cheekbones. She seemed too elegant to be a prostitute, Minki thought, with a fine, almost aristocratic bearing, long delicate fingers and graceful movements. Her accent was unusual too... Russian perhaps.

Although nervous, Minki felt emboldened by her first sip of port. She proffered her hand to the woman. 'My name is Minki Sommer... it's very nice to meet you.'

'I am Franziska zu Reventlow,' replied the woman grandly, shaking Minki's hand. 'I am an artist, but no one has any vision any more.' She sighed as she took a sip of her port. 'So, if my paintings don't sell, I have to sell myself instead...'

Minki blushed. Again, the woman threw her head back and laughed, her auburn curls gyrating. 'Oh, I've shocked the little convent girl.'

'How do you know I went to a convent?'

'It's obvious. I can tell by your clothes – that grey jacket does nothing for you. You might as well be wearing a nun's habit. Plus, your stockings are made of lisle, your shoes are flat and dull. Frankly darling – you scream "convent girl". Am I right?'

'You are. I don't particularly like my clothes – my father bought them for me before I started at university.'

'Didn't your mother have a say in it?'

'My mother died when I was a child.'

The woman's manner changed suddenly, and she reached across the beer-stained table and stroked Minki's cheek. 'You poor little thing. I'm so sorry. To lose your mother at such a tender age must have been dreadful.'

'It's all right,' replied Minki bravely. 'I survived...' She was surprised to see tears in Franziska's eyes.

'You're such a pretty girl – you're wasting yourself in those awful clothes. I could lend you something, if you like.'

'Oh no – I couldn't possibly...' Minki stammered.

'Don't be ridiculous. I have plenty of clothes. Drink up and follow me – I only live upstairs.'

The woman led the way to her room on the first floor. Opening the door, Minki felt she was entering a chaotic but exotic Aladdin's cave. Clothes lay in tangled heaps on the floor. Feather boas and large hats hung from nails in the wall. The pink satin counterpane on Franziska's bed was covered with a selection of pastel satin nightwear. In one corner of the room was an artist's easel, on which stood a half-finished oil painting of a female nude.

'Is this your work?' Minki asked, admiringly.

'It is... Do you like it?'

'It's very good... is it a self-portrait?'

'Of course. I usually paint myself – models can be so diffi-cult and expensive. I'll paint you though, if you'd like.'

'I'm not sure my father would approve,' replied Minki hurriedly. 'Not painted like that, anyway.'

'You're very funny,' said Franziska, laughing. 'You don't care what people think, do you?'

'Not always,' replied Minki, blushing.

'Well now, let's find you a pretty coat.' Franziska rummaged in her overstuffed wardrobe, and finally brought out a dark blue coat, trimmed with a brown fur collar. 'Try this on.'

'Oh, I really couldn't,' said Minki.

'Of course you could! Besides, blue has never been my colour. Try it.'

Minki removed her tweed jacket, and slipped the coat over her cotton shirt and skirt. Standing in front of the mirror, she saw that the colour brought out her blue eyes and the cut of the coat – narrow over the shoulders and waist – fitted her perfectly.

'It is lovely,' said Minki wistfully. 'Perhaps I could buy it from you.'

'Don't be so insulting! It's a gift.'

Minki began to remove the coat. 'That's very kind, but it's also silly. You've already said you're short of money, and I have an allowance – please let me pay.'

'I ought to be offended,' said Franziska, smiling, 'but... all right – if you insist.'

Over the next few days, Minki found herself drawn to the café and often spent time with Franziska.

'What's it like living here?'

'Noisy,' replied Franziska. 'But it's free – so I put up with it.'

'Free? How did you manage that?'

'The patron and I have "an understanding".' Franziska winked. 'He gives me room and board, and I give him what he wants. He calls me "The Queen of Schwabing" – in fact that's what they all call me round here.'

'*I'm* looking for somewhere new to live,' said Minki. 'Are

there any other rooms for rent above the café?'

'Oh, no darling, I don't think that's a good idea. Gerhard, the owner, would think he'd died and gone to heaven if you moved in. No, we'll find you somewhere more suitable. Wait here...'

Franziska walked out into the street, and returned ten minutes later, carrying a key. She slammed it down on the marble-topped table. 'There you are. I've arranged for you to live in the attic above the tailor's shop three doors down. He's a nice man, a widower – but respectable. His son's a bit odd, but he won't be any trouble. I negotiated a good price too.'

'Thank you – I'm so grateful...'

'There's a bathroom of sorts on the landing, and a tiny kitchen. But if you like, you can eat your meals here with me.'

Minki picked up the key and put it in her handbag. 'Why are you being so kind to me?'

The woman studied Minki for a few minutes. 'Perhaps I see myself in you. Even I was young and innocent once.' She smiled, but her face took on a wistfulness that Minki had not noticed before. 'I've not always lived this way, you know. I come from a good family, but sometimes things don't work out quite as one imagines.'

The following weekend, Minki moved into her new lodgings. The room was small but comfortable, and Franziska helped to make it more homely. She lent Minki a couple of her feather boas and a spare counterpane for the bed. Although old enough to be Minki's mother, 'The Queen of Schwabing' behaved more like an elder sister. Over the coming weeks, she taught her new protégée how to dress, how to drink, how to flirt and, most importantly, how to laugh. Minki had never enjoyed herself as much as when she was in the company of 'The Queen'. Soon the café and its inhabitants became a sort of home from home. It was here that Minki enjoyed her first sexual encounter – with a tall, shy young man she had met only a few hours before. Both participants were drunk and the act itself was a fumbling affair that took place standing up in the dark corridor at the back of the café. When it was over, Minki was not entirely sure what had happened. She and the young man soon drifted apart, but the experience, though not romantic, had given Minki the taste for sex. And wanting sex made her one of the crowd – most of the girls who frequented the café and the surrounding area were sexually active. It also filled a void in her life – for affection.

At the start of the new term, Minki invited Leila to her new lodgings. 'It's not exactly grand, and the furnishings are appalling, but at least I can come and go when I please. Living with the professor and his awful housekeeper was like being in jail...'

Light and laughter spilled out into the dusk from Café Stephanie as the two girls turned in to Minki's road. 'Are you hungry?' she asked Leila.

'A little.'

'Why don't we eat here first, and then go and chat in my room.'

As the two girls entered the café, the clientele called out. 'Hi, Minki... sit over here, Minki... Is that your girlfriend, Minki?'

Minki had a cheerful word for all her admirers – laughing, kissing the men on the cheek and hugging the girls. While she stood at the bar, ordering their drinks, Leila sat nervously at a table in the corner. The café was unlike anywhere she had ever been. At one table, two women were kissing one another. Elsewhere, half-dressed women draped themselves over men before disappearing upstairs; even Leila understood they must be prostitutes. Meanwhile, groups of men and women were engaged in heated discussions about philosophy and politics. It was a different world from the staid, cosy environment in which she had been brought up.

Minki returned with the drinks, putting two glasses of schnapps down on the table. 'Prost!'

'Prost,' Leila replied nervously. She had never tasted schnapps before. Her only experience of alcohol had been the occasional glass of sweet wine. Her nose wrinkled with disgust as she took the first sip.

'Oh, don't you like schnapps? I'm sorry,' said Minki.

'It's fine... I'll get used to it.' Leila blushed, feeling foolish. 'What... an interesting place.'

'Well, it's not a respectable restaurant like Café Luitpold, that's for sure. It's much more fun. You're not shocked, are you?'

'No... not at all.' Leila was anxious not to appear too innocent.

Minki reached over and took her hand. 'These people are my friends, Leila – just as you are. What I love about them is that they don't judge – either themselves or me. But they are all interesting and great fun.'

Leila smiled uncertainly.

'I know...' Minki went on, 'why don't we find you a boyfriend. I'm sure there are heaps of men here who'd love to go to bed with you.'

'I don't want a boyfriend,' Leila protested.

'Why ever not? You don't want to leave university still a virgin.'

Leila blushed again. 'What's wrong with being a virgin?'

'Everything!' declared Minki.

In spite of their differences, the two girls were united in two things: their love of writing, and sheer ambition to succeed.

Both were still leading lights of the student newspaper, and within a year Minki had become editor, and asked Leila to be her deputy.

Leila was flattered but uncertain. 'Are you absolutely sure, Minki?'

'Of course,' said Minki. 'You're better than all the boys here. We'll make a fine team.'

Despite the distraction of student journalism, the two friends studied hard and were rewarded with good degrees. On their final day at university, they hugged one another, aware it was the end of an era.

'I can't believe I won't see you tomorrow, Minki,' said Leila tearfully.

'What do you mean? I'm not going anywhere... we can still see each other.'

'But surely your father is expecting you to go home.'

'He might expect it, but I'm not doing it. I suppose he'll cut me off, but I don't mind... I'm already looking for a job here in Munich.'

Leila smiled. 'Why does that not surprise me? But I'm relieved – I couldn't bear the thought of not seeing you again. As for me, I have no idea what I'm going to do with the rest of my life. If my mother had her way, I'd be married to the next nice boy I brought home.'

'Would you like to get married, Leila?'

'Yes, I suppose so... one day. I mean, I want children and a home... is that so odd?'

'No, it's perfectly normal, which I suppose is why I can't imagine myself doing it.'

'Oh Minki... you do say the funniest things. But seriously, you're so beautiful – you're bound to marry one day.'

Minki shook her head. 'Not me... I'm going to be independent, and free of any man. As for you, darling Leila – just listen to your heart, and follow your instincts...'

2

MUNICH

Leila Hoffman stepped gingerly around the puddles that were forming on the pavement. The rain, which had been falling in a gentle drizzle all afternoon, now gushed from the darkening sky, splashing the backs of her calves with mud, and soaking her brown leather brogues. She wished now she had worn her winter boots as her mother had advised that morning. Pulling the belt of her raincoat tightly around her, she took a silk scarf from her handbag and tied it over her hair. She had spent the afternoon visiting her old English professor – a man of great wisdom and integrity – to ask his advice about a possible career.

'I could teach, I suppose,' she suggested as they sipped tea together in his study.

'Teaching is a vocation, Leila. You can't do it if you don't love it.'

She smiled. 'Do you love it, Professor?'

'Absolutely. It's my life – to help young people discover and develop their intellect. So, if not teaching, what else might excite you?'

'Well... if it doesn't sound too silly – I'd like to write.'

'That's not silly at all. You have great skill as a writer, I always said so.'

Leila blushed with pleasure at her mentor's approbation. 'That's kind, but you can't just... become a writer, can you? I mean, novelists take years to learn their craft.'

'Have you considered journalism? You wrote for the university paper, didn't you? I always thought your pieces rather good.'

'Do you really think so?'

'I do. I also think there has never been a more important time for any intelligent young person to get involved with explaining what is happening in our country. We need people who are prepared to stand up for the truth.'

Leila looked up at the old man, searching his face with her dark eyes. 'You think it's really that important?'

'Of course. We live in troubled times, Leila. Have a think about it.'

Heading home in the rain that evening, Leila mulled over what the professor had said. She had certainly enjoyed her time on the university newspaper, but was it really something she could turn into a career? Minki had been looking for work as a journalist since the summer, and as far as Leila knew had so far failed to be offered a job. More worrying, might Minki be angry or envious if Leila chose the same path? She could just imagine Minki's reaction: 'You're only going into journalism because I want to do it and you can't think of anything else.' Now Leila wondered if that might be true. Whatever her professor thought of her abilities, did she really have either the talent, or the determination, to make it work?

And what would her father make of such a career choice? She recalled a conversation with her parents back in the summer after she had been awarded her degree. To celebrate, her father had opened a bottle of wine – a rare treat – and toasted her. 'To my darling daughter. I feel sure you will one day do important work.'

'What do you mean, important work?' Leila had asked.

'I don't know... simply that you'll become a person of importance – a teacher, or doctor, or a politician.'

'Goodness, Papa. I'm not sure how I could become a doctor with an English degree.'

Her father had tutted. 'You know what I mean...'

'To be honest,' added her mother, 'I'd be quite happy if you found a nice boy and settled down.'

Now Leila wondered what her parents would make of her decision. Would her father consider journalism 'important work'?

Lost in her own thoughts, Leila was walking down Marienplatz towards the town hall square when a crowd of men suddenly materialised from the side streets on either side of her. At their head, and shouting at the top of his voice, was an unremarkable-looking man wearing an old dun-coloured raincoat, his hair plastered flat by the rain. Alarmed, Leila ran into the nearest shop doorway, and hid in the shadows. As the crowd ran past, chanting and yelling, they smashed shop windows and jeered at passers-by. Leila waited until the last stragglers had disappeared before ducking out from the doorway and running home as fast as she could. She crossed the river on the Luitpold Bridge and within minutes was rushing down the elegant nineteenth-century street where her parents lived. Once inside the apartment building she ran up the main staircase, taking the steps two at a time. Fumbling with her keys, she finally managed to unlock the door, and literally fell into the hall, panting heavily.

Her mother found her a few moments later, on the floor. 'Leila, darling. What on earth is the matter?' She took Leila's arm and helped her to her feet.

'Oh... Mutti, I was on my way home, and a huge crowd of men rushed past me, heading for the Alter Hof. They were jeering and shouting – smashing shop windows. It was awful. I ran all the way home.'

'You're soaking wet. Take off your coat.' Hannah shook the raincoat on the tiled floor.

'I'm afraid this is wet through as well,' said Leila, handing Hannah her headscarf.

'I'll hang it on the mantelpiece in the sitting room – I've got the fire lit, and then I'll get you some tea – you've obviously had a shock.'

'I hope Papa's all right,' Leila said. 'I think the crowd might have passed his shop.'

Leila's father Levi owned a jewellery business just off the fashionable Marienplatz, and often stayed late after the shop had closed, expertly repairing rings, bracelets and brooches.

'Well, we must just pray he will be all right,' said her mother, disappearing into the kitchen.

An hour passed before the two women finally heard Levi's key in the lock. 'Thank goodness,' sighed Hannah. The pair listened as he went through his normal routine – removing his coat, and stowing his umbrella in the metal stand. But when he came into the room his face was white and drawn.

Hannah stood up, her arms outstretched. 'Levi, darling, you look exhausted. Sit down.'

He sank down into an armchair by the side of the fire. 'I'm glad to see you both here, safe and sound.'

'Did that awful crowd of men come past your shop, Papa?'

'Yes, they did.' He took his pipe out of his jacket pocket and sucked on it, soothing his nerves.

'Who were they, do you think?' asked Leila. 'I got caught up in it too, but managed to get away. It was very frightening.'

'Thank God for that.' Levi filled his pipe with tobacco from the pouch in his pocket. He tamped it down with his thumb, and struck a match. The smoke billowed around his head. 'I was about to close the shop, and had just put the lights out when the mob raced up the road. Thank God I did, because they passed by without incident, but poor Mr Lepmann – you know, the tailor opposite – was still hard at work, and the mob saw him through the window, and hurled bricks through the glass.'

'Through his window?' interjected Hannah. 'But why?'

'Because he is Jewish,' replied Levi matter-of-factly.

Hannah blanched. 'Oh, no... surely not. Who would do such a thing?'

'National Socialist thugs.'

'Was Mr Lepmann all right?' asked Leila.

'He was shocked, of course, but not hurt, fortunately. I helped him clear away the shattered glass, but he was worried people might break in – he has some lovely bolts of cloth in there. We moved most of his stock into the back room and locked it. Then we nailed some old pieces of plywood across the broken window. He said he'd get someone in the morning to replace it.'

'But why are these awful people so angry, and why tonight, Papa?'

'I think they were headed for the Bürgerbräukeller – that big beer hall near the square,' said Levi, relighting his pipe. 'I'd seen a poster earlier in the day advertising a speech by von Kahr – the commissioner of Bavaria. I suspect that crazy Austrian – what's his name, Adolf Hitler? – was on his way there, with his thugs, clearly intent on making trouble.'

Leila was now fiddling with the radio, trying to tune it to get a signal. 'Will there be something about it on the news, do you think?'

'I doubt it,' replied her father. 'The government won't want to give these rebels any publicity.'

'But it's a disgrace,' Leila persisted. 'People should know about it.'

'Of course... but what can we do?' Her father raised his hands and shrugged his shoulders. 'Now, Hannah, what's for dinner? I'm starving.'

Leila was unable to sleep that night. Tossing and turning in bed, she pictured Mr Lepmann trying to protect his stock and his shop; she thought of her father standing in the darkness as the mob ran by, wondering if he would be next. It was a miracle he had not been attacked. Surely, she thought, the government must do something about these awful people. And why were they so angry with Jews in particular? Her father had told her that Jews had lived in Munich since the twelfth century. 'We have as much right to be here as anyone, Leila.' But now, it seemed, their rights were under threat.

What she had seen that day crystallised her decision about her future career. As her professor had said – there had never been a more important time for journalists to expose the wickedness in their country.

Her only worry was what Minki would make of her decision. She hoped she would be happy for her. Perhaps they might even work together one day – as they'd done at university. With that comforting thought she turned out the light, and finally fell asleep.

3

MUNICH

Minki was searching her tiny wardrobe for something suitable to wear. She had finally found a part-time position as the diary editor for a local Munich newspaper, and as a young professional woman she wanted her image to reflect her new career. She hauled out the old woollen skirts and Bavarian jackets that her father had considered suitable when she first started university, and laid them on the bed. The skirts were too long – fashions had changed, and hem length was now firmly mid-calf, or even above the knee. The jackets too were the wrong style, and made of sensible tweed, more suited to country walks than the sort of parties she would be required to attend as a diary editor. Although money was tight, she was determined to rid herself of her past, and new clothes were the first step on that path.

Minki bundled her old clothes up, tying them with a piece of string to take to a second-hand clothes shop she knew. Its owner would always pay a fair price for good-quality clothing, and might even agree to take her old clothes in return for something more stylish.

The shop was on a quiet side street. As Minki approached, her eye was drawn to the mannequin in the centre of the window display, wearing a simple teal-blue shift. Minki decided it would suit her very well.

Weighed down by her bundle of clothes, she greeted the shop owner cheerfully. 'Good morning, Helga. I've brought some things I no longer wear and I wondered if we might do a deal – perhaps swap some of them for the dress in the window?'

Helga smiled. 'Yes Minki... in fact, I thought of you when I bought that dress. A most elegant woman brought it in – similar shape and colouring to you. I'll get it for you.'

While Minki tried it on in the changing room, Helga sorted through the bundle of clothes.

As soon as Minki stepped back into the shop, Helga beamed at her.

'Oh, yes – that's wonderful. Here, try this with it.' She grabbed a long silk scarf in shades of green and blue and hung it round Minki's neck. 'What do you think?'

Minki admired herself in the mirror. 'I like it. Can we do a swap?'

'Yes, of course. In fact, I'll give you a little extra cash too. One or two of your jackets are very good quality... someone will want them.'

Back home, Minki tried on the ensemble again, adding a string of her mother's pearls. She twirled delightedly in front of the mirror. The dress was perfect – it emphasised her blue eyes, and contrasted well with her bright blond hair. All that was missing was a suitable coat to complete the outfit. On her last visit home, she had persuaded her father to hand over her mother's fur coats, still languishing in Greta's wardrobe so many years after her death. Minki knew he was only keeping them for sentimental reasons. 'It's such a shame, Papa... they just hang there attracting moths,' she had insisted.

Reluctantly, her father had agreed, and Minki had returned

to Munich with a silver fox fur coat and a cream mink evening jacket. Minki threw the fox fur coat artfully round her shoulders, and pirouetted in front of the mirror. Gone was the dowdy student – in her place was a glamorous professional woman.

She rushed downstairs to the communal telephone in the hall. 'Leila, come and meet me at Café Luitpold. I've got something exciting to tell you.'

'Oh, don't make me wait till then, tell me now,' urged her friend.

'Oh, all right, if you insist. I've got a job.'

'A real job?'

'Yes, of course it's a "real job". I'm the new social and diary reporter for the *Munich Latest News*. Meet me at eleven?'

Minki rushed outside, only to find that snow had begun to fall. Glancing down, she realised she was wearing her best black suede shoes. She should have been wearing her old leather boots, but they wouldn't go with the dress or the coat, so instead of going back upstairs and changing, she set off across the park. The snow was already thick on the ground by the time she arrived at Café Luitpold. Leila was waiting for her outside, shod in sensible snow boots, Minki noticed. She was stamping her feet to keep warm.

'What are you doing out here, Leila? Let's get inside, I'm starving.'

They settled at a table next to the window and ordered coffee and cakes.

'Tell me everything about your new job,' said Leila eagerly.

'Well, it's not full time, you understand... and, to be honest, it's a crummy little paper, but it's a start.'

'So, what does it entail?'

'Oh... diary pieces, gossip – you know the sort of thing.'

'Well, I'm very impressed. And if anyone knows about gossip, it's you.'

'Is that a compliment? I'm not sure.' Minki laughed.

'Yes, of course.'

'To be honest, it's also a relief. I really need the money. My father has decided to cut me off after Christmas. He thinks that now I've finished my degree I should become the de facto chatelaine of his enormous house in Augsburg until I find a husband.'

'I'm sorry. But we knew that was on the cards. Still, without an allowance how will you afford your rent?'

'That's not a problem. My landlord, the old tailor, is very kind. I'm sure he'll allow me a bit of leeway. And I'll have my salary, of course.'

'You know, if money is tight, you could always stay with me and my parents.'

'That's very sweet, Leila, but I don't think your mother would like it. Besides, I've lived on my own for so long I don't think I could live with other people – I'm far too selfish.'

'You're not selfish at all.' Leila paused, realising that now would be the best time to tell Minki of her own job ambitions. 'I'm glad we met up... because I have something to tell you.'

'Oh yes, what?' asked Minki, sinking her teeth into a slice of chocolate torte.

'I met with our professor recently, to get his advice about what I should do, now we've finished our degrees.'

'And what did he suggest?'

'That I should become a journalist...' Leila glanced at Minki nervously, waiting for her response.

'How marvellous,' Minki exclaimed happily. 'I think it will be grand for us both to be doing the same thing. Have you started job-hunting yet?'

'Well, I did apply to a couple of papers last week, but was rejected by both.'

'Why?'

'Lack of experience was what they said, but I fear it was simply that they would rather hire a man. At the interview, there was a waiting room full of male applicants. But I expect I'll get something eventually.'

'I'm sure you will. You're far cleverer than most men.'

'Minki, you're sure you don't mind about me becoming a journalist too?'

'Of course not! I'll be more successful than you, anyway!' Minki laughed and snatched the last piece of cake from Leila's plate, ate it in one bite, before wiping her mouth on a napkin.

'Now, Leila, I want to ask you a favour. I've been invited to a literary *soirée*.' She pronounced the words with fake grandeur. 'It's being held this evening, at a smart restaurant. Do come with me. I have a pathological fear of going into a room full of strangers unaccompanied. And besides, you never know who you'll meet. Most of the guests will be publishers and writers – one of them might give you a job. I'm certainly hoping I'll find someone who can give me a leg-up.' She laughed uproariously, and lit a cigarette.

Leila had noticed that Minki had a habit of drinking too much at parties and was often reluctant to leave. 'All right,' she agreed finally, 'as long as we don't have to spend all evening there – I've got a couple of application letters to write tonight.'

'We'll leave by nine, I promise.'

The smell of cloves and mulled wine filled the air as Leila followed Minki into the market square that evening. The Christmas market was in full swing and the stalls were packed with enthusiastic shoppers stocking up on seasonal treats like roasted chestnuts and gingerbread.

'Oh, do come on, Leila,' shouted Minki breathlessly over her shoulder. 'I don't want to be late.'

Leila, whose new velvet evening shoes were a bit too tight,

was struggling to keep up. 'You go ahead,' she called out, 'I won't be far behind.'

'It feels like snow,' said Minki breathlessly, peering up into the starless sky. 'I can't believe I'm about to ruin a second pair of shoes.'

The event was being held in a private room above a restaurant in the main square. The noise of party chatter spilled out onto the street. Standing at the bottom of the stairs, Minki looked up and noticed the guests were standing on the staircase, smoking and drinking. Leila arrived a few minutes later and, after checking their coats, the two girls went to the ladies' room to comb their hair and touch up their make-up.

'It looks packed up there,' said Minki, applying red lipstick. 'I can't wait to see who's here.'

'I thought you had a "pathological fear" of parties where you don't know anyone,' teased Leila, tidying her hair.

'Oh, I just said that to make you come with me. Now hurry up – let's get in there.'

Minki ran up the stairs, and plunged enthusiastically into the main room, leaving Leila standing in the doorway feeling nervous and shy. She had a momentary flash of envy at her friend's extraordinary social confidence. After a few moments, a tall man with kind hazel eyes approached her. 'You look a bit lost.'

'Oh, do I?' Leila smoothed the skirt of her emerald green cocktail dress. 'I came with a friend, but she's disappeared already. She's a journalist – looking for gossip, I suspect.'

The man smiled. 'Well, she's come to the right place. The room is full of potential gossip. I'm Viktor Labowski, by the way. And you are?'

'Leila... Leila Hoffmann. Nice to meet you.' She smiled up at him, brushing her hair away from her dark eyes. As he held her gaze for a moment, she blushed in spite of herself. He was handsome in a middle-aged sort of way, with dark hair silvering slightly at the temples. Gallantly, he took her hand and kissed it. 'It's a delight to meet you, Leila. I'm surprised we've not met before. Are you a journalist too?'

'Not yet, but I'd like to be. I've been for a couple of interviews, but no luck so far...'

'Well, I'm sure you'll get something eventually. Let me introduce you to a few people. There are lots of journalists, publishers and editors here.'

Viktor took her by the elbow and ushered her around the room, introducing her to one person after another. Although initially shy, she gradually became bolder and more confident. When she made an intelligent comment, or a witty remark, Viktor smiled at her, she noticed, like a proud parent of a child who had said something clever to the grown-ups at dinner. At a break in the conversation he whispered in her ear: 'See those men in the corner?'

She nodded.

'The one on the left – with the splendid moustache and beard – is called Erhard Auer. He's the chief editor of the *Munich Post*. He's also leader of Munich's Social Democratic Party. Have you approached them yet for a job?'

'No,' Leila replied nervously. 'I imagined a paper as erudite as that would only employ people with lots of experience. Of course – I read it every day.' That wasn't the complete truth, but she did read the paper from time to time.

'Good. Let's go and talk to him. Erhard is a good friend of mine and I'm going to ask him to give you a job.'

'Oh, no, you can't do that. It would be too embarrassing.'

'Don't be silly, how else do you think people get jobs,' replied Viktor, taking her arm and leading her across the room.

'Erhard, I'd like you to meet Leila. She's an eager young reporter and is looking for a job. If I were you I'd snap her up before some other lucky beggar gets her.'

'Oh, Viktor,' said Leila, colouring with embarrassment, 'you do exaggerate.' She turned to the bearded man. 'He's right, Herr Auer – I am looking for a job, but I have absolutely no professional experience – and that's the truth.'

Auer smiled at her. 'Well that's honest, and I like that. And don't worry – I'm used to Viktor's enthusiasm about people. Do you read the paper?'

'Yes, of course.'

'Good to hear. We don't have as much support here in Munich as I'd like.' Lowering his voice, he added: 'Being a Social Democrat in the birthplace of National Socialism is a dangerous business these days.' He smiled faintly, but Leila could see the strain behind his kind eyes. She felt drawn to him.

'We are facing unprecedented pressures,' he went on. 'Hitler's putsch at the bierkeller was just the beginning. These National Socialists mean business and their thugs aren't going to stop. Our offices at the *Post* were subjected to a particularly sustained attack that night.'

'That's awful – but why?' asked Leila.

'Because we are the enemy,' Auer replied calmly. '"The Jewish Newspaper", they call us, or sometimes the "Munich Plague". They want to destroy us – along with every other Jew in Germany.'

'Do you really believe that?' asked Leila.

Auer shrugged. 'You mark my words – it can only get worse—'

'My dear fellow,' interrupted Viktor, 'I didn't know they had attacked your offices – what exactly happened?'

'It's not really suitable party conversation,' said Auer. 'I don't want to alarm the young lady.'

'I don't mind, sir. Please tell us,' Leila insisted.

'Well... on the night of the putsch a group of Hitler's thugs arrived at our offices, demanding entry. My business manager, Ferdinand, who lives in the flat on the top floor, came downstairs and was held at gunpoint until he agreed to open up – the poor man was terrified. Once the gates onto the street were unlocked about two hundred of Hitler's storm troopers poured into the courtyard, armed to the teeth with pistols, rifles and even hand grenades. The place was completely surrounded and Ferdinand had no choice but to open the main doors. Once inside, they ransacked the place – cutting the phone lines, smashing desks, knocking over filing cabinets, and throwing ink on the walls. After smashing all the panes of glass in the windows with their rifle butts, they threw our papers and files – even our records with details of our subscribers – out into the street and set fire to them. They stole our typewriters and quite a lot of cash. Then they broke into the garage and tried to steal the car. Fortunately they couldn't get it started, but they took the tyres.'

'What about the printing presses?' asked Viktor.

'Ah... well, they tried to take them – I hear they were intending to hand them over to a more sympathetic newspaper, but a policeman finally turned up and interrupted their orgy of violence. After that they decided to storm my apartment.'

'No!' said Leila.

'I was not at home that evening – I'd been tipped off they were looking for me, and was staying with my lawyer that night. But my wife and family – two daughters and my grandson – were at home. Naively, I had assumed that if they found I wasn't there they'd leave. But I underestimated them. They held my poor wife at gunpoint, demanding to know where I was, and where we kept valuables – that sort of thing. They ransacked the apartment, and woke up the little boy who was terrified. My daughter kept asking them, "what are you looking for? Tell me, and we'll give it to you." They opened the safe but there was nothing in there except a few papers – at least nothing of any real importance. Nevertheless, they seized everything they could and left, shouting at my daughter, "We are the masters and we govern now."'

'How awful,' said Leila, 'your poor family. My father's neighbour was attacked that night too. His shop was all smashed up.'

'Was he taken hostage?' asked Auer.

'No, fortunately.'

'He was lucky. Sixty-four Jews were taken that night – and held at the bierkeller.'

'I didn't know,' said Leila, shaking her head. 'I'm just grateful that Hitler is in prison now. Surely, he'll be tried, found guilty and put away forever. Won't that be an end to it?'

Auer smiled. 'I don't think it will be quite that simple. He has amassed a big following. People are angry – they have no jobs, they feel dispossessed, voiceless. It's easy to blame others – in this case, the Jews. Hitler represents something they want to say, something they feel... almost viscerally.'

'But not everyone feels that way, surely?'

'No. The intelligentsia don't agree with him. But things are finely balanced. His popularity has grown remarkably since he first came on the scene. He's got the judiciary in his pocket. You know his other name for us – at the *Post*?'

'No...'

'"The Poison Kitchen".'

'But why?'

'I think he's trying to suggest we're mixing up a brew of poison against him.'

'And are you?'

'No, not really. When I began in journalism, I thought it was so simple. Basically, one just tells the truth. But Hitler and his followers lie all the time, and, in order to fight back, I too have had to lower my standards slightly. Sometimes a story comes my way that I know will damage Herr Hitler. In my youth I'd have looked for a second or third source to confirm it. But nowadays I'll just print it. I have to use everything I can to fight that man and his thugs. If that's poison, so be it.'

'He often uses that word – poison – about Jews, doesn't he?' said Leila quietly. 'The eternal poisoners of the world – that's what he calls us.' She fell silent.

Viktor took her arm. 'Come on now, Leila, none of that. Hitler's just one man – a nasty, vicious little crook of a man, but still just one man. We can't let him intimidate us.'

'But he's not just one man, is he, Viktor?' said Auer passionately. 'He's a movement... and it's growing, believe me.'

Leila could feel tears welling up in her eyes, and wiped her cheek with a finger.

'Perhaps we ought to change the subject, old boy,' said Viktor, 'this is supposed to be a party.'

Auer nodded. 'Of course – forgive me.' He smiled sympathetically at Leila.

'So, tell me, will you give Leila a job?' asked Viktor enthusiastically.

'Viktor!' Leila blushed. 'You shouldn't...'

'No, my dear – it's all right. I know Viktor of old, and we *are* looking for some fresh recruits as it happens – trainees and so on. Come and see me next week and we'll talk, all right?'

Auer moved on and Viktor and Leila chatted to the other guests. Leila spotted Minki from time to time among the crowd, laughing and drinking, her pretty face pink with excitement and alcohol. Glancing at her watch, she realised it was well past nine o'clock, the time they had agreed to leave. She worked her way over to her friend.

'Are you all right, Minki?'

'Of course, darling. I'm having a wonderful time. And you seem to have found a friend.' Minki nodded towards Viktor. 'He's a top book publisher you know; you should grab him.'

'I know, and he's very nice, but I really think we ought to go now. We agreed on nine, and it's already half past. You did promise.'

'Oh, don't be such a bore, Leila. You go if you want to, but I've just met someone and he's not given me his address yet.' She kissed Leila's cheek airily, and drifted away across the room.

Leila turned to Viktor. 'It's been lovely to meet you, but I really ought to be going.'

'Can I see you home?'

'I don't want to drag you away.'

'You're not, I assure you.'

'Well, that would be very kind... if you're sure.'

'What about your friend?'

Leila watched Minki draping her arms round the neck of a pale-faced man. 'I really ought to drag her away, but she's pretty determined to stay. Better not to argue with her. She'll be all right.'

Walking through the moonlit streets, Viktor offered Leila his arm. As she hooked her arm through his, it felt natural and comfortable.

'Did you enjoy the party, Leila?'

'Yes – and thank you for introducing me to so many people. But I was troubled by what your friend Erhard had to say.'

'He takes these things to heart. He had a terrible experi-ence, obviously. But the paper's back on its feet. He still has a lot of support from the Social Democratic Party – and he's determined to carry on.' He smiled down at her and patted her hand. 'Try not to let it worry you too much.'

As they walked along the riverbank, Leila found herself wondering whether Viktor was married perhaps, with children? Was he the sort of man who left his wife at home and seduced pretty girls at parties? She hoped not, but realised she needed to find out a little more about him.

When they arrived at her parents' apartment, Leila unhooked her arm from Viktor's. 'Well... this is me. Thank you for walking me home. I hope you don't have too far to go?'

'Oh no... as it happens I only live a couple of blocks away.'

She held out her hand. 'Well... goodnight then.'

He took her hand. 'Leila,' he began nervously, 'would you think me very forward if I asked to see you again?'

'No, not at all,' she replied. 'But won't your wife mind?'

'My wife?' He looked slightly shocked. 'Oh... I should have explained earlier. I used to be married, but my dear wife, Saskia, died five years ago.'

'Oh... I'm so sorry.' Leila blushed. 'That was crass of me.'

'Not at all! Why would you not think I was married? For your information – I'm forty-one, my wife died when she was only thirty-two, and I miss her very much. We had no children, which in some ways is a blessing, but in other ways less so. They would have given me somebody to love...' He looked wistful suddenly. 'No, I asked you out because I like you. I feel comfortable with you and, if I'm honest, you're the first person I've wanted to spend time with since Saskia died.'

Although surprised, Leila was delighted. 'I'd be pleased to see you again, Viktor. Really.'

'How about Saturday? We could have dinner if you like.'

'Perfect.'

'I'll pick you up here, shall I? At seven?'

'I'll be waiting outside.'

She walked up the few steps to the main front door. As she slid her keys into the lock, she turned and watched as Viktor walked away down the street, feeling that something momentous had just happened.

4

MUNICH

On the morning of her job interview with Erhard Auer, Leila hurried along the quiet street in Munich Old Town, towards the offices of the *Munich Post*. She nervously checked her wrist-watch, and was relieved to see she had a few minutes in hand. Pausing, she stood to admire the building's impressive entrance – a pair of sturdy black iron gates set into a wide stone archway engraved with the word MÜNCHENERPOST. Despite the recent attack by Hitler's storm troopers, the building still looked imposing.

She crossed the road and gave her name to the uniformed guard.

'Go through the courtyard and into the building on the left,' he told her. 'The newsroom is on the first floor.'

Upstairs, she was met by a young receptionist. 'Welcome to the *Munich Post*, Fräulein Hoffman. Herr Auer is waiting for you in his office. Please follow me.'

As the young woman opened the newsroom door, Leila was assaulted by the thunderous sound of half a dozen jaded-looking men pounding away at their typewriters. They barely looked up as Leila walked past. The room was still festooned with gaudy Christmas decorations, and a few empty beer bottles lay abandoned on a desk by the door.

'Sorry, we had a bit of a party last night,' explained the young woman apologetically, stopping at an impressive oak door. 'This is Herr Auer's office.'

She knocked.

'Come!' said a gruff voice inside. The receptionist opened the door, revealing Auer seated behind a wide leather-topped desk.

'Ah, our new recruit,' he said, rising to his feet. 'Do please sit down.'

Leila nervously sat down opposite him and surveyed the room. Auer's desk was covered with paperwork. A bookcase stretched along one wall, filled with fat files bulging with papers, and opposite his desk was a huge window overlooking the newsroom.

Auer followed Leila's gaze. 'All the better to keep an eye on them,' he said, winking. 'So... did you have a good Christmas? Or perhaps you celebrate Hanukkah.'

'Well, both really, sir. Yes, it was very good, thank you.'

'Perhaps I should tell you a little about what we do here at the *Post*?'

Leila nodded.

'We're only a small paper in terms of circulation and income – fifteen thousand subscribers at the last count – but we have influence, and I believe we are important. Here at the *Post* our current mission is to tell the truth about what's going on in Munich. And in particular, to expose the appalling discriminatory and, frankly, frightening polices of Hitler and the National Socialists. Everyone we employ has to sign up to that purpose. Do you understand?'

Leila nodded. 'Yes, of course.'

'Good. Have you written much before?'

'I wrote for the university newspaper,' she replied eagerly. 'I have brought a few articles with me.' Nervously, she reached into her bag and withdrew a sheaf of papers, laying them on his desk.

He studied them for a few minutes before looking up. 'Not bad – nice style. Bit florid perhaps. You need to learn that "less is more".'

She frowned slightly.

'Journalism requires brevity,' he explained. 'Readers have a short attention span. Give them the headline, tell them what the story's about and then sum it up for them.'

'I understand.'

'What made you want to be a journalist?' he asked.

'I don't know... I suppose I am interested in lots of things and journalism is a way of dipping in and out of lots of subjects, isn't it?'

'That's one way of looking at it, I suppose.'

'And I want to make a difference,' she added hurriedly, 'if that doesn't sound too pompous – or ridiculous. I want to do something important.'

'That's good – we need people like that. But journalism is an increasingly dangerous game. There are people out there who want to stifle debate and suppress the truth. Here at the *Post*, we are doing our best to hold out against censorship, but it's a constant battle.' He leaned forward, elbows on his desk. 'What you need to understand is that things could get rough, Leila, so I need journalists who are up for the fight. I sensed the other night that you might be one of those people...' He fixed her with his twinkly blue eyes, a slight smile playing on his lips.

Leila felt butterflies fluttering in her stomach, her palms growing damp with excitement. She was flattered by the editor's comments, and proud to feel that she could be part of his "mission to tell the truth", but she couldn't deny that she also felt anxious – frightened even. 'Yes,' she replied quietly. 'I think I might be one of those people...'

He smiled gently. 'You're still very young. Do you really understand what I'm asking? Hitler's trial is coming up, and we'll have a front-row seat. Hitler's supporters will be out to convince the people of Munich that he's a freedom fighter. It's up to us to prove the opposite – that he's a dangerous man, determined to rule by force and inflict totalitarianism on the people of this country. Journalists like us will be fair game.'

'I'm not afraid,' said Leila bravely – not completely convinced by her own answer.

'Good. I'll give you a three-month trial, all right? It will give us both a chance to work out if this is the right place for you.'

'Thank you, Herr Auer.'

'You can start in a few days' time – on the first of January.'

Viktor had arranged to take Leila out for supper the following evening. She spent much of the afternoon preparing, surprised at how excited she felt. As she curled her hair and chose her dress – a mid-calf shift made of red velvet – she thought about Viktor's wife, Saskia, wondering if she had been as beautiful as her name might suggest. She was a little jealous, which was ridiculous. How could she possibly be envious of a dead woman? But there was something about this man that made her want to be the most important person in his life.

Just before seven o'clock she went to say goodbye to her mother. Hannah was in the sitting room by the fire, mending one of Levi's jackets.

'You look very nice,' she observed, laying her sewing on a side table. 'Where are you off to? Out with Minki again?'

'No... not this evening. I'm having dinner with a man I met the other night. He's a publisher.'

Hannah looked slightly surprised. 'A publisher? So, he's not a *young* man then?'

'Not exactly,' replied Leila, pulling on her evening gloves. 'He was married before, but his wife died five years ago. I like him a lot.'

'But you've only just met him, Leila.'

'I know. But I have a good feeling about him. And before you ask: yes, he is Jewish.'

'Well, that's something at least,' replied Hannah. 'But don't be too late home, all right?'

'Of course not. We're just going out for dinner.'

'Why not invite him in afterwards?'

'Not this evening, Mutti. Next time, maybe.'

At precisely seven o'clock Leila emerged into the cold night air, to find Viktor standing beneath a lamp post, his hat pulled down over his eyes, the collar of his coat up around his ears. Her stomach lurched with butterflies when she saw him.

'Good evening,' he said, walking towards her, his hands outstretched. 'Erhard told me the good news about your job. I'm so pleased. Are you happy to walk to the restaurant? It's still a fine evening. Or perhaps we should get a taxi?'

'It depends where we're going... I'm wearing evening shoes – not the most sensible footwear, I realise, for a long walk.'

'I'm taking you to the Ratskeller. Have you been there before?'

'Yes, but not for ages.'

He looked disappointed. 'Oh that's a pity... I was rather hoping you hadn't. I like giving people new experiences. But given your pretty shoes, I think it's best if we take a taxi. Let's walk along the river as far as the bridge – I'm sure we'll pick one up there.'

. . .

The sound of noisy diners rose up the stone stairs as the pair pushed open the restaurant doors from the street above.

Making their way down to the famous basement dining area, they were met by the head waiter. 'Good evening, Herr Labowski. How good to see you again. Your table is ready. Please follow me.'

The waiter led the way through a series of interconnecting rooms, each one accommodating a few tables. Along the basement walls were smaller, more intimate booths with just one table inside, illuminated by flickering candles. The waiter stopped at one. 'Will this be all right, sir?'

'Perfect, thank you, Hans,' replied Viktor.

Leila slid along the wooden bench seat and looked across at Viktor. 'My parents brought me here when I was accepted at university. It was a special treat.'

'Good, so you'll know the kind of food they serve here. It's all delicious.'

Once they had ordered, and the wine had been poured, Viktor sat back and smiled at Leila. 'It's really lovely to see you,' he said. 'I have to admit that I've missed you. Isn't that strange? I've only just met you and I miss you already.'

Leila felt herself blushing. She bit her lip, temporarily tongue-tied. 'I missed you too,' she replied eventually. 'As soon I left Erhard's office, I was dying to tell you everything.'

'Tell me now,' he said, leaning forward, resting his chin on his hands.

As she recounted her interview with Erhard Auer, Viktor listened attentively. Finally he sat back. 'Well, I think Erhard has got himself an excellent trainee. What's he given you to do?'

'He suggested I start with court reporting.'

'Ah... the standard way in for all rookie reporters. If you can bear to sit through boring court cases and make good stories out of them, you'll have learned the basic skills to be a good journalist.' He smiled. 'I've just realised though... it's the Hitler hearings coming up, isn't it?'

'Yes. I've been told to spend the next six weeks reporting on ordinary cases – thefts, petty burglaries and so on – to get my hand in. Then once the big trial starts – at the end of February – he'll send an experienced journalist to cover it, but said I might be allowed to attend occasionally. "To watch and learn," he said.' She looked across at Viktor nervously.

'That sounds eminently sensible – and what a case for the start of your career.' He raised his glass to her. 'To the lovely Leila Hoffman – a name that one day will be famous, I'm quite sure.'

When the waiter had cleared away their dessert plates, Leila plucked up the courage to ask Viktor about his first wife.

'Saskia made me the happiest of men,' he said wistfully. 'Her death was a terrible shock. We had no idea she was even ill until the end... she had ovarian cancer, you see – the silent killer, they call it.' He looked across at Leila with tears in his eyes. 'There are times when I still feel her presence, you know? But I have to accept that she's gone. And she would want me to be happy. Before she died, she begged me to marry again.'

As Viktor talked of his wife, Leila felt ashamed of her earlier feelings of envy. Instead, she felt a bond with Saskia, as if Viktor was describing someone Leila had already met and cared for – a cousin, perhaps, or even a sister. What they had in common was their affection for this kind, intelligent man. 'She sounds a remarkable woman,' Leila said wistfully. 'I wish I could have met her.'

The candles on the table began to sputter, and the waiters were clearing the tables around them, when Leila checked her watch.

'Look, I really ought to be getting home. I promised my

mother I wouldn't be late. Besides, I have a feeling they want to close the restaurant.'

'Yes of course,' he replied. 'I've been rather selfish keeping you out so long.'

'No! I've loved being with you, honestly. But I should go now.'

Outside, they were met by a dense blanket of fog which had descended over the city during the evening.

'I can hardly see my hand in front of my face,' complained Leila. 'How on earth will we get home?'

'There'll be no taxis running. I fear we will have to walk.'

'How will we find our way?' asked Leila.

'By instinct,' Viktor replied, laughing. 'Come on, hang on to me.'

Arm in arm, they walked gingerly round the edge of the square, feeling their way along the buildings. As they clung closely to one another, Leila could smell Viktor's coat – a warm fragrance of wool and cashmere. As they attempted to cross what Viktor assured her was a road, a car suddenly loomed out of the yellow fog. Leila yelped in fear, and Viktor wrapped his arms round her and pulled her clear. 'I've got you,' he whispered.

Finally, they arrived at the Hoffmans' apartment building, and stood wrapped in each other's arms beneath the dim glow of a nearby ground-floor window. Viktor looked down at Leila. 'Do you know what I've wanted to do all evening?'

'No, what?' Leila replied teasingly.

'This.' He kissed her tenderly on the mouth.

She, in turn, yielded herself to him, wrapping her arms around his neck and pulling him towards her.

'Oh, Leila,' he murmured after a few moments, caressing

her hair, kissing her ear. 'I know it's mad, but I think I'm in love with you.'

She felt tears spring into her eyes. It seemed unreal some-how, that this wonderful man should declare himself to her so soon. She considered replying, 'I love you too,' but held back. Something about the speed and the ferocity of their feelings for each other frightened her. She felt the need to control the emotions whirling inside her.

'I should go in,' she said quietly.

He pulled away. 'I've offended you.'

'No! Not at all,' she said, kissing his cheek. 'I'm flattered and a little overwhelmed, if I'm honest, Viktor. I've never had a proper boyfriend, you see. The occasional young man has made advances, but nothing like this. I have no experience of the world in that way.'

'I'm sorry – I'm rushing you. It's just... from the moment I met you, I knew, do you see? I thought I'd never fall in love again. I had loved the same woman for twelve years, and when she died I truly believed her to be irreplaceable. But when you sauntered into my life at that party – all that changed. It sounds mad but I just can't get you out of my mind.'

She smiled in the darkness. 'Give me a little time, all right?'

He nodded. 'Of course. Can I see you again – soon?'

'Yes,' she said with a laugh. 'Perhaps on Monday? I have to buy a new suit for work – but I should be free in the afternoon.'

'Let me buy the suit for you. I'll pick you up and we'll have lunch and then I'll take you to a wonderful dress shop I know. And we can have supper afterwards. After all, it will be New Year's Eve, so we can celebrate it together.'

'Oh, I've just remembered... I was supposed to go to a party with Minki that night.'

Viktor looked at her, his eyes imploring her to change her mind.

'But I'm sure she'll forgive me,' Leila added quickly. 'She

scarcely notices me once we're at a party anyway. So, I'd love to have dinner with you on New Year's Eve. But I'll buy my own suit, if that's all the same to you.'

At that moment the fog lifted, and the moon slipped out from behind a cloud, illuminating the pair.

'Well... Goodnight Viktor,' she said, gazing up into his hazel eyes. 'See you on Monday.'

'I'll be here at one,' he replied, kissing her hand.

She ran up the steps to the apartment building, and unlocked the door. Before opening it, she turned round. Viktor was still standing there, watching her, and smiling. He blew her a kiss. 'Goodnight, my love.'

'Goodnight, Viktor. Now go home. It's cold – you'll catch a chill.'

'I love you,' he called out, before walking away. It struck Leila then that perhaps, by a quirk of fate, she had met the man she would marry – the man who might one day father her children. It seemed absurd – it was too quick, too easy. And yet, as she walked up the communal stairs towards her parents' front door, she couldn't help but dream...

5

MUNICH

Minki woke with the sun filtering through the thin curtains. She peered at the bedside clock. It was eight thirty. Her head was throbbing and her mouth felt sandpaper dry. She opened her eyes and pulled herself up against the pillows. To her surprise, buried beneath the duvet in the bed beside her was the distinct shape of a body. Minki had been to a New Year's Eve party at the café up the road the night before, but she had no memory of coming home with anyone, let alone inviting them into her bed.

She shivered as her naked feet touched the cold lino. Pulling on a silk kimono that lay abandoned on the floor, she stood up unsteadily, her stomach grumbling, and crossed the room to the small bathroom. At the door she turned and studied the shape in the bed. Untidy brown hair poked out from the bedding, but the face was obscured. 'The shape' groaned slightly and rolled over. As the duvet fell away, his features were revealed. He was fine-boned and pale-skinned, with deep-set eyes. Suddenly she remembered him. He had been leaning up against the bar of the café when she had arrived at the party. Although a complete stranger, he had gently grabbed her hand as she passed by, and kissed it theatrically, declaring, 'You are the most beautiful girl I've ever seen.'

Minki had intended to go to the party with Leila, but her friend had cried off at the last minute. Irritated, Minki had gone alone and got too drunk, too fast. Consequently, most of the evening was a blur, but as she studied the man in her bed random episodes slipped into her memory. She remembered him kissing her outside the café, had a vague recollection of walking with him back to her apartment. After that it was a blank.

Locking the bathroom door behind her, she studied her face in the mirror. Her thick blond hair was lank, her skin was grey, and her eyes, which were normally the colour of forget-me-nots – or so she had been told – were bloodshot. She brushed her teeth, splashed her face with water and ran a bath. Slipping beneath the surface, she allowed the hot water to cover her face. Swooshing up from the watery depths, she heard loud banging on the bathroom door.

'Minki – what the hell... open the door. I need a pee.'

'Sorry,' she called back. 'Hang on.'

She hauled herself out of the bath, wrapped herself in a large towel and unlocked the door. The naked man pushed past her and stood at her lavatory, peeing noisily. He was slight and slender – not her usual type at all – and walked with a slight limp, she noticed. Something about the way he was relieving himself turned her stomach, and she hurriedly left the bathroom. Closing the door behind her, she slumped down at her cluttered dressing table, muttering to herself: 'I really must stop picking up strange men.' She prayed he had taken precautions. The idea of getting pregnant now, with no husband, and when she was just starting out on her career, would be a disaster.

When the man came out of the bathroom, he picked up his underwear and began to dress.

'Do you have anything to eat?' he asked.

'No,' she replied blankly. 'I'm sorry.'

He sighed.

'Look...' she began, 'I know this sounds awful, but did we... you know, last night?'

He smirked slightly and pushed his dark brown hair away from his high forehead. 'I should say so. You're a remarkable girl, Minki.'

She blushed. 'I'm afraid I can't remember your name... isn't that awful.'

'Joe... Joseph Goebbels – we met last night. I'm a writer.'

'Ah, yes, of course... you're writing a novel, aren't you?'

'It's more of a diary, but I'm hoping to turn it into a novel one day.'

'I'm a writer too – at least I want to be.'

'I know – we talked about it last night.' He pulled on his shirt. 'Don't you remember anything?'

'Bits and pieces.' She sighed and shrugged. 'Too much schnapps, I'm afraid.'

He laughed and hauled on his trousers.

'Do you live here in Munich?' she went on. 'I was just thinking it was odd we hadn't met before.'

'No, I'm from Rheydt... a small town in the north. I came down here on political business and someone invited me to the party.'

Minki's reporter brain whirred into gear. 'What sort of political business?'

'Meeting a few people.' His reply sounded evasive.

'Hitler's people, you mean?'

'Possibly... are you shocked?'

'No, why should I be?'

'I just thought... maybe you are a liberal. Most writers are.'

'Not me... I'm a nothing. I'm completely agnostic when it comes to politics and religion alike. Lots of my friends are shocked by Hitler and his little gang, but I like to keep an open mind. In fact, I think the man is rather interesting – possibly mad, but definitely interesting.' She laughed.

Joseph now sat on the edge of the unmade bed, and lit a cigarette. 'You're a fascinating girl. I'd love to see you again.'

'Well, that's very flattering. But if you don't mind, I really ought to get on. I need to wash my hair.'

'Don't let me stop you,' he replied, tying his shoelaces, the cigarette hanging limply from his lips. 'I know where you live – I'm sure I'll find you again quite easily.'

Minki headed for the bathroom, and climbed back into the bath, where she soaped her hair. She tried to decide if she found Joseph attractive or not. Something must have drawn her to him the previous evening, apart from the drink. He was obviously intelligent, but then so were most of her friends. But there was something oddly persuasive about him. When she finally returned to her room, she was relieved to see that he had gone. All that was left of him was an ashtray full of cigarette stubs.

Naked beneath her silk kimono, Minki ran down the three flights of stairs to the narrow entrance hall of the apartment building and unlocked her postbox. The tailor's son peered out through the glass door that led from the hall to the tailor's shop, ogling his father's pretty tenant.

'Good morning,' Minki called out gaily. The young man shrank back from the glazed door, embarrassed to be caught snooping on his glamorous neighbour. Laughing, Minki ran back upstairs and, alone in her tiny kitchen, made herself a pot of coffee on her little two-ring stove. Flicking through her post, she noticed there was an envelope with a Nuremberg postmark. Inside was the letter she had been hoping for – from the editor of a newspaper called *Der Stürmer*. Right wing, and with a dubious inclination towards risqué stories, it had only been going since the spring of '23, but had already attracted a lot of attention, and its circulation was growing. The letter invited her to an interview later that week, and offered to put her up in a local hotel the night before.

Her heart racing slightly with excitement, she slurped her coffee and reread the letter. Nuremberg was at least two hours away by train, so if she were to take the job she would effectively be leaving all her friends behind. On the other hand, it was a great opportunity. Sipping her coffee, she mused on what Nuremberg would be like. She had a vague memory of visiting the town many years before with her father. It was pretty enough, she remembered, medieval in origin, but not famous for its nightlife; she would undoubtedly miss Café Stephanie and her friends. Nevertheless, it was the first step on the ladder to success and if she were offered the job she would take it.

In her bedroom, she flung open the wardrobe door to plan what she would wear for the interview. She debated what image she wanted to present – intellectual, or feminine? In the end, her choice was somewhat limited. Her father had stuck to his guns and refused to give her an allowance, and her meagre salary from the part-time diary pieces barely covered her rent. But she did have her mother's furs – and they could add glamour to any outfit.

Rifling through her clothes, her eye fell on a fitted suit made of lavender-coloured wool that she had retained from her university days. She had taken it to a dressmaker, who had shortened the skirt to a more fashionable length and altered the line of the jacket. With her mother's mink wrap draped over her shoulders she looked elegant, with a touch of glamour. She hung the outfit on the outside of the wardrobe door while she dried her hair in front of the gas fire. Then, dressed in a casual woollen day dress, she threw on her mother's silver fox coat and went out to celebrate at Café Stephanie.

From there, she called Leila's number. Her mother answered the phone.

'Hello, Frau Hoffman. Is Leila there?'

'Who is this?' asked Hannah.

'It's Minki. Happy New Year.'

'And to you,' said Hannah coolly. 'I'm afraid Leila's not here. She started her new job at the *Post* today.'

'Oh, of course she did. I forgot. Thanks... I'll pop over there and see her.'

'Oh, I shouldn't...' Hannah began, but Minki had already put the phone down and was heading for the door.

She arrived at the *Post*'s offices to find the gates locked, with a uniformed guard standing watch.

Minki smiled charmingly. 'I'm here for a meeting with Leila Hoffman.'

'Is she expecting you?'

'Of course.'

The guard unlocked the gates, and Minki crossed the courtyard and ran up the stairs into the newsroom. She spotted Leila immediately, her head buried in her work. Passing by the other journalists' desks, Minki attracted a lot of attention.

'Morning, darling,' she said, perching on the edge of Leila's desk, and lighting a cigarette.

'Minki! What are you doing here... and how did you get in? Look, you really ought to go, I'm supposed to be working.'

'But it's nearly lunchtime,' Minki replied, picking up Leila's notebook and scanning its contents. 'I thought we could go out somewhere.'

'It's far too early for lunch – it's not even mid-day yet.' Leila snatched back her notebook and closed it firmly. 'Besides, I've got a meeting in ten minutes.'

'Well, I only dropped by to give you the good news.'

'What good news?'

'I've got an interview this week – for a new paper called *Der Stürmer*.'

'Oh, that *is* good news. But don't you already have a job?'

'Oh, that... it's only part-time and pays virtually nothing. But this job has a proper salary. The only problem is that it's based in Nuremberg.'

'Nuremberg! But that's so far away... I'll never see you.'

'It's not that far. We can meet up at weekends. Anyway, I may not even get it. I'm off there on Tuesday – they're putting me up in a hotel. I'll let you know how it goes.' She bent down to kiss her friend's cheek.

'Minki, darling... is that schnapps I can smell? Isn't it rather early?'

'Oh don't be a bore,' said Minki. 'I'm celebrating!'

It was early evening when Minki stepped off the train in Nuremberg station. Taking a taxi into the centre of the city, she found herself enchanted by the beautiful medieval architecture. Winding its way down a narrow street, the taxi finally drew up in front of Hotel Elch – a traditional half-timbered building with a high tiled roof.

Her room was up in the eaves. Once she'd unpacked her small valise, she went down to the dining room for dinner. As the only woman eating alone, she attracted a lot of attention. Other women looked on disapprovingly, while their husbands found themselves fascinated by the beautiful blonde drinking copious quantities of white wine.

After dinner, she wandered through to the bar and sat at the long counter on a tall stool. She lit a cigarette and looked around. A fair-haired man – young and rather handsome – was sitting in a booth to one side and caught her eye. Within a few moments, he was coming towards her. 'Hello,' he said, leaning an elbow on the bar next to her.

'Good evening,' she replied.

'I don't think I've seen you here before.'

'That's because I've not been here before.'

'Can I buy you a drink? My name is Friedrich, by the way.'

'Thank you, Friedrich... a schnapps, please.'

The next morning, Minki woke up to find a note on her pillow:

This is my office number. Call me when you're next in town.

Minki felt a twinge of sadness. These encounters with strange men were enjoyable enough at the time, but often left her with a sense of emptiness – an aching gap where love should have been. She wondered if she would ever call Friedrich again. He'd been a good enough lover, but she hadn't felt any real connection. He was 'in sales', she remembered, and had no interest in either art or literature. Screwing up his note, she threw it in the wastepaper bin, and started to prepare for her interview.

Minki arrived at the *Der Stürmer* building promptly at nine o'clock and was shown into the office of Julius Streicher, the newspaper's editor and owner.

Bald, with a moustache and deep-set eyes, he was scribbling something in a notebook and scarcely looked up when she arrived. Not used to being ignored by men, Minki stood awkwardly opposite his desk, and coughed quietly to attract his attention.

Streicher looked up distractedly from his work. 'Who are you?'

'Minki Sommer,' she replied, 'I'm here for an interview.'

He frowned slightly, and studied his diary. 'You're a reporter?'

'Yes.'

He raised his eyebrows. 'Well, you'd better sit down.'

Minki perched on the edge of the chair, unnerved by Streicher's mild hostility.

To her consternation, he resumed his writing, and it was some minutes before he put down his pen and closed his notebook. Leaning back in his chair, he studied his interviewee. 'So, tell me... what experience do you have, Fräulein?'

'I've been the diary editor of a local paper in Munich since I left university, and I edited the university paper.'

'Mmm... Do you have any examples of your work?'

Minki opened her handbag and removed a sheaf of newspaper clippings, laying them in front of him. He flicked through the pages, smiling occasionally, and even laughing once or twice.

'You write well, Fräulein. What are your politics?'

'I don't have any,' she replied simply.

Streicher took a cigar from a box on his desk and lit it. 'Oh, excuse me, do you smoke? Would you like a cigarette?'

'Yes please.'

He opened a silver cigarette case and held it out to her.

'Thank you.'

She took out a cigarette, but, as he leaned forward to light it for her, she noticed his hand shaking slightly. The man was clearly not as composed as he had at first seemed.

'I want people working here who are up for the fight,' he said with sudden passion. 'When Adolf Hitler was arrested, the Bavarian state authorities shut my newspaper down. But I fought them tooth and nail, and now we're back. If you work for me you need to be a fighter. I have no cowards on my team.'

'That's good,' replied Minki, 'I don't think anyone could describe me as a coward.'

He looked her in the eye. 'No... I don't suppose they could.' He took another puff on his cigar. 'So, the job: I need someone to get the dirt on our enemies – politicians, liberals, Jews... those kind of people. It's tough work – nasty sometimes – could you do that?'

'I presume you mean, would I sleep with a man to get a good story.'

'How you do it is up to you, but yes... something like that.'

'As long as the pay is good, I get to write my own copy, and have my own byline – then I'd do pretty much anything. I've slept with men for far less.'

Streicher's eyes widened with surprise.

Terms were agreed. The paper would offer her a loan against her first month's salary and would supply a list of apartments she could rent.

'I think that's everything,' said Streicher. 'My secretary will make all the arrangements. Can you start next week?'

'Yes, that should be no problem.' Minki gathered up her handbag, preparing to leave. But Streicher hadn't finished.

'Fräulein, I hope you realise what we do here,' he began, leaning forward conspiratorially. 'I'll be honest with you – I don't like Jews. I don't like the way they dominate every area of cultural and business life – the theatre and the cinema, the world of banking, even the newspaper business. This is my paper – I own it, I edit it. Some might find what we do here offensive. Frankly I couldn't care less. The readers love it and I'm making money. I hope we understand each other.'

'Completely,' replied Minki. But her confident answer belied her true feelings, for the truth was she was torn. Her best friend Leila was one of the people Streicher despised – a Jewish liberal journalist – and now she would be required to disown such people... to write vitriol about them – even to lie. But, on the other hand, Streicher was giving her a great opportunity, and the money was good. Besides, she didn't have to believe everything she wrote. They were only words, after all, and words couldn't really hurt people.

She stood up, and shook Streicher's hand. It was slightly damp, she noticed, and she wondered if she made him nervous. He seemed so powerful, but underneath all men were the same... helpless when faced with a beautiful woman. As she left his office and crossed the newsroom, she heard him shouting for his secretary, barking orders: 'The new reporter starts next week. Find her an apartment, and arrange for her desk to be just outside my office. I want her near to me so I can keep an eye on her. I think she's going to be rather good...'

Smiling to herself, Minki left the newsroom and returned to her hotel. As she packed up her things, she pushed any negative feelings she might have about the new job to one side. Her dream of being a reporter was now a reality, and that ultimately was all that mattered. She was an independent woman, free of her father's control, and as such she needed an income. Some women – like her friend Franziska – sold their bodies; Minki was selling her talent as a writer – both were simply doing what was necessary to survive. As the taxi drove her back to the station, she began to plan how she would spend her first month's salary.

6

MUNICH

With Hitler's trial due to start at the end of February, Leila was given a swift introduction to newspaper reporting by the daily editor, Martin Gruber. A short stocky man in his early fifties, with a friendly, almost round, face, Gruber had edited the paper for over two decades.

'The *Post* is in my blood, Leila. It was the first paper I worked for, and I became its editor within ten years.'

'I feel I have so much to learn from you,' she replied earnestly, '... and so much to live up to.'

Gruber smiled. 'We stand for the small people here, and against authoritarianism – that's the key. Remember that and you won't go far wrong.'

'I will, I promise.'

'We're going to start you off with court reporting – burglaries, fraud, petty theft, that sort of thing. Have you ever been to court before?'

She shook her head. 'No, sir,' she murmured.

'Well, it's fairly simple... you make a note of the offence and make sure you get the names of the perpetrator and the victim right. Then summarise the cases for both defence and prosecution. Oh, and try not to be out of the room when they pronounce judgment.' Gruber smiled sympathetically. 'And don't look so worried – I'm certain you'll manage perfectly.'

Over the next few weeks, Leila was sent to cover a wide variety of cases in the local courts – mostly involving petty burglary. Returning to the office full of excitement, she would spend hours reconstructing the case, describing everything from the atmosphere in the court to the attitude of the witnesses and the defendant. But she soon discovered this was not what her editor was hoping for.

'Leila Hoffman,' Gruber shouted across the newsroom one afternoon, waving a sheet of paper in the air. 'Did you write this?'

Leila stood up nervously. 'If it's the case of the man caught stealing a kilo of apples, then yes, I did.'

'That's the one... look, you'd better come into my office.'

Leila nervously followed him and sat down gingerly opposite his desk.

Gruber read out loud from her text: '"Standing in the dock, the defendant appeared small and slight in stature. He crumpled slightly as the judge read out the charges against him, and his eyes filled with tears – not of shame, but of fear. To think he had descended to this and all for a kilo of apples..."'

Gruber sighed and looked at her over the top of his pince-nez spectacles. 'Leila, you make him sound like the protagonist in a Tolstoy novel.'

'I'm sorry,' she replied, her eyes stinging with tears. 'Do you think there's too much description, then?'

'Leila... I don't want to be discouraging – and believe me when I say that you write very well – too well really. The thing is, you're reporter, not a novelist. I need facts, and that's all. They can be written with energy and flair, but you can't interpret, or imagine, what the man is feeling. How do you know, for example, that he feels either fear or shame?'

'Well, I don't, but I would... in his situation,' she replied timidly.

'But *he* may not feel those things. He may simply have wanted apples, and decided to take them. You can't ascribe noble motives unless you have evidence for it.'

'But he looked so poor,' protested Leila. 'His clothes were so shabby, and his boots had holes in them. Inflation means that ordinary people can't afford even basic things like food. My father is a jeweller with a good business, but my mother says it's getting harder to manage on her housekeeping by the day.'

'The fact that inflation is rife is, of course, true, and your empathy does you credit, Leila. But you can't conflate the two stories. Our job is to present the facts and allow readers to make up their own minds. Anything else is pure supposition. Effectively, what you've written is unwarranted editorialising. Do you understand?'

The tears that had been welling in Leila's eyes spilled down her cheeks. 'I see... yes. I'm so sorry.'

Gruber stood up and came round to the front of his desk, where he perched, laying his hands on Leila's shoulders. 'Now don't start weeping on me,' he said gently. 'You need to be tough, remember?'

She nodded.

'Go away and rewrite this – but take out all the stuff about "crumpling" and "tears". Just give me the facts. If the defence can prove that this man had been an upstanding member of society who has been unjustifiably fired from his job, for example, then we say that. Or, perhaps, if an unprincipled landlord had thrown him out of his home, then we can report that. In either case, the reader will feel justifiable sympathy for this man, anger even. But if there is no such defence, and he's just a little low-life, then that's what we write. Uncompromising truth – remember?'

She nodded again, and Gruber took a handkerchief from his pocket and handed it to her. 'Here, wipe your eyes. Those vultures out there won't admire you if you cry. You've got to toughen up, Leila. Show no fear – all right?'

'All right, sir, and thank you.'

One morning, Leila arrived in the newsroom and was surprised to find a dark-haired young man sitting at her desk. He leapt up as she approached.

'Good morning,' he began, 'I'm sorry... is this your desk?'

He spoke good German, but he had an odd accent, which she couldn't place.

'Yes it is. How can I help you?'

'Martin Gruber told me to find a desk, and I saw this was empty.'

'Are you working here?'

'Yes, but only temporarily. I'm covering the Hitler trial for an American newspaper – the *New York Times*. Martin has kindly offered me house room for the duration.'

He began to gather up his notebooks and stuffed them into a battered leather briefcase. 'My name is Peter Fischer, by the way.'

'I'm Leila Hoffman. It's nice to meet you. I'm hoping to cover the trial too.'

He smiled, and they shook hands. 'As you've probably worked out from my accent, I was brought up in America. My parents are German, but we moved to New York when I was a small boy. We often spoke German at home, so I grew up fairly fluent. It's been pretty helpful...'

A spare desk was found for Fischer just a few feet away

from Leila's. Over the next couple of days she was able to see
how he worked, admiring the large number of local contacts he
seemed to have, and how much inside information he obtained
about Hitler and his Party.

Intrigued to discover more about this self-assured young
man, Leila invited him to join her for lunch one day at a nearby
café, where they ordered bratwurst and beers.

'You seem to know far more about our country and its politics than I do,' she said honestly. 'It makes me feel rather
ashamed.'

'I've been at the job a long time.'

'But you're still so young...'

'I'm thirty-two – been doing this job since I left college.
Because I speak fluent German, along with some French and
Italian, I've covered a lot of foreign news stories. I spent quite a
lot of time in Europe during the Great War.'

'What do you think of Hitler's chances – in his trial, I
mean?'

'I'd say they're evens. Everyone back home thinks he'll be
executed, or at least jailed for life. Most of my colleagues believe
that the putsch marks the end of his career. But I fear it's just
the beginning. Don't underestimate Adolf Hitler.'

'What makes you say that?'

Peter sipped his beer. 'A few things, I guess, but mostly just
the evidence of my own eyes.'

'Like what?'

'Well... I was at the bierkeller the night of the putsch, along
with a crowd of foreign correspondents. We'd gone there to
listen to Gustav von Kahr, the state commissioner of Bavaria –
you know him?'

Leila nodded.

'Hitler thought the commissioner was going to rabble-rouse
for his cause – support the National Socialist vision – but I
think von Kahr got cold feet. Either way, Hitler and his storm

troopers broke into the hall, shouting "The German revolution has begun," and bundled von Kahr into a back room.'

'I heard about that...'

'And that wasn't the worst of it... Göring gave an electrifying speech demanding the end of "Jewish" government in Berlin. He got the audience very riled up, at which point the storm troopers pushed all of us – the correspondents and press – to the front of the hall, and held guns to our heads, shouting "The press are all Jews."'

'You must have been terrified, Peter.'

'I'm not sure we had time to be frightened. One of my colleagues demanded they release us immediately, but Hitler refused. "We waited five years, surely the press can wait," he shouted. Then the crowd in the hall started singing nationalistic songs and shouting, "What a pity there are no Jews to kill."'

'The *Post* was subjected to terrible violence that night,' said Leila. 'And my own father – who is a jeweller in the town – was caught up in the mob. His neighbour's shop was vandalised.'

'The violence that night was appalling,' said Peter. 'I wasn't surprised it ended with so much killing – of policemen as well as Hitler's supporters.'

'People say Hitler will use the death of his men for propaganda – to make martyrs of them.'

'He will, for sure. The thing is – when you see him in the flesh, he looks so uninspiring. I wrote a piece for the *Times* the day after the putsch, describing him as "overwrought and dead tired, a little man in an old waterproof coat with a revolver at his hip, unshaven and with disordered hair"'.

'I thought exactly the same!' said Leila. 'I saw him that night too, leading the mob, and that's just how he appeared to me – just a dull little man in an old raincoat.'

'But be in no doubt,' Peter went on. 'That guy has power coming out of his fingertips. When he starts to speak he is mesmeric. And he has the luck of the devil.'

Leila shivered slightly. 'What do you think will happen at the trial? Will he get off?'

'I can't see it. There's no way he can clear his name completely. After all, people were killed that night. On the other hand, this trial will present him with a platform. He knows everyone is watching and waiting for the outcome, and this will give him exactly what he wants – an opportunity to speak to the world.'

'So what should we do, as reporters? Would it be best not to cover the trial?'

'Well, no – I mean, the trial is one of the biggest stories ever. It will sell papers. But it's how we cover it – that's what will matter.'

'But we must simply tell the truth, surely? That's what is most important.'

'But which version of the truth, Leila? Hitler's or ours?'

Leila had arranged to meet Viktor that evening. He had promised to collect her from her office and take her out to dinner. She was sitting on Peter's desk, deep in conversation with him, when Viktor arrived. 'Hello there,' she said, leaping off the desk, 'is it seven o'clock already? I'd completely lost track of time.'

Viktor stared pointedly at Peter. 'I don't think we've been introduced...'

'Oh, I'm sorry,' replied Leila. 'Viktor Labowski, this is Peter Fischer. Peter's from the *New York Times* and he's over here to cover the trial. Peter – Viktor is a very good friend, and a rather grand publisher here in Munich.'

Peter stood up, and shook the older man's hand. 'It's good to meet you, sir.'

'You too,' replied Viktor, before taking Leila's arm. 'Darling... we ought to go. I booked a table.'

'Yes, of course. I'll get my things.'

Viktor was silent as they walked towards the restaurant, and Leila sensed his irritation. As they were shown to their table, she decided to broach the subject. 'Viktor – has something upset you?'

'No, no...' he replied hurriedly.

'Don't be silly. I can see you're upset. What is it?'

Viktor paused while the waiter poured water into their glasses, and then ordered a bottle of hock. When the waiter had finally left them alone, he breathed deeply. 'That man – Peter... how long has he worked with you?'

'A week or so, why?'

'It's just... you hadn't mentioned him before.'

'Why should I? He's just a colleague.'

'Are you sure? I got the impression you were rather close.'

Leila sat back in her chair. 'Don't be ridiculous, Viktor. I'm working with him, and he's teaching me so much. We're covering the trial together. But there's nothing between us. I can't believe you're even suggesting it.'

She sipped her water, and irritably drummed her fingers on the starched tablecloth as the waiter, who had returned with the wine, now laboriously poured it into their glasses.

'I'm sorry,' said Viktor, as soon as the waiter left. 'I can't help it. I see you with a young man like that and I realise... that's the sort of man you should be with – someone nearer your own age. Not an old fossil like me.'

Leila reached across the table and took his hands. 'Viktor, darling – stop this. Stop being so silly. I like Peter, of course – he's a very nice man, and a good journalist – full of passion for his work. But I feel nothing for him, I promise. It's unlike you to be jealous. I'm here with you now – what more do you want?'

'Marry me?'

Leila rocked back in her chair. 'Marry you? But I've only known you a few weeks.'

'You know I love you. But do you love me?'

Leila paused, considering her answer. She made it a rule to never lie. Looking across the table at Viktor now, she realised that she did love him. She was never happier than when she was in his company. 'Yes, Viktor – I do love you, but I'm about to start work on the most important trial of the century. I can't think about marriage now.'

Viktor looked downcast.

'Look,' she said gently. 'Don't think that marrying me will bind me to you. I'm with you because I want to be. Just be grateful for what we have. And if in a few months we decide to marry – then that will be wonderful. But don't spoil it because of petty jealousy. You're bigger than that, Viktor.'

7

MUNICH

Before starting her new job, Minki gave a farewell party in an upstairs room of Café Stephanie. The guests were an eclectic mix: friends from her university days rubbed up against writers, artists and singers, along with the women who plied their trade from the café, including the legendary 'Queen of Schwabing'.

The air in the room was foetid with cigarette smoke, and Minki threw open the window, allowing the sound of jazz music and laughter to filter out into the dreary rain-sodden street. Peering out, she spotted Leila and Viktor.

'Leila, darling,' she shouted down, 'here you are at last – do hurry up!'

'I brought Viktor with me,' Leila shouted back. 'I hope that's all right?'

'Of course, darling.' With a wave of her hand, Minki disappeared inside.

She was waiting at the top of the stairs as the couple entered the café below. 'Hang your coats on that rack in the hall,' she called down to them, 'and come up.'

They added their coats to the mountain of garments, and climbed the stairs.

Minki was wearing a sequinned grey dress with a matching feather boa, and wafting a long mother-of-pearl cigarette holder with abandon.

'You look wonderful,' said Leila, kissing her, 'like an ethereal blond angel.'

'Isn't she adorable?' said Minki, turning to Viktor. 'She says the sweetest things. I'm going to miss her terribly.' She grabbed a couple of cocktails from a passing waiter and handed one to each of her guests. 'Have one of these... they're dynamite. You'll hardly be able to talk once you've drunk it! Now, you must meet some people...'

Minki pushed her way into the room, pulling Leila behind her. Loud American jazz music came from a gramophone on a table, and, in spite of the open window, the air was still grey with cigarette smoke. Looking for someone suitable to introduce Leila to, Minki spotted her sometime lover leaning languidly against a bookcase.

'Joseph darling, you must meet my best friend, Leila Hoffman. Leila, this is Joseph Goebbels.'

The young man bowed slightly and kissed Leila's hand. 'Enchanted,' he said, before nodding politely at Viktor.

'And this is her boyfriend – Viktor Labowski,' said Minki. 'Viktor's a publisher. Perhaps he'll publish your novel.'

'You've written a novel?' asked Viktor politely.

'Yes... well, I've written a diary that I'm thinking of turning into a novel,' replied Goebbels tentatively.

'Most writers are inclined towards the autobiographical at the start of their careers,' said Viktor kindly. 'Are novels the form you wish to concentrate on?'

'I would like to write plays, ideally,' replied Joseph, 'and I write poetry too, of course.'

'Whom do you most admire?' asked Viktor, 'as a writer, I mean?'

'The Russians obviously – Tolstoy, Dostoyevsky... and the Scandinavians. Oh, and Hesse, of course. I thought his novel *Beneath the Wheel* summed up the predicament of all young people – the struggle of finding one's place in the world. It felt as if he had entered my mind, seen my thoughts, and written them down.'

'That's very insightful,' said Viktor. 'You must send me something you've written – I'd be more than happy to take a look.'

'There, you see!' interjected Minki. 'I told you he'd be interested in publishing your novel. Now, I'm bored with all this work talk. This is my party and you men have been monopolising my best friend for too long. Leila, come and dance with me, darling.'

It was well after midnight when the guests began to drift away. Minki's mascara was smudged, and her dress was torn at the hem from dancing too energetically. As she mixed yet another cocktail, Leila whispered in her ear.

'Viktor and I really must go. I've got an early start...'

'Oh, must you?' replied Minki miserably. 'I really am going to miss you.' Her eyes filled with tears.

'And I'll miss you too – every day.'

'You'll come and see me in Nuremberg, won't you?'

'Of course.'

At that moment Viktor appeared, carrying Leila's coat. He wrapped it tenderly round her shoulders, kissing her cheek as he did so.

'You're so lucky,' said Minki sadly. 'I wish I had someone who loved me as much as Viktor seems to love you.'

'You'll find someone... maybe Joseph?' suggested Leila,

glancing at Goebbels, now standing alone in the corner of the room.

'Oh no! Not him. He's hugely intelligent, of course, and a good lover, but he's so earnest... and he lives miles away – somewhere in the north. Besides, I think he already loves someone else... he's always talking about her – Else, I think he said her name was. Are you going to publish his novel, Viktor?'

'I'll take a look at his work, certainly.'

'You are kind,' said Minki.

'Not at all – you never know what you'll find, so it's important to keep an open mind. He seemed interesting and intelligent. Who knows, he might be the next big thing...'

As Minki stood at the top of the stairs watching her best friend depart, Joseph Goebbels slipped his arm round her waist, and stroked her cheek. 'It's been a wonderful party. I wondered if you wanted me to stay... you look a bit sad.'

'No, not tonight,' replied Minki, removing his arm from her waist. 'I've got too much to do in the morning.'

'Oh... but we always have such a good time together.' Goebbels kissed her ear.

'No, Joe... not tonight,' she said firmly. 'Besides, you've already got a girlfriend. And while, in principle, I have no objection to sleeping with another girl's man, I'm bored with playing second fiddle to whatsherface.'

'If you mean Else, I'm not sure that's really going anywhere...' said Joseph miserably.

By now, most of the guests had left, revealing broken glass and cigarette stubs scattered across the floorboards. Empty bottles had been stacked half-heartedly in one corner, and a couple of girls slept fitfully on the sofa.

Minki sank down on a small chaise longue next to the now silent gramophone, and motioned to Joseph to join her.

'Do you want to talk about her – Else, I mean?'

'I don't know...' he replied, slumping down beside her. 'I

care for her deeply, but she's Jewish... on her mother's side. It makes things complicated. I've loved her for a long time, you see, and I can't quite reconcile myself to letting her go.'

'Well, don't let her go. Marry her if you're so in love with her.'

Goebbels shook his head. He looked momentarily misty-eyed. Minki leant towards him and touched him gently on the shoulder.

'Look, Joe, I really ought to get home. I'm off to Nuremberg tomorrow afternoon.'

Goebbels looked up into her eyes, pleadingly. 'Are you really going to work for that awful rag?'

'Yes... have you actually read it?'

'I've seen it, if that's what you mean. Most of it appears to be in pictures – cartoons and hideous drawings. It's not really a newspaper, it's just a sordid little comic.'

'Well, it's also a job and it's paying quite well. I need the money. Besides, it will be fun. What about you – have you found a job yet?'

'No.' He stared gloomily into the middle distance.

'Did Viktor say he'd help?'

'He offered to read my stuff, but it's unlikely to lead to anything.' He paused, before adding: 'He's Jewish, isn't he?'

'Yes, both he and Leila are. What of it?'

'You do realise the man who owns *Der Stürmer* hates Jews.'

'Well, so what?' Minki shifted uncomfortably on her seat. 'Leila is my best friend, and *Der Stürmer* printing a few vitriolic articles won't do anything to change that. Besides... they're only words, aren't they?'

Joseph studied her carefully. 'Minki, you must know that's not true. Words are the most important thing in the world. They are how we communicate, how we persuade, argue, reason, coerce. Words make things happen.'

'Yes I know,' replied Minki irritably. 'But what I mean is

that it's just his opinion. Most of the press is run by Jews – so you could argue that he's simply balancing things out a bit.'

Goebbels smiled. 'That's one way of looking at it. But, seriously... you must understand that a newspaper like *Der Stürmer* is articulating what many important people in our society believe – that Jews should be eradicated from German society.'

'People like Hitler, you mean?'

'Him... and others.'

'I'm hoping to be allowed to cover his trial,' said Minki, changing the subject.

'Won't they give that to a more experienced journalist?'

'Perhaps... but I suspect I can persuade Julius, my editor. Plus, I don't think he has many "experienced" journalists on his team.' She smiled quietly to herself.

'Julius! Is that what you're calling him? Have you slept with him already?'

'No! But I have to say that, if I had, it would be none of your business. Now, I'm sorry, Joe... If you have nowhere to stay tonight, I'm sure you can squeeze onto the sofa over there with those two lovely girls. In the meantime, I've got to get home and get packed.'

'Will I see you again?'

'I expect so. Come to Nuremberg, and we'll see...'

The following morning Minki woke to the sound of rain thrumming against the window. It matched the throbbing in her forehead. Her mouth was dry and she was desperate for water. Suddenly she recalled Goebbels trying to persuade her to let him stay the night, and had a momentary panic that she had relented. She ran her hand over the other side of the bed and was relieved to find it cool and empty.

Swinging her legs out of bed, she picked up her grey sequinned dress, which lay in a tangled heap on the floor.

Folding it carefully, she laid it with a pile of other clothes, ready to be packed away in her suitcase. Pulling on her dressing gown, she wandered through to the small kitchen and surveyed the open shelves. Her only concessions to domesticity were a coffee pot, two cups and a few mismatched plates – oddments she had bought at junk shops. She would leave them all behind, she decided. Nuremberg was a new start – a chance to earn some real money and buy herself new things.

A couple of hours later, she hung up her key in the lobby of her apartment building, and went out with her suitcases to get a taxi to the station, ready to start a new chapter in her life.

8

MUNICH

The snow that had fallen overnight had already turned to slush as Leila hurried towards the courtroom. The leaden sky cast a gloom over the city, but Leila hardly noticed the bad weather; she was filled with excitement and a sense of being part of history in the making, for today was the day that Adolf Hitler and his nine co-defendants were to begin their trial, charged with treason against the state.

Leila's excitement was due, in part, to her relief at getting a pass to attend. The journalists at the *Munich Post* had been on tenterhooks waiting to see if they would get an allocation. They knew how much the right-wing judiciary hated their newspaper.

'Three hundred journalists have applied for passes,' Martin Gruber told his team at the morning meeting, 'but only sixty will be granted – we'll be lucky to get any at all.'

The day before the trial began, Leila arrived in the news-room to find Gruber in consultation with his political editor,

Edmund Goldschagg, and the cultural editor Julius Zerfass. On the desk between them lay just two passes for the courtroom.

'Ah, Leila,' said Martin, 'there you are. We've got our allocation for tomorrow – just two passes, I'm afraid.'

'You might have to sit this one out, for the first few days, Leila,' said Edmund. 'Martin wants me there as political editor, of course, and either he or Julius should attend every day. But as the trial progresses, we'll apply for more passes. I'm sure you'll get your chance.'

Leila did her best to hide her disappointment.

'I've got two passes,' Peter Fischer interrupted. 'She can have one of mine...'

Leila smiled appreciatively at Peter, then glanced questioningly at Goldschagg.

'All right,' he said. 'And thank you, Peter. It would be really helpful to have Leila there – to take notes and share them with me at the end of the day.'

'I won't let you down,' Leila said earnestly.

The trial was taking place at a military academy – an impressive red-brick building. Outside, mounted state police formed a protective cordon. Leila approached nervously.

'Pass,' demanded one of the policemen, his horse rearing slightly.

Leila handed up her blue press pass and was relieved when the policeman returned it to her, nodded and, pulling on the reins, moved his horse slightly, allowing her through. Inside the cordon, she saw a long line of people queuing to get into the building. She soon spotted her *Post* colleagues near the front of the queue, together with Peter. She raced to join them.

'My goodness,' said Leila, 'what a crowd!'

'Only to be expected,' said Edmund.

As they waited for the doors to be opened, Leila looked around anxiously.

'Is something the matter?' asked Peter.

'My friend Minki... I thought she would be here by now. She rang me last night and asked me to keep her a seat.'

'Is she a journalist?' asked Peter.

'Yes... of a kind,' replied Leila quietly. 'She works for a paper in Nuremberg.' Leila wondered what Peter would make of Minki working for *Der Stürmer*. He would doubtless consider it beneath contempt.

Many of the queuing crowd were ordinary members of the public, keen to witness the trial. Passes were issued on a daily basis, and the lead judge, Georg Neithardt – a prominent right-winger – had personally vetted the attendees, stacking the public gallery with Hitler supporters.

Finally, the journalists were admitted and directed up two flights of stairs and along a corridor lined with armed state police.

At the entrance to the press gallery, which overlooked the courtroom, Leila and her three colleagues were subjected to a search. Leila, who had never been searched before, felt shocked by this invasion of her privacy, but her excitement overcame any shyness. Edmund led the way to the front of the raked seating, and the group took up their places. Eager to imprint every last detail on her memory, Leila glanced eagerly around. One half of the gallery had been set aside for journalists, the other for the spectators. Once the journalists had taken their seats, members of the public excitedly rushed in, clambering over one another to get the best view. Leila was surprised by how many well-dressed women had turned out to support Hitler. They craned their necks peering into the hall below, touching up their make-up and chattering to one another excitedly, like a theatre audience at a first night. The atmosphere was electric.

From her vantage point in the front row Leila had a

perfect view of the courtroom below. Two-thirds of this converted dining hall had been arranged with seating, presumably for the many witnesses, families of the defendants, and important guests. At the far end of the hall stood a long baize-covered table, behind which were five impressive chairs.

'Are those for the judges?' whispered Leila to Edmund.

'Yes... and the verdict of the judges is final. There's no appeal.'

By eight o'clock the viewing gallery was almost full. Leila looked around anxiously for Minki. She had saved her a seat – fighting off several irritated journalists in the process – so was relieved when she heard Minki's unmistakeable voice from the back of the gallery.

'What do you mean you want to search me?'

Turning, she saw her friend standing with her arms above her head as a state policeman patted her body, searching for weapons.

Finally released, Minki strode into the gallery, like an actress making her entrance on the stage. She wore a suit of cream wool crepe, and a matching coat with a fox fur collar. Sixty pairs of eyes in the press gallery turned in her direction and watched as she walked down the aisle towards the front row and slid into her seat next to Leila. At the same moment, the judges entered the courtroom, led by Georg Neithardt, in his distinctive black robe and cap.

'Talk about making an entrance – almost as good as yours,' muttered Leila.

Minki smirked. 'Thanks for keeping my place, darling.'

'No problem – cutting it fine, as always,' Leila whispered back. 'But *you* look very well. I love the outfit! You look like a movie star.'

Minki preened visibly. 'I bought it specially – important to stand out, I think.'

Suddenly there was a murmur, as Hitler entered the court. The spectators craned their necks to get a good look at him.

'Good God... he looks like a travelling salesman,' whispered Minki, 'dressed in that ghastly suit.'

She giggled quietly to herself, but Leila didn't join in. She was too busy studying Hitler's face and demeanour. He showed no fear; in fact, he was poised, calmly scanning the room with his bright blue eyes, as if acknowledging his supporters. His gaze travelled up to the gallery, taking in the spectators, and then along to the journalists. For a second, it seemed to Leila that he locked eyes with her – a cold blue stare that caused her to shiver involuntarily. She was relieved when the prosecutor, Hans Ehard, began to read the indictment.

The defendants would be charged with high treason, he announced, singling out Hitler as the 'soul of the whole undertaking'. His evidence against Hitler went on for so long – nearly two hours in total – that the spectators began to nod off, and even the press lost interest and gazed into the middle distance.

By mid-morning, just as the audience were readying themselves for the case for the defence, the chief prosecutor, Ludwig Stenglein, leapt to his feet and demanded the case be held in private. 'It is a threat to national security and public order,' he declared. The spectators woke up from their daydreaming, and the journalists began to scribble frantically in their notebooks.

The courtroom was cleared and Minki, Leila and the others were led downstairs, and into a press room at the end of a long corridor.

'I don't understand,' Leila whispered to Peter, 'why does the prosecutor want the trial held in private?'

'Because he realises that having journalists and the public in the courtroom gives Hitler a platform. The prosecutor can't stop Hitler speaking up for himself, or interrogating witnesses – that's his right under German law – but he can deny him an audience.'

Minki, who was leaning against the wall lighting a cigarette, turned her gaze on the young American journalist. 'I don't think we've been introduced.'

'Oh, I'm sorry,' said Leila. 'Minki Sommer, this is Peter Fischer. He's here covering the trial for the *New York Times*. He's borrowing a desk at the *Post*.'

'How lovely to meet you,' drawled Minki, taking Peter's hand. To Leila's surprise, he blushed.

Two hours later, Neithardt emerged from his chambers to announce his decision: 'The trial is to be public.' Proceedings would begin that afternoon.

'Hitler won, then,' murmured Peter, when they heard the news.

'It was inevitable, I'm afraid,' said Edmund. 'Neithardt was never going to allow a private hearing. He knows this is the perfect opportunity for Hitler to put his case to the world.'

Martin Gruber had now settled himself at a table in the press room, and laid out his notebooks. 'Edmund, shall we make a start on tomorrow's lead?'

'Do you want my notes?' asked Leila.

'No, Leila, it's all right,' replied Martin. 'You go and have some lunch. We'll see you later.'

Outside the courtroom, journalists and members of the public poured out, all keen to have lunch before the afternoon session.

'There's such a crush,' said Leila. 'We'll never find some-where with a table to spare.'

'Don't worry,' said Minki, taking Peter by the arm. 'There's a little place I know. The owner is a bit of a fan...'

Minki guided the group to a little bar in the backstreets. It was full, but Minki pushed her way through the crowd. 'Heini... Heini!' she called out to a man wearing an apron, carrying a tray of beers.

'Minki! How good to see you. We've missed you.'

'And I you. We need a table – can you find us one?'

'Of course,' he shouted back. 'Follow me.'

Depositing his tray of beers on the bar counter, Heini led the group to a private room at the back of the bar where there was an empty table. 'Will this do?'

'Perfect... and could you bring over three beers, a plate of sandwiches and a glass of schnapps for each of us.'

'Well found,' said Peter, as the owner scurried off to fetch their order.

'It helps to have connections everywhere, don't you think?' said Minki, lighting a cigarette.

'So, where are you staying while you're in Munich?' Leila asked her, as they settled at the table.

'Oh, a friend has lent me his flat. He's gone to Paris for a month or so.'

'That was lucky. Will you stay to cover the whole trial?'

'I doubt it. Streicher, my editor, is not that keen on the ins and outs of politics. He adores Hitler, of course, so we'll be putting a positive spin on things. I'll stay for the opening statements, and hang around for some of the evidence – and the judgment, of course – but I can't see myself sitting through those endless diatribes every day.'

'Do you mean Julius Streicher – editor of *Der Stürmer?*' interjected Peter incredulously. 'You're working for him?'

Minki nodded.

'You know that Streicher has been giving speeches in support of Hitler recently. Are you a fascist, like him?'

'No, I'm totally apolitical,' replied Minki casually.

'What nonsense,' he retorted. 'No one is apolitical.'

Minki fixed Peter with her clear blue eyes. 'Look, Peter... unlike you and Leila, who work for intellectual beacons of the liberal left, I'm just a hack.'

'Oh, Minki,' declared Leila. 'You're not a hack – you're far better than that.' She turned to Peter. 'She was a brilliant editor of the university newspaper, you know.'

Peter looked doubtful.

'It's all right,' said Minki quickly. 'I'm sure you despise me, Peter, and I understand, I really do. I work at *Der Stürmer* because I have to earn a living – but I don't have to like everything they print... and to be honest, most of it's utter rubbish.' She inhaled deeply on her cigarette and stubbed it out just as the bar's owner returned with their order. 'But as far as I'm concerned, this job is just the first rung on the ladder.'

'We all have to make a living, but that doesn't make it all right to work for someone like Streicher,' said Peter quietly. 'What he prints is pure invention most of the time, and what makes it worse is people believe it. He has too much influence.'

'All newspaper editors have influence,' Minki retorted. 'I'm sure even your paper is capable of twisting the truth occasionally to fit its point of view. I'm not defending Streicher, but I'll tell you this – he's going to turn that little rag into a national sensation. Its circulation is small at the moment, but it's rising. The working man loves it. He represents them, you see – the forgotten masses who have been ignored for too long by the government in Berlin. As for me, I have no idea how long I'll stay there. As I said, it's just a job.' She picked up her schnapps. 'Prost!' she said, before downing it in one.

Back at the courtroom, they resumed their seats in the front of the gallery. Hitler was called to the stand and invited to make his opening statement.

'This is the moment he's been waiting for,' whispered Peter to Leila, 'the chance to speak to the world.'

Hitler's speech began with a lengthy description of his early life – his artistic ambition, the devotion of his mother, his military service in the Great War – followed by an extensive elaboration on his vision for Germany and its people. His voice shook with emotion, as he raged against racial minorities and communists, declaring them 'not even human'. The government in Berlin, he claimed, were responsible for the poverty gripping their country. It had 'practically robbed the people of their last pennies...' Finally, thumping his fist on the edge of the table in front of him, he thundered: 'Policy is made not with the palm branch, but the sword.' The spellbound onlookers, who until that point had been quelled into silence, gasped audibly. The journalists scribbled frantically, keen to record Hitler's every word. His opening speech would be front-page news the following morning all over the world.

It was already dark when Minki, Leila and Peter emerged from the courtroom at the end of the day's proceedings.

'God, I need a drink,' said Minki, lighting a cigarette.

'I really ought to get back to the office,' declared Leila. 'Edmund will be waiting for my notes. He wants this on the front page tomorrow.'

'I'll come with you,' said Peter.

'Oh, that's a shame,' said Minki. 'I thought we could spend the evening together.'

'Well, not tonight,' said Leila. 'Besides, don't you have copy to file?'

'Yes... I'll call something through later. Streicher will only be interested in Hitler's main points. I can sum them up pretty quickly.'

'We'll see you tomorrow then.' Leila kissed Minki goodbye, took Peter by the arm, and the pair headed back to the office. At the corner of the road, she turned to wave at her friend. Minki looked wistful, and rather forlorn, standing alone in the empty road, the fur collar of her cream coat pulled up around her neck against the cold.

'I hope Minki will be all right, Peter.'

'I'm sure she will be fine. She's as tough as old boots, isn't she?'

'Oh no,' replied Leila, 'you don't understand Minki at all. She comes across as tough and uncaring, but deep down she's soft as butter. I think she's one of the most vulnerable people I know...'

～

Minki watched the pair leave, and was just wondering how to spend her evening when she heard a familiar voice calling out. 'Minki Sommer... what a delight.'

She turned to find Joseph Goebbels heading towards her.

'Joe! What on earth are you doing here?'

'I might ask you the same... I thought you'd moved to Nuremberg.'

'I thought *you* lived in Rheydt – wherever that is – with your little Jewish girlfriend.'

Goebbels coloured, clearly irritated. 'I came here to listen to Adolf,' he replied firmly. 'I thought he was extraordinary, didn't you?'

'If you really want to know, I think he's a monstrous egotist, and a bit of a bore. All that guff about racial purity,' replied Minki. 'I'd have thought – with your girlfriend being Jewish – you'd have hated it too.'

Joseph raised his eyebrows. 'Well, I...' he stammered.

'Oh, come on Joe, let's not squabble. I'm dying for a drink. You coming?'

Goebbels followed her to a nearby bar. A fire glowed in the hearth and Minki grabbed two seats, one on either side. 'Order us a schnapps, Joe. And ask the barman if we can take the bottle. We might need more than one glass.'

Settled by the fire, Joseph poured them each a drink. 'Did you really see nothing inspirational in what Adolf said?'

'Not especially. That first hour, with Hitler telling us about his past, was pathetic – the poor little Austrian boy with a mother fixation, and a failed artist to boot.'

Joseph flushed with fury. 'I have to disagree. He fought for our country in the war.'

'He was a mere despatch driver!' protested Minki. 'Nothing particularly heroic about that. I don't suppose he ever got shot at.'

'He was gassed,' argued Goebbels.

'Only incidentally. You can't convince me that he suffered like the front-line German troops. One of my cousins died in that war. Hitler's still alive.'

'That's a childish argument, Minki – you can't blame the man for surviving. The point is – Hitler knows what it is to suffer under the boot of the foreigner. The German people were humiliated after the war. That treaty made at Versailles, and its punitive war reparations order, has destroyed our economy, denying us any chance of supporting our own people. We owe money to everyone and have nothing left for ourselves. You may not realise this, but where I come from in the north-west we're now under foreign control. The Belgians and the French have taken over the Rhineland. Can you imagine what it feels like to live under the control of a foreign power?'

Minki shrugged, and refilled her glass.

'Hitler wants to give us back our pride. And as for the putsch, he took full responsibility for that – as a brave leader should.'

'He's got you heart, body and soul, hasn't he?' Minki said. 'You've quite fallen in love with him.'

Goebbels blushed. 'Don't be absurd.'

'I don't mean sexually – I mean that you adore him, almost worship him.'

'I wouldn't put it like that, Minki, but I admire him enormously. What is liberating about him is the way he commits

himself as a truly upright and honest personality. That is so rare
in a world dominated by party interests. Hitler is an idealist. A
man who will bring new self-belief to the Germans... He'll find
a way, all right.'

'Well, enough about him,' said Minki, lighting another
cigarette. 'How about you – how's the job-hunting going?'

Goebbels looked downcast. 'Not much luck I'm afraid. I
applied to the newspaper publisher Rudolf Mosse a couple of
weeks ago, but they turned me down.'

'Mosse is a Jewish publisher, you know,' Minki pointed out.
'I'd have thought that might prove a problem to someone like
you?'

'Well, whatever I feel about them, they didn't want me. I've
even been turned down for a teaching position. It's absurd – I
have a PhD in philosophy, for heaven's sake!'

'Well, I'm sorry,' replied Minki. 'Maybe you're barking up
the wrong tree. Perhaps your future lies in politics. Your obsession with Hitler suggests you have a passion for it. Whatever I
think of Hitler – and it's not much, I admit – he clearly is
making a name for himself. Maybe you should join him and his
little band of Brownshirts.'

'Maybe,' replied Goebbels, staring into the fire, 'perhaps
you're right. Perhaps it's time to take stock...'

'Well, I'd better be getting back to my flat.' Minki stood up
and pulled on her coat.

'Can I come with you?' Goebbels gazed longingly at her.

'I really shouldn't,' she said. 'I promised myself I wouldn't
sleep with you again – at least not while you're involved with
someone else.'

'I may not be involved for long,' Goebbels replied. 'I'm not
sure Else and I have a future. She has no style, no class. She's a
bit of a human dumpling, if I'm honest.'

Minki sniggered. 'She sounds frightful.'

He stood up and stroked Minki's neck. In spite of herself,

she shivered slightly, aroused, yearning for physical comfort and human contact. Goebbels, though not classically handsome, was certainly an attentive lover. 'Oh, all right,' she said. 'You can come back. But don't think it means anything... it's just for tonight.'

'Just for tonight then.'

9

MUNICH

Two weeks into the trial, the long hours of evidence were beginning to take their toll on spectators and journalists alike. Leila, Peter and Edmund attended the courtroom each day, with either Martin Gruber or Julius Zerfass taking it in turns. But Minki, predictably, flitted in and out, filing copy erratically between 'private engagements', as she called them.

'What do you do when you're not in court?' Leila asked Minki one evening as the three young journalists strolled into the centre of town after a day in the courtroom.

'Oh, I meet people, hunt out stories, that sort of thing.'

'But the real story is in the courtroom,' protested Peter.

'Hitler's trial yes – but there are other stories that Streicher is more interested in.'

'What sort of things?' asked Leila.

'Oh, nothing that would interest you,' replied Minki evasively. The truth was Streicher had asked her to follow up a lead about a Jewish ritual murder cult. She knew it was complete nonsense, of course, but she had to investigate.

She quickly changed the subject. 'Why don't we all have a drink and chew the cud a little? I'd love to hear your views on the case, Peter.'

'I really shouldn't, I've got work to do.'

'You don't like me, do you?' Minki said suddenly, staring accusatorily at Peter, her blue eyes challenging him to answer her honestly.

'Oh, Minki.' Leila blushed with embarrassment.

'I hardly know you,' Peter replied. 'So, there's nothing to like, or dislike.'

'Then get to know me – have a drink with me, at least. Leila, you'll come too, won't you?'

Leila had observed in the past how all men ultimately fell under Minki's spell. She combined an almost ethereal feminine beauty with a certain boldness not often found in a woman.

Peter smiled. 'All right... But just a quick one.'

Minki led the way to a small bar she knew. It was packed with journalists, fresh from the trial. She pushed her way through the crowd towards the back, and confidently parted a heavy embroidered curtain, revealing a private room. In the centre was a table big enough for six people. 'Sit here,' she told them, 'I'll order the drinks.'

'How did you find this place?' Leila asked, when Minki returned.

'A friend brought me here once,' Minki replied. 'This area's normally reserved for private meetings, but they know me here... they won't mind.'

'You really are full of surprises,' said Leila admiringly.

The waitress soon arrived with their beers.

'Prost,' said Minki, chinking her glass with Peter's. 'So, Peter... what would you like to know about me?'

'Well, I suppose the obvious question is how on earth you can work for that awful paper?'

'Quite easily – I've already told you, it's a job, and the pay's good.'

'Are you committed to their beliefs?'

'Of course not,' she replied baldly. 'I don't have any beliefs. I'm not committed to anything, or anyone.'

'That can't be true. Everyone believes in something.'

'I don't.'

'What – you don't care about anything?'

'I care about individual people, of course,' she retorted. 'This girl for a start.' Minki grabbed Leila's arm and pulled her towards her, kissing her cheek. 'I adore her.' Leila flushed with pleasure.

'I have many friends, Peter,' Minki went on, 'from all walks of life – academics, prostitutes, singers... If they are loyal to me and make me laugh, I return the favour. I don't discriminate, and I don't pigeonhole people based on their political views. Fascists, communists – none of it matters to me. All authoritarian governments, whether left or right, want the same thing – to take control of other people's lives.'

'That's why I work for a paper run by the Social Democrats,' interjected Leila.

'And I know you believe you can do some good working for them,' replied Minki, 'but do they really have the stomach for the fight? It seems to me they will fall at the first hurdle when faced with a truly authoritarian government.'

Keen to avoid an argument, Leila tried to move the conversation on. 'Well, I don't know... you might be right. But we're none of us politicians, we're just journalists. Why not switch to another paper, Minki? You have such talent – I'm sure you could work for a paper like the *Post* if you really wanted to.'

'I seriously doubt they'd hire me,' replied Minki. 'Besides, I might give it all up... or go in another direction entirely.'

'Mysterious, as ever,' said Leila, standing up and draining her glass. 'Well, thanks for the drink, Minki. I ought to get back to the office and give Edmund a hand with the trial story. Then I'm meeting Viktor for supper.' She waited, expecting Peter to join her, but he remained seated. 'Peter... are you coming?'

'In a little while,' he replied.

As she left the room, Leila turned at the curtain to wave goodbye, and noticed that Minki had wrapped her long lean leg round Peter's shin. He was grinning like a cat.

That evening, Leila arrived at Café Luitpold to find Viktor already seated at the table.

'I'm so sorry I'm a bit late, Viktor. I had to give my notes to Edmund.'

'Of course,' he replied. 'Work is all that matters – especially now. How's it going?'

'Well, it's fascinating of course. I feel so privileged to have a ringside seat in the place where such an important event is happening – to be part of it. And Martin and Edmund are both wonderful. I've learned such a lot.'

'They're good men,' replied Viktor. 'And how's our friend from the *New York Times*?'

His voice betrayed a tinge of anxiety. Leila knew he had been jealous of Peter, and, however hard she tried to convince him that she had no interest in the younger man, Viktor somehow never looked entirely convinced.

'You'll be glad to know that Minki's set her cap at him.'

Viktor laughed. 'Poor chap. He doesn't stand a chance.'

'I just left them together in a bar before coming here. I fear you're right – he's fallen completely under her spell.'

'I'm surprised it's taken him this long.'

'Well, they are diametrically opposed politically. He despises *Der Stürmer*.'

'So does Minki, I suspect,' replied Viktor.

'That's very insightful of you.'

'Well, it's obvious. That girl is many things, but stupid is not one of them. She's got a sharp intellect, and is using that paper, just as they are using her. I'm sure she won't stay long...'

'Well, I think she and Peter make an unlikely pair.'

'I think it will be good for her,' said Viktor. 'It's probably exactly what she needs.'

On the final day of evidence, the courtroom was packed. The atmosphere was electric, as first the judges and then the defendants filed back into court.

Hitler was allowed to make a final statement. Once again he spoke with passion, as if addressing the entire courtroom:

'The hour will come when the masses who stand in the streets under our swastika flag will unite with those who fired at us on November eighth... the army we have formed is growing from day to day.'

A murmur of approval rippled around the spectators. Hitler continued, his voice rising with emotion as he made his final plea to the assembled court.

'Even if you pronounce us guilty a thousand times, the eternal goddess of the eternal court of history will smilingly tear up the proposition of the prosecutor and the verdict of the court: she will acquit us!'

The courtroom erupted into thunderous applause. The spectators in the gallery leapt to their feet and cheered, while those seated in the courtroom below surged forward, desperate to shake hands with the man in whom so many had placed their faith.

The journalists looked on in astonishment. 'My God...' murmured Leila, 'they really love him, don't they?'

Peter reached across, squeezed her hand and whispered back: 'One day they'll realise their monumental mistake.'

As the spring sunshine streamed through the large windows

of the courtroom, the judge called for order, announcing that he would defer sentencing for five days.

Edmund Goldschagg immediately leapt to his feet and pushed past the others towards the end of the row. 'I'm sorry,' he said, 'but I must get back and start work.'

Minki, Leila and Peter filed out of the courtroom and stood together outside in the street.

'Shall we have a drink?' asked Leila.

'Not today,' replied Minki, 'I've got to be somewhere.'

'So have I, I'm afraid,' added Peter.

Slightly dispirited, but not surprised by the refusal, Leila turned to leave. When she got to the end of the street, she looked back. Minki and Peter were kissing passionately.

Returning to the office, Leila found the newsroom in an uproar.

'What's going on?' she asked.

'The authorities have banned us from going to press until after the sentencing. We're too left-wing, apparently,' said Julius Zerfass.

'Can they do that?'

'It seems they can,' he replied. 'They've also banned an extreme right-wing paper here in Munich – which was even-handed of them, I suppose. They're scared of whipping up dissent, apparently.'

'It's a disgrace, an absolute disgrace!' Martin Gruber shouted across the newsroom, before retreating to his office and slamming the door.

Through the glass window of his office, the reporters watched as he and Edmund, along with the chief editor Erhard Auer, paced the room, locked in what looked like a fierce debate.

Leila dutifully wrote up her notes and placed them on Edmund's desk.

'Go home,' Julius told her. 'There's nothing more we can do here. It's not the first time this has happened. We've walked this sort of tightrope before. The last time was just after the war. Then it was the communists demanding we cease our work. It's absurd really – all we want to do is tell the truth. But don't worry, Leila. The ban will be lifted in time for the sentencing and that's all that really matters.'

With no work to do, Leila spent the weekend with Viktor. The bars and cafés of Munich were filled with people discussing the trial, and the couple couldn't avoid eavesdropping on the neighbouring tables over lunch. To their surprise, they found there was a huge groundswell of support for Hitler and his fellow defendants.

Strolling through town in the late afternoon spring sunshine, they passed the Hofbräuhaus. A poster outside announced a cabaret starring the famous comedian Weiss Ferdl.

'Shall we go in?' asked Leila.

'Why not? It might be interesting.'

The hall was packed as Leila and Viktor squeezed into two spare seats near the back. Ferdl was already on stage, making his views on the trial, and Hitler's innocence, clear. 'What have they done wrong?' he harangued the audience. 'Can it really be a crime to try to save one's Fatherland from disgrace and despair?'

The audience went wild with approbation, standing and cheering. Unnerved, Leila tugged at Viktor's arm. 'I think we should leave, don't you?'

Outside, as dusk fell, police were already patrolling the streets. 'I had heard the authorities are braced for trouble,' said Viktor, 'and after that cabaret, I can see why. Hitler has divided the people. Some think he is their saviour, others – the devil.'

'I just don't recognise my city any more,' said Leila nervously. 'It used to be such a peaceful, quiet place to live.'

Viktor put his arm round her. 'We'll be all right, darling. Try not to worry. Let's get a drink somewhere – and something to eat.'

He guided her to a favourite bar, where they sat in a small private booth near the back.

'I thought you might be interested in these,' said Viktor, opening his briefcase and taking out a few copies of foreign papers. He laid them out on the table in front of them, picking up a magazine. 'This is a new magazine from America, called *Time*. The journalist writing the story seems to think Hitler will get away with it: "The authorities almost encouraged the putsch," is what he says.'

Leila picked up *Le Petit Parisien*. 'The French describe the trial as "a comedy of justice".' She threw the paper down angrily on the table. 'This country is a laughing stock, Viktor.'

'It's extraordinary really. The world's press can all see it for what it is – Hitler's made a fool of everyone – and worse, he's had the perfect opportunity to convince the world that right is on his side.'

'Oh, Viktor, I just want it to be over, to see that awful man in prison, so we can all get on with our lives.'

Viktor reached over and squeezed her hand. 'Darling, I fear that it will not be so simple.'

10

MUNICH

As the first day of April dawned, Minki, who had slept fitfully, threw back the covers and climbed out of bed. Opening the curtains of her borrowed third-floor apartment, she had a perfect view of the Munich skyline. The sun was just rising over the rooftops, casting an apricot glow across an opalescent blue sky. This was the day the judge would deliver his final verdict on the Adolf Hitler case, and the trial would come to an end. She would go back to Nuremberg, and Peter – with whom she had fallen hopelessly in love – would return to America.

As she brewed a morning pot of coffee, she reflected on the new, and sometimes bewildering, emotions that now swirled inside her. She was used to feeling passion, lust and occasionally even affection for her lovers, but had never felt such love and devotion. She tried to analyse her feelings. Peter was handsome, of course, and a tender lover, but more than that, he represented something good in the world. He was an honourable man, with a strong sense of morality. And much as she liked to ridicule such values, in her heart she was beginning to admire the charming American.

They had spent much of the last month together. In public he had maintained an air of detachment from her – something she had found frustrating at times. But he was a private man, and she had tried to understand his reluctance to make their love affair public. His work, as he often told her, took precedence. He would attend court during the day, spend the evening at the offices of the *Munich Post*, file his copy, and then late at night visit her apartment, where they would drink and make love. Early in the morning he would return to his hotel room to shower and change. In this way, they appeared to have separate lives. But the truth was they had been together almost every night... until last night.

The five-day adjournment of the trial, while the judges considered the evidence, had given Minki and Peter a chance to spend more time together. Peter still worked during the day, spending several hours at the offices of the *Munich Post*, but in the evenings they would meet for supper, enjoying long languid meals in restaurants around town. It gave them an opportunity to talk of their lives and hopes for the future – in particular how Peter's life had been changed by living in America.

'You'd love it there,' he assured her. 'I can imagine you in New York – it's full of energy and dynamism – you'd fit in well... in fact, I think you could be a huge success. You have the necessary drive to make it.'

Minki took this as a sign that Peter might be considering a possible future for them both in America. She began to wonder if she had finally met the man she was destined to marry.

But on that final Sunday – the day before the verdict was due – Minki woke to find Peter dressing hurriedly.

'Where are you going?' she asked, peering at the clock on the bedside. 'It's seven o'clock in the morning.'

'I have to go to work...'

'So early? Must you, Peter? It's Sunday, after all.'

'I still have work to do – copy to file. '

'I know... it's just I had hoped we could go to the Englischer Garten later – it's such a beautiful day.'

'Not today, I'm afraid.'

'But surely... the verdict is due tomorrow and there's nothing much you can do until that's announced.'

He smiled, buttoning his cuffs. 'It's not that simple, Minki. I have to consider every possible outcome and prepare articles accordingly. If Hitler is found guilty and sentenced to life imprisonment that's one article... if he's let off with a slap on the wrist, that's quite another.' He stooped down to check his hair in the dressing table mirror.

'You'll come back later though?' she asked.

'I'm not sure...' He glanced at her reflection in the mirror.

'But I was going to cook us supper tonight. Please say you'll come... You won't be disappointed.' She allowed her silk kimono to slip off her shoulders, revealing her firm white breasts.

He removed his jacket from the back of the chair. 'It's a tempting offer, Minki, really, but I don't want to make a promise I can't keep.'

Hurt at being rejected, Minki pulled her kimono tightly around her and got out of bed. 'I just thought... supper would be nice. Most of the time we only make love, and I want you to see a different side of me. I am capable of being domestic, you know.'

She wandered through to the kitchen and lit the gas ring under the coffee pot.

Peter followed her, pulling on his jacket. Standing behind her, he slipped his arms round her waist and whispered in her ear. 'Can you really cook, Minki? I've never even seen you boil an egg.'

'Of course I can.' She turned to face him, wrapped her arms

round his neck and kissed him. 'Oh, please say you'll come over later?'

To her surprise, she felt him resisting.

'Oh don't come then,' she snapped. 'Go to work – I don't care.' She turned away and discreetly wiped the tears from her eyes, before clanging the coffee pot onto the countertop and pouring them both a cup of coffee. 'Here... you'd better have this before you go.'

'Thanks.' He picked it up with both hands, and blew on the steaming black liquid before drinking it down in one. 'Look, Minki – I'm sorry if you're upset, but I'll see you tomorrow at the court, OK?'

'Sure... that will be nice.' Her voice was clipped, controlled.

He reached down and kissed her cheek. 'You're lovely.'

Minki spent the rest of the day alone in her apartment, anxiously pacing the floor. What had just happened? Was he telling the truth and he really had work to do, or was it something more serious? Had she misunderstood his affection? Had he fallen out of love with her? She hated herself for feeling this way – for needing him so badly. That evening, she drank a bottle of wine, fell into bed and cried herself to sleep.

She woke periodically throughout the night, tossing and turning, her mind racing. Finally at dawn she gave up trying to sleep, and climbed out of bed. Gazing out of her third-floor window at the Munich skyline, she felt a little ashamed of her petulant reaction the day before. Peter was a professional, she told herself; of course he had to work. But once the trial was finally over, the pressure would be off them both, and then they would have time to talk and discuss their future together.

Feeling more optimistic, and determined to make a last dramatic entrance on the final morning of the trial, she dressed with care, selecting a figure-hugging navy blue dress and matching hat. She hoped it struck the right note of elegance mixed with seriousness. If Peter was ever going to see her as a potential wife, she must dress like one.

Hurrying to the courtroom, Minki could see the queue to the press gallery already stretching round the block. Leila was standing near the front alongside Edmund, Martin... and Peter. Minki's heart leapt. She hurried to insert herself into the group, standing right next to Peter, their hands almost touching.

'Goodness Minki,' said Leila, glancing at her watch, 'I'm impressed... for once you're early.'

Minki blushed. 'I thought I ought to show willing as it's judgment day.' She glanced up at Peter, but he chose that moment to light a cigarette, exhaling the smoke away from her. After what had happened the day before, this apparent indifference gave her a frisson of anxiety.

There was no time to brood, for moments later the courtroom doors opened, and the journalists rushed up the stairs that led to the press gallery. Edmund and Peter forged ahead, and took up their positions in the front row, with Minki, Leila and Martin following behind. As they slid into their seats, Minki was delighted to find herself sitting between Leila and Peter. Hoping for a sign of affection from her lover, she pressed her leg against his, but he turned away to Edmund and began discussing the case.

Embarrassed at being ignored, Minki switched her attention to the gallery and studied the spectators, some of whom were chatting volubly about Hitler as if he were a film star. Giggling, she nudged Leila. 'I just overheard one of those women on the other side of the aisle saying: "I'd like to share a bath with him, wouldn't you?"'

'God, how odd,' said Leila.

'And her friend replied: "Oh yes... to soak his back, to feel his legs around one's own. Oh, the thought of it..."'

Leila and Minki giggled, but Peter shushed them. 'Can't you take anything seriously,' he said coldly.

At that moment, the doors to the courtroom opened and the defendants entered, followed by their lawyers, and finally the five judges. The room fell silent; even the two 'Hitler fans' in the gallery stopped talking and leaned forward eagerly, waiting for the verdict.

But Judge Neithardt took his time. His summing-up was long-winded, his voice monotonous, and Minki struggled to concentrate. She could think of nothing but seeing Peter at the end of the day and where they would go that evening. Perhaps they would start off in a bar, before dining somewhere romantic. Later, they would end up in bed, as they always did, and he would make love to her, whispering such sweet things in her ear. Might this be the night when he proposed, or at least invited her to come back to America with him? She glanced across at Peter, hoping for some sign of affection, but he seemed intent on writing up his notes.

Finally the judge pronounced he would give his verdict. Minki sat up and took her notebook and pen out from her bag. In ponderous tones, Neithardt declared Hitler guilty of high treason. Immediately, the courtroom erupted with cries of 'Unacceptable!' and 'Scandalous!' The two ladies in the gallery who had spoken so amorously of Hitler began to weep theatrically. 'It's a disgrace,' one of them screamed. Minki made a note of their reaction – fine headline material, she thought.

When the sentences were announced, the journalists in the press gallery gasped. Hitler would go to prison for five years.

'Is that all?' muttered Peter.

Edmund shook his head mournfully. 'With the four months he's already served, it won't even be that long. The whole thing is a farce.'

.   .   .

Outside the courtroom, the *Post*'s journalists stood mutely together – almost in a state of shock.

Edmund finally broke the silence. 'It's unbelievable... five years for Hitler and his co-conspirators, one year for the others, and one acquitted completely. And you know what makes it even more disgraceful? By law, here in Bavaria, treason should result in a lifetime sentence – but somehow Neithardt and the other judges have bent the rules.'

'What sickens me is the hypocrisy,' added Martin. 'Do you remember, last year, the case of that left-wing Jewish journalist Felix Fechenbach? He was convicted of treason and sentenced to eleven years with hard labour. I'm ashamed of the legal system in this country.'

'Well, there's nothing we can do about it,' said Edmund. 'I suppose we'd better get back to the office. The ban should be lifted on the *Post* by tomorrow morning, and we need to be ready. Are you coming, Leila?'

'Yes... in a moment. Minki, are you staying in town much longer, or going straight back to Nuremberg?'

'I'm not sure,' Minki said, looking nervously at Peter.

'And what are your plans, Peter?' asked Leila.

'I'll come back to the newsroom shortly,' he replied.

'All right then, I'll see you both soon.' Leila strode off, leaving Peter and Minki alone together.

'Shall we go somewhere for lunch, Peter?' Minki ventured.

'I can't really spare the time.'

'Oh, that's a shame,' said Minki, trying to hide her disappointment. 'Perhaps we can meet later, after work.'

Peter flushed. 'I'm not sure that will be possible, either.'

'What do you mean?'

'Well, I'm leaving Germany tomorrow – I have to get back to New York. I need to pack... and so on.'

Minki felt the blood draining from her face; her legs began to buckle beneath her.

'Are you all right?' asked Peter, grabbing her arm.

'Yes... It's just I had thought we were...' She paused, unsure what to say. Everything she had imagined about their relationship now seemed absurdly unrealistic.

'Minki,' he began, 'I think there may have been a misunderstanding.'

She turned to him, her blue eyes flashing with tears, her voice pleading but strident. 'What can I possibly have misunderstood? We've been together for the last month – sleeping together almost every night. We've even discussed me visiting you in America. I thought we had a future together...'

'Oh, I see. Oh dear.' Peter ran his hands nervously through his hair. 'I hadn't realised you felt that way. I had assumed – what with me living in America, and you in Germany – that you would understand. It's been fun being with you, but...'

'But what?' The tears were now spilling down her cheeks.

'Minki... I'm so sorry.' He wiped the tears from her face. 'Come on... Let's go and have a drink.'

He wrapped his arm round her shoulders and led her to a favourite bar. He bought her a glass of brandy and set it down in front of her. He lit a cigarette and placed it between her lips.

She wiped her eyes, sipped the brandy and inhaled deeply on the cigarette. 'I feel an absolute fool,' she said at last. 'I've fallen in love with you, you see. I've never felt this way before. You've altered my whole view of the world. You've changed me.' She reached across the table, and took his hand. 'Please don't leave me now... I need you.'

'Minki, sweetheart... the thing is... I already have a girl back home.'

'What? I don't understand...'

'Yes, she's called Mary. We got engaged a few months back.'

Minki stood up suddenly, and threw what was left of her brandy in his face. 'You bastard! All these weeks we've been together, and you never mentioned another woman. The things you said to me... I believed you loved me.'

Not waiting for an answer, Minki stormed out of the bar. Stopping at the end of the road, she looked back, half expecting him to follow her... perhaps even to apologise and beg her forgiveness. But there was no sign of him. She stumbled back to her apartment engulfed in tears.

Once inside, she fell hysterically onto the bed, pummelling the pillow with rage. 'How could I be so stupid,' she wailed, over and over. Finally, sheer exhaustion took over and she lay on her side, her legs curled up like a child, realising that all her hopes had evaporated. The happy married life she had envisaged with Peter had been nothing but a fantasy and all that was left now was a broken dream.

Desperate now to get away, she threw her belongings into her suitcase and ran downstairs. Outside she hailed a taxi. 'Munich railway station please.' She would take the night train to Nuremberg.

11

MUNICH

Early the next morning, Leila hurried to Minki's rented apartment, anxious to see her before she returned to Nuremberg. The main door to the apartment building was open, and Leila ran up the stairs. She knocked on Minki's door.

There was no answer. 'Minki, Minki...' she called out. 'Are you there?'

After a few minutes, she gave up and came downstairs. In the hall, she tapped on the caretaker's door.

He opened it a few moments later, pulling on his braces. 'What do you want?'

'I'm looking for Minki Sommer... she was renting the apartment on the third floor.'

'She left... last night, I think.'

'Did she say where she was going?'

'Back home, I suppose.'

It seemed odd that Minki should leave Munich without a word. Now, as Leila walked towards her office, she wondered why Minki had left so suddenly. Perhaps her boss had demanded her presence urgently. More likely, it was triggered by something personal. It had been obvious for some time that Minki had developed a crush on Peter. But as Minki had never discussed it with Leila, there was no way of knowing how serious her feelings had become. Perhaps the couple had rowed and parted on bad terms. Either way, Leila resolved to discuss it with Peter when he came in.

Settling herself at her desk, she began to write up an article for that evening's print run, all the while keeping an anxious eye out for Peter. He finally arrived before lunch, and began to pack his notebooks into his briefcase.

'I'm so glad you're here,' Leila whispered. 'There's something I need to talk to you about.'

'Of course... I'll be a while yet.'

Martin Gruber wandered over to Peter's desk. 'So, you're finally leaving... we'll miss you.' He shook Peter's hand.

'Thank you, Martin. It's been a pleasure working with you all. And good luck to you – fighting the good fight.'

'We'll need it,' replied Gruber ruefully. 'The National Socialists look as if they're going to take many of the seats at the next election. Hitler and his friends have not gone away...'

'I heard from a friend who works for the US consul here in Munich that Hitler's conditions at Landsberg are very comfortable,' said Peter. 'He has the largest room in the prison, with a view of the garden. And, conveniently, his co-conspirators are housed on either side of him. They call it "the commander's wing", apparently.'

'That's what we're up against,' replied Gruber. 'I fear he will not receive any punishment there. This is just a chance for him to regroup.'

'I hope it gives you the chance to do the same,' said Peter. He picked up his bulging briefcase. 'Well... I suppose I should get going – I have a train to catch.'

The assembled journalists all duly gathered around Peter's

desk. He smiled and shook hands. But as he took Leila's hand, he kissed her cheek. 'It's been a great pleasure to meet you.'

'You too,' she said.

'There was something you wanted to say?'

'Oh... it will keep,' said Leila, embarrassed to raise the subject of Minki in front of her colleagues.

But as Peter left the newsroom, Leila chased after him. 'Peter,' she called out, 'wait a minute.'

'Yes...'

'I just wanted to ask... did you have a chance to say goodbye to Minki?'

'In a way... but it didn't go well.' He flushed slightly. 'You probably know we had a sort of fling.'

'Minki never talked about it, but it was obvious from her behaviour that she liked you. I'm a bit worried, because she left Munich without saying goodbye. It's not like her.'

'I think I may have upset her. I didn't think Minki was the sort of girl to take love affairs so seriously. She seemed so independent – almost blasé.'

'She always has been in the past, but I think she felt differently about you.'

'I didn't mean to hurt her – you must believe that. Can you tell her I'm sorry?'

'Maybe you should tell her yourself.'

'I tried yesterday, but she was upset and ran off. I should have gone after her. But I was worried that if I did, we'd just end up in bed together. I adore her you see, but the fact is, I've got a girl back home.'

Leila flushed with shock. 'Someone important?'

'Yes.' Peter looked guiltily down at his shoes. 'You disapprove...'

'Well, I'm surprised – put it that way. I thought you were an honourable man, Peter.'

'I am... or at least, I like to think I am.' He dropped his briefcase on the floor and ran his hands through his hair. 'It was wrong, I see that now. But I allowed myself to believe that an affair with Minki was all right – a transient thing that Mary, my fiancée, need never know about. But that was so selfish. I hadn't considered Minki's feelings in all this. I want you to know – I do care for Minki. I admit that at first I didn't even like her, but, somehow, she bewitched me, and then things got out of hand.'

Leila felt a tinge of sympathy for Peter. She had observed how her friend had ensnared many men over the years, while displaying an air of indifference, which they interpreted as strength and lack of emotion. Nevertheless, Leila was surprised by Peter's admission. Whether he loved Minki or not, to sleep with her when he had a girl back home was just wrong.

'Look, Leila... I've got to leave Munich today. I'm getting the train to Paris this afternoon, and then travelling on to London. I'll be back in New York in a couple of weeks. I genuinely feel very guilty about Minki. Will you talk to her for me, Leila, and try to explain things?'

'I'll try,' said Leila. 'But it won't be easy.'

'I feel terrible... she seemed so strong and untouchable, but I think it's all just a mask.'

Leila nodded thoughtfully. 'Look, Peter... you'd better go. I'll write to her, and explain that you didn't mean to upset her. I'm not sure what else we can do.'

Peter put down his briefcase, and kissed Leila on the cheek. 'You're a good friend. And good luck with your career – you have the makings of a fine journalist.'

In spite of her concern for her friend, Leila felt a sense of renewal and hope on her walk to work every morning – that her country had a chance to root out the evil that Hitler represented. Of course, there was still, and probably always would be, anti-Semitism. After all, Hitler's followers had not disappeared, but they had, for now at least, been suppressed. As a young Jewish woman, Leila had to believe that her future as a journalist looked more promising than ever.

One evening towards the end of April, Leila and Viktor walked together in the Englischer Garten. The flower beds were filled with tulips, the trees were in their first flush, their leaves a bright, almost acidic green. Inhaling the scent of newly mown grass, Leila took Viktor's hand in her own. She drew him towards her and kissed him.

'What was that for?' he asked.

'For being the most wonderful man in the world.'

'Hardly.' He laughed. 'I'm forty-one, have a bad back and a weak chest... what's wonderful about that?'

'You are also the most kind, patient, intelligent man I've ever met, and I love you.'

'You do?'

'You know I do. I'm sorry if I've been rather withdrawn over the last few months. The new job, the trial – there was so much to deal with, so much I needed to learn and understand. I had little space left for anything else. Forgive me?'

'There's nothing to forgive.' He kissed her.

'Do you remember a question you asked me... a few months ago?'

'A question – what question?' He frowned, as if struggling to remember.

'Oh Viktor... you know... *The* question – that I was too busy to consider?'

She waited patiently, but Viktor continued with the farce of not being able to remember. 'No... I'm sorry,' he said, smiling, 'you'll have to remind me.'

'Oh, Viktor, stop teasing! I'll have to ask you if you won't ask me...'

'Then go ahead,' he said.

'All right.' She gazed up into his hazel eyes. 'Viktor Labowski... will you marry me?'

He pulled her towards him and held her tightly to his chest. 'I thought you'd never ask,' he whispered into her hair.

Leila suggested she should break the happy news to her parents immediately.

'I'll come with you,' said Viktor.

'No,' she told him, 'I want to do this alone. Come for supper tomorrow and we can celebrate properly.'

'Maybe we'll be commiserating,' he said. 'After all, they might not agree to the marriage.'

'Don't be ridiculous,' she scolded him. 'I'm twenty-two and an independent woman. Of course they'll agree.'

But as she walked back to her parents' apartment that evening, she did wonder if they would be as happy about her impending marriage as she was.

Coming into the hall that evening, she heard the familiar, comforting sounds of her parents chatting in the sitting room. Hanging up her coat, she listened as her mother scolded her father gently about spilling his pipe tobacco on the arm of the chair. Leila stood for a moment, realising that, if she were to marry, she would soon be leaving this place – that these sounds and sights would no longer be part of her daily life – and she had a momentary flash of sadness.

'There you are,' said her mother as Leila entered the sitting room. 'We were just wondering if you'd be back in time for dinner.'

'Yes... sorry I'm a bit late.'

Her father was standing in front of the fireplace, throwing a log onto the fire. 'Do you want a drink?' he asked.

'Yes, thank you... if there's time before we eat?'

He poured her a little glass of wine from a cut-glass decanter.

'Prost,' she said, taking a sip. 'I have some good news.'

'Oh?' Her mother looked up.

'I'm getting married... to Viktor.'

Hannah's eyes widened in surprise. 'Oh... how wonderful. When was this decided?'

'Just now... I asked him in the park.'

'You asked him?' interjected her father. 'Isn't that the wrong way round?'

'Oh, that doesn't matter,' said Leila casually. 'He'd asked me before and I said I wanted to wait a little. Well, I've waited quite a while now and I know it's the right thing to do.'

'If you're sure?' Her mother sounded anxious.

'Of course I'm sure... why wouldn't I be?'

Leila glanced at her father, hoping for a more positive response.

'Well... he seems very nice,' Levi began, 'but is he perhaps... a little old for you?'

'Oh, Papa – don't be silly. I've met a man I adore and who adores me. He makes me feel safe, secure and admired. We work in similar areas – we understand one another. We are two sides of the same coin. What more could I ask?'

Hannah laid her needlework aside and glanced over at Levi, who nodded. She stood up, holding her hands out to her daughter. 'What more indeed? Darling Leila – of course, we give you our blessing.'

12

NUREMBERG

Minki was experiencing unfamiliar emotions – misery at being rejected by Peter, along with regret at the missed opportunities he represented. Her feelings ate away at her. She slept badly, and struggled to concentrate at work. When she got back to her empty flat at night, her life felt devoid of meaning. Nuremberg had none of the distractions of Munich. She missed Café Stephanie and her friends. She tried to imagine what advice the 'Queen of Schwabing' would have given her about Peter.

'Move on, darling,' she would have said, 'he's just a poor little writer with no prospects. Don't throw yourself away on him.'

And yet the time she had spent with Peter had changed her. His sense of moral purpose was inspirational, and made her feel ashamed of her cavalier attitude to politics and morality. She daydreamed about what life would have been like if they had married. They would have lived in New York and over time he would have helped her get a job. Or perhaps they would have moved to the country and had children. She had never before considered having a family – always assuming she was unsuited to the task. Her own mother had died so young she had no blueprint for how to be a mother and had thought it better never to try. But with Peter at her side, perhaps she could have managed it. The missed opportunities – which in reality had never been offered, or even suggested – nagged at her, like a wound in her side.

One morning, she received two letters. The first one she opened was from Leila.

> *I spoke with Peter after the trial and he was rather upset. He didn't mean to hurt you and I know he feels bad for leading you on. But deep down, he's a good man – don't think too harshly of him. I fear, in some ways, he regretted getting involved…*

Minki angrily threw the letter into the bin without finishing it. How dare Peter regret their relationship? He had made love to her almost every night for a month. She remembered the things he had said when they were at their most intimate – most of them loving and apparently sincere. He never said he loved her, it was true, but he had shown her love. Now, to find he wished it had never happened broke her heart.

Fighting back the tears, she picked up the second letter. It had a Rheydt postmark – Joseph Goebbels' hometown. Intrigued, she ripped it open.

> *My darling Minki,*
>
> *It has been a while since we saw one another and I do think back on our times together most fondly. I wonder if I could persuade you to visit me? I do so miss you. I have been busy since we last met and have founded a local National Socialist group here in Rheydt.*

I am filled with enthusiasm for the project. As the NSDAP has been banned since November last year, we are technically an illegal organisation. At our first meeting we discussed anti-Semitism – a subject that unites the Germans and the Russians. I have been doing a lot of reading... Henry Ford's anti-Semitic tract The International Jew *is fascinating. But I am troubled, for so many people I admire are Jewish – Trotsky and Marx being two of the most famous examples. Lenin, of course, is not, but either way, for so many of one's idols to be part of the group one is supposed to hate is most difficult.*

Minki smiled. How like Joseph to write a letter that was intended to be romantic, and end up pontificating about politics. Nevertheless, there was an energy about him that was intoxicating. Perhaps she had been too harsh on him. For the first time in weeks, she felt some stirring of interest. Peter might not want her, but Goebbels was still keen. 'Damn Peter,' she muttered under her breath. She would visit Goebbels, she decided, and with luck he might also make a good feature subject for the paper.

She went in to work that day with a little of her old spark, and offered the story to her editor.

'Why this man particularly?' Streicher demanded.

'He is interesting,' she told him. 'Goebbels is an intellectual, and like you a huge fan of Hitler. He's making his name through public speaking and has already set up his own branch of the Party in the north-west. I tell you – he's going places.'

'I'm not interested in intellectuals,' Streicher argued. 'Find me an industrialist who wants to support this country with his money – that's what my readers want.'

'I think you're wrong,' Minki ventured.

Streicher raised his eyebrows in surprise. 'Well, you've got nerve, I'll give you that. All right... convince me.'

'Intellectuals might not be interesting in themselves to your readers, but the Party need people with brilliant minds to convey even the simplest message. Goebbels understands that. He has a genius for communication.'

Streicher inhaled deeply on his cigar and leaned back in his chair, studying his beautiful reporter. 'All right,' he said at last. 'But you'd better make it worth our while.'

Minki wrote back to Goebbels that she would like to visit him and possibly do a feature about him for the paper. He replied by return, and arranged to meet Minki off the train.

Minki arrived at Rheydt station to be met by a man wearing a crumpled grey suit and brown trilby, waiting outside in an old pony and trap. It took her a few moments to realise that this was Goebbels. He looked utterly incongruous wielding a set of reins and a whip. He jumped down as soon as she saw her and embraced her.

'Good God, Joseph,' she exclaimed, laughing, 'what on earth is that?'

'A pony and trap... I borrowed it,' he replied, looking slightly downcast. 'I don't have a car, you see, and I wanted to show you the sights.'

Minki surveyed the motley passengers milling around the simple railway station. 'I can't imagine there are any sights here that might be of interest to me...'

'You'd be surprised,' said Joseph, taking her bag. He helped her up onto the seat and climbed aboard beside her.

'I've booked myself into a hotel in the town,' she told him. 'Could we go there first?'

'No, later,' he said. 'There's somewhere I want to take you first – while it's still light.'

The pony and trap set off at a fast pace, trotting through the streets of the little town. Some of the shops were boarded up and the people looked downtrodden, wearing shabby clothes, their skin pale and pasty. There was none of the elegance of Munich, or even Nuremberg. Minki was relieved when Goebbels cracked the whip and they headed out into the countryside, passing fields of wheat, the young green shoots now poking above the brown soil. Finally, Goebbels pulled sharply on the reins, guiding the pony down a long avenue lined on either side by tall plane trees.

'Where are we going?' asked Minki.

'Just wait.' Goebbels smiled gleefully. 'You'll soon see.'

Peering ahead, Minki glimpsed a pinkish structure through the trees. At the end of the avenue, Joseph brought the pony and trap to a halt, leapt down, tied the pony to a nearby tree and helped Minki down onto the ground. In front of them stood an impressive rose-coloured castle, surrounded by a moat.

'Joe, what on earth are we doing here?'

'Patience,' he said. He took her hand and together they crossed a stone bridge over the moat; the water was filled with large orange carp, their scales flashing brightly in the afternoon sun. Passing beneath a stone arch, they emerged into a large courtyard, where colourful peacocks strutted and squawked aggressively. One large male fanned out his tail feathers as if to say, 'keep out'.

Minki instinctively grabbed Joseph's arm.

'Don't be frightened, he's just protecting his women.' Goebbels pointed at the brown females lying sleepily in the sun. He guided Minki past the sleeping birds and they walked through a second archway. In front of them was a stunning castle with turrets at each corner, and a romantic stone loggia down one side.

'What is this place?' asked Minki. 'It doesn't look German.'

'It dates back, originally, to the eleventh century, but in the sixteenth someone rebuilt it in Italian Renaissance style. Look at that loggia... It's wonderful, isn't it?'

Minki nodded. 'Fabulous. Very romantic. Who does it belong to?'

'It was in the same family for generations, but they couldn't afford to keep it up, so the local authority took it over – they own it now.'

'And why have you brought me here?'

'Because I intend to live in it one day,' said Goebbels, smiling broadly.

'You? How on earth would you be able to afford a place like this? You can't even scrape enough money together to move out of your parents' house.'

He grimaced slightly – with embarrassment, she presumed. 'I don't know exactly, but I just have a feeling, you know...' He took her hand and kissed it. 'Let me show you around.'

'Are we allowed?'

'There's a door they sometimes forget to lock... follow me.'

He led her to the side of the loggia, and pulled aside a thick wall of ivy, revealing an oak door. As he turned the heavy handle, the door opened onto a dark, dusty corridor. 'Ah... just as I thought,' he said, beckoning her to follow him.

In the fading afternoon light, he guided her through the deserted rooms. The once magnificent parquet floors were now covered in dust, and what little furniture had been left was hidden by dustsheets. Lifting one corner, she found a gilded sofa, now eaten away by mice, its wadding spewing out of the faded silk upholstery.

'How sad,' said Minki, as they walked from room to room. 'It was obviously a beautiful house. It should be filled with people – children and parties. It's awful seeing it abandoned in this way.'

'I agree...' He took her in his arms. 'Perhaps you and I might fill it one day?' He kissed her lips tenderly. 'Oh, I'm so happy to see you, Minki. I thought you'd abandoned me.'

'Well, perhaps I did for a while,' she replied shyly. 'Besides,

I thought you had abandoned me. Are you still seeing that other woman?'

'Else, you mean? Yes, from time to time.'

Minki pulled angrily away. 'So you're not really interested in me at all, are you?'

'I am, Minki... it's just difficult.' He sounded pained.

'Why? You're never very complimentary about her. What did you call her... a human dumpling?'

He blushed at the memory. 'I'd forgotten about that. It's true – she's not the most intellectual woman... and she's Jewish of course.'

'So, what's the allure?'

'I don't know... I am addicted to love, I suppose.' He took her hand again and kissed it. 'Like you, perhaps?'

Minki laughed. 'I suppose that's fair. Come on then, show me the rest of the house.'

From the main reception rooms on the ground floor, he led her down a set of steep stone steps. 'The cellars are fascinating... they run the whole length of the house.' He lit a match, illuminating the darkness.

Minki stopped on the bottom step. 'I don't like it down here, Joe... Let's go.'

Reluctantly he agreed. 'All right. I'll take you to your hotel.'

They talked in her room for the rest of the day. Minki, notebook in hand, was determined to get under Goebbels' skin – to explore his philosophy of life.

'You intrigue me, Joe. You're as poor as a church mouse and yet you have this inner belief that you will be successful.'

'You're laughing at me.'

'No, I'm not, truly. You have something about you... potential, I suppose. Is that how you see it?'

'That's kind. There are times when I despair, but then my

belief in the nation and the German spirit rises, phoenix-like. Whether my future will be in literature or politics I can't say. But I have to believe I will succeed.'

She allowed him to stay with her that night. When they made love, it was more tender than before. Minki gazed into his large brown eyes, and wondered if she could ever love him in the way she had loved Peter. Perhaps Joseph was her destiny, after all.

Sitting on the train back to Nuremberg that Friday afternoon, she opened her handbag, and found a note from him. He must have put it there that morning over breakfast.

I adore you. You have bewitched me, but I know you are not the marrying kind. Until we meet again... JG

Back at her apartment, she unpacked her small suitcase, then sat down at the kitchen table, going over her notes on the interview. It had the makings of an interesting piece. Suddenly, the bell to her apartment rang from down below. Peering out of her window, she saw Leila and Viktor standing in the street outside.

'Leila!' she called out, 'what are you doing here?'

'We've come to see you. We have some exciting news... Didn't you get my letter?'

'Hang on,' replied Minki. She ducked back inside, tipped the kitchen rubbish bin upside down and found Leila's abandoned letter. She speedily read to the end.

May we come and visit you soon? Viktor could drive me up on the weekend of the 20th. Do say we can come. I'm so worried about you and want so desperately to make sure you're all right. All my love, Leila.

Filled with remorse, Minki raced down the stairs of her

apartment building and threw open the door. 'Darling Leila, and dear Victor... how wonderful to see you. Please do come up.'

She led the couple up the staircase to her apartment. In the tiny hall, she took their coats. 'Where are you staying?'

'In a hotel round the corner,' replied Viktor.

'How very liberated!' Minki joked. 'Staying in a hotel together...'

'Very funny,' replied Leila. 'You'd better tell her, Viktor...'

Viktor held up a bottle of champagne. 'We have some good news and brought this... do you have glasses?'

'Oh, of course,' replied Minki, leading the way into her tiny kitchen, where she opened the cupboard and took out three glass tumblers.

Leila stared at the open cupboard. 'Minki darling... you have hardly any china, or glassware. How on earth do you live like this?'

'Quite easily,' replied Minki. 'I don't bother to cook – I just go out.' She placed the glasses on the countertop. 'So what are we celebrating?'

Viktor poured the champagne and handed each of them a glass. 'We are celebrating the fact that your dear friend has agreed to be my wife.'

Minki put her glass down and embraced Leila. 'Oh darling, that's wonderful.'

Leila beamed happily. 'I'm so glad you're pleased. I'm never very sure if you approve of marriage.'

'I approve of other people's marriages.' Minki laughed, taking a swig of her champagne. 'Mmm, delicious. Now, let's finish this bottle and then we'll go out and celebrate in Nuremberg's finest restaurant. The owner's a good friend of mine.'

13

MUNICH

Plans for Leila's wedding proceeded apace. Her mother had insisted on a formal wedding at the local synagogue, and Leila naturally asked her best friend to be her bridesmaid.

'Minki, I can't think of anyone I'd rather have with me on that day. Can you spare the time to come down to Munich one weekend and help me choose my outfit? My mother wants to use a local seamstress she's been going to for years. I might need some moral support.'

A few weeks later, on a hot summer's day, Minki duly arrived at Munich station, and went straight to Leila's parents' apartment.

Hannah made coffee for the two girls in her kitchen. 'I have it all arranged,' she said. 'Leila's dress will be made by Frau Becker. She's the best dressmaker in Munich. I've made an appointment to see her in an hour's time.'

Leila smiled at Minki and whispered, 'There's no point arguing.'

'She is also making my own outfit,' Hannah went on,

handing out cookies. 'Lilac silk, very elegant. Now, drink up girls, we don't want to be late.'

Emilia Becker lived and worked in an elegant first-floor apartment overlooking a verdant square in central Munich. A delicate, fine-boned woman with neat blond hair, she opened the door wearing a beautifully cut grey suit.

'Welcome, Frau Hoffman. I'm delighted you have chosen my little atelier for such an important occasion.'

She led Hannah and the girls through to the living room. In the centre was a walnut table covered in bolts of cloth, and around the walls were cream calico dressmaker's dummies – like a silent audience, Leila thought. The three women sat down on a high-backed silk sofa, and Frau Becker showed them samples of silk, lace and chiffon.

'Leila, I would suggest pure white with your colouring,' she said. 'And as for the fabric, lace is always a good choice – delicate to the eye, and yet quite a sturdy fabric. I would back it with silk, of course, and might I suggest pure white chiffon for the veil?'

Leila picked up the lace, feeling it between her fingers. 'It sounds wonderful – I'll take your advice.'

Once Leila had been measured, the dressmaker drew a quick sketch of the outfit she proposed – a simple sheath, with three-quarter sleeves and dropped waist.

A later appointment was made for Leila to try on a 'toile' – a mock-up of the dress, she explained, made in simple calico.

Then it was Hannah's turn. She too was measured and the whole procedure was performed again, but this time the choice was between three different shades of lilac cloth.

'I love the silk crêpe de Chine,' said Leila.

'Yes... but will it crease?' asked her mother.

'Not at all,' Frau Becker assured her. 'I'll line it, and you'll see – it will hang beautifully. Come back with your daughter in two weeks' time and I'll have a toile ready for you to try on.'

'Now, what about Minki?' asked Leila eagerly.

Hannah pursed her lips. 'I didn't realise I was paying for Minki's dress too...'

'Oh, no, you're not,' Minki answered quickly. 'Not at all. I'll buy something ready-made. There's a dear little shop I know... not far away near my old apartment in Schwabing. It's a funny little place selling all sorts of things – most of it second-hand, but it often has a few gems. Leila and I can go there later and find something to tie in with her dress – but not as beautiful of course,' she added diplomatically.

Leila reached across and squeezed her friend's hand. 'Thank you, darling.'

The main business of the day duly completed, Hannah offered to take the two girls to lunch at a small café nearby. They settled themselves near the window.

'So, Minki... any chance of you getting married soon?' Hannah asked.

'Oh, Mutti, don't be so nosy,' said Leila.

'It's all right.' Minki laughed. 'It's a fair question – and no, Frau Hoffman, I fear not. I don't seem to have Leila's luck with men.' She smiled and winked at her friend, before lighting a cigarette. 'The men I love don't love me and the men who do love me leave me cold.'

'Maybe you expect too much,' said Hannah, waving Minki's smoke away from her face.

'Mutti! That's so rude,' interjected Leila.

'No it's all right, Leila. You might be right, Frau Hoffman,' replied Minki, stubbing out the cigarette. 'But in matters of the heart, you have to follow your instinct, don't you? You can't look at a man and say to yourself, "he may not be what I really want, but he earns enough money, or has nice hands, or owns a lovely dog." No, if you're going to marry a man, you must really love him. My mother didn't love my father. I think she married him because he was rich and would give her a comfortable life. But he was also a bit of a bully, and he made her life hell. I'm sure that's why she got ill.' She looked momentarily wistful, and lit another cigarette.

Leila reached across the table, and took her friend's hand. 'Don't think about it, Minki.' Then, glaring at her mother, she added: 'Let's stop talking about marriage, shall we?'

After lunch the two girls headed off to find Minki's bridesmaid dress at the second-hand shop. Helga, the owner, rummaged along the rails and pulled out a pale-blue dress, its skirt made of tiers of silk chiffon.

'This would suit you,' she said. 'I bought it from a rich woman the other day – she had gambling debts, so I got it for a good price. I can pass the discount on to you. Try it on.'

Emerging from the makeshift changing room, Minki stood in front of the mirror. The chiffon skirt rippled as she moved.

'Oh, Minki,' said Leila. 'You look wonderful.'

'Do you think so? I worry it's a little tight...'

She yanked the dress down over her hips. 'I must be eating too much.'

'Maybe the straps need to be lengthened a little,' suggested Helga, releasing one strap and pulling the dress down a few centimetres. 'I can do that for you in an hour or two.'

'What about a hat?' asked Leila, looking around the shop.

'Oh, I don't want to buy a hat,' said Minki. 'I'll go and see my friend Franziska tomorrow – you remember her, the "Queen of Schwabing"? She has heaps of lovely things buried away in her bedroom.'

·   ·   ·

'You look like an angel,' Franziska declared, admiring Minki in the bridesmaid's outfit the following day.

'I just need a hairpiece or something to finish it off,' said Minki, running her hands through her blond hair. 'Feathers perhaps?'

'No, I have a better idea.' Franziska moved a picture on the wall of her bedroom, revealing a small metal safe. Fiddling with the combination lock, she opened the metal door. Reaching in, she took out a tiara. It was made of white and blue stones, which shimmered and gleamed in the light.

She turned and held out the delicate tiara. 'I think you should wear this.'

'My God... Is it real?'

'Of course it's real. It's made of diamonds and aquamarine. Here – take it.'

'No... it's too much, I couldn't possibly...'

'Try it on at least,' Franziska urged.

Minki took the tiara and studied it, fondling it gently in her hands. 'Franziska... this is extraordinary. Where did you get it?'

'I inherited it.'

'Who from?'

'My mother, of course.'

'Your mother?'

'Don't look so surprised. I've always told you I come from good stock. My real name is... the Countess von Reventlow.' She smiled tightly.

'You... are a countess?'

Franziska nodded. 'I am. My family had to flee Russia after the revolution. My parents, my brother... they were all murdered. I am the sole survivor.'

'Franziska – why did you never tell me this before?' asked Minki, wrapping her arms round her friend.

'Shame, I suppose. To fall so far from grace is embarrassing. Now try the tiara on. I know it will suit you.'

Minki threaded the tiara through her hair.

'It looks wonderful on you,' said Franziska. 'My mother also had a wonderful tiara made of emeralds and diamonds. That was my favourite – but sadly... it didn't survive.'

'Look, Franziska... I'm so grateful, but I really couldn't borrow it. What if I lost it? I'd never forgive myself.'

'You won't lose it. Wear it and enjoy it and give it back to me after the wedding.'

'But it must be worth a fortune. And I know how short of money you are... why don't you sell it?'

'A lady never sells her jewels,' replied the countess grandly, 'particularly if they are inherited. They are capital assets, not to be frittered away on everyday things like food and fuel. My father sold too much of the family treasures – and far too cheaply. This tiara is all that's left. I'll never part with it.'

'Well, if you're absolutely sure, Franziska, I'd love to borrow it.'

'I just hope it hooks you a rich husband.'

'I don't need a husband.'

'Don't be absurd – of course you need a husband.' The countess reached across and patted Minki's stomach.

'What do you mean?'

'Oh, darling, don't be so naive. You're obviously pregnant – I can tell.'

Minki sank down on the edge of the bed. She removed the tiara and laid it on the dressing table. 'Pregnant...' she muttered quietly. 'Maybe you're right. I haven't had a period for...' Her eyes filled with tears. 'Oh God... what am I going to do?'

'Do you know who the father might be?'

Minki shrugged. 'Possibly. It's one of two people.'

'Might one of them marry you?'

Minki shook her head. 'It's unlikely. One lives in America... and besides, he's engaged to someone else. The other...' She paused, wondering what Joseph Goebbels would make of this news. He had told her he adored her, but she knew that he too loved someone else.

'If marriage is impossible, you have only one option. You must get rid of it.'

'An abortion you mean. But how?'

The countess shrugged. 'There are ways and means. I know someone who can help.'

Minki gasped. 'Oh, I couldn't... I mean, it's a sin.'

'So the little Catholic girl is still in there, is she? I thought you didn't believe all that nonsense any more.'

Minki stood up, studying her profile in the cheval mirror. She could see it now – a small bump projecting beyond her hipbones. 'You don't think I could just be a bit fat?'

'No, my darling, you are pregnant! Now listen. I have the name of a doctor here in Munich. I suggest you go and see him straight away.'

Minki made an appointment that afternoon. As she lay on the examination table, answering the doctor's intimate questions, she tried to work out which of her two lovers might be the father. It had been three months since she had slept with Peter and less than two since her last night with Joseph.

After the examination, the doctor disappeared into the next room and she heard him washing his hands. She climbed off the bed and rearranged her clothes. When the doctor came back into the room, she was already sitting anxiously in his visitor's chair. He resumed his seat behind his desk.

'I'd say you're approximately ten to twelve weeks pregnant, although it's hard to be exact. Could be more, could be less, but certainly no more than fourteen.'

Minki, now sitting opposite him, felt her head spinning. 'So I am definitely pregnant then?'

'My dear girl... of course you are. The question is, what do you want to do about it?'

Tears came into Minki's eyes. 'I don't know...'

'Well, you have three options. You're unmarried, I presume?'

She nodded.

'So, first – you can have the child, but you run the risk of ruining your reputation. Do you have parents who might support you?'

She imagined her father's furious reaction to her news, and shook her head.

'In that case, option two is to go away and have the child, and give it up for adoption. But that takes a lot of planning, and a certain amount of money.

'The final option is to get rid of it. I can help with the last, but I'd advise not leaving it too much longer.'

'I'd like a little time to think about it,' she said quietly.

'Very well. You can telephone me when you've made your decision. The procedure will only take a short time – no more than an hour. But you'll need somewhere quiet and safe to recover. It can get a little messy.'

Minki felt her stomach churn. 'I understand.'

The doctor stood up and held out his hand. 'My receptionist will give you my bill on the way out.'

Back in her small apartment in Nuremberg, Minki mulled over the news. The timing made it clear that Peter was the father. Peter... the man she had once loved... still loved. The thought of aborting his child was unthinkable, but so were the other two options the doctor had suggested. Each night when she went to bed, she prayed she would be saved from making such an appalling decision – perhaps by having a miscarriage. Her normally flippant, casual attitude evaporated, and in its place she felt weak, abandoned and frightened. The worst part was that she could not share the decision with Peter. What would be the point, after all? He was back in America, and engaged to someone else.

She considered telling Joseph it was his child. Perhaps he would marry her out of a sense of duty? But she knew he was not in love with her – the woman he still loved was Else. What had he written in that note, the last time they'd met? 'I adore you... but you are not the marrying kind...'

In her heart she had agreed with him. How could she now go to him, and implore him to marry her?

Somehow, in the midst of this emotional turmoil, she managed to write the article about Goebbels and submit it to her editor.

'It's not bad,' Streicher declared, throwing her typescript down on his desk in front of her, 'but it's not exactly crackling with energy, is it? As I feared, it's all about how intellectual, knowledgeable and well-read this man is. My readers are neither intellectual, nor well-read – why should they be interested in him?'

'I'm sorry, Herr Streicher – shall I rewrite it?'

'No, don't bother – I'll lose it somewhere inside the paper. But you'd better sharpen up, Minki. I don't pay you to write ordinary little articles. I expect something better of you.'

His comment felt like a slap in the face.

'Perhaps you're not really suited to a paper like ours, after all,' Streicher went on. 'Maybe it's time to look for another job. You might be better suited to women's issues – cooking, sewing, children... that sort of thing.'

Depressed, Minki went home and opened a full bottle of schnapps. She climbed into bed, and worked her way through the bottle, tossing and turning, feverish and weeping, racked with indecision and guilt. The following morning, she rang the office and told them she was sick.

Desperate to confide in someone, she decided to share her predicament with the one person she could always rely on – Leila. She took a piece of paper, and propped up against pillows in bed, began to write.

My dearest friend,

I have the most awful problem, which I can hardly bear to disclose.

I am pregnant with Peter's child. What on earth am I to do?

Within a few days, Leila was standing on Minki's doorstep with Viktor.

Still in her nightgown, Minki ran downstairs, opened the front door and fell into Leila's arms, sobbing.

'I'm so glad you wrote to me,' Leila whispered into her hair. 'Now let's get upstairs and we'll talk.'

The two friends huddled together in Minki's bedroom, leaving Viktor outside in the tiny kitchen.

'I just don't know what to do...' Minki began.

Leila held her hand. 'I understand. It's an awful situation. You're sure it's Peter's?'

Minki nodded miserably.

'Might he be persuaded to come back and look after you?' Leila knew the answer but felt she had to ask the question.

'What do you think?'

'Well, he's an honourable man...' Leila began.

'But possibly already married to someone else... no, that's not the answer.'

'You could keep it. You've never been conventional. We'd support you – Viktor and I.'

Minki shook her head. 'It would be the end of everything – my chance of marriage, my career. And my father would never speak to me again.'

'Abortion then.' Leila winced as she uttered the word.

Minki stared into Leila's kind brown eyes. 'I can't bear the thought... not Peter's baby.'

Throughout their discussions, Viktor brought them cups of tea, and later glasses of wine.

Finally, towards the evening, the pair emerged.

'Viktor,' Leila said softly. 'I have something to ask you. Come with me?'

She led him downstairs and out into the street. Minki watched the couple from her kitchen window, and wondered what they were talking about. Leila was waving her hands around, gesticulating, her expression earnest, but at the same time pleading. Viktor, meanwhile, listened attentively, his face impassive. Finally, he held out his arms to Leila and embraced her, kissing the top of her head.

They returned to Minki's apartment, Leila smiling broadly. 'Minki – Viktor and I would like to suggest an idea that might solve a lot of problems. How about if he and I look after you while you wait to have the baby, and when it's born we'll take care of it – just until you get yourself sorted out. One day, I'm sure you'll get married and then you will take the child back. But in the meantime, you can see the baby whenever you want.'

Minki was shocked. 'Would you really do this for me?' Her eyes darted between the two of them.

'Of course,' replied Leila.

'I'm stunned, and so grateful – but there are so many possible problems. For example, you might fall in love with it, and then could you really bear to let it go?'

'Minki, don't be ridiculous. I will love your child whether I am responsible for it or not. Viktor and I are simply offering to be guardians – an extra set of parents, if you like – to give you a chance to work, to meet someone, to make a proper go of your life.'

Minki, exhausted from her days of emotional turmoil, suddenly burst into tears. She took Leila's face in her hands and kissed her. 'You are the best friend any woman has ever had.'

14

MUNICH

Leila woke early on the morning of her wedding with the bright summer sun filtering through the thin curtains in her childhood bedroom. She lay, enjoying the brief moment of quiet, aware that the day would be filled with intense activity, and that her life was about to change forever. Tonight she and Viktor would be alone together in a hotel room as a married couple; and tomorrow they would go on their honeymoon. Viktor had booked a hotel in Ascona – a smart town on the shores of Lake Maggiore in Switzerland. Leila's clothes for the trip had been laid out on a small sofa in her bedroom for a week. She and her mother had debated endlessly about which dress would look most elegant for dinner in the smart hotel restaurant, which suit would be most practical for sightseeing, which trousers could be worn for hiking up the mountains behind the town.

Today, and indeed the rest of her life, would be filled with 'firsts' – her first night as a married woman; her first trip out of the country; her first proper holiday – for her father had never seen the point of such indulgences.

'Leila...' Her mother knocked on the door.

'Yes, Mutti – come in.'

Her mother bustled in carrying a tray loaded with a teapot, a pile of toast and eggs.

'Breakfast in bed?' Leila sat up and rearranged her pillows. 'I've only ever had that when I was sick.'

Her mother smiled. 'Enjoy it, but don't take too long – there's a lot to do.'

Later that morning, dressed in her lace wedding gown, Leila studied her reflection in the mirror, while her mother kneeled at her feet making final adjustments to the hem. 'That's done now, Leila,' she said, standing up to admire her. 'You look beautiful.'

Leila smiled. She had to agree that, just for once, she did look beautiful. Beauty was not something she had ever claimed, or desired. She had always been considered attractive enough, and was happy with that. But today, her skin glowed, her eyes sparkled and her newly bobbed hair gleamed. She and her mother had visited a hairdresser a few days before and Leila had asked for a radical new style.

Her mother had been dismayed. 'Oh, don't try anything new before the wedding. Your long hair is so lovely.'

'Chin-length is more fashionable, Fräulein,' suggested the hairdresser, picking up Leila's long tresses and eyeing them, scissors in hand.

'Chin-length!' said Hannah, alarmed. 'Oh surely not.'

'I think it's a good idea,' said Leila. 'It will be easier to manage – it's such a bore having to pin it up all the time. Besides, Mutti, I'm a modern woman now and I need a modern haircut. Chop it all off!' she instructed.

Even Hannah agreed that the new bob looked good, framing Leila's pretty face and emphasising her large dark eyes and neat bow mouth. Now dressed for her wedding, with the long silk veil held in place by a headpiece covered in seed pearls, she looked gamine, and yet sophisticated.

'You look a bit like Clara Bow, the film actress,' Hannah had to admit.

Leila smoothed down the long lace skirt of her dress, which finished mid-calf, revealing matching white lace shoes. 'I love the dress, Mutti. Thank you so much.'

'It's such a shame you'll probably never wear it again,' said her mother. 'Perhaps we could dye it after the wedding...'

'Oh, Mutti... what a thing to say – today of all days.'

The ceremony was due to take place at the synagogue on Herzog-Max-Strasse. Leila had tried to persuade her mother that she and Viktor would prefer a non-religious ceremony, but once again Hannah won the argument, and insisted on following tradition.

'What would your aunts and uncles say if you didn't have a proper wedding?'

Outside, Leila and her parents climbed into a waiting Mercedes and headed for the synagogue. As they arrived, Leila could see Minki standing on the pavement, wearing a pale-blue chiffon dress, a sparkling tiara nestling in her blond hair. She rushed forward and helped Leila out of the car, holding the veil off the pavement. 'You look beautiful, Leila,' she whispered.

'So do you,' replied Leila, kissing her. 'A vision in blue...'

In retrospect, Leila wondered how she had missed the tell-tale signs. Minki looked as she always did – exquisitely dressed, her hair gleaming – and yet... there was something about her that was not quite right. Her face was paler than usual, her eyes a little sunken.

· · ·

After the wedding ceremony, the guests moved on to a smart hotel in the centre of Munich. In the ballroom, Leila and her new husband made their entrance – to rapturous applause. The guests were a mix of family and friends from the worlds of press and publishing. They dined on consommé, followed by trout with new potatoes, roast goose and a dessert of cake and ice cream.

Leila and Viktor led the dancing and soon the room was filled with unlikely couples. Uncles danced with secretaries, aunts with editors. It was a joyous occasion – just as it should have been. Minki, normally an enthusiastic dancer, refused all invitations to join in. Leila suspected that she might be self-conscious about her pregnancy. But when a particularly hand-some young man asked her to dance, Minki finally relented. As he twirled her around the room, there was an audible gasp from the other guests, and shocked looks in her direction. Leila could see a dark red stain spreading across the back of Minki's beau-tiful blue dress. She rushed across the ballroom, wrapped her arms round her friend's shoulders and guided her out of the room. 'Darling, come with me, quickly.'

'Why?' asked Minki.

'You're bleeding. Come.'

By the time they reached the ladies' powder room, the blood was an unstoppable flow. It dribbled down Minki's legs, staining her shoes. She sat down heavily on a small stool, the blood pooling at her feet, her blue dress crimson, her face white as a sheet.

Two ambulancemen soon arrived, and stretchered her downstairs to the hotel lobby. Leila watched from the top of the stairs, clutching her friend's diamond tiara. Minki looked up and called out from the stretcher: 'Remember to give it back to the countess for me. I promised I'd return it.'

. . .

Visiting Minki in hospital the following morning, Leila was relieved to find her friend sleeping peacefully. She sat by the bed for a while, watching her. Finally, Minki opened her eyes.

'Hello darling,' said Leila. 'How are you?'

'I'm not sure...' whispered Minki. 'Have I been asleep?'

'Yes... it's what you needed.'

Minki looked around her. 'Where am I?'

'Hospital. Don't you remember?'

Minki touched her stomach. 'The baby,' she said flatly.

'It's gone, Minki... I'm sorry.'

'I see... But why are you here? Aren't you supposed to be on your honeymoon?'

'We've cancelled it.'

'Oh no! Not because of me, I hope. Oh, don't do that.'

'We can go another time... it's not important.'

At that Minki began to weep. 'I don't deserve you. I ruined your wedding – and after all you've done for me.'

'You didn't ruin it... besides, everyone was very concerned.'

Minki turned away. 'Now they'll all know.'

'Don't worry about that. You've never concerned yourself with what others think. It's one of the things I love about you.' She smiled, and reached across the bedclothes to take Minki's hand.

'That's true,' said Minki, wiping her tears away. 'What do I care what people think? Did you give the countess back her tiara?'

'Yes, I went there this morning. She sends her love, and was most concerned about you, obviously.'

'She hoped I'd snare a husband with that tiara.' Minki smiled ruefully. 'Fat chance of that now.'

'Look, darling, you just need to get your strength back and then things will regain some perspective. Miscarriages happen. You'll have another chance.'

Minki turned away again, tears streaming down her face. She bit her lip and buried her head in the pillow. 'I need to sleep,' she said quietly.

'Of course,' replied Leila, standing up. 'I'll come back later.'

'Don't,' said Minki. 'I'm going back to Nuremberg later today.'

'You can't go – not yet,' replied Leila.

'I can, and I must. I have to put this behind me. Get on with my life... work.'

'But Minki—' Leila persisted.

'No – don't try to argue with me. I'll be all right, really. Go on honeymoon with Viktor, and forget about me for a while. I'll write in a few weeks, I promise.'

Viktor was waiting in Hannah and Levi's apartment when Leila returned from the hospital; she fell into his arms. 'Oh, Viktor, I'm so glad to see you.'

'How was she?' he asked.

'Fine... but odd.'

'In what way odd?'

'She just seems to want to put the whole thing behind her, as if nothing had happened. She's going back to Nuremberg today. Oh, and she doesn't want us to change our plans.'

'Well, it's her decision, I suppose.'

'But Viktor, she's lost her child. She must be devastated. I know I would be.'

'The two of you are so very different. It's one of the remarkable things about your friendship with her. You're so unalike and yet you are as close as sisters.' He chuckled. 'I always knew that by marrying you, I was in some senses taking her on as well. You'll be close to her for the rest of your lives. But she is entitled to make her own decisions, Leila. What would be right for you might not work for her. Let her go. She'll cope. She's strong. And she's right – we should go on honeymoon; we deserve it. You deserve it. So, go and pack your bags. If we hurry we can still catch the afternoon train.'

PART TWO

1930–1934

The press is like a piano in the hands of the government,
on which the government can play.

JOSEPH GOEBBELS, 1933

15

BERLIN

Minki Sommer waited at the side of the road for a tram to pass. As it snaked away, a gust of wind caught the brim of her trilby hat. Clutching it to her head, she darted across the road and into the offices of *Deutsche Allgemeine Zeitung* – a conservative newspaper, based in Berlin. As deputy features editor of the women's pages, she wrote articles that reflected the interests of Germany's womenfolk, focussing on child-rearing, house-keeping and fashion. It was not, if she were honest, her ideal metier; instinctively she was drawn to political reporting. But after her time at *Der Stürmer*, with its poor reputation, she had found it hard to be taken seriously as a political journalist.

Minki had no regrets. Her new job was relatively well paid, came with a private office and phone line, and the hours were compatible with having a social life. Her colleagues were exclusively male, and many of them had tried to persuade her to go out with them, but so far she had refused them all. She had long ago made the decision not to marry a journalist. Instead, she was looking for a man with status and money.

Home was a charming one-bedroom apartment on the first floor of an elegant building in the centre of town. It was furnished with eclectic items she had found in junk shops – little gilded sofas jostled for position with Moroccan inlaid side tables. As in all her previous apartments, the kitchen cupboards were relatively bare, with just a couple of plates, cups and saucers. There was no need for more, as she ate out most evenings. Her one concession to domesticity was to grow geraniums in her window boxes – a relatively new passion. In the summer, she would throw open the windows and admire the cheerful scarlet flowers bobbing in the breeze.

One morning in early September, Minki settled at her desk, lit her first cigarette of the day and flicked through her notes for the piece she was intending to write. Her article would attempt to explain how a good German housewife could make one joint of beef feed a family of four for a week. After the relative hedonism of the late 1920s, economising was once again top of the German people's agenda. The world financial crash in 1929 had heavily impacted the German economy, and explaining to readers how they could save money had become increasingly important. It amused Minki that she was responsible for providing culinary advice, for she rarely cooked. Instead, she had befriended a network of professional chefs who provided her with useful recipe ideas. As she fed a piece of paper into her typewriter, ready to start work, she was startled by the noisy jangling of her private phone.

'Good morning, Minki.' It was Joseph Goebbels.

Since Hitler's release from prison at the end of 1924, Goebbels had risen swiftly through the ranks of the National Socialist Party. No longer the impoverished, unemployed writer, he was now the Gauleiter of Berlin – effectively the leader of the Party in the capital and one of its most influential voices.

'Good morning, Joseph,' said Minki. 'What can I do for you?'

'I want you to come for dinner – tonight. I'm holding a small party in my apartment, and I want you to be there.'

It sounded more like an order than an invitation, but no journalist could possibly turn it down. Elections for the Reichstag were coming up later that month, and Minki's close friendship with Goebbels put her in pole position to get the inside story on the Party's election strategy. Although she was not herself a political journalist, having inside information increased her status at the paper. The editor would be intrigued by her perspective on the elections, knowing that her information came from the top.

'Well, can you come to dinner?' Goebbels persisted. Ever the tease, Minki made a small pretence of checking her diary.

'Mmm, let me see... yes,' she said eventually. 'I think I can squeeze you in. What time?'

'Eight? And wear something beautiful...'

The phone went dead.

Minki leaned back in her chair, exhaling cigarette smoke. 'Wear something beautiful,' she mused. 'What on earth is he up to?'

Back in her apartment after work, Minki quickly looked through her wardrobe. She pulled out a selection of dresses, wondering which one would be the most alluring. She finally chose a dress of dark blue velvet. Fashionably cut on the cross, it clung to her body, emphasising her broad shoulders, long limbs and full bosom.

She hoped Joseph would like it. Although it had been some months since they had slept together, she interpreted his instruction to 'wear something beautiful' as an invitation that he would like her to stay. If that were his plan, she would probably agree. She enjoyed his company, and sex with him was pleasant enough. Occasionally, she had even wondered what it would be like to be married to him. They had much in common, after all. Both were writers, and understood the frustration of unemployment. Both had struggled at the start of their careers, but were now on the up. But was that enough? She admired his mind, but did she really love him? More importantly, did he really love her?

One of the perennial stumbling blocks in their relationship was his inability to be faithful to one woman at a time. Through all the years they'd known each other he had two, three or even four women on the go at any one time. Minki could put up with this sexual incontinence as one of his occasional lovers, but not as a wife.

Goebbels had finally abandoned the hapless Else, confiding in Minki: 'How on earth could I marry a Jewish woman – Hitler would find it quite unacceptable.' With Else out of his life, he had soon revived a previous relationship with a woman named Anka, who by then was married to another man and had a child. But that too fell apart, and since then numerous other women had come and gone. What they all had in common, it seemed to Minki, was their ability to 'love him like a mother'. That was Goebbels' constant refrain; but Minki was not a motherly sort of woman.

She finished dressing – selecting black suede shoes and a small velvet evening bag – and brushed through her thick blond hair, admiring her own reflection. Should she make a play for Goebbels? She wasn't in love with him, but there was no doubt he was a catch. He was increasingly powerful, and with power came riches. In many ways he was everything a sensible woman could want in a husband.

Putting on her fur coat, she recalled the advice the countess had given her just before she left Munich all those years before. 'Don't marry for money, Minki, but marry where money is...' It was good advice, but was it enough?

Goebbels opened the door to his apartment wearing a dark double-breasted suit with his red Nazi armband prominently on display.

'Minki, it's wonderful to see you, as always.' He kissed her delicately on the lips – something he always did. It was his way of saying, '*I know you, I have made love to you, so I'm entitled to kiss you this way.*'

'It's lovely to see you too, Joseph.'

He removed her fur coat, revealing the blue dress, and gasped. 'I see you took me at my word – blue is definitely your colour, Minki. Now, come through, there is someone rather important I want you to meet.'

Entering the large wood-panelled drawing room, Minki looked around at the assembled guests, and was startled to see Adolf Hitler standing by the fireplace. In all the years she had known Joseph, he had never introduced her to 'the great man'. So why now? Perhaps that was the reason behind his instruction to 'wear something beautiful'. Was she perhaps being set up as a future mistress for the Party leader?

'Everyone, this is Minki Sommer,' Joseph announced. 'Minki's an old friend.' He put his arm round her shoulders and kissed her cheek – *laying claim to me again*, Minki thought. She smiled and nodded to the assembled guests, meeting Hitler's gaze last.

He studied her for a few seconds, then strode towards her, his hand outstretched. 'Enchanted,' he said, bowing slightly to kiss her hand. 'Joseph has told me all about you. You're a journalist, I hear?'

Minki blushed involuntarily. Hitler was not handsome, but

there was something powerful about him, a strength and masculinity, which was almost erotic. She recalled the women in the spectators' gallery at his trial, fantasising about sharing his bath, and began to understand the appeal. 'I'm delighted to meet you at last,' she said. 'I've followed your career with interest.'

'Who do you write for?' asked Hitler.

'*Deutsche Allgemeine Zeitung*. I'm the deputy features editor – but only of the women's pages,' she added almost apologetically.

'She's wasted there,' said Goebbels, handing her a drink. 'She would make a wonderful political reporter... she has all the right instincts. I've tried to persuade her to join my own newspaper, but she's reluctant. Maybe you can convince her?'

'Oh, Joseph really...' said Minki, laughing. Joseph had founded the National Socialist Party newspaper *Der Angriff* a few years earlier, and had tried in vain to persuade Minki to join its ranks.

Hitler gave a tight-lipped smile, but his bright blue gaze never left Minki's face. 'I wouldn't dream of telling the lady how to live her life,' he said. 'But I hope we can get better acquainted this evening.'

When the guests moved through to the dining room for dinner, they found little place cards had been laid out above each place setting – each printed with a tiny swastika. To her surprise, Minki found her place card next to Hitler's. He pulled out her chair for her before sitting down beside her. While wine was served, she surveyed the other guests. They were a predictably dull group. Goebbels took up his position at the head of the table with Hitler on his right. To his left was a dumpy little woman with mousy-coloured hair and a lavender dress. Next to her sat a tall thin man with a slit of a mouth and an unnaturally high forehead. They introduced themselves to Minki as Hilda and Otto Schneider and announced, proudly, that Otto owned a steel factory outside Berlin.

Goebbels had long since abandoned his libertarian, artistic friends. These people were obviously devoted Party supporters – the women were dressed conventionally in prim cocktail dresses, and the men wore smart dark suits. But one man, seated at the far end of the table, stood out. Resplendent in an elegant black dinner jacket, he was fair-haired and well built. He was chatting amiably to the woman on his right, but kept glancing up the table towards Minki. They smiled at one another, each acknowledging the other as somehow outside this group of dreary, conventional-looking people.

The conversation over dinner revolved around the coming election. Predictably, Hitler took the lead, his voice deep and sonorous. 'This election in a week's time is our chance. We must take it with both hands. People are beginning to get disillusioned. Money is tight and unemployment is on the rise. We can offer them an alternative: the chance of a better life.'

'How can you possibly promise that?' asked Minki boldly.

Hitler turned to her, once again fixing her with his powerful gaze. 'I will make Germany a great European power again. I will take back the territory that was stolen from us after the war. I will put the people back to work, and build up our industries. The people of this country will be proud to call themselves German again.'

The diners all murmured their approval, and the woman opposite suddenly blurted out, 'Heil Hitler.' Surprised and a little shocked by her intervention, the other diners fell silent. The woman blushed with embarrassment, and her husband placed his hand on his wife's arm, muttering, 'Hilda, my dear, please...'

But Hitler, clearly delighted by this outburst, was all smiles. 'I thank you, dear lady. It is women like you who are the backbone of this country. You are the wives and mothers who give love and succour to the men who will make Germany great again. I salute you.' He held up his glass and toasted her. The woman giggled, covering her mouth with her hand, while her husband beamed proudly.

Hitler then turned to Minki. 'You are also important, Fräulein,' he murmured softly. 'You write articles for women – yes?'

'Yes.'

'My Party understand the importance of sending the right message to the homemakers of this country. You have a vital part to play in helping us to succeed.'

Minki laughed. 'You really think that writing articles about how to make a good dinner out of cheap ingredients will help?'

'Of course. We must all work together now to make Germany great. Running a house properly is as important as running the country, something women instinctively understand. That's why they are essential to our victory. The National Socialists will never win elections without the support of women.'

After dinner the group retired to the drawing room. Goebbels sat at the piano and proceeded to play. Minki recognised it as a Beethoven piece – 'Für Elise' – which had been part of her own mother's repertoire. Minki had never heard Goebbels play before and was surprised at his hidden talent. He really was the most remarkable man, she thought. He finished the piece with a flourish of his hand, stood up and acknowledged the applause of his guests. The handsome man in the dinner jacket stood up and sauntered over to the piano. 'It sounds a fine instrument, Joseph. Might I play?'

'Of course, Max.'

The man sat down, flexed his fingers, and began to play a much more complex piece of music.

The other guests listened attentively for a few minutes, but soon began to chat among themselves. Minki, however, was mesmerised. She wandered over to the piano and draped herself across it. 'That's wonderful,' she said. 'What is it?'

'Schubert,' replied the man. He reached the end of a phrase and stopped. 'I don't think we've been properly introduced. My name is Max von Zeller.'

'Minki Sommer. It's nice to meet you. Please, don't stop... do carry on.'

He made space for her beside him on the long piano stool, and continued his performance. She listened with rapt attention, enchanted by his dexterous hands and obvious affinity with the music.

At the end of Max's recital, the assembled guests applauded politely. 'Enough, I think,' he said, closing the lid on the piano keys. 'People can only be polite for so long.'

'Well, I think they must be philistines if they didn't love it,' said Minki. 'Is that what you do for a living – play the piano?'

He laughed. 'No. I learned as a boy and like the chance to show off. But I *am* in the arts.'

'Oh, really? What do you do?'

'I am a film producer at the studios in Potsdam.'

'How fascinating. What sort of films?'

'Love stories, romances, comedies – anything and everything.'

She glanced across the room and saw Goebbels watching her intently. 'Have you ever worked for Joe?'

'Not yet... but I'm sure it won't be long before he comes to me with a project.'

Minki laughed. 'He once had ambitions as a dramatist, you know.'

'Did he? Yes, I can imagine that.'

'He wrote a play years ago, as well as a novel called *Michael* – perhaps you've read it?'

'No, I haven't. How fascinating. Was it any good?'

Minki hesitated. 'It was... interesting. It was written in the form of a diary, and the central character was a man not unlike the Party leader.' She nodded towards Hitler, who was now deep in discussion with Goebbels. 'They hadn't met at that point,' she went on, 'but the likeness is remarkable. It was as if Joseph conjured him up – brought him into existence.'

Max studied her closely. 'What a fascinating woman you are,' he said, touching her hand gently. 'You've obviously known Joseph for some time?'

'Yes... we met in our early twenties – both of us were impoverished and frustrated writers at the time.' Minki paused. She didn't want to discuss her relationship with Goebbels; she was more interested in Max's marital status.

'Did you bring your wife tonight?' she blurted out, blushing with embarrassment at her own boldness.

'I'm not married,' he replied, smiling. 'Are you?'

'No.'

'I thought perhaps you and Joseph were together.'

'No. As I explained, Joseph and I go back a long way – but we're just friends.'

A few moments later, Goebbels appeared at her side. 'Minki, darling – come and say goodbye to Adolf...' He took her arm and guided her across the room, whispering in her ear: 'He is most impressed...'

'Ah, Fräulein Sommer,' said Hitler, taking her hand and kissing it again. 'It was a delight to meet you. I hope we will meet again.'

'Yes... I'd like that.'

With Hitler gone, Max also prepared to leave. 'Well, Joseph, I should be making a move. It was a delightful evening, thank you.'

'My pleasure, Max. We must have that meeting soon. There are things to discuss.'

'Of course.'

Max bowed to Minki. 'It was a great pleasure to meet you, Fräulein. I wonder... might I give you a lift?'

Minki instinctively looked at Goebbels for approval. He nodded, and shrugged his shoulders, as if to say, *fine, it's nothing to do with me*.

Downstairs, Max led Minki by the arm to his parked Mercedes and ushered her into the passenger seat. As soon as he had taken his place behind the wheel, he reached across, took her in his arms and kissed her. When he finally released her, he murmured: 'I've been wanting to do that from the moment you walked in this evening.'

Minki smiled. 'Well, you can do it again if you like.'

16

MUNICH

Leila held Sofia's head over the lavatory basin. 'Try to be sick, Sofia, it will make you feel better.'

The child retched, then looked up at her mother. 'Can I have a glass of water please?'

Leila held the glass to the girl's lips, and patted her brow with a damp flannel. 'Are you feeling better now?'

Sofia nodded silently. Leila picked her up and carried her through to the bedroom she shared with her younger brother. Although it was early in the morning, the boy was already awake, sitting cross-legged in his pyjamas, banging a metal toy train loudly on the wooden floorboards. The noise tore through Leila's thumping head – it had been a long night caring for Sofia.

'Axel, sweetheart, stop doing that. Sofia's not well and she's tired.'

Axel shrugged and wandered out of the room. 'Daddy, Daddy,' he called out. Within minutes Viktor appeared at the children's bedroom door. 'How is she?'

'She was sick again. I don't think there's much left, poor little thing. I'll get her into bed. Perhaps I should stay at home today...'

'There's no need, Leila. I can do that. I've got a new manuscript to start editing. I can do it as easily here as in the office – more easily really.'

'Oh, all right. But what about Axel – won't he disturb you? Perhaps I should I take him to my mother?'

'Yes, that's a good idea – she can take him to the park to run off a bit of steam. I can collect him later.'

Leila reached up to her husband. 'You're the nicest man, really you are.'

'Don't be silly.' He leaned down and kissed her. 'Now, go and get ready. I'll look after this little one.'

Leila and Viktor had now been married for just over six years. Their daughter, Sofia, was born nine months after their wedding celebrations – almost to the day. Leila had, of course, been delighted to find she was pregnant – having children had always been important to her. But the early arrival of a child had left little time for her and Viktor to be together as a couple, and there was a tiny part of her which regretted that. Axel had arrived two years later and the pair decided that their family was now complete. With each child Leila had only taken a couple of months off from the *Munich Post*, and it was a constant juggling act. Leila's parents had been a huge help and stepped in when necessary, but without Viktor's constant and flexible support life would have been impossible.

There were times when Leila would watch her husband cuddling Sofia and Axel on the sofa before supper, or listen to him reading bedtime stories, and think to herself that she was the luckiest, most contented woman in the world.

. . .

Later that morning, Leila dropped Axel at her mother's apartment. As she hurried to work, she glanced down at her watch, and she realised she was over an hour late.

The newsroom was already bustling with activity by the time she arrived.

'Ah, there you are, Leila,' said Julius Zerfass. 'Martin was looking for you earlier – he's in his office.'

Leila hurried over to Martin Gruber's office. He and Edmund were studying some papers as she arrived.

'Good, Leila, here you are,' said Martin. 'Come in... take a seat.'

Leila sat down gingerly, and instantly began to apologise. 'I'm sorry I was so late... Sofia's not very well.'

'Don't worry about that. She's all right now?' Martin asked.

Leila nodded.

'Good, because I need to talk to you about the Reichstag elections next week.'

'What about them?'

'I want you to go to Berlin with Edmund.'

'Me... go to Berlin? Are you sure?'

'Yes, of course. It will be good experience for you, and Edmund will need an assistant.'

'I'd be honoured, obviously,' she replied.

'What about the children – will Viktor mind?' asked Martin.

'Of course not. It's my job – he'll understand. And my mother can help out.'

'Excellent. We're just going through the list of parliamentary seats, working out our plan of action. Here are the details.' Martin handed her a file of papers. 'The National Socialists are throwing everything at this election. The financial crash has created the perfect environment for them to make ground. We have seven million unemployed in Germany now, and it's only going to get worse. There's a good chance that Hitler and his Party will take a considerable number of seats.'

Leila was aghast. 'Could they win a majority?'

Martin shrugged. 'Unlikely, but you never know.'

Leila sighed. 'When Hitler was arrested back in '24 we thought it was all over, didn't we?'

Martin eyed Leila closely, peering over his glasses. 'You may have hoped that my dear, but I had no such illusions. The monster was merely sleeping. Our work is just beginning in earnest now. It's up to us, and papers like ours, to expose his evil. You have a couple of days to get prepared. My secretary will organise your accommodation. You and Edmund will go up to Berlin as soon as you can – all right?'

'Yes... And thank you for your faith in me.'

As Leila settled into her seat on the train opposite Edmund the following Sunday, her excitement was tinged with anxiety about leaving the children. They had wanted to go to the station in Munich and see her off, but she had begged Viktor to keep them at home.

'I'm not sure I could leave at all if I saw them there on the platform. It's better if I can imagine them here at the flat with you and Mother, knowing they're happy, playing safely. Do you understand, Viktor?'

'Yes, darling. But you mustn't worry so. I'm quite capable of looking after them. I can take Sofia to school each day before work, and Axel is thrilled to have his grandmother all to himself for several days. Don't worry – just try to enjoy the sense of freedom, and the chance to concentrate on work and nothing else. It will do you good.'

Now, as the train pulled out of the station, Leila knew she had made the right decision. Viktor was right – the children would be fine, and she was looking forward to the next few days. She sat back, took out her notes and lost herself in her research.

On the way to Berlin, the train stopped at Nuremberg. Peering out at the bustling passengers on the platform, Leila recalled the last time she had been there, visiting Minki. What an odd time it had been, she thought – Minki's revelation of her pregnancy, Leila offering to take the child. Looking back, she realised how misguided she had been in offering to take the baby. It was the naive gesture of a young woman who had no concept of the responsibility of motherhood. What was remarkable was that Viktor had been prepared to go along with it. Now they had two children of their own, she saw how generous he had been in even considering it.

In the months following her marriage, with so much to do and think about, Leila had lost touch with her closest friend. But when Sofia was born, she had been thrilled to receive a letter.

> *I heard on the grapevine that you are a mother. I can only say that your child is the luckiest child in the world.*
>
> *I am now living in Berlin – quite settled and happy. I work on the women's pages of* Deutsche Allgemeine Zeitung. *Isn't that funny? Me – writing articles about knitting and cookery. It's laughable really, but I rather enjoy it. There is no stress at all, apart from the pressure of having to concoct these ridiculous stories. I have a wonderful little apartment, with geraniums in the window boxes. Can you believe it – me with flowers? Do come and see me if you're ever in Berlin.*
>
> *With all my love,*
>
> *Minki*

Leila had been relieved to get her friend's letter. Minki

sounded like her old self, she thought, cheerful and optimistic. After that, they had occasionally written to each other, but Minki never again suggested they meet. The physical distance between them was the major barrier, but sometimes Leila wondered if the disparity in their situations – one happily married with children and a career, the other unmarried, possibly still mourning a lost child – made meeting too painful for Minki.

Now, as the train rumbled north towards Berlin, Leila decided to surprise her friend and drop in on her as soon as she got there.

Once settled in her hotel, Leila studied a map and saw that Minki's apartment was nearby, overlooking the Tiergarten, the large park in the centre of Berlin. She headed out and soon found the address. She noticed two windows on the first floor, with scarlet geraniums trailing from the window boxes. She knew in an instant that this was Minki's apartment.

Leila rang the bell at the side of the entrance door, her heart thumping slightly. It had been six years since they had last seen each other. Would Minki have changed? Would they still like one another? What if she didn't even want to see her? Suddenly, she heard a window opening above.

'Hello. Who's there?'

She looked up to see Minki leaning out of the window.

'It's me, Minki... Leila.'

'Leila! Wait there. I'm coming down.'

Moments later, the main door was flung open, and out came Minki, beaming, her arms outstretched. 'Leila... darling Leila.' They hugged each other closely, laughing and giggling.

'Come inside,' said Minki, almost hauling Leila up the stairs and into her first floor apartment.

Through the tiny entrance hall, Leila followed Minki to the kitchen, where she poured two large glasses of white wine. 'Let's go the sitting room,' said Minki, leading Leila by the hand.

They sat together on the tiny sofa. 'Oh, Leila, I can't believe you're actually here.'

Leila laughed. 'Neither can I really. Oh, it's so good to see you, Minki, and I love the apartment – it's utterly charming. And you look wonderful too.'

Minki blushed with pleasure. 'You're too kind. I could say the same about you. So how are Viktor and the children – and what brings you to Berlin? You must tell me everything.'

The pair sat up late into the night. Minki listened happily as Leila shared the delights of motherhood and family life. Shyly, Minki shared her own news.

'I think I've finally met someone.'

'Really?' replied Leila excitedly. 'Oh, tell me all about him.'

'It's very early days... He's a film producer – not my usual sort at all. I met him at Joe's...'

'Joseph Goebbels?'

'Yes... that's right.'

'I didn't realise you had stayed in touch. He's quite high up in the Party now, isn't he?'

Minki nodded. 'Yes, very.'

'Are you still... lovers?'

'No – not for a while now, anyway.'

There was an awkward silence. The mere mention of Goebbels had highlighted the huge division between them.

'Are you a supporter of the Party?' Leila asked tentatively. It was a risky question and she wasn't sure she wanted to know the answer.

'No, not at all,' replied Minki firmly. 'I remain politically neutral – agnostic – as always. I'm an interested observer, that's all. And you know me... the inner "hack" inside me is always looking for stories. Joe invited me to dinner the other night and sat me next to Adolf Hitler himself.'

Leila felt her stomach churn. To her, and the rest of her

press colleagues, Adolf Hitler was the enemy. To share a dinner table with him was unthinkable.

'He was very charming,' Minki continued airily. 'Quite handsome in an odd sort of way – very powerful, you know, with a very deep voice – rather masculine. He thinks they stand a good chance at the elections.'

'So I understand.' Leila wondered if Minki understood how hurtful her comments were. How could she not see the danger of mixing with a man well known for his hatred of Jews who was now on the cusp of taking power? Should she challenge Minki, she wondered. Fearful of damaging their relationship, she decided against saying anything. Instead she stood up, pulling on her gloves. 'Well, it's getting late, and I really must go. I've got a long day tomorrow.'

'Shall I see you again while you're in Berlin?'

'Perhaps... it depends on the work. We'll be very busy, and as soon as we finish I'll be desperate to get back to Munich. I already miss the children, and I've only been gone a few hours.' Leila smiled nervously.

'Well, if I don't see you again while you're here, Leila, take care, won't you. And give Viktor my love.'

'I will.' Leila headed for the door, but turned back to Minki. 'Darling... you will be careful, won't you? These people you're involved with... they are not what they seem. They are danger-ous. They have bad intentions.'

Minki hurried across the room and hugged Leila tightly. 'Don't worry about me. I'm a survivor and I don't easily get taken in. As I said, I merely watch from the sidelines. It's what journalists are supposed to do, isn't it? To be impartial observers.'

Leila nodded, but she wondered if Minki really understood. Sometimes, to be an impartial observer was not possible.

Outside in the street, Leila looked up at Minki's apartment. She was waving goodbye, her cheery geraniums in the window boxes still glowing in the half-light. Leila waved back, but, walking away across the park, she felt profoundly uneasy. If intelligent people such as Minki could not see the threat that Hitler posed, then the world was about to get very dangerous indeed.

17

BERLIN

November 1930

From the moment Minki and Max had met, theirs had been a whirlwind romance. Max – clearly smitten with the beautiful journalist – had sent Minki flowers and presents; he had squired her around town, taking her to all the best restaurants and introducing her to his wide circle of friends and colleagues. Inevitably, Minki was flattered and excited. It had been a long time since a man had shown her such unbounded affection. Her only other true love had been Peter, the American journalist who had stolen her heart six years earlier and the father of her lost child. After he had gone back to America, she had promised herself she would never let a man get so close to her again. His abandonment had left her broken, and with an unfamiliar sense of failure – she was normally the one who did the 'leaving' in any relationship. It had taken her years to recover – years in which she had grown an impermeable outer shell to shield herself from love. She had even denied herself sex in order to avoid getting close to anyone.

But when Max came into her life, it was as if a switch had

been turned. She found him irresistible. They spent hours making love, exploring one another's bodies. He was both experienced and generous. She responded in kind, and he often told her that she was the most exciting lover he had ever had. But was unbridled lust the same as love? Neither had ever declared their love for the other. Curiously, this didn't bother her. Her love for Peter had been desperate at times, but ultimately ended with a broken heart. Whereas she and Max made no real emotional demands on each other, and the relationship worked all the better for it. Max made her feel good about herself; he was also fun, handsome and rich. But whether she would spend her life with him... that was another matter.

One evening, as they dined at the Romanisches Café – famous among Berlin's sophisticates – Max reached across the table and took her hand. 'Minki, do you think you'll ever marry?'

'I'd like to think so,' she replied, laughing. 'Why... are you asking?'

He smiled – a broad, happy smile – took her hands in his and kissed them. 'Perhaps...'

It was typical of Max to tease her in this way. And she, being cynical and still nervous of exposing her feelings, found it easier to tease in return. So rather than encourage Max's proposal, her response was typically flippant. 'You really are the most irritating man, Max.' Again, she laughed it off.

Max suddenly became serious. 'You do realise I'm proposing to you? I've been mulling it over for a while now and can't think of anyone I'd rather marry – you're perfect, Minki. You must know I love you.'

She was taken aback by his solemnity and sudden declaration of love. But still, she couldn't quite bring herself to reciprocate.

'Well, I admit, it's a tempting offer.'

He leaned across the table, took her hand in his and kissed it. 'Are you going to make me beg?'

'Perhaps... how much do you love me?'

'With all my heart, Minki.'

'Do you really, Max? You've never said it before...' Behind her smile, she was trying to decide if he really was the man for her. She was a strong, independent woman, with a mind of her own; she would never be happy as a mere accessory to a man. Would Max accept that? More importantly, did she truly love him as she had loved Peter?

'Is there someone I should ask for permission?' he asked.

'How ridiculously old-fashioned you are, Max.'

'Your father perhaps?' he persisted. 'You rarely mention him, but I know he's still alive – you went to visit him a few months ago.'

'You can ask him, I suppose. He'd like that. He's a very traditional sort of man – I suspect that's why we never really got on. He was appalled when I said I wanted to go to university. He would have preferred me to stay at home and look after him and the house. But, unfortunately for him, that was the last thing I was prepared to do.'

'I have some sympathy with your father.' Max smiled.

'What *are* you talking about?'

'Well... most men like the idea of a beautiful woman taking care of them.'

'If it's a housekeeper or mother figure you're looking for, Max – you've got the wrong woman. May I have a cigarette?'

She reached across the table for his silver cigarette case, at the same time as Max reached into his pocket and removed a small leather box. He laid it on the table between them. 'I want neither a housekeeper nor a mother, Minki. I want you...' He opened the box, revealing a diamond solitaire ring.

'Oh, Max... it's very beautiful.'

'Like its wearer,' he replied, placing the ring on her finger.

She held out her hand, admiring the ring sparkling in the lights of the restaurant, while considering how to respond. The ring was certainly impressive, but Minki had never been the sort of woman to marry only for money.

Suddenly, Max was kneeling at her side. The whole restaurant seemed to turn and look at them.

'Oh, Max, this is embarrassing,' whispered Minki. 'Do get up.'

But he refused to move, instead taking her hand. 'Minki Sommer – I would be honoured if you would consent to be my wife.'

Minki gazed into his clear blue eyes and felt her resolve weakening. It would be perverse to refuse him – marriage to Max to would be so easy... so comfortable.

'You understand the sort of woman I am, don't you?'

'What do you mean, exactly?' he asked.

'Independent, opinionated. I won't just be your wife – I have a career, and a mind of my own.'

'I know, Minki... that's why I love you. Please say yes.'

She smiled. 'Oh, all right, Max. Yes, I'll marry you.'

'Well, that's a relief,' he said, rising to his feet. 'For a moment or two there I thought you might turn me down.'

'Well... it was a possibility, I suppose. But I do love you, Max.' The moment the words were out of her mouth she realised that it was true.

'You've never said it before.'

'Neither had you, Max – until tonight.'

'Well, we're even then,' he said, sitting back down.

There was a murmur of approval from the diners sitting nearby, and one or two clapped.

'Now look what you've done,' said Minki. 'You've made a complete spectacle of yourself.' She laughed and held out her hand, admiring the ring.

'So... about meeting your father?'

'Well, dear Max, if you really want to meet him, I suppose we'll have to drive down to Augsburg.'

The pair arranged to visit Minki's father the week before Christmas.

Snow lay on the ground, as Max's Mercedes crunched up the long drive to her family home. Minki was suddenly transported back to her younger self – no longer the impressive, independent career woman, but a nervous child. She gripped Max's hand as they pulled up outside the house. 'Why did we come here?' she murmured, suddenly anxious. 'I've never got on with my father... let's just go to Munich and forget all about it.'

'Don't be silly, sweetheart. He knows we're coming... it would be rude just to drive away. Besides, I'd like to meet him.'

Pulling her mother's fur coat round her, Minki led Max to the grand porch and rang the bell. Max wrapped his arm protectively round her shoulders, kissed her forehead and smiled encouragingly.

To her surprise, her father opened the door himself, smiling broadly. 'Minki... how lovely. And this must be your young man.'

'Max von Zeller, sir,' said Max, holding out his hand. 'It's an honour to meet you.'

'Gunther Sommer,' he replied, shaking Max's hand. 'Well, come in, come in, both of you, don't let all the cold air in.'

He ushered the couple into the hall, where a maid took their coats.

'We've lit the fire in the sitting room,' he said, 'so it's nice and warm. And lunch will be ready in an hour or so.'

'That sounds excellent,' said Max. 'But I wonder if, first, I might speak with you privately, sir?'

Gunther glanced over at his daughter. 'Does he mean what I think he means?'

Minki shrugged. 'I suspect so. Max wants to ask you for my hand in marriage. I told him it was none of your business – but he's an impossible romantic, and old-fashioned to boot.'

'Minki!' whispered Max. 'There's no need to be quite so outspoken.'

Gunther smiled. 'My daughter is nothing if not headstrong and opinionated, Max. You'd better come into my study – we can talk man to man in there. Minki, you can wait for us in the sitting room.'

Minki knew there was no question of her father refusing Max, but nevertheless the idea of her future being discussed by these two men was irritating. To distract herself, she studied the silver-framed photographs in the sitting room. Arranged in groups on various side tables, and on the grand piano, most were of her mother, Greta. They chronicled much of her adult life until her untimely death, aged just thirty-five. There were pictures of her on her wedding day, standing ramrod straight in a long Edwardian gown and large straw hat. Another showed her laughing gaily, wearing a silk evening dress, with feathers in her hair. Another of her hiking on a Bavarian hillside, and fishing on a lake. Minki wondered who the photographer had been – it must have been her father, she presumed, and yet she struggled to imagine him with this joyous, energetic woman.

Above the fireplace was an oil portrait of Greta that she knew well. Her mother's blue eyes followed the viewer around the room. They matched her pale-blue day dress exactly. Had that been that artistic licence, Minki wondered, or were Greta's eyes really that shade of blue? So many years after her mother's death, she struggled to remember.

There were only two photographs of Minki herself. One had been taken when she was a child, dressed in corduroy trousers with a mop of blond hair, astride a fat little pony. Her mother, looking impossibly beautiful in jodhpurs and a fitted jacket, was holding the reins. Minki tried to recall where the photograph had been taken. She had never owned a pony of her own, so they must have been on holiday. It distressed her that she couldn't remember the details.

The second photograph took her by surprise. It was a picture of her receiving her degree. Minki had no memory of it being taken. Perhaps her father had been proud of her achievements after all.

Looking at the photograph now, it struck her how much she resembled her mother. They had the same smile, the same shaped face and hair colour. They even had a similar taste in clothes – a mixture of elegance and flamboyance. Minki's eyes suddenly filled with tears, saddened by all the experiences her mother had missed – Minki finishing school, her first party, and graduating from university. She felt sure her mother would have been proud of her – and how happy she would have been to meet her daughter's future husband.

'Well, Minki,' said her father, leading Max back into the room, 'I must congratulate you on your choice. This young man is an excellent prospect.'

'Oh, Papa – what a ridiculous thing to say,' said Minki sharply, blinking away tears. 'I'm not marrying Max because of his prospects. I love him – it's as simple as that.'

Standing behind Gunther, Max beamed at Minki, and mouthed the words, 'I love you, too.'

Lunch was served in the formal dining room. Gunther sat at the head of the table, with Max and Minki on either side of him. The conversation was dominated by the two men: they discussed Gunther's business, Max's work and his ambition for the future. Minki felt, as she often did, ignored by her father – as if her own career, her own life had no meaning.

When dessert was cleared away, Gunther finally turned his attention to his daughter. 'Well, Minki, I hope that once you're married you might come home and see your old father a little more often.'

'Yes, Papa. Although I do work, you know.'

'Not after you're married, surely?'

Minki's irritation bubbled to the surface, and she was about to reply when Max hurriedly interjected. 'Gunther, as I explained, Minki will do as she pleases after we're married. I'm sure she can manage to be a wonderful wife alongside her career.'

'Well, that's as maybe,' replied Gunther, 'but I hope I'll be able to see my grandchildren from time to time – you'll make time for that, I imagine, Minki.'

'Grandchildren! We're not even married yet, Papa.'

'Of course, Gunther,' said Max, hurriedly. 'As soon as we have children, you'll be the first to meet them.'

As the couple drove away later that afternoon, Minki breathed a sigh of relief. 'Well, thank God that's over.'

'Oh, it wasn't so bad,' said Max. 'I rather liked your father.'

'Did you?' muttered Minki, staring gloomily out of the car window.

'What's the matter, darling? You seem rather sad...' Max reached across and squeezed her hand.

'I'm sorry. It's just that my father makes me feel worthless somehow. That meeting today was the nicest he's ever been to me. Perhaps because I've finally done what he always wanted – become an appendage to a man. I was his appendage, of course, for the first eighteen years of my life, and now, as far as he's concerned, I belong to you. But for the years in between, it's as if I didn't exist. My career, my apartment, my independence have all counted for nothing. He's never told me he was proud of me – not once. Clearly I should just have married years ago, then he might have loved me more.'

'Well, I love you and am very proud of you, darling,' said

Max, kissing her hand. 'And I will never think of you as a mere appendage – I promise you that.'

Max had booked them into a smart hotel in Munich for the night before returning to Berlin. Minki persuaded him they should take the opportunity to drop in on Leila and Viktor, and rang her to make the arrangements. The next morning they drove to the Labowksis' apartment. Standing on the doorstep, Minki gripped Max's arm.

'Now you must be nice, Max. Leila is my oldest and dearest friend. You promise, don't you?'

'Of course,' he replied. 'Why would I be anything else?'

The door opened, and there was Viktor, smiling broadly. 'Minki, my dear, how wonderful to see you. And this must be the new friend I've heard so much about – it's Max, isn't it? Welcome, both of you.'

The pair were ushered up to the apartment, to find Leila doing a jigsaw with her children in the sitting room. 'Minki,' she exclaimed, leaping to her feet. 'What a wonderful treat. Are you sure you can only stay for lunch? Couldn't we persuade you to spend the night and go back tomorrow?'

'Oh, no, Leila – it's a flying visit, I'm afraid. Max has to be back in Berlin this evening. We came down to see my father. Max wanted to ask him something.' She smiled shyly.

'You're getting married,' said Leila, grabbing Minki's left hand. 'Oh, what a beautiful ring. Congratulations, both of you. Oh, Minki, I'm so happy for you.' She turned to Max. 'You must promise me to look after her, won't you? She's very precious.'

'Of course I'll look after her,' he said, cradling Minki's shoulder. 'And I agree – she is very precious indeed.'

'So, when is the wedding?' asked Leila.

'Oh, I don't know,' replied Minki. 'We've not really discussed it.'

'Soon,' said Max. 'Why wait?'

'Why wait indeed,' said Leila happily. 'Well, Minki, as I've only got you for a short time, let's go and have a private chat while we make lunch. I'm sure the men can amuse themselves.'

'Absolutely,' said Max. 'I imagine Viktor and I have a lot to discuss – you're in publishing, I understand, Viktor? You must show me a couple of your latest books.'

The two men settled down together and Leila pulled Minki into the kitchen. 'Max seems very nice,' she said when they were alone.

'He's marvellous,' replied Minki sincerely. 'I've been lucky to find him.'

'Are you hoping to start a family soon?'

'Yes, I suppose so. Max is keen.'

'Was he understanding about... the miscarriage?'

Minki glared at Leila and closed the kitchen door tight shut. 'I've not told him about that,' she whispered. 'And you're not to say anything.'

'All right. But surely Minki, a marriage shouldn't start off with secrets.'

Minki glared at her friend. 'It's my marriage and I'll handle it my own way.'

'Of course, of course,' said Leila hurriedly. 'I just meant... oh, never mind. I'm sure you'll be very happy.'

Driving back to Berlin later that afternoon, Minki reflected on Leila's advice. She was sure that Leila and Viktor had no secrets from one another. Whereas a part of her past would always be hidden from Max – he simply didn't need to know she had ever been pregnant.

· · ·

Back in Berlin, Minki adjusted to the idea of being engaged and getting married, but it occurred to her that her old lover Joseph Goebbels might not be so enthusiastic. How would he react to the news of her impending nuptials? He had always made his claim on Minki rather obvious. And while she knew he wasn't interested in marrying her, she worried he might perversely be annoyed that another man had finally claimed her.

She rang him one afternoon and invited herself over that evening. 'I have some good news, Joseph. Can I come and see you?'

Goebbels was surprisingly friendly. 'Of course. Come after work, about seven.'

Arriving at his apartment, the pair embraced, and Goebbels took her coat. 'Come through to the living room – we can talk there.'

Passing his study, Minki noticed an attractive dark-haired woman seated at his desk.

'Who's the new secretary?' Minki whispered.

'She's not a secretary,' he replied sternly, ushering her into the sitting room and closing the door. 'Her name is Magda Quandt, and she is here to help me sort out my papers.'

'Well, she's very beautiful,' said Minki, settling herself on a sofa.

Goebbels smiled. 'Do you think so? I agree – she is lovelier than any woman I've ever met. Even you, my dear Minki.'

'Joseph! I think you might be a little in love with your new paper sorter.'

Goebbels blushed slightly as he sat down.

'Your silence speaks volumes,' said Minki. 'If I'm honest, I hope you are a little in love with her, because it will make what I'm about to say much easier.'

Goebbels leaned forward eagerly. 'Go on...'

'I'm engaged to Max. I hope you'll be happy for us.'

'Dear Max... of course, I couldn't be any happier. You'll

make a marvellous couple. Congratulations, my dear. As it happens, I have an idea that Max might be helpful to us one day – in the Party.'

'Doing what?'

'His skills will come in very useful as we take the German people with us. Film, you know, is a marvellous medium for propaganda.' Goebbels smiled quietly.

'But Max doesn't do propaganda. He makes elegant, exciting films.'

'Precisely... Now he can do both.'

It was a beautiful spring day; the air was heady with the fragrance of daffodils and early blossom as Minki and Max emerged, smiling, from the registry office. To cheers from their guests, Max kissed his bride, before driving them back to his house near Potsdam for the reception.

As Leila and Viktor walked into the elegant drawing room, they each took a glass of champagne from a silver tray. 'I can't see anyone I recognise,' murmured Leila, searching the crowd for a familiar face. 'It's a shame the countess isn't here... she was such an important figure in Minki's life when we were young.'

'People drift apart,' replied Viktor sagely. 'Minki looks happy though...'

Leila had to agree. The bride, wearing a close-fitting dress of white duchesse satin, radiated happiness. Flitting between guests, she kissed cheeks, laughing gaily.

Finally catching sight of her best friend, she raced towards them, her arms outstretched. 'Leila, Viktor – how wonderful to see you, and so good of you to come all this way. Now, who can I introduce you to?' She surveyed the room, before lowering her voice to a whisper. 'I'm afraid most of the guests are rather dull business associates of Max. But my father's here... do you remember him, Leila?'

'Yes, we met a couple of times when you and I were at university.'

'Well, come and chat to him. He doesn't know a soul, and would so like to see a familiar face.'

Gunther bowed politely as Minki introduced the couple. 'Papa, you remember Leila – my best friend from university – and this is her husband Viktor Labowski – he's a very grand publisher in Munich.'

'Ah yes, Leila... we met once or twice, I seem to remember.'

'How are you, Gunther?' asked Leila.

'Oh, well enough. Relieved to see this daughter of mine finally settled.' He turned towards Viktor. 'So, publishing. How's business?'

As the two men chatted, Leila looked around the room. Out of the corner of her eye, she noticed Joseph Goebbels, standing alone in one corner of the drawing room. Much as she loathed the man's politics, the journalist in her couldn't resist the opportunity of talking to him.

'Would you excuse me a minute,' she said to Viktor. 'There's someone I must speak to...'

'Oh... who?'

'Joseph Goebbels,' she replied under her breath.

'Are you sure that's a good idea?' murmured Viktor, his eyebrows raised. 'Your paper has not exactly been his greatest fan.'

'Don't worry,' she whispered into his ear.

She crossed the room, and touched Goebbels' arm. 'Excuse me... you probably don't remember me, do you?'

He looked at her blankly.

'I'm Leila Labowski... an old friend of Minki's. My husband Viktor is a publisher in Munich. We met at one of Minki's parties many years ago. You asked Viktor to read one of your novels...'

Goebbels studied Leila's face. 'Ah, yes, I do remember you. He didn't publish it.'

'No, but I remember he thought it showed great promise.'

'Did he? Is he here?'

'Yes, he's over there, talking to Minki's father.'

'You're a journalist, aren't you? Who do you work for – remind me?'

'The *Munich Post*.'

He stared at her contemptuously.

Leila nervously filled the uneasy silence. 'You must be pleased with the results of the election. To have gained over a hundred seats is pretty impressive.'

'Yes, we made great headway,' replied Goebbels coolly. 'But there is still much to do. I seem to remember your paper was not exactly enthusiastic.'

In spite of herself, Leila flushed with embarrassment. 'It's true that we've had a combative relationship over the years. But surely it is the role of the journalist to challenge?'

'Well, despite your best efforts, I expect an even better result at the next election. Your paper will soon be a lone voice crying in the wind.'

Anxious to avoid a pointless political argument, Leila tried to change the subject. 'Minki looks beautiful, doesn't she? And so happy.'

'She does,' replied Goebbels, glancing over at his old mistress. 'But then, she has always been beautiful.'

'I thought once that you and she might marry.'

He snorted. 'Oh, no, Minki's far too independent. Will you excuse me – there is someone I need to speak to.'

Goebbels strode away across the room, gathering up an attractive woman on his arm. This must be Magda, Leila realised. Minki had told her all about the man's latest love affair with the glamorous divorcée, who she had described as

Goebbels' perfect woman – 'passionate about the National Socialist cause, rich as Croesus and motherly to boot!'

Magically, Viktor appeared at his wife's side. 'Are you all right, darling?'

'Yes, I'm fine. But I fear we are deep in the midst of the enemy.'

'What do you mean?'

'Viktor, have you noticed we are the only Jewish people here?'

'Are we? How can you tell? Do we all go around with a sign on our heads?'

'Oh Viktor, don't be silly. I just know. It makes me feel... uncomfortable.'

'So, would you like to leave?'

'I shouldn't, but yes, I would.'

'We should say goodbye at least...'

Leila looked across at the stunning bride, now laughing gaily with her handsome new husband and Goebbels. 'No, Viktor. Let's just slip away quietly.'

Driving away from Max's house, Leila again felt the sense of anxiety that increasingly accompanied her meetings with Minki. Her friend had become immersed completely in a world that was quite alien to her. A world dominated by the Party and its acolytes. A world, she felt sure, that would drive a wedge between them.

18

BERLIN

Minki emerged from the bathroom, her face white, her eyes bloodshot. Max was lying on their bed, reading the newspaper.

'Darling... are you all right?'

'No, not really.'

'Is it the baby?'

'Probably... that's the sixth time today I've been sick. I thought it was supposed to be morning sickness. Mine appears to last all day. It's really unfair. I'm four months gone at least... it should have stopped by now.'

'Poor you,' said Max. 'Maybe it's worst with your first?'

Minki had a flash of guilt. She had never told Max about the first pregnancy, which had caused no morning sickness at all. Perhaps the fact she was so unwell this time was a good sign, meaning her body was adjusting properly to being pregnant. She pushed the memories of her first lost child away and sat down at the dressing table, studying her face in the mirror. 'I'm not sure I can go out tonight, Max.'

'Oh, darling, we must go. You know what Goebbels is like...
he's expecting us – and you in particular. He adores you.'

'He adores Magda Quandt. He's quite forgotten me.'

'Don't be so silly – you'll always hold a special place in his
heart. Besides, I have business to discuss with him.'

Minki swung round on the padded seat. 'Max, I sometimes
think you only married me for my relationship with Goebbels.'
She didn't really mean it – wasn't even sure where the idea
came from – but Max flushed, with anger or embarrassment,
she couldn't tell which.

'Don't be absurd,' he said furiously. 'That's a stupid thing to
say.'

'All right... I'm sorry. It was just a joke. But do we really
have to go?'

'I told you – I have to see him.'

'Can't you just go and see him at his office?'

'It's better at a party – more relaxed.'

'Why is it so important?'

'He's talking about setting up a special unit – a film department for the Party. He hasn't said as much, but I think he's
going to ask me to head it up. I'm keen to show my face – let
him see I'm interested.'

'But why would you want such a job? You're already a
successful film producer.'

Max smiled. 'You can be a little naive sometimes, Minki. A
job like that would bring both influence and money.'

'But you already have money, Max, and what do you care
about influence?'

'In this business you are only as good as your last film. I can
see the way the wind is blowing. Hitler and his Party are gathering support every day. I feel sure they'll win the next election
and, if they do, Goebbels will be very powerful. He is talking
about taking control of the arts in Germany. I need him to see

that I can be useful. So, please darling – hurry up and get dressed.'

The party that evening was being held in Magda's glamorous flat on Reichskanzlerplatz – the circular ring road in the fashionable centre of Berlin that surrounded an elegant park. Max parked the car and the couple walked towards the apartment building.

'I hear Hitler has been invited,' said Max. 'So be on your best behaviour.'

'All right,' said Minki. 'I've not seen him for a while – not since the night I met you, in fact.'

'Oh yes... that glorious night,' Max wrapped his arm round Minki and kissed her cheek.

'I thought I was being set up as Hitler's mistress, you know.'

'Really?'

'Yes... Goebbels certainly gave me that impression. But I think I've been superseded in Hitler's affections by the lovely Magda.'

'Really – Magda and Adolf? Are you sure?'

'So I've heard...'

'You're not jealous, are you?'

'Of course not.'

'Good – because while attractive, Magda's nowhere near as beautiful as you.'

'Oh, Max, you do say the sweetest things.'

The couple arrived outside Magda's apartment building and rang the main doorbell.

'I suspect part of her appeal is her devotion to National Socialism,' murmured Max, 'which is not something we could accuse you of.'

Upstairs, a maid ushered them in and took their coats.

Minki, still feeling queasy, was relieved when the dinner gong was rung; food always made her feel better.

The guests were the usual coterie of Party faithful. Guest of honour was Adolf Hitler himself, who was seated at one end of the table between Magda and Goebbels. Minki and Max were placed at the other end. While making polite conversation with her neighbours, Minki was fascinated by the dynamic between Magda and the evening's two leading lights. Interestingly, Hitler appeared obsessed with Magda: he couldn't keep his eyes off her, hanging on her every word, while Goebbels looked increasingly uneasy.

After dinner Goebbels invited Minki to join him on the sofa in the opulent drawing room. Magda, meanwhile, sat a little apart from the rest of her guests on a small sofa in the window, locked in conversation with Adolf Hitler. She was listening intently to the Party leader, laughing at his jokes as she fiddled with her dark brown hair. Any casual observer, Minki thought, would assume they were lovers.

Goebbels began to mutter, his face colouring with fury. 'I think she's letting herself down a little,' he said sourly, motioning towards Magda.

'In what way?' asked Minki innocently, interested to hear his analysis.

'Flirting with Adolf so obviously. It's unseemly. She's always like this with the boss.'

'You shouldn't let it upset you, Joe.'

'It's just not very ladylike. I worry sometimes...' He looked away, and Minki thought she saw a tear in his eye. 'I worry that she might be unfaithful to me. How would I cope if they were to become lovers? How could I stop them?'

Minki smiled. 'It's quite funny really – you being jealous of Adolf. You're one of the most unfaithful men I've ever met.'

He shook his head. 'Not any more. I haven't made love to

another woman since the day I met her. I have sleepless nights about her when we're not together.'

Minki squeezed Goebbels' hand. 'I'm sure she loves you, Joe. Besides, she's in a very difficult position. It's obvious Hitler is mad about her. How is she supposed to deal with it – tell him to get lost? I think she's just flirting to keep him happy. I feel quite sorry for her.'

'Do you really think so?' Goebbels gazed deeply into Minki's blue eyes.

'Yes... I really think so. She's a woman of the world, who knows how to make a man happy – and I mean that kindly. She's doing what any of us would do in that situation.'

'I suppose so,' replied Goebbels sulkily.

'Adolf never seems to have a woman of his own, does he?' mused Minki. 'Maybe he's happier borrowing other people's. Less responsibility, or something.'

'You're right, Minki... He doesn't have much luck with women. He's too soft, you see? Women don't like that.' His face softened. 'I shouldn't really begrudge the boss a little affection, should I? It's so lacking in his life.'

'That's very generous of you,' replied Minki. 'But I, for one, think that Magda is the right woman for you. She clearly has something that none of your other lovers ever had... me included. You were never this sick with jealousy about me, or even Else. And what was the name of the other one you kept going back to? Anka, that's it – the married one – you were wildly in love with her.'

'Anka got in touch recently, you know. She wanted me back but I told her it's too late. I'm with Magda now, and I'm staying with her.'

Driving home, Max was unusually quiet. Minki finally broke the silence. 'Are you all right?'

'Yes,' he mumbled.

This monosyllabic response unnerved her. Normally after a party, they would share gossip and stories from the evening.

Finally, Max broke the silence. 'You and Goebbels seemed to have a lot to talk about this evening.'

'Yes... Poor Joseph.' Minki sighed. 'He's being driven mad with jealousy about Magda. He thinks she's having an affair with Adolf.'

'Is she?'

'I don't know, but I do think she's one of those women who are drawn to powerful men. It's a sort of aphrodisiac for them. Her first husband was so much older than her – I suspect she married him just for his money. Now, she's more interested in power.' She glanced across at Max. 'Did you manage to speak to Joseph about the job?'

'No,' he replied sulkily. 'He was too obsessed with you and his girlfriend.'

'Never mind, darling. Maybe go and see him at his office. Dinner parties and business deals don't mix.'

A few weeks later Minki had taken a day off work, and was resting on the sofa after lunch when she was woken by the ringing of the telephone. Sleepily she stumbled into the hall and picked up the receiver. 'Hello.'

'Minki?'

'Yes, who's that?'

'It's Joseph... I have news.'

'How exciting – go on.'

'Magda and I are engaged.'

'Oh, that's wonderful. You must be thrilled.'

'I am.' He sounded uncertain, his voice suddenly flat and dull.

'You don't sound very pleased, Joe. What's the matter?'

'Nothing really... it's just that it was quite odd.'

'What was?'

'Well, she told both Hitler and her ex-husband that we were to marry before even mentioning it with me. I was presented with a sort of fait accompli.'

'A woman who knows her own mind, obviously...' said Minki quietly. 'But you want to marry her, don't you, Joe? I mean... you love her desperately.'

'Oh, yes – very much.'

'And how did Adolf take it?'

'Surprisingly well, I think. I was worried at first – thought it might come between us – but he and I had a good conversation the other evening. He told me I was a "lucky devil". Those were his exact words. He loves Magda, you see, but doesn't begrudge my happiness. In his eyes I got there first and that's that.'

'Well, that's one good thing. When are you getting married?'

'Soon, I suspect – before Christmas. It won't be a big affair. There's a lot of politics going on at the moment. But we'd love you and Max to come.'

'Really?' replied Minki, flattered. 'Are you sure?'

'Of course – we're very fond of you both. Anyway... How are you?'

'Me? Oh, getting fatter.'

'When's the baby due?'

'Just after Christmas. Honestly, I think I must have got pregnant on our wedding night.'

'You'll be a wonderful mother.'

'Do you really think so? I worry that I'm too selfish.'

'Well, if you are, having children will cure you of it.'

'Will you and Magda have children?'

'We hope to. Magda is very keen, I'm glad to say. But she must have a little operation first.'

'Oh, nothing serious, I hope.'

'No, just some woman's problem... I'm sure it will be all right.'

The Goebbels' wedding was held at the Quandt family estate a couple of hours' drive from Berlin. Magda had been granted right of residence to the fine red-brick manor house by her ex-husband as part of the divorce settlement.

The night before the wedding Max and Minki checked into a local hotel. The following morning, as Max lay on the bed, working his way through a pile of newspapers, Minki studied her outfit in the mirror. She had chosen a long purple dress, which was stretched tightly over her large bump.

'My God, Max,' she said, turning left and right, 'what on earth induced me to bring this ghastly dress? I look awful.'

Max leapt off the bed and wrapped his arms round her pregnant bump. 'Darling girl, you look magnificent,' he said, kissing the side of her neck. 'Like a regal ship in full sail.'

'Exactly... like a huge purple whale. At least my fur coat will conceal the worst of it.'

'You can't wear a fur coat for the entire day. You'll have to take it off when we get inside. Now stop being silly. The colour suits you wonderfully.'

'Magda will look ravishing, of course,' said Minki gloomily.

'As she should – it is her wedding day, after all. Now, if you'll excuse me, I'm going down to the dining room to get some breakfast.'

Max disappeared downstairs, and Minki applied the finishing touches to her make-up. Suddenly tired, she flopped down onto the bed and picked up a copy of the *Munich Post*. Her eye was caught by the headline:

JEWS IN THE THIRD REICH

The article had been written by the political editor, Edmund Goldschagg, with added reporting by Leila Labowski. Minki scanned it, her heart thumping:

The National Socialist Party leadership has, in the eventuality of taking power, drafted special guidelines for the 'Solution of the Jewish Question'.

Although the National Socialist Party leaders had tried to keep the plans secret, they had been leaked to the newspaper. The details made chilling reading:

Jews living in Germany will have no right to citizenship... No Jew can have a government job. A Jew cannot give testimony in a German court... All Jews will be subject to special laws. They are to pay a special tax. Jews are forbidden to give medical treatment to Christians. Marriages between Jews and Christians will be declared invalid. Jewish children are not allowed to attend German schools or universities... The German state reserves the right to intern or deport undesirable Jewish denizens who violate the interests of the German people.

As part of the *final solution*, the document continued:

...it is proposed to use Jews in Germany for labour and reclaiming German moorlands... under the control of the SS.

Minki stood up and ran to the bathroom. Clutching at the edges of the basin, she retched violently, but her empty stomach yielded nothing but water. She sank down on the edge of the bath, her head in her hands. It seemed incredible that the Party could be capable of such vindictiveness and cruelty. How could Joseph be any part of it? After all, he had once been in love with

a Jewish woman – Else– who he had loved almost as passionately as he now loved Magda. How could those feelings of love
have been replaced with such hatred? Was his lust for power so
all-consuming that he was prepared to abandon his humanity?

Minki thought of all the impressive Jewish people she knew
– in particular, of Leila and Viktor. She tried to put herself in
Leila's position – writing an article about evil policies that
would impact her own life so severely. What courage, she
thought – and what a contrast to herself. Minki had always
taken such pride in standing aloof from politics, convincing
herself that her objective stance was in some way noble. But in
reality, it was just cowardice. Instead of challenging the philosophy of the National Socialist Party, she had stayed silent, and
wasted the last few years of her life writing trivial articles about
housekeeping. Now she felt ashamed.

Moments later, Max came into the bathroom and found his
wife with her head in her hands. 'Darling, are you all right?'

'What?' She looked up at him blankly. 'Yes... I suppose so.'

'Well, come on, hurry up. We have to leave in half an hour.
We can't be late for Joe's wedding.'

'No, of course not.' She got to her feet, her legs trembling
beneath the purple dress. 'After all, we don't want to upset the
great man, do we?'

19

MUNICH

Just after Christmas, Leila was made deputy political editor of the newspaper. It was a huge honour, and to her delight the new job came with its own office – a tiny space off the main news-room. She also had a secretary, named Katja, who looked after both her and Edmund Goldschagg.

The article she had written with Edmund revealing the 'Jewish plan' had caused a huge stir. Martin Gruber, the paper's editor, was determined to keep up the pressure and insisted that his political journalists use all their contacts to find similar stories.

One day, Edmund was sent secret details of an order issued by Heinrich Himmler about eugenics – one of the National Socialists' new policies on racial superiority. Himmler was head of the SS – an elite corps of men who swore personal allegiance to Hitler. The directive contained details of how the Party intended to put the policy into action.

'Listen to this,' Edmund called out to the newsroom. His colleagues gathered round. 'I'll read you a few extracts...

'"No SS member may marry a racially inferior woman. He must check first with an SS specialist in genetics, to ensure he marries only someone who is free of hereditary disease, and possesses Nordic and German characteristics..."'

'Good God,' muttered Julius.

'Oh, and there's more,' said Edmund: '"The future of the German people depends on the selection and preservation of healthy blood."'

Martin was keen to run the story the following day. 'I've already got the headline: "Nazi Breeding Facility – Foretaste of the Third Reich".'

Reading the final text before it went to press, Leila felt a deep chill running through her body. She looked over at Julius Zerfass, that day's news editor. 'This story Edmund's written, it's almost unbelievable. Do you think people will understand what it means?'

Julius shook his head and shrugged. 'I fear most people are simply unwilling to open their minds to this sort of evil. They would rather bury their heads in the sand, and carry on with their daily lives, than challenge the authorities.'

'If the National Socialists get into power this will become law...'

Julius nodded sadly. 'It's up to us – and papers like ours – to try and stop that happening.'

Leila had just returned home that evening when the phone rang in the hall. She ran to answer it. 'Hello... yes.'

'Leila?'

'Yes.'

'It's Max... I wanted you to know that Minki had her baby last night – a girl.'

'Oh, that's wonderful news. Are they both OK?'

'Minki's tired, obviously.'

'And the baby?'

He paused.

'Max?'

'I think the baby's all right. It was a Caesarean. The baby needed oxygen.'

'Well, these things happen, Max... but it's not out of the ordinary,' Leila reassured him.

'Yes, you're probably right.'

'Max, please give Minki our love. I'm not sure how easy it would be for us to come and see her right away. We're both very busy, but I'll write.'

'She'd love that. And I suspect we'll be down in the spring to visit her father – so hopefully you can see them both then.'

A few days later, Leila arrived at work and found Martin Gruber striding around the newsroom in a rage, waving a document in the air and shouting, 'It's unbelievable... bloody outrageous...' Finally he disappeared into his office, slamming the door behind him.

'What's the matter with Martin?' Leila whispered to Julius.

'Someone's just sent him a copy of a report from a doctors' conference in Leipzig.'

'And?'

'The main speaker – a Professor Staemmler – opened his lecture by discussing the dangers of allowing "inferior" Jews and Germans to breed. Marriages between Germans and Jews, he suggested, must be made illegal. The problem he identified was how to determine who was a Jew.'

'I'm sorry – but this sounds too ridiculous,' said Leila.

'Ridiculous, but true. The professor has come up with a theory based on the amount of Jewish blood a person has in their system.' Julius glanced down at his notes. 'Yes, here it is... you are considered Jewish if you have either a Jewish parent or grandparent. You only escape the classification if your Jewish ancestry is more distant – such as traceable to a great-grandparent.'

'I see,' said Leila, sinking down onto her chair.

'Oh... but there's more. Jews are not Staemmler's only target,' Julius went on, 'he also believes that all serial criminals, prostitutes and those suffering from heritable diseases should be sterilised. Martin is furious and is writing the story himself. Expect fireworks when the paper hits the streets tomorrow.'

Early the next morning, Leila ran down to the communal hall to fetch her copy of the paper. The banner headline was printed in a huge typeface.

EUGENICS IN THE THIRD REICH

Walking back upstairs to her apartment, she skim-read the first paragraph.

> *Prof Staemmler's lecture focussed on the need to purify the German race. In his view breeding between 'inferior' Jews and Gentiles should be made illegal. Further, he proposes sterilisation of anyone with either a mental or an inheritable physical disease.*

In the kitchen, she laid the paper on the table and began to prepare the children's breakfast.

'Morning, Mutti,' said Sofia, standing behind her mother and wrapping her arms round Leila's waist.

Realising she had left the newspaper on the table, Leila swung round anxiously, hoping to remove it. But Axel had already sat down at the table, and was reading the front page. 'Mutti, what's E... U... GEN... ICS?'

Leila was at a loss. Although she had always wanted to be open with her children, some subjects were just too horrific for their young minds to cope with.

To her relief, Viktor came into the kitchen. 'Come on children, eat up. I've got a meeting in half an hour, and I've got to drop you both at school first.'

The newspaper headline was lost in the kerfuffle of cramming food into mouths and finding school bags and shoes. But when everyone had left, Leila opened out the newspaper and read the whole article with growing disbelief. The concept of 'Jewish classification' and the proposal to make marriage between Jews and Gentiles illegal was appalling, but so was the idea of sterilising anyone with an inheritable disease. What counted, she wondered, as an inheritable disease? Leila had met a couple of children at Sofia's school who had problems. There was a delightful deaf boy called Pieter, who often came back to the apartment with Sofia. He used sign language and, to her credit, Sofia was doing her best to learn it. Another friend had problems reading. 'The teacher gets so cross with her, Mutti,' Sofia had told her, 'but it's not fair, because she's really very clever. She can tell marvellous stories, she just can't seem to read the words in a book.'

Would those children be classed as suitable for sterilisation, Leila wondered.

It suddenly occurred to her that she had not heard from Minki since the birth of her baby girl. Max had sounded so worried when she was born; now Leila wondered if there was still a problem with the baby. Anxious to be reassured, she put through a long-distance call to Berlin.

'Hello.' Minki's voice sounded strained.

'Minki – it's Leila. Max told us about the baby, and I just

wanted to give you our congratulations – you must be thrilled. How are you?'

'I'm all right.' Minki sounded monosyllabic and tired.

'It's just...' Leila went on nervously, 'I was a bit worried when Max mentioned the baby had needed a bit of oxygen. Is everything all right?'

Leila could hear sobbing at the end of the phone.

'Minki... oh, sweetheart... what's the matter?'

There was a brief silence. Finally, Minki blew her nose and answered tearfully. 'The baby was a Caesarean. She was breech, you see – the wrong way round. I was put to sleep, so it was the next day when I saw her. She was in a box... with oxygen... struggling to breathe.' Minki began to weep hysterically. 'Oh Leila, Leila... it's all my fault.'

'No... Don't be silly. How could it be your fault? I'm sure she'll be all right.'

'Are you? I'm not.'

'Is the baby home now?'

'No, not yet. Maybe next week, they said. I don't know. Oh, it's all my fault. It's a punishment from God.'

'Now, Minki, don't say that. Why would you say that?'

'I'm being punished for aborting that child.'

Leila gave a sharp intake of breath. She had always assumed that Minki had miscarried. The thought of her deliberately ending the life of her baby was so upsetting that for a moment she didn't know how to respond. How could Minki have kept this from her – kept it from everyone? But finally, hearing Minki sobbing uncontrollably on the end of the phone, she felt she had to say something – anything – to comfort her. 'Surely, God doesn't punish people for things like that, Minki.'

'I never went to confession afterwards. I am a sinner, Leila. I murdered my child, and now my darling girl is damaged. I'm so frightened.'

Leila could hear the panic in Minki's voice. She was no

longer the brave, strong woman Leila had known for so long. She was a frightened girl, crazed with grief and guilt.

'Minki... you must calm down. Your feelings of regret are natural, of course. And I can barely comprehend what you went through all those years ago, but that is not the reason your baby is unwell now. You're not being punished for some past mistake. Lots of babies are born by Caesarean and need oxygen. You must have a little faith.'

'I'm trying... but it's so hard.' Minki continued, sobbing loudly.

'Now listen to me, Minki. You must think of the baby and not yourself. Your job is to protect and love your child. You're one of the strongest people I've ever known. You can do this, Minki, but you need to pull yourself together. Have you seen the baby today?'

'No. I've not seen her since I left hospital... I can't face it.'

'You must face it. Have a bath, get dressed and go to the hospital now. Sit with her, talk to her, feed her. She's your flesh and blood and it's your job to be there for her, and bring her up. I'll telephone you later, all right? Promise me you'll go?'

'I promise,' Minki replied through tears.

In the following days, while Minki's baby remained in hospital for observation, Leila did her best to encourage her friend over the phone. After a couple of weeks she received a letter.

My dearest Leila,

I'm just writing to tell you that Clara – yes, that is the name we've chosen for our beautiful girl – is back home at last.

I feel ashamed of my initial response. I think I panicked – it all felt so new and unfamiliar. But you gave me the courage to spend time with the baby in hospital and I must thank you

for that. She's improved hugely and now sleeps and feeds well,
and smiles all the time.

Her name means 'bright and clear' – did you know that? It
suits her so well.

Max has employed a nurse, which is a great help. It allows
me to rest and I'm hopeful that in a few months I might even
get back to work.

All my love,

Minki

Inside the envelope Leila found a photograph of mother
and baby. The child was the image of her mother. Even in black
and white her fair hair and bright eyes shone out. There was a
beauty and strength about her, and Minki, after all her despair,
looked truly happy, beaming at the camera. Leila propped the
photograph on her desk in the sitting room, and sat down to
write.

Dearest Minki,

Thank you for your letter and for the lovely photograph. What
a beautiful child Clara is; she is the image of you. And you
both look so well and happy. I'm so relieved. I knew in my
bones all would be well.

If you're planning on going back to work soon, can you try
to come down and see us first? If Max is too busy to drive you,
perhaps you can bring Clara on the train. We'll collect you,
and put you up.

A visit was arranged that spring. Leila collected Minki and
Clara from Munich station in Viktor's old Mercedes. As Minki
settled herself in the passenger seat, Leila was thrilled to see

how much her friend obviously adored her child, cradling Clara in her arms as if she were the most precious creature in the world.

'I've put you both in the children's room,' said Leila. 'They can spend the night at my mother's.'

'Oh no,' replied Minki. 'I don't want to put you to that trouble. I could easily go to a hotel.'

'No, don't be silly. They're thrilled about staying with my mother – she spoils them so. Besides, I want to be able to concentrate on you and the baby this evening.'

Back at the apartment, Minki handed her the sleeping bundle.

'She's exquisite,' said Leila, 'the prettiest baby I've ever seen.'

'Isn't she?' said Minki, unpacking her suitcase. 'I can't believe it sometimes – that she's here with me. I'm so grateful to you – you gave me the courage to be a proper mother. Now, I'm in love with her, completely and utterly. She's all I can think about, the only thing that matters. I'm not even sure I want to go back to work.'

'Gosh,' said Leila. 'That is a surprise.' The baby opened her eyes, stared quizzically at the stranger holding her and began to whimper. 'Oh, dear – I've upset her,' she said.

'Here... let me,' said Minki, taking the child. 'She needs a feed, I suspect. And she's still very sleepy. Do you think she's OK?'

'I'm sure she's fine. She's just a baby, Minki. Babies do sleep a lot, you know. Take advantage of it – and when she sleeps, try and get some rest yourself. Now, you feed her, while I get dinner ready.'

Half an hour later Minki came into the kitchen, and sat down at the table. 'She's fast asleep... should be down for a few hours, I hope.'

'Well, enjoy it. Have a glass of wine.' Leila poured two

glasses of Riesling and slid one across the table to Minki. 'Here's to baby Clara – may she be as bright as her name would suggest.'

'I'll drink to that,' replied Minki, raising her glass.

'And Max, is he pleased?'

'Oh yes, he's thrilled. But he's so busy at the moment he has very little time for either of us.'

'That's a shame – what's he doing?'

'Oh, he's producing a brilliant new detective film, so that keeps him busy.' Minki sipped her wine, before adding quietly, 'that and one or two other projects.'

'What sort of projects?'

'Oh, just documentaries about various things. He's about to start filming one about how young people can help farmers in the countryside.'

'By young people, I presume you mean the Hitler Youth?'

'Yes,' replied Minki, blushing slightly. 'He's also been asked to follow Hitler around the country, filming him as he speaks at rallies. Thousands of people come and see him, apparently. It's a huge undertaking.'

'It sounds like one of Goebbels' ideas... am I right?'

'Yes.' Minki nervously took another sip of Riesling. 'I know you never liked him.'

'That doesn't surprise you, I hope. Goebbels is a clever man, but he's also deeply manipulative. At the *Post*, we've heard he has been tasked by Hitler to control all aspects of our cultural life if they get into power. Is that your understanding?'

Minki nodded.

'Doesn't that terrify you, just a little?'

Minki shrugged and drained her glass, refilling it herself.

'You do know what their plans are for Jewish people like me and Viktor, don't you?'

Minki nodded, and bit her lip. 'I read that article you wrote a few months ago. It's quite wrong, I know. I wish they would stop demonising people.'

'Have you challenged Goebbels about it? He always used to listen to you.'

Minki shook her head. 'I'm not really in a position—' she began.

'I'm working on a new piece now,' Leila interjected, her anger suddenly rising despite herself. 'It's about the Nazis' obsession with creating a pure race of people – whatever that means. If it wasn't so sick you'd say it was a kind of insanity.' She wondered if Minki knew about Staemmler's proposal to sterilise people with disabilities. Should she mention it now? 'If people like us don't fight back, Minki, these ideas about racial purity will become the law... do you understand the seriousness of the situation?'

At that moment Clara began to cry from the bedroom.

'I'm sorry...' Minki muttered, rising to her feet. 'I must go to her.'

Viktor arrived home shortly afterwards, and no more was said about politics, but the division between the two friends lurked under the surface. Leila cooked supper, they ate together, drank wine, laughed a little, but all the while Leila wondered what Minki's real opinion was about her National Socialist friends. She was grateful when Minki crept off to bed, professing a headache.

In bed that night, Viktor wrapped Leila in his arms. 'What's the matter, Leila? You were so looking forward to seeing Minki, but it's obvious that all is not well between you.'

'Yes, I was looking forward to seeing her, and the baby – who is adorable, by the way – but politics came between us. Did you know that Max is making propaganda films for Goebbels now?'

Viktor shook his head.

'It means that Max, and by default Minki, have become the enemy. How can we possibly stay friends?'

'That's a bit harsh. What do you expect her to do? Leave her husband?'

'I don't know. Stand up to him, maybe. Show some courage... demand he stops what he's doing. Something has to shake her awake. It's as if she's sleepwalking into disaster.'

'Darling, you can't hope to control the way she thinks, or acts. Just be a friend to her. She'll do the right thing, when the time is right.'

'You really think so?' Leila shook her head. 'I'm not so sure any more. Something has changed since the baby was born. She's become weak and soft. She used to be such a rebel. When I was young, she was such an inspiration to me – she was independent and fearless. But now... It's as if Max's money and Goebbels' influence is just too seductive, too easy. She used to say she was 'above' politics – was proud of the fact. "An observer," she used to say. I believed her then – in fact I admired her for it – but now I think she's just a coward... a coward who won't face reality.'

Minki left early the following morning. On the surface, the friends were affectionate, promising to 'see each other soon', but, as she waved Minki goodbye, Leila was relieved. The last few hours together had opened up a wound that Leila feared would never heal.

Over the following weeks, an outpouring of revelations about the National Socialists' policies was leaked to the *Munich Post*. The Party had a secret plan to set up 'collection camps for people who were unwilling to work, or were politically unreliable'. Effectively, they intended to create a prison state.

But was there an outcry from the public? To Leila's amazement there was not. Far from her countrymen rising up and denouncing the Party, the National Socialists instead grew in popularity.

Arriving home one evening, Viktor found Leila in the kitchen, close to tears. 'What's the matter, my love?'

'I just don't understand, Viktor... What's wrong with people? Day after day, we're publishing stories that make my blood run cold. And where's the outcry? Where's the fury? It's as if everyone is asleep. They need to wake up!'

'Most people are not asleep, my love, they are simply out of work,' Viktor replied patiently. 'Millions of people are without a job in this country. They would vote for the devil if he promised to put food on the table.'

'I suppose you're right. It's just... I'm frightened, Viktor. For the first time, I'm really frightened.'

'Come on now. We'll survive.'

'But how? The worse the economy gets, the more popular that evil man becomes. The terrible things he's planning simply get brushed under the carpet. But one day we – and our children – could be imprisoned for merely existing.'

He held out his arms to her. 'It won't come to that.'

She allowed him to hold her, absorbing his strength. She loved him at that moment more than ever before. 'Viktor, if anything ever happened to you I just don't think I could survive.'

'Of course you could,' he said, kissing the top of her head. 'Your strength will see you through anything, darling. Trust me... things will get better.'

She looked up at him, her eyes filled with tears. 'Will they? I wish I had your faith, Viktor, I really do.'

20

BERLIN

Minki stood with a glass of champagne in a large reception room in the Reich Chancellery, admiring the elegant Baroque architecture. Hitler had just been appointed Chancellor of Germany, and she was one of an intimate group of friends who had been invited to celebrate.

Max had sent a car to take her to the reception. Driving through the streets, Minki had been amazed by the vast crowds standing on either side of a wide boulevard, watching a torchlit parade. The car was forced to a snail's pace and eventually had to stop. 'If you want to get to the Reich Chancellery at all tonight, Madam, I'm afraid you'd be better off walking,' said the chauffeur.

She climbed out of the car and was soon swept along with the throng. Peering over the excited crowds, she caught sight of thousands of men in matching brown uniforms marching in perfect formation, their flaming torches held aloft – like a river of fire.

Finally arriving at the Reich Chancellery, Minki showed

her invitation to the guard, and was escorted up to the reception room. Through the open French windows leading to a balcony, she could see the back of the new chancellor, arms raised, acknowledging the roars of approval from the crowd below. After a while they broke into a rendition of the national anthem: 'Deutschland, Deutschland über Alles.'

Taking a glass of champagne from a silver tray, Minki looked around nervously for someone she knew. Max had warned her that she would be alone for much of the evening, as he was filming the whole event for Goebbels.

Out of the blue, she heard a voice behind her. 'Minki... how lovely.' It was Magda, who took her by the shoulders and kissed the air on either side of Minki's face. 'Isn't this evening wonderful?'

'Yes... marvellous,' replied Minki uncertainly.

'They estimate there will be twenty thousand supporters out there this evening... all ex-soldiers, SS troops – men who've fought for their country and love what Adolf is doing for them.'

'It's very impressive.'

'I'm glad you're here... we've not seen you in ages.'

'No, I've been quite busy with the baby. And how is your new arrival?'

Magda had given birth to her and Joseph's first child the previous autumn. 'Oh, the new baby is no trouble. I've done it all before, of course. Harald – my older child – was a very difficult birth, but he's such a joy now. He's quite grown up and is away at school, you know. My focus is Joseph... and Adolf, of course. He's always at our house – he can't keep away.' Magda smiled proudly.

Minki had heard the rumours that Magda was secretly Hitler's mistress. Some said that her marriage to Goebbels was merely one of convenience – to enable Hitler to have a secret liaison with her. Magda often acted as hostess at Hitler's events, and her marital status protected her from idle gossip. It was no surprise to find her here on such an important night as this.

The two women chattered inconsequentially, but Magda seemed distracted, her eyes darting constantly to Hitler, who was now addressing the jubilant crowd from the balcony. His delivery, Minki noticed, was harsh and staccato – not at all like his normal deep, sonorous voice. Finally, his speech came to an end, followed by a crescendo of applause and cheers. Magda turned to Minki. 'Will you excuse me... but I must speak to Adolf. He'll want to know what I thought.'

As if on cue, Hitler swept into the room and made straight for Magda.

'How was it?' He sounded anxious, Minki thought, like a child asking for his mother's approval.

'You were marvellous,' Magda assured him, squeezing his arm.

He beamed and led her across the room, where they joined a group of the Party faithful.

Minki desultorily exchanged a few words with the other guests, but their attention was on the new chancellor, and all were keen to grab a few seconds with the great man. She was relieved when Max and Joseph finally arrived. Both looked exhausted, but triumphant.

'What a night!' said Goebbels, kissing Minki fleetingly on the cheek. 'I'm sure Max will tell you all about it – but if you'll excuse me I must find Adolf...' He looked anxiously around the room.

'He's over there, talking to your wife,' said Minki, motioning to the far side of the room.

Goebbels hurried away, leaving Max and Minki together.

'Isn't it fantastic, darling?' enthused Max. 'Have you had a wonderful time?'

'Oh, yes, wonderful,' murmured Minki sarcastically. 'Magda has kept me entertained...'

'The whole event will make a marvellous film,' Max enthused. 'Joseph is delighted. He's hoping Hitler will give it his seal of approval.'

Minki looked across the crowded reception room at Joseph, now standing beside Magda and Adolf. He seemed nervous, she thought, gazing adoringly at the new chancellor. She'd seen that look before, when he was unsure of himself, and wanted something – a woman, or a job...

'I'll let you into a secret, Minki,' said Max, whispering into her ear. 'Joseph is in discussion with Hitler about the possibility of a big job in the government – to become the Minister for Propaganda. He's doing much of the role already, of course, but he's anxious for it to be formalised. Hitler won't commit, and the tension is driving Joseph mad.'

'Ah, I thought there was something – a slight sense of desperation about him.'

'I'm sure Joseph will persuade him in the end,' Max went on. 'He's the perfect man for the job. And he has great plans to control all parts of the media – radio, film... even the newspapers. They must all be brought under his control – that's what he thinks, and I agree with him. Everyone must be brought into line with our way of thinking.'

'*Our* way of thinking?' she challenged him. 'Max, I'm not a National Socialist, and I wasn't aware you were either.'

'I am now. I've just joined the Party.'

Minki's jaw dropped.

'Oh, don't look so shocked, Minki. I'll do whatever it takes... be whatever they want me to be.'

At that moment, a member of Hitler's security squad tapped Max on the shoulder. 'Excuse me, Herr von Zeller, but the chancellor has asked if you would like to join him.'

'Of course,' said Max, straightening his tie and smoothing his hair. 'I'm sorry, darling, but I'd better go. Will you be all right on your own for a short while?'

'Oh, I'll be fine,' said Minki coldly. 'Well, hurry up... you don't want to keep the boss waiting.'

As Max hurried across the room to join Goebbels and Hitler, Minki took a glass of champagne from a passing waiter and found an armchair in a quiet corner of the room. She needed time to think. 'I'll do whatever it takes... be whatever they want me to be,' Max had just said. Hearing the words spoken so baldly came as a shock. Suddenly she was faced with the harsh truth – that both she and Max had compromised their principles for the sake of advancement and an easy life. Minki reflected on what Leila had said months earlier, and her fears of what was happening to their country. Leila had stood up for what she believed in, risking her own safety to challenge National Socialism and all it stood for. Minki, by contrast, had closed her mind to the political upheaval around her, and had used motherhood as an excuse not to confront it.

At that moment, it was as if a switch had been turned in Minki's brain. She realised she had lost her way in accepting an easy life. But that life came at a cost, and the cost was betrayal – the betrayal of people like Leila and Viktor. It was time to put a marker in the sand, she realised. Time to engage once again in the real world and stand up for what was right, however painful and difficult that might be.

21

MUNICH

FEBRUARY 1933

THIS IS HOW THE PRESS IS MUZZLED

That bold headline dominated the front page of the *Munich Post* on 5 February.

Within days of the formation of the new government coalition, a decree was passed to suspend the publication of newspapers Hitler perceived as a threat.

Martin Gruber gathered his team together in the newsroom that morning. 'Ironically, the government is calling this bill: "For the Protection of the German People" – as if it's for the people's benefit. When in fact it's old-fashioned censorship. You can see the way this is going – their intention is to silence us. We will obviously do all we can to fight the ban, but I warn you – things will get rough.'

Two weeks later, the *Munich Post* was temporarily shut down.

The following day the newswires reported that the Reichstag had gone up in flames. A Dutch anarchist had been arrested, and accused of arson.

'Hitler claims it's a communist plot,' said Martin that morning, reading from the teleprinter. 'He's arrested over four thousand members of the Communist Party. But I think this Dutchman is being set up. I wouldn't be surprised if Hitler organised the fire himself.'

'But why would he do that?' asked Leila.

The teleprinter again chattered into life. Martin tore out the message.

'This is why,' he said. 'Listen to this: "Hitler's cabinet has approved an emergency decree to be known as the Reichstag Fire Decree, suspending many civil liberties, including the freedom of the press and freedom of assembly".'

Martin turned to the room. 'You see how this works? In a single day Germany has gone from a democracy to an authoritarian state. '

As soon as they were allowed to publish once again, the *Post* hit back with a front-page banner headline and defiant editorial:

WE WILL NOT BE INTIMIDATED

Banning our newspaper was totally unjustified... The Munich Post *will continue to engage in a battle for social democracy and for the freedom-loving working class.*

Leila was proud of Martin and the rest of the team for showing such fearlessness, but she was also a realist, and she understood the danger they were in.

That night she shared her anxieties with Viktor. 'Martin is determined we will carry on. We're back on the newsstands, so you could argue we've won this battle – but they'll just shut us down again. In the end, they hold all the cards.'

Viktor poured out a large glass of wine and handed it to his wife. 'I had some visitors myself, today.'

'Oh yes?'

'Men from the National Socialists, based here in Munich. They came with a message from Goebbels. He objects to the books I publish, apparently. He seems to think he is entitled to tell us all what we can read or write.'

Leila slumped down onto a chair at the kitchen table. 'Did they threaten you?'

'Not physically, but they were pretty intimidating. They demanded a full list of all the authors I publish.'

'I can't believe it... and particularly after he asked you to publish his awful novel, for God's sake.'

'Perhaps I should have done... it might have kept him onside,' Viktor said ruefully.

'I don't think anything would have kept that man onside. The trouble is that I can't see any of this ending well. Every outcome I can imagine ends up with us being silenced... or worse.'

'What I don't understand is why they care about someone like me. I'm a small-time publisher, specialising in esoteric authors. Yes, some of them are Jewish, some are liberals, but they're intellectuals, academics. I'm doing no harm.'

'They don't care about that. Your books challenge their views – that's all that matters to them. Perhaps you should consider shutting down for a while?'

'I'll never do that, Leila. And I'm shocked you should even suggest it. No, I'm more worried about you. Martin and the rest of you are really goading Hitler. Your headlines, and the stories you run, make it clear you're never going to back down. The elections are coming up in a few days. If Hitler gets control of parliament, I dread what will happen.'

'If I'm honest, Viktor, so do I.'

A few days later Leila was in her office, trying to write an editorial about how Hitler's new government was intent on removing freedom of speech from the press, and with it many of the rights of the German people. As she wrestled for the umpteenth time with the opening sentence, she suddenly felt as if she had received an electric shock.

'Viktor!' she said out loud. Her hands suddenly sweating, she stood up unsteadily, and hurriedly opened the door that connected her to the outer office. 'Katja,' she called out.

Her secretary stopped typing and looked up. 'Yes, boss.'

'Could you get my husband on the phone for me please.'

Leila went back to her blank piece of paper, her heart racing with anticipation, as she waited to hear Viktor's voice on the phone.

Katja put her head round Leila's door. 'I'm sorry Leila... I tried the number but there was no reply.'

Leila tapped her fingers nervously on her desk. It was absurd to worry, she told herself. She checked her watch – it was two o'clock. Viktor had probably just popped out, perhaps to the pharmacy, she reassured herself. He had been unwell for a few days and still had the remnants of a cold. But she couldn't stop herself feeling something had happened to him. After all, he had personally been threatened by Hitler's thugs, and was married to a woman who worked for the very newspaper that had been attacking the government. Rumours were flying around Munich of liberals being arrested on the flimsiest of pretexts.

Unable to contain her anxiety any longer, she picked up her handbag, and grabbed her coat. 'I'm just going out for a moment, Katja, I won't be long.'

She hurried over to the news editor. 'Julius,' she began, 'I'm sorry to bother you...'

He looked up absent-mindedly. 'Yes, Leila?' He was in his shirtsleeves, his glasses on the end of his nose, surrounded by paperwork.

'I know you're waiting for a thousand words from me, but I've got to go out for a moment.'

'Fine,' he replied, waving his hand in the air indifferently. 'See you later.'

Leila ran the four or five blocks to their first-floor apartment. She unlocked the main door of the building and raced upstairs. Her hand shook as she fiddled with the lock. *Why does it always stick when you're in a hurry*, she thought, resolving to get it fixed as soon as possible. The door finally swung open. Pale winter sunlight streamed through the window at the far end of the corridor, glinting on the oak parquet floor. The apartment felt empty.

'Viktor,' she called out. 'Viktor, darling. It's Leila...'

There was no answer.

Her heart thudding, she went into the sitting room, and noticed the book he had been reading the night before was still lying open on a side table, his spectacles folded neatly on top. But the small glass of brandy he had been sipping had been knocked over, pooling its contents on the inlaid table. She righted it, licking her fingers.

'Viktor... Viktor...' she called out as she went from room to room. The bed was unmade, as if he'd recently got out of it. His pyjamas were strewn on the floor. In the kitchen, crumbs were evidence that bread had been eaten. A cup of left-over cold coffee sat on the countertop. But there was no sign of him. She returned to the hall. If he had gone out, why was his coat still hanging on the rack by the door? It was cold outside, and it had been raining on and off all day. Surely he wouldn't be so stupid as to leave without a coat – especially when he still had a cold. She picked up the phone to call his secretary at the publishing house, her hand shaking.

'Michaela... it's Leila. Is Victor with you?'

'No, I've not seen him all week – I thought he was at home... ill in bed.'

'He was... he has been. But I've just got home and he's not here. He didn't take his coat. I'm rather worried.'

Michaela was silent for a few moments. 'OK...' she began tentatively. 'That does sound odd, I agree, Leila. But could he have popped out to the shops – to get some medicine, perhaps?'

'That's what I wondered, but without his coat? It's starting to rain again.'

'He can be forgetful...'

'Yes, I know. Look, Michaela, I'll stay here, in case he gets back. Could you call me if you hear from him?'

When Axel and Sofia arrived home from school, they threw their school bags down noisily and retreated to their room. Leila, anxious not to alarm them, tried to concentrate on her column. She sat at Viktor's desk, typing furiously – the words came easily now, suddenly released in a torrent from her brain. '*If Fascism wins*,' she wrote, '*basic citizens' rights will come to an end for the foreseeable future.*'

She finished the piece within an hour and dictated the text to the sub-editor over the phone. Whatever the circumstances, she was a professional and couldn't let Julius down.

It wasn't until they sat down to dinner that the children noticed their father's absence.

'He's had to go out... with colleagues,' Leila explained. 'Now, as soon as you finish your homework, it's into bed with both of you.'

'Oh, but Mutti,' pleaded Axel, 'you promised we'd play cards tonight.'

'I know I did... but I've got work to do. I'm sorry, sweetheart.'

Her son sulkily got to his feet and the children sloped off to their room.

With the children in bed, Leila sat alone in the sitting room, her heart thudding with fear, desperately hoping to hear the sound of Victor's key in the lock. But there was silence. She needed someone to talk to, and rang Julius. 'Did you get my column?'

'Yes, it was very good... powerful. I think it will create quite a stir.'

'Not too much of a stir, I hope.' Her voice was quiet and frightened.

'Are you all right, Leila? You sound upset.'

'It's Viktor... it's nine o'clock and he hasn't come home yet.'

'Is that unusual?'

'Yes – very. He's been ill and he'd never have gone out without leaving a note, or calling me.'

'I'll come over – I've just got to put the paper to bed. Won't be long.'

The moment Julius arrived, Leila fell into his arms. 'I just know something's happened to him... I can feel it. Someone's taken him.'

'Now there,' he said, rocking her gently, 'you don't know that. Let's just try to stay calm.'

'No!' She pushed him away and began to pace the floor. 'Something's happened to him, I tell you. His glass had been knocked over. He didn't take his coat or his spectacles. Oh God... where is he?'

'I agree, it's odd – but that's not exactly evidence, is it? He might be out with a client, or friends.'

'Without telling me? No, he'd never do that.'

'Look, Leila, try to get some sleep. I'll go back to the office now, and see what I can find out.'

'How?' she asked desperately.

'Contacts in the police – that sort of thing. I'll call you as soon as I know anything.'

Leila dragged an armchair into the hall, next to the telephone, and wrapped herself in a blanket. When the phone finally rang, she was woken from a dreamless half-sleep. 'Yes... yes,' she said urgently.

'Leila, it's me, Julius. Sorry to ring so late, but I thought you'd want to know right away. You were right... Viktor has been arrested. He's at the police station at Ettstrasse. We can't get in to see him now, but the police will permit a lawyer visit. I've arranged for a criminal lawyer I know to go first thing in the morning. He's a good man – they won't mess with him.'

Leila stumbled from the hall into her bedroom. She lay in the half-dark, dreading the coming dawn, and agonising over what she could tell the children. She imagined the scene: at seven they would get up, go to the bathroom, brush their teeth, squabble over who deserved more time in front of the mirror. She would hear them getting dressed, going into the kitchen. 'Mutti,' they would call out. 'What's for breakfast?'

How could she stay cheerful and calm? 'Oh, let's have some eggs,' she might suggest. She had to hope they would not notice their father's continued absence.

At dawn she rose and dressed. In the kitchen she prepared a pot of coffee for herself, and breakfast for the children. When they joined her, they behaved as normal, arguing over who would sit where, buttering their toast, cracking the shells of boiled eggs. But Leila's mind was elsewhere, picturing Viktor miserably locked up in a police station.

'Mutti... Mutti!' Sofia was tugging at her mother's sleeve.

'I'm sorry, darling,' said Leila. 'I was miles away. Have you finished breakfast? Go and get ready for school.'

The children stood up from the table but, as Sofia reached the kitchen door, she turned and asked softly: 'Where's Daddy?'

'Oh... he's at work.' Leila kept her voice light, and, to her relief, Sofia seemed to accept the explanation.

The children gathered up their school books, and were just putting on their coats in the hall when the phone rang. Leila answered it, her hand shaking. 'Hello...?'

'Leila, it's Julius. I've arranged for us to meet to meet the lawyer just before nine at the police station. Can you manage that?'

'Yes, of course. I'll just take the children to school.'

She went into the sitting room and picked up Viktor's glasses and the book he had been reading, hoping to give them to him while he waited to be released.

'Why have you got Daddy's glasses?' asked Sofia, as Leila locked the apartment door.

'He left them behind this morning – I'll drop them at his office on my way to work.'

As calmly as she could, Leila walked the children to school, but as soon as they disappeared through the wide school gates she ran to the police station. She arrived breathless, bursting through the double doors. To her relief, Julius was waiting for her in the lobby.

'Ah, here you are,' he said, getting to his feet. 'Leila, can I introduce you to Manfred Adler – one of our lawyers.' He turned towards a slight, fair-haired man, who stood up and shook Leila's hand.

'Thank you so much for coming, Herr Adler,' said Leila. 'Do you have any news of Viktor? Are they going to release him today?'

The lawyer shook his head. 'I'm sorry – I was just explaining it all to Julius. It seems they've accused him of being an enemy of the state. I've got a hearing with a judge tomorrow.'

Leila's eyes filled with tears, and she sank down onto a hard wooden chair.

'I'm sorry it's not better news,' Adler said gently, sitting down next to her.

Leila stared into space. 'You said... not till tomor-row... Thursday. That's something, at least... that he'll be out by tomorrow night. Out for the weekend.'

Adler took her hand. 'I don't want you to get your hopes up. It's just a hearing, you understand. I have no idea what evidence they have against Viktor. We'll have to see... take it step by step.'

Leila felt her stomach churn, the panic rising. 'I understand, but I'm disappointed, obviously. I hoped we might get him out today.'

Adler smiled sympathetically. 'It's awful for you, I know, and I'm so sorry. But I'm not sure there's much else we can achieve today.'

'But surely they'll let me see him? I brought his glasses...' She took the glasses and Viktor's book out of her handbag.

'I'll ask them.'

Adler spoke to the desk clerk but returned a few minutes later, looking downcast. 'I'm sorry, Leila, but they won't let you see him. They will allow us to leave his glasses... but not the book, I'm afraid.'

'But why? Why are they being so petty and cruel?' She began to sob, gulping down her the tears, as if a dam of self-control had finally broken.

Adler took Viktor's glasses and deposited them on the desk clerk's desk. 'Please see that Herr Labowski gets these,' he said firmly. Sitting back down with Leila, he put his arm round her. 'At least now, Viktor will realise you've been here, that you know what's going on. I'll telephone you after the hearing tomorrow – hopefully a judge will see our side of the argument.'

Glancing at his watch, he stood up. 'I'm afraid I must go... I have another appointment.' Bowing, he handed her his business card. 'Please call me at any time.'

After Adler had left, Julius took Leila gently by the hand and led her outside into the street. 'Leila... I'm so sorry. I don't know what to say.'

'There's nothing to say, is there?' She looked up at him and tried to smile. 'I feel so responsible, Julius. I'm sure they're targeting him because of me.'

'I really don't think that's likely, Leila. There could be so many reasons they want to put pressure on him.'

'Some of Hitler's henchmen visited him a few days ago. We should have got him out of Munich then... he could have gone to his sister's in Freiburg – anywhere but here. Why were we so relaxed? How could we have been so stupid?' She began to sob again.

Julius grasped her arms firmly, and looked deeply into her eyes. 'We are dealing with monsters, Leila. None of us could have seen this coming. You need to stay calm... for the sake of your family and your own sanity. Adler will do everything he can. It will be all right, you'll see.'

'I wish I shared your optimism,' replied Leila, wiping away tears. 'Look, Julius, I need to think a few things through. Mainly, how I'm going to cope for the next few days without Viktor. The children, you know – I'm so used to him being there, collecting them and so on. I need time to think. Can I join you at the office in a little while?'

'Of course, Leila. Take your time. I'll see you later.'

Leila sat in a coffee shop for a couple of hours, mulling over the options, trying to stay calm, as Julius had advised. She paid her bill and began to walk towards the *Munich Post*'s offices. As she turned the corner into Altheimer Eck, two trucks roared past her and screeched to a halt outside the newspaper's building. A dozen brown-shirted storm troopers clambered out of the first truck, and formed a human chain across the road, effectively corralling the pedestrians. Leila ducked into the shadowy doorway of a haber-dasher's shop on the opposite side of the road. A second truck threw open its rear doors, and another dozen Brownshirts ran into the newspaper's offices. Leila watched as the windows on the upper level of the building were thrown open and typewriters, desks, chairs – even the bedding from the business manager's apart-ment on the top floor – were thrown down into the yard below. Finally, to her horror, she saw Julius Zerfass being frogmarched out of the building and bundled into a waiting truck. Moments later, the junior staff ran out screaming and scattered down the road.

Leila's legs turned to jelly. She thought she might collapse. Fumbling for the door handle of the shop, she almost fell inside.

'What's going on out there?' asked the woman behind the counter. 'There's always some trouble these days...' she muttered, not waiting for an answer. 'Can I help you with anything?'

'No... no,' Leila stumbled. 'I was just looking.' She wandered around the shop, absent-mindedly examining reels of coloured ribbon, and fingering the bolts of cloth – pink gingham and red velvet. On a happier day she might have bought a metre or two to make a dress for Sofia. But her mind was elsewhere. Where were they taking Julius? If he had been arrested, would the other editors be next? Would she also be taken? At that moment, she wanted nothing more than to get back home, to see her children and know they were safe.

Leila ran all the way back to the apartment and collapsed on the hall floor, sobbing. The apartment was agonisingly silent. Crying, she wandered the rooms, touching Viktor's desk, stroking his clothes in the wardrobe. But finally the panic subsided, and she began to think more clearly. If they were arresting the editorial team of the *Post*, she was certainly in danger. The apartment was the first place they would look. She decided to flee. After packing a few clothes for herself and the children, she locked the apartment behind her and hurried to her parents' apartment a few blocks away.

The main door to the building was open, and she ran up the echoing stone staircase to her parents' apartment and banged loudly on the door.

When her mother opened it, Leila fell into her arms.

'Oh Mutti... thank God you're here.'

'Darling, of course I'm here. Whatever is the matter?'

Sobbing, Leila explained what had happened. When she had finished, Hannah took her by the hand and led her to the kitchen where she made tea.

'The trouble is, Mutti, I could be next – and what would happen to the children then?'

'You must stay here with us, out of sight,' said her mother firmly. 'I'll collect the children from school today.'

'They might look for me here, and the last thing I want is to bring you and father into danger.'

'Why would we be in any danger? Your father and I have done nothing wrong. Besides, your place is with us.'

Somehow Leila got through the rest of the day. She rang Adler, but he had no news of Viktor. Frustratingly, the judge had deferred the hearing until the following Monday.

'But that's four days away,' Leila protested.

'I know... But there's really nothing I can do.'

'What about Julius, where is he?'

'He's being held at the same police station.'

'And what of the others – Martin, Edmund and Erhard... were they arrested too?'

'No, fortunately they got away – they're in hiding somewhere.'

'Well, that's something, I suppose.'

'I'd advise you to leave your apartment...'

'I already have, I'm at my parents' apartment at the moment.'

'I suggest you keep on the move. It's the only way.'

'But where can I go?'

'I'm sorry Leila, I can't really help with that. And it's better I don't know where you are. Call me on Monday evening, and I'll let you know what happened at the hearing.'

The prospect of four long days with no news of Viktor stretched ahead. The thought of him, frightened and alone in a cell at the police station, was unbearable. And how would she explain it to the children?

That afternoon, her mother went out to collect them from school. Leila was alone in the sitting room when she heard them come back. She listened quietly as Hannah explained that Viktor was away on business. 'Your mother thought it would be more fun if you spent the next few days with Grandpa and me. Let's have something to eat, shall we?'

With the children settled in the kitchen, Hannah brought Leila a cup of tea in the sitting room. 'How are you feeling?'

'Worried... frightened. Are the children all right?'

'They're fine – doing some colouring at the kitchen table. Don't worry about them. Now, what are you going to do about Viktor?'

'What can I do? The hearing isn't till Monday. I'm powerless...'

'Can't your friend Minki help? She knows all the top people, doesn't she?'

'Minki... yes of course!' Leila leapt to her feet and kissed her mother's cheek. 'You're absolutely right, Mutti. I've been in such a panic, I didn't think of Minki. Can you keep the children busy while I call her?'

Leila dialled the Berlin number from the phone in the hall. She listened to the telephone ringing at Minki's house for what seemed an interminable time. Finally someone answered. 'The von Zeller residence.'

'Minki... is that you?'

'Yes, who's that?'

'It's me... Leila.'

'Leila! How lovely...'

'Minki, this is not a social call. Something awful has happened.'

'Go on.'

'Viktor's been arrested, accused of being an enemy of the state. It's quite ridiculous, of course. One of my editors has also been arrested – a man called Julius Zerfass. I'm in hiding with the children – at my mother's – and I need your help.'

'Oh, Leila, I'm so sorry...'

Minki fell silent, and all Leila could hear was her breathing.

'Minki... you will help me, won't you? I don't know where else to turn.'

'I want to help, obviously, but I'm just not sure what I can do.'

'Speak to Goebbels, I beg you. He's your friend, and he has the power to get Viktor and Julius out. Please do that for me.'

'Speak to Goebbels... Yes, well, I can try.'

'Please, Minki. I'm begging you – you must try. You're my only hope.'

22

BERLIN

Minki sat by the telephone for some time, thinking through the implications of Leila's phone call. It was true that she knew Goebbels well, and her husband was now part of his inner circle. But she suspected one of the reasons they remained friends was that she had never tried to 'use' Goebbels' position for her own advantage. If that changed, so might his feelings.

Max came home that evening filled with excitement. 'The new film is going to be marvellous – Goebbels loves it. Joining forces with him was the best thing I've ever done.'

'How wonderful, darling,' said Minki, pouring them both a drink. 'Come and sit down with me. There's something I need to talk to you about.'

'Go on,' said Max, settling down next to her on the sofa in the drawing room.

'It's about my friend Leila... the journalist, you know?'

'Yes, I know... what of her?'

'Her husband, Viktor, has been arrested by the Munich

police and is being held on some trumped-up charge. I need to help her...'

'Well, I don't see how. What can you do?'

'We're not exactly without friends in high places, are we?'

Max narrowed his eyes, sipped his brandy, but said nothing.

'Could we... speak to Joseph, do you think?' she ventured.

'What's it got to do with him? It's obviously a local police matter.'

'Well, for a start, he knows Viktor personally. They've met a couple of times – Viktor was nice enough to read Joe's novel. And both men were guests at our wedding.'

'There's been a lot of water under the bridge since then,' said Max darkly.

'Oh, Max, for heaven's sake... The point is, Goebbels has power – he could order Viktor to be released.'

'He's a Jew, isn't he, Viktor?'

'Yes, what of it?'

'Well, Goebbels won't like that. And more importantly, things are at a very delicate stage between him and Hitler. Joseph has been negotiating for months for a senior position in the government. He won't want to rock the boat – not now. It's just not a good time.'

'But Leila is my friend. She and Viktor have been so good to me – so good to us. When the baby was born Leila was a rock for me. We have to help them, Max.'

'Well, I'm not prepared to speak to Goebbels. If anyone can persuade him, it's you. Call him, if you like, but don't push it. We need to keep him onside.'

'I'll call him then,' Minki said uncertainly. She finished her drink, went through to the hall, and spooled through her address book until she found Goebbels' number. She dialled with trembling fingers.

'Hello.' It was Magda, her voice, as always, icy cool.

'Oh, hello, Magda. How lovely to hear your voice. It's Minki. Is Joe there?'

'Joseph... yes he's here.'

'Might I speak to him?'

'I'll get him.'

Minki felt sick with nerves, her palms sweating.

His voice, when he came on the line, was dark and suspicious. 'Hello.'

'Joseph... It's Minki.'

'Yes, I know, Magda told me. What is it?' He sounded impatient and irritable.

'I just wondered... I have a small favour to ask... oh, it's rather difficult.'

'Just spit it out, Minki, I'm busy.'

'I'm sorry. It's about my friend, Leila – you remember Leila... dark hair, very pretty – you met at my wedding. She's married to Viktor Labowski, the publisher.'

'Yes, I remember.'

'It seems that Viktor has been arrested – charged with being an enemy of the state or something. I'm sure it's a ridiculous mistake. I mean, he publishes esoteric authors and academics. A less treasonable man you couldn't find.'

'Well, he must have done something. The police don't tend to make mistakes, you know.'

'Oh, Joe... you know that's not true.' It was the old Minki speaking – the one who saw herself on the same level as Joseph, the brave journalist who stood on the sidelines observing life. But challenging him was not the way to 'keep him onside' and she regretted the comment instantly.

There was a long pause. When Goebbels spoke again his voice was clinical and cold. 'I'd be very careful if I were you, Minki. You and Max are in a privileged position. But things can change, you know.'

Minki's instinct was to answer back, but she knew that

would be reckless. Nevertheless, she needed him to be clear – to spell it out. 'So you can't help, then.'

'No, Minki, I can't. Goodbye.'

She collapsed onto the stool by the phone table and sobbed, her head in her hands.

Max came through from the sitting room. 'What's the matter, sweetheart? Did you speak to him?'

'Yes...'

'And?'

'Nothing. He won't help.' She looked up at Max, tears rolling down her face. 'Oh God, Max, I hate him sometimes. How could he be so cruel?'

'Now, Minki, don't be rash. Joseph's in a difficult position – he can't go intervening all over the place. There's a system – a process – that has to be followed. I'm sure Viktor will be all right. It's probably just a warning. They're rapping his knuckles... pulling him into line.'

Minki stared up at him, wiping her face with the back of her hand. 'Do you really believe that?'

'Well, of course I do. Don't fuss so. You've done all you can. Dry your eyes and let's have dinner. I'm starving.'

He reached down to help her up from her seat, but she pushed him angrily away.

'Go away, Max. Leave me alone – I must think.'

'What's there to think about? There's nothing you can do. You must see that.'

'Before I met you, Max, I wouldn't have thought twice about what to do. I'd have gone to see Joseph, begged him if necessary – done anything to help Leila and Viktor. They need my help, and I can't desert them now.'

'Might I remind you that marriage to me has given you stability and security, perhaps for the first time in your life. And you're a mother now, Minki. That's your primary job, taking care of Clara, not helping your Jewish friends.'

He turned and disappeared into the dining room, where the maid was laying the table.

Minki ran tearfully upstairs and stood at the end of the baby's cot. Clara lay on her back, legs waving in the air, clenching her fists, making delightful gurgling noises. Seeing her mother, she reached out her hand. Minki leaned over the cot, and inserted her finger into her daughter's grasp.

'Hello, my best darling,' Minki whispered. 'You ought to be asleep.'

The child smiled up at her mother, revealing a couple of tiny teeth that were beginning to push their way through her gums. She pulled Minki's finger towards her mouth, and bit it gently.

'Ow,' Minki said, smiling. But she left her finger in the child's mouth, enjoying the sensation of Clara claiming a tiny part of her.

Her mind swirled with doubt. Perhaps Max was right. Could she really risk her baby's safety for the sake of her friend? Max was obviously not going to help her, and now Goebbels had turned his back on her. Without their support, what could she actually do? She could go to Munich to be with Leila, and argue with the police, but would it achieve anything?

Reluctantly, she decided her only course of action was to write to Leila and explain that she had tried her best to persuade Goebbels, but that he had refused to help. Retrieving her finger from her baby's mouth, Minki kissed her forehead and slipped quietly away downstairs to join Max in the dining room.

23

MUNICH

The four days before the hearing stretched away interminably. Leila had initially put all her hopes in the lawyer. But Adler had not sounded overly optimistic, and she was becoming increasingly anxious that Monday might come and go with no resolution.

As for Minki, Leila was troubled by their phone call. She had hoped for an unequivocal declaration of support. But Minki had sounded tentative and nervous. Leila just had to hope that her friend would decide to help her, and that her guile and beauty would work its usual magic. She had always been able to wrap Goebbels round her little finger. If anyone could persuade him to show mercy and get Viktor out of jail, it was Minki.

The children, believing their father was away on business, went happily enough to school on Friday, accompanied by their grandmother. Left alone in the apartment, Leila would normally have relished the chance to sit and write, but she had no work. Following the arrest of Julius Zerfass, and the disappearance of the senior editorial team, the *Munich Post* had been forced to close. Any hopes of it reopening had been dashed when Hitler suddenly enacted a law making it illegal for Jews to work as journalists. Without work, Leila had no income, and Viktor's legal fees would need to be paid. She and Viktor had some savings, but they would soon be whittled away. Reluctantly, Leila came to the conclusion that she might not even be able to keep up the rent on their own apartment.

That afternoon, her mother returned with the children and a basket of shopping. While Axel and Sofia relaxed in the sitting room, Leila helped her mother unpack the groceries. 'Mutti, I've been thinking... I may have to give up the apartment. I'll go and collect a few more of the children's things.'

'But I thought the lawyer had said you should stay out of sight. Let me go instead.'

'No, it's all right. I'll take a taxi, and I won't be long. It's easier for me – I know what they'll need.'

'But do you need to go at all? Viktor might be out on Monday.'

'We can hope he'll be out, but we have to be prepared for the possibility that he might not.'

'Oh, darling...' Hannah reached across the kitchen table, and squeezed Leila's hand.

'I think I'll have to be honest with the children too. I know you meant well telling them that white lie about a business trip. But if he doesn't get out, they'll have to know, and it would be better if they got used to the idea over the weekend.'

'If you think so, dear... I was just trying to protect them.'

'I know, and I'm grateful, but I think we need to be realistic.'

.   .   .

Carrying a pair of her mother's empty suitcases, Leila took a taxi to the apartment and hurried inside. It felt eerily quiet, and she tearfully went from room to room railing at the injustice of her situation. But slowly she pulled herself together. She cleaned and tidied the kitchen, taking a couple of the children's favourite mugs and placing them in one of the suitcases. In her own room, she packed up the few items of jewellery Viktor had bought her over the years, along with more clothes, a pair of comfortable boots and a spare coat. In the children's room, she packed the second suitcase with more clothes, one or two of their favourite toys and some books. Finally, she folded up the children's bedcovers – patchwork quilts her mother had made when they were babies – and lay them in the suitcase. It would make them feel more at home. Locking the front door, she began to weep again, but she had recovered by the time she arrived back at her parents' apartment.

When the children came home from school, Leila sat them down at the kitchen table. 'I've got some bad news, I'm afraid... about Daddy. He's been arrested and is in jail, but it's only temporary,' she added quickly. 'There's been a mistake. Daddy has done nothing wrong and the lawyer says he'll be out by Monday. So I don't want you to worry. In the meantime we'll stay here with Granny and Grandpa... just till Daddy comes home.'

Axel, who had been playing with a toy car on the table, frowned and looked up at his mother with his dark-brown eyes. 'Why did they make a mistake?'

Leila shrugged. 'They just did. They thought Daddy had done something wrong, but he hadn't. Like at school – if a teacher blames someone for doing something when they're actually innocent. Grown-ups do make mistakes sometimes.'

Sofia, Leila noticed, said nothing. She was doodling in a little notebook, drawing a series of concentric circles with a pencil.

'Sofia... is there anything you want to ask?'

But the girl simply shook her head.

After tea, Leila began to busy herself rearranging the bedroom she was sharing with the children. It had been her old childhood bedroom, and still had its original single bed. Her father had managed to get hold of two extra mattresses for the children. Now, she covered each with a quilt.

Sofia came in and flopped down on one of the mattresses, watching her mother squeezing some of her clothes into the wardrobe. 'Why did you bring over so many of our things? I thought we were only staying for the weekend.'

'Well, we might need to stay a little longer.' Leila tried to keep her voice light and carefree.

'But you said Daddy will be out on Monday.'

Leila kept her back to her daughter, aware that her eyes were filling with tears. She was determined not to show Sofia any fear. 'We *hope* he'll be out on Monday,' she said quietly, 'but we don't know for certain.'

'Is Daddy going to die in prison?' asked Sofia suddenly.

'No, darling, of course not!' Leila swung round and faced her. 'You mustn't think that. It's just that the legal system works slowly – we have to be prepared. And I thought it would be better if we were here, with Granny and Grandpa, so that I can really concentrate on helping Daddy. Do you see?' She tried to smile encouragingly.

Sofia nodded. 'I see,' she mumbled.

'You like living here, don't you?' asked Leila.

'Yes, I love Granny and Grandpa, but I miss my room at home.'

'I do understand darling, but I promise it will all be over soon.'

'Will it really?' Sofia asked doubtfully, her eyes filling with tears. 'I'm just so frightened, Mutti. What if he doesn't get out on Monday? Papa is old... he won't like prison.'

Leila lay down on the mattress next to Sofia, and hugged her tight. 'Papa might be older than me, but he's also fit and strong. You mustn't worry so. We'll get him out. The lawyer is a clever man and the police have no reason to keep Papa in prison. You'll see – it will be all right.'

Sofia appeared satisfied, and went off to join her brother, but Leila realised that if there was no good news on Monday, she would struggle to keep the children's spirits up – and her own.

Finally, Monday morning came. Leila woke at dawn, and lay in her childhood bed watching the sun strengthen through the window. The children, thankfully, were sleeping peacefully. She tried to imagine how the day might unfold. Her fantasy ending involved Viktor running towards her, free at last. She thought of how they would celebrate that night – drinking champagne, eating well and making love. She smiled and looked down at her children. Perhaps not making love, then. But her optimism soon faded and hard reality set in. Leila knew Viktor's chances of release were not good. And she had heard nothing from Minki since their phone call. If Goebbels couldn't or wouldn't help, all her hopes would have to be pinned on Adler getting Viktor out of prison.

She climbed silently out of bed, circumnavigating the sleeping children, and went into the sitting room. Through the large window that overlooked the street, she could see the rising sun glinting on the River Isar below. It was a beautiful sight, and so familiar: the swirl of the water, the handsome buildings on the opposite bank, the little boats and tugs chugging up and down the river. She loved it, and the city it carved in two. But as the sunlight grew stronger, she realised with total clarity that, if she were lucky enough to get Viktor out of prison, they must leave Germany immediately. There really was no other option.

However much they loved Munich and their homeland, they would never be able to live their lives in safety while Hitler was in power. And if the last few days had clarified anything, it was that nothing mattered more than the safety of her husband and family.

In the kitchen, the family gathered for breakfast, but the children were sullen and silent.

'I've made you hot chocolate, and cinnamon toast,' said Leila cheerfully, laying the food on the table.

'I'm not hungry,' said Sofia, pushing the plate away.

'I'll have yours,' said Axel.

Hannah, who was busy packing up the children's school bags, glanced anxiously at Leila. 'You must eat something, Sofia... you'll be hungry later.'

The girl shook her head.

'Well, if you're not going to eat, you'd better get your coats on,' said Hannah. 'We have to leave for school in five minutes.'

Axel crammed the last piece of toast into his mouth, pulled his heavy school bag onto his back and went out into the hall, but Sofia lingered in the kitchen. She kissed her mother's cheek. 'He will get out today, won't he, Mutti?'

'Of course, darling. Now go to school and work hard.'

Once Hannah and the children had gone, Leila's father got up from the breakfast table. 'I really ought to open up the shop, but I hate to leave you. Will you be all right on your own?'

'Yes of course. I'll get on with some work.'

'All right, if you're sure.' He put on his overcoat, and kissed his daughter on the forehead. 'And try not to worry... things have a way of working out in the end.'

Leila washed the dishes and tidied their bedroom. Her instinct was to write, but with the paper shut she felt purposeless. Her thoughts turned to Minki. Why had she not rung? It suddenly occurred to her she may have sent a letter instead. She hurried down to the communal hall to check the postbox. To her delight there was a letter with a Berlin postmark, which had just been delivered. 'At last,' she thought. Eagerly she ripped it open, praying it contained good news.

Darling Leila,

I have been thinking of you constantly.

As promised, I spoke to Goebbels, but I'm afraid he simply refused to get involved. He insists it's a police matter and he cannot interfere. In all honesty, I don't know what more I can do.

It must seem inexplicable to you that I cannot make this problem go away, but things are not straightforward. Being close to the seat of power is not always an easy place to be.

I want to assure you that I care for you both so much, but you must understand my position. Max is sure that Viktor will soon be released. It's a 'show of strength', he told me, designed to intimidate, not destroy. He sends you both his best.

So stay strong my dear friend. I feel sure Viktor will be home soon.

Know that I am thinking of you and wish you well.

Your loving friend,

Minki

Leila threw the letter down on the floor in a fit of rage and despair. How could her friend have abandoned her? Gathering up the sheet of paper, she staggered back upstairs to the apartment. Inside she went straight to the kitchen, opened the waste bin, and tore Minki's letter into tiny pieces, throwing them onto a pile of potato peelings. Her only hope now lay with Adler.

As the morning wore on, she wrote a few notes for a possible book about the way the government were controlling the population through propaganda. It was just an idea at this stage, but it gave her something to focus on.

When her mother returned, Leila joined her in the kitchen. 'Have you heard anything?' her mother asked, as she made coffee.

'Of course not,' Leila snapped. 'I'd have told you if I had.'

'I'm sorry,' said Hannah, 'I didn't mean...'

'No, I'm sorry, Mutti.' Leila wrapped her arms round her mother. 'I just feel so desperate.'

'I know, *liebling*...'

At lunchtime, Hannah prepared some soup, but Leila couldn't eat. Finally, abandoning any thought of work, she spent the rest of the afternoon sitting by the phone in the hall, waiting for Adler to ring and give her the news she was so desperate to hear.

She was still sitting by the phone when her mother returned with the children. Axel followed Hannah into the kitchen, but Sofia lingered with her mother. 'Is he out of prison yet?' she asked softly.

'I'm not sure, darling. I'm still waiting to speak to the lawyer. Go and have some tea in the kitchen.'

Reluctantly, Sofia left. As soon as she was out of earshot, Leila dialled Adler's number. 'You hadn't rung, so I thought I should call you. What's happening?'

There was a pause. 'It's not good news, I'm afraid, Leila. They won't release either Julius or Viktor.'

Leila felt a sharp pain in her ribs, as if she had been kicked. She could barely breathe. 'Why not?'

'I don't know – there's absolutely no logic to it. It's almost as if the judge has been pressured into it. All I know is that they are going to be sent to Stadelheim Prison – it's not far away, just in the southern suburbs.'

'I know where it is...'

Sofia put her head round the kitchen door. Leila, struggling to contain her emotions, smiled bravely at her.

'You'll keep trying to get them released?' she asked Adler.

'Of course. I'm preparing an appeal now – I'll let you know how it goes. I'm so sorry it's not better news. Please stay safe yourself, and call me in a few days – I might know more by then.'

24

BERLIN

MARCH 1933

Minki's guilt at failing her friend ate away at her. Leila had always been so supportive, ever since they had met one another. She had been there for Minki when Peter Fischer had deserted her, when she was first pregnant, and when her beloved child was born – and had never asked Minki for anything in return. Yet the first time Leila had asked for help, Minki had let her down.

There was clearly nothing Minki could do to persuade Goebbels to change his mind and intercede for Viktor, but she could, in some small way, repay Leila by re-entering journalism and opposing the growing totalitarianism around her. Clara was now fourteen months old – happy and healthy and cared for by a young nursemaid called Ida. It was time to get back to work – not her old job as women's editor, but real journalism – political journalism. What was the point of writing articles about cookery and knitting when terrible injustices were being meted out to innocent people like Viktor and Leila?

Although Hitler had suppressed dissident newspapers like

the *Munich Post*, more centrist papers still existed. The *Deutsche Allgemeine Zeitung*, for example, where she had worked as editor of the women's pages, though increasingly right-wing, had a reputation for objective reporting. She decided to call her old editor and sound him out about a job, but first she needed to discuss it with Max.

Minki was waiting for him in the sitting room when he came back from work that evening. He seemed excited as he poured them both a drink. 'It's finally official. Goebbels has been appointed "Minister for the People's Education and Propaganda", he announced grandly. 'He's planning on initiating daily press briefings. He's really going to crack the whip with the press, show them who's boss.' He laughed, and downed his first brandy of the evening. 'There's a new broom in town and its name is Joseph Goebbels.'

'I don't see what's so funny, Max. Personally, I find it rather alarming. This obsession Joseph has to control everything is blatant censorship.'

Max looked startled, but she persisted. 'You can't keep the lid on truth forever, Max. It always comes out in the end. Joseph seems to think he's justified in suppressing anything that doesn't fit with his world view.'

'He's simply doing his job, Minki. We need to control information, direct people to accept the truth as we see it.'

'We, Max?'

'Of course, "We". I'm a member of the Party now, remember. My job is to support their initiatives.'

Max went over to the drinks tray and poured himself another brandy. Minki studied him with something approaching despair. She had understood that his joining the Party was pure expediency. Now it seemed he was a true believer. It struck her that she should keep quiet about her plan to enter political journalism. It was clear they were on different sides, and, if he knew she intended to write about politics, he would be bound to disapprove, or even prevent her returning at all.

'I've been thinking, Max, that perhaps I ought to get back to work.'

'Back to your women's pages, you mean?'

'Yes... that sort of thing.' She kept her tone light-hearted. 'Ida seems good with Clara. What do you think?'

Max shrugged his shoulders. 'I think it's a splendid idea. I've said for ages you should go back to work. It would be good for you – give you less time to brood about those Jewish friends of yours. Go back to your knitting and cooking column, darling – distract yourself, have a bit of fun.'

Irritated at being so patronised, Minki nevertheless bit her tongue. 'I'll call my old boss, then – first thing in the morning.'

Helmut Müller, Minki's old editor on the *Deutsche Allgemeine Zeitung*, was delighted. 'We've missed you, Minki. The women's pages haven't been the same without you.'

'Oh, good. Perhaps I could pop in later and we could discuss it.'

'Marvellous. Come in after lunch... around two?'

Settled in her editor's office, Minki explained her proposal. 'You know I've been very happy editing the women's pages in the past, Helmut, but I wonder if it's time to move on... change tack, as it were.'

'What, leave knitting and cooking to one side?' He gave a wry smile. 'I have to say, I was always surprised by your enthusiasm for all matters female, as you clearly have good political instincts...'

'It's as if you read my mind, Helmut. You're right, I've always been fascinated by politics. But my time on *Der Stürmer* all those years ago rather stymied any aspirations I might have had in that area. No decent newspaper would look at me after that.'

'Well I'm looking at you, Minki. Through your friendship with Goebbels, you've given us some good leads over the years, and I'd be happy to discuss a change of direction.'

Minki smiled. Did she consider her relationship with Goebbels to be a friendship? Not any more... Goebbels was more like the enemy. But it would be better if Helmut didn't know her true feelings. 'Yes, it's useful meeting him socially. His guard can slip occasionally and one gets useful titbits of information that way. Which brings me to my proposition... If you agree, I'd like to ask you to put me on the political team.'

Helmut smiled, gently raising an eyebrow.

'I realise I'm inexperienced, so I don't expect any privileges. I'll start at the bottom and work my way up. But I can give you the inside track – for example, my husband tells me that Goebbels is about to launch daily press briefings and I think if I were to attend I could offer you a novel perspective.'

Helmut studied her for a moment. 'You do realise these briefings might be incredibly dull. And I'm not sure how much freedom we'd have to be critical of the government, for example.'

'I realise that... but I'd like to see if there's a way of challenging the official line – not in a dangerous way, but to subtly call into question the Party's view of the world.'

'It's worth a try, I suppose. That is, after all, what journalism is supposed to be...'

'One other thing... I think it would be best to keep my real identity secret. I'm not sure I should use my real name.'

'Why ever not?'

'Well, for a start, would readers accept a political story from a woman who's spent the last few years giving them household advice?'

'Good point.'

'And secondly, I'd prefer that neither Goebbels, nor my husband – who works for him – knew what I was up to. For a start they'd be furious, which would destroy my value to you. So it would be better if I were... undercover.'

'How intriguing.' The editor sat back in his chair and studied her. 'If you're to attend these briefings, we'll have to get you an accredited press pass – and create a bit of a backstory. Make you out to be a new rookie reporter. And you'll need a false name, of course.'

'So you think it could work?'

He smiled. 'Yes possibly... but surely, won't Goebbels recognise you?'

'I've thought of that... I think some sort of disguise might be in order.' She laughed. 'It might be fun, and don't worry about a name – I'll think of something.'

'Well, I'll leave the finer details to you,' said Helmut, standing up, indicating the meeting was over.

'Thank you, Helmut, for being so open to the idea. I appreciate it.'

'Something's happened to you, Minki. You've changed.'

'Perhaps I have. Or maybe it's that the world around me has changed.'

On the way home Minki stopped at an optician and bought a pair of clear spectacles – little round tortoiseshell glasses that quite altered her appearance. At home, she went to her wardrobe and pulled out a dull grey suit that she rarely wore – the colour did nothing for her complexion or eyes. On the top of the wardrobe she found an old brown trilby hat belonging to Max. When she put on the whole ensemble, she looked less like her former glamorous self, and more like the earnest political journalist she hoped to become.

· · ·

The first Reich press conference was held in the elegant neoclassical royal palace on Wilhelmplatz. This stunning building was now the headquarters of the grandly titled Reich Ministry of Popular Enlightenment and Propaganda.

Minki, dressed in her disguise of 'the earnest reporter', boldly showed her new press pass. She had chosen the name of Greta Schreiber. Greta, after her mother, and Schreiber meaning 'writer'. The press conference took place in the ballroom, a room adorned with statues and paintings of classical Greek and Roman gods and goddesses. It was typical of Goebbels, she thought, to choose such a splendid location for his first formal encounter with the press. He had always had pretensions to grandeur.

A stage had been erected at one end of the ballroom, with a dark lectern in the centre, in front of which was a forest of microphones. Settling herself in the middle of the room, Minki looked around. She had been out of the journalism loop for so long that she recognised none of the other reporters – which was just as well, she thought, as no one would see through her disguise. In the old days she might have attended such an event with Leila. They'd always had fun together in their different ways – Leila, the serious one, earnestly taking notes, and Minki whispering in her friend's ear, mocking the participants, barely able to control her laughter.

On the dot of ten o'clock, a functionary announced the start of proceedings, and the room fell silent. All heads turned to see Goebbels entering from the back, walking up the central aisle. In spite of his slight build and subtle limp, he cut an impressive figure in a well-cut charcoal grey suit, his dark hair slicked back to reveal his high forehead. Perhaps it was the grand surroundings, or possibly the reverential hush in the room, but it seemed to Minki that the man had been transformed. Gone was the impoverished, nervous young writer who had once been her lover and in his place was a self-confident politician about to address the nation's top journalists.

Goebbels took his place behind the lectern. His stance was confident, almost imperious, as he threw his head back, preparing to speak.

He began with a welcome. He appeared friendly enough at the start, but within minutes it became clear that he saw the press people in that room not as journalists, but as propagandists for the government.

'The purpose of these press briefings is to provide you with information on a daily basis. But you'll also be given instructions how to report the news to reflect the Party's opinion. We don't want any independent reporting, or so-called "investigations".' Goebbels raised two fingers to indicate quote marks. 'In short, we will tell you what to report and how.'

A murmur went around the room. The man on Minki's right, a journalist from a centrist paper in Berlin, leaned across and whispered in her ear.

'Who the hell does he think he is, giving us instructions. Is he mad?'

'No, sadly – he knows exactly what he's doing,' she replied. 'And I fear he's just getting started.'

Over the following months, 'Greta Schreiber' attended all of Goebbels' daily press briefings. She always sat near the back, in her disguise of fake glasses and dull clothing, and was never recognised. Sitting through these dreary events – in which Goebbels effectively harangued the press, demanding they print exactly what he wanted – made her realise the country was being taken over by a totalitarian regime. They weren't really press conferences, but propaganda instructions. As a result the newspapers were reduced to printing almost identical stories, their texts almost word for word the same. Unsurprisingly, newspaper sales plummeted, angering the few press barons still publishing. Minki was surprised that Goebbels had not spotted the obvious flaw in his strategy. That he, of all people – someone who had once been a writer himself – had effectively made journalism redundant.

Towards the end of April, Max and Minki were invited to a grand dinner party at Goebbels' state apartments. Minki was intrigued to find out whether Goebbels had any inkling that she attended his press conferences. After dinner she sought him out among the guests.

'What a lovely party, Joseph.'

'I'm glad you could come,' he replied. He looked thoughtful for a moment. 'I'm sorry about the last time we spoke... I was rather impatient with you. I was under a lot of pressure at the time.'

'That's all right. It was rather unrealistic of me to think you could help Viktor. A man as important as you is far above sorting a little local difficulty.'

'I'm glad we understand each other. Max tells me you've gone back to work.'

Minki blushed slightly. 'Yes... I'm trying to find my niche.'

She must be careful, she realised, not to be too specific. Goebbels had a way of sniffing out the truth.

'I've not seen your byline recently – have you abandoned the women's pages?'

'No, not at all,' she replied hurriedly. 'I'm overseeing a junior writer. I'm in more of a strategic role now.'

He studied her with his piercing gaze. 'Perhaps you should come and work for me on my paper?'

'Why? Is *Der Angriff* running a cookery column now?' She laughed.

'Good point. I was thinking more of the political side – you know I've always thought you were wasted on the women's pages.'

'Well, it's a flattering offer, Joe. And if things don't work out I'll be sure to consider it.' She paused, before adding, 'I hear you're running press conferences now. How's that working out?'

He smiled. 'All going according to plan... it's a way of keeping journalists in line. Quite honestly, Minki – between you and me – any man with even a modicum of honour would be a fool to become a journalist.'

'Joseph!' said Minki, with mock seriousness. 'I'm shocked.'

'No, you're not,' he replied, smiling. 'You're a realist, like me. That's why you write about cooking. There's just no point in being a political journalist any more.'

A couple of weeks after the party, Minki heard that university students all over Germany were being encouraged to 'cleanse' public libraries and bookshops of authors they considered 'un-German'. Thomas Mann, H.G. Wells, Helen Keller and Ernest Hemingway were among the authors chosen to be banned. The writers had nothing in common, apart from the fact that their views did not correspond to the National Socialist vision for Germany. Once confiscated, the books would be burned publicly on a particular evening in May. In Berlin, the location chosen for this event was the square outside the State Opera House.

Minki was keen to cover the event, and hurried to the scene that evening. A huge fire had already been set, and she watched, appalled, as young men threw books onto the flames by the dozen. Nearby, a group of students made great show of swearing an oath to 'combat un-German literature'. The watching crowd cheered as the pile of burning books grew higher and higher. Soon flames were leaping three or four metres into the darkening sky.

A podium draped in a swastika flag had been erected on the steps of the Opera House. Here stood Joseph Goebbels, his face lit up by the flames. Dressed casually in a white shirt, his skin glistening with beads of sweat, his eyes gleamed with excitement. When he began to speak, his voice rose with emotion as he declared: 'The age of pretentious Jewish intellectualism is over... We in the Third Reich say, "No to decadence and moral corruption."'

The students cheered and raised their arms in salute, as Goebbels continued: 'In the future, the German man will not just be a man of books but also a man of character, and it is to this end we want to educate you.'

The students screamed their approval. It seemed to Minki that they were more than just enthusiastic acolytes – it was as if they were hypnotised. What Goebbels was saying was the opposite of a real education. Books were the precious repository of all learning, of all human thought. Why were these presumably intelligent young people so terrified of any information their government had not sanctioned?

Standing in the shadows, notebook in hand, Minki felt outraged. But another part of her – the dispassionate 'outside observer' – was astounded at the ease with which Goebbels could manipulate the populace. By encouraging the students to do the burning, he was able to create the impression that it was the people rising up spontaneously against a liberal belief system, whereas in fact it was obviously a state-organised operation.

Her mind went back to the young Joe Goebbels she had met a decade earlier at a literary party in Munich. He had been so earnest, so desperate to succeed, so open to new ideas. What on earth would he have then said about burning books? Minki felt sure he would have been horrified. As she watched the feverish crowd hanging on to Goebbels' every word, she wondered how someone with so much promise – someone with a doctorate in philosophy, no less – could have become the controlling propagandist she saw before her. Was it simply ruthless ambition? Or a determination to break away from a working-class background? Having been born, herself, into a relatively wealthy and comfortable family, perhaps she had no right to judge him. She didn't know what it felt like to pull oneself up from the gutter, using nothing but sheer drive and intellect.

Nevertheless, what Minki had witnessed profoundly shocked her, and she returned to the office that evening and wrote an excoriating piece, which she entitled 'The burning of un-German books is un-German'.

> *We are a nation of thinkers, writers, poets and philosophers. To see the minds of university students so blinded by state propaganda is both frightening and shocking.*

It was well after ten o'clock at night when she laid it in front of her editor.

Helmut read it, before scoring it with a red pen and throwing it into his wastepaper bin. 'I'm sorry, Minki, but I can't print this. Editors are ending up in concentration camps for less. I'm as keen on journalistic truth as the next man, but I have a wife and children, for God's sake. I'm not going die on the altar of your opinions.'

'But Helmut, what I saw tonight was an outrage. Surely we must be allowed to say so.'

'Privately, I agree,' he said, shaking his head. 'But I still can't run it… I'm sorry.'

'But what's the point of doing our job if we can't tell the truth?'

'It's a balance… we must choose which battles are worth the fight – and this isn't one of them. Rewrite the piece but leave out your opinions – simply report what happened. Let readers make up their own minds.'

Minki felt deflated. As she turned to leave, she stopped at the door. 'I so wanted to make a difference.'

'Perhaps you can... but not like this. Believe me, Minki – now is not the time for heroism.'

'Isn't it? You see, I'd have thought it was exactly the right time, but perhaps heroism is no longer possible in journalism.'

Minki rewrote her article, just as Helmut had instructed, and left it on his desk. The piece, though factual and accurate, was dull and uninspiring. It would never change hearts and minds. Pulling on her coat, preparing to go home, she realised how misguided and naive she had been to imagine she could use her position as a journalist to influence society. As she looked around the empty newsroom, her job suddenly seemed pointless. Sitting down at her desk, she inserted a new sheet of paper into her typewriter and wrote a letter of resignation.

It was late when she got back home. Max was already asleep in bed, and the house was silent and peaceful. She went to Clara's room and stood at the end of her cot, watching her little girl sleeping. 'I'm sorry, my little darling,' Minki whispered. 'I tried... I tried to make a difference, but the world won't let me.'

Her mind still racing, and knowing she would struggle to sleep, she decided to write to the one person who always understood her.

My dearest Leila,

You have been on my mind for so many months. I feel so guilty that I was unable to help Viktor. We live in an evil world and it is incumbent on us all to do what we can to make a differ-

ence. You knew that from the start, and I admit that I have taken longer to arrive at the same conclusion. Finally, I realised I must do something to fight back, and so I joined the political team on my old newspaper – the Deutsche Allgemeine Zeitung. I hoped to demonstrate the stranglehold National Socialism has on the German people through my articles – but as you know, the press is now so constrained by Goebbels that even that proved impossible.

This evening I witnessed a horrific sight – book-burning on a grand scale on the streets of Berlin. It was appalling. Here were university students, for God's sake, burning the works of Hemingway and Thomas Mann. I wrote an article condemning it, but my editor refused to publish. I understand why – he is frightened – but it is a terrible disappointment. What, after all, is the point of political journalism if one is not allowed to tell the truth.

I realised that the only solution was for me to resign, and I have done so this evening.

You and Viktor stood up to the bullies in the National Socialist Party. You were prepared to be brave and to be counted, and you have suffered for it. But I want you to know that in spite of walking away from my job, I will carry on, in some small way, fighting the good fight. I will not abandon either you, or my country.

Write and tell me how you are – and more importantly how Viktor is. I presume he is still incarcerated, or I would have heard. He is strong, darling, and will survive, I'm sure of it.

With love,

Your friend,

Minki

25

MUNICH

DECEMBER 1933

Leila gingerly drove Viktor's battered old Mercedes on the icy road leading out of Munich towards the village of Dachau. The route was familiar, as she and Viktor had often visited the village in happier days. It sat amidst pretty countryside, and on many summer Sunday afternoons the family would picnic on the banks of a river. There, the couple would lie in the shade of low-hanging willows while the children paddled and fished for minnows. It seemed horrifying that this place – once associated with such happy memories – had now been chosen for the Nazis' first internment camp.

Throughout Viktor's incarceration at Stadelheim, and now at Dachau, Leila had written to her husband – sometimes as much as twice a week – but she never received a reply. Through her lawyer, Manfred Adler, she made frequent requests to visit him, but they were constantly rebuffed.

So she was astonished when she received a letter from her lawyer telling her that the authorities had finally agreed to let her visit Viktor at the new camp. She should present herself, along with her identity papers, at the entrance to Dachau at 10 a.m. on 21 December.

As Leila drove up the narrow bumpy lane that led to the camp, snow began to fall from a darkening sky. Finally, the road petered out, and ahead of her she saw a clearing, surrounded by barbed wire.

A uniformed guard flagged her down. 'Papers.'

She handed over her identity papers, along with Adler's letter.

He studied the documents ponderously, before nodding and handing them back. He peered in the back of the car as if checking for uninvited visitors. 'You're early. Park the car here by the fence, and wait. When the others arrive, you will be given admittance.'

She waited nervously, watching the snow settling on the car's windscreen and bonnet.

A black Volkswagen soon drew up next to her. Inside she could make out Charlotte, Julius Zerfass's wife. Leila braved the thickening snow and knocked on her car window. Charlotte smiled, beckoning her into the passenger seat, and the two women hugged each other firmly.

'I wondered if you'd be here, Leila.'

'And I you... I'm so glad to see you. It's all rather unnerving, isn't it?'

Charlotte nodded, her green eyes filling with tears.

'We must stay strong for them,' said Leila, taking her hand.

'I know.' Charlotte wiped her eyes. 'Have you been before?'

'No... you?'

Charlotte shook her head. 'But I did receive a letter from Julius.'

'Oh, what did it say?'

'Not much – I suppose they censor them. He just said he and Viktor were working in the gravel pits.'

'That must be hard work,' said Leila quietly.

'Brutal, I'd have thought...'

Leila, who until then had managed to keep hold of her emotions, began to weep.

'Oh, I'm sorry,' said Charlotte hurriedly, 'that was crass of me. I'm sure they'll be OK.'

Leila wiped her eyes. 'I hope so. And although Viktor is much older than Julius, he's very fit, you know. And our lawyer assures me they'll be out by the summer. We just have to be patient.'

'Yes... of course, you're right.' Charlotte hugged Leila to her tightly. 'We must have hope – we're finished once that's gone.'

The clearing began to fill up with people, some arriving on foot despite the weather. At precisely ten o'clock, four guards marshalled the whole group towards the camp gates. Set above the entrance was a metal arch inscribed with the words Arbeit Macht Frei – 'Work sets you free'.

Charlotte and Leila linked arms as they were funnelled into a guardroom to the right of the gates. Here they again had to show their papers, before being searched. 'It's as if they think *we* are the accused,' murmured Leila.

The group was herded through the snow across a large parade ground, into a wooden hut on the perimeter. As they filed inside, Leila detected a smell that she couldn't quite place – sweat, perhaps, or urine. The room was gloomy, dingy and depressing. It was also freezing cold and Leila was grateful for her fur coat and warm gloves. She wondered how Viktor – who had always suffered from a weak chest – could possibly cope without his own warm winter coat.

Long trestle tables had been laid out in parallel rows, with chairs on either side. The visitors were ordered to sit at the tables, all facing the same direction. Leila looked around as everyone took a seat. They were almost entirely women – wives, mothers, daughters, sisters, she presumed. As they removed their headscarves and hats, shaking the snow onto the floor, some looked anxious, others hopeful and expectant. One or two even took out powder compacts and powdered their noses. It was an act of touching normality, thought Leila. Like her, these women had probably not seen their menfolk for months, and simply wanted to look their best.

Two stony-faced guards stood at either side of a pair of double doors at one end of the hut. At half past ten precisely, they opened the doors, and Leila could see a gaggle of prisoners gathering behind them, dressed in beige prisoner uniforms. She knew these men were not real criminals, but politicians, writers, clerics, academics, lawyers – brave men who had openly criticised Hitler's new regime.

Leila found it curious that they did not rush into the room to see their visitors. Instead they appeared tentative, peering nervously from the doorway, as if they were frightened of what was awaiting them – a punishment perhaps? But as each man began to recognise his visitor, the anxiety left his face and he hurried in. Sitting opposite their loved ones, the men instinctively reached out to hold hands, or stroke faces. But the guards slapped whips down on the table between them, shouting, 'No touching.'

The seats around Leila began to fill up, but there was no sign of Viktor. Finally, she saw him at the doorway. She had to prevent herself from gasping out loud – he was so changed. Standing forlornly in his shapeless beige jacket and trousers, he appeared to have lost a huge amount of weight. As soon as he recognised her, he shuffled towards her. She could see his once-dark hair was white, his face was lined and tanned. He sat down heavily on the chair opposite his wife, gazing in wonder at her, as if she were someone from another world.

Fearful of the guards, but desperate to touch her husband, Leila tentatively reached across the table, her fingertips just connecting with his own. 'Darling, I'm so sorry I've not been before – they refused me until now.'

Viktor nodded.

'Tell me what it's like in here.'

He shook his head. 'You don't want to know.'

Leila was shocked by how weak his voice sounded. 'I do... you must tell me.'

He shook his head again.

His hands, resting on the table, were scratched, rough, raw and blistered. From her conversation with Charlotte, she knew exactly why, but she was desperate to make Viktor say something. 'Do they put you to work here?'

'Yes... in the gravel pit – that's where the Jews get sent. Julius and I are together. It's good to have his company.'

'His wife, Charlotte, is here – we were chatting before coming in. Look she's over there with him.' Leila could see Julius gazing at his wife with the same look of bewilderment as Viktor.

But Viktor didn't react; it was as if he was unable to hear her.

'I'm glad you've got each other for company,' Leila said gently.

He looked up. 'How are the children?' His voice cracked with emotion.

'They miss you. Sofia has matured a lot in just a few months. She studies hard – to distract herself, I think. Axel didn't understand what had happened at first, but he does now... he's angry – a typical boy, I suppose.'

'Take them away, Leila. Leave Germany.'

'No! We can't leave without you.'

'Forget about me. I'll either survive or I won't. If I survive, I'll follow you. But in the meantime, take the children and go... please.'

'No, I'll wait for you. I want to leave Germany, but we'll go together. Manfred Adler says you'll be out by next summer.'

Viktor sighed. 'We'll see.' He touched her fingertips again. 'You must do what you think is right, darling.'

The guards strode between the tables, shouting, 'One minute left. Time to say goodbye now.'

Some of the women wailed in protest, but the guards' stony faces made it clear that there would be no kindness shown that day. Leila felt a rising sense of panic. There was so much she still wanted to say... so much she had planned to say. 'Oh God.'

Viktor squeezed her fingers. 'Listen, Leila, I want to say something. Thank you for coming into my life. You have made me so happy for the last ten years – happier than I could ever have imagined.'

Instinctively, Leila took Viktor's hand and kissed it. 'Darling, you know I feel the same – you have made me so happy.'

There was a sudden crack as the guard brought his whip down hard, catching the back of Leila's hand. She yelped, but instantly bit her lip, not wanting to give the guard the satisfaction of seeing her weep.

At that moment, the double doors opened. 'Prisoners out,' shouted the guards.

Viktor stood up. 'Leila, take the children and leave Germany, I beg you...'

He turned and walked away, joining the hunched figures returning to an existence Leila could not imagine. She felt her resolve crumbling, and her whole body began to shake with emotion.

The guards locked the double doors behind the retreating men, and turned back to the room. 'Everybody out, now... *Schnell, schnell.*'

The women stood up quietly, wiping their eyes and noses, putting handkerchiefs away in bags, tying headscarves on heads

– trying to put on a show of dignity, refusing to be bullied by the guards.

Leila glanced across at Charlotte, who smiled back bravely. But instead of leaving straight away, Leila placed her hands on the table where Viktor's hands had just been, almost as if she wanted to absorb some part of him.

'Shall we go?' whispered Charlotte.

But Leila's legs refused to cooperate. Part of her was desperate to get out of this place, and home to the children, but another part wanted to stay there until they let her see Viktor again. She wanted to scream: 'Take me prisoner too – let us at least be together.' But she kept quiet. They would only ignore her, and in any case, what use could she be locked away? Who would care for the children then?

Charlotte took her arm. 'Come on...'

Leila, her face streaming with tears, finally allowed herself to be led towards the door.

When they reached their cars, Leila hugged Charlotte tightly. 'I'm so glad you were here today. I'm not sure I could have coped alone.'

'I know...' whispered Charlotte.

'As you said... we must just stay strong and have hope. That's really all we can do.'

26

BERLIN

CHRISTMAS 1933

Minki was sitting at the kitchen table early one morning, writing a list of jobs for the staff, when Max joined her for breakfast. They were hosting a special Christmas dinner party that night, and the guests of honour were Joseph Goebbels and his wife Magda.

'It's quite a coup to get the golden couple,' Max said, as he poured himself a cup of coffee. 'Goebbels' social circle is rather less ecumenical these days. He and Magda normally only dine with really important people.'

'Well, he obviously thinks you're a "really important person",' said Minki, with just a hint of sarcasm. But Max missed the sneer, hearing only approbation.

'That's kind, darling, but he's very fond of you too, you know. He was surprised when I told him you'd given up working at the *Deutsche Allgemeine Zeitung* – you know he has always thought you had great talent as a journalist.'

Minki had never revealed the true nature of her job at the newspaper and was determined it wouldn't come out now.

'That's very kind of him, I'm sure. But, as I told you when I left the job back in May – it seemed to me that writing a column about how to run a house properly was less important than actually doing it myself... do you want something to eat?'

'Yes... just some bread, and maybe a boiled egg.'

Minki passed the bread basket, and cracked a hard-boiled egg onto Max's plate. 'In any case,' she went on, 'I really don't miss working. Taking care of Clara is far more important.'

Clara, who was nearly two years old, had turned into a bright, cheerful child with boundless energy. She was a quick learner too, and much to Minki's delight was already speaking in simple sentences, and had even mastered her alphabet.

'I'm pleased, obviously, that you find motherhood so fulfilling,' said Max, buttering his bread. 'All I meant was that Goebbels thinks you have talent. He would have loved you to work on his own paper.'

'Yes... so he's often said. But I can't see myself working for him. One sycophant in this house is quite enough, don't you think?'

Her cutting remark took Max by surprise. 'I hope you'll keep opinions like that to yourself this evening, Minki.'

'Of course, Max. I'll be the perfect hostess, don't worry.'

'Good,' he said, pouring himself another cup of coffee. 'On that subject – I've done a seating plan for the table.' He pulled a piece of paper from his inside jacket pocket, and laid it between them on the table. 'I'd be grateful if you could stick to it... it's all rather strategic.'

To her irritation, Minki saw that Max had placed her next to Goebbels. 'Are you sure Joe should sit next to me? There must be more interesting people he'd rather talk to?'

'Don't be ridiculous, Minki. It's your place as hostess to have Joseph on your right. Besides, the key guest, from Joseph's point of view, is sitting on your left... he's a scientist called

Professor Staemmler. Goebbels has important business with him.'

'I see,' said Minki, picking up her list of jobs and the table plan. 'Well, if there's nothing else, I'd better go and sort out the dining room... there's a lot to do.'

The dining room was oak-panelled, topped by a sparkling chandelier. Lena, the housemaid, had already laid a white linen cloth on the long table, and arranged silver vases and candle-sticks along the centre.

'Christmas roses would be nice in those vases, I think,' said Minki. 'Can you pick some from the garden?'

'Yes, madam.'

'We'll be fourteen in all. I've got a table plan and will write out some place cards this morning. And please use the best silver cutlery and crystal... all right?'

The maid bobbed her head.

Once she was satisfied with the arrangements, Minki went upstairs to Clara's room. Ida, the nursery maid, was already running a bath for the little girl.

'I'll bathe her today, Ida. You can go and help Lena downstairs.'

While the child splashed happily in the bubbles, Minki mused on her conversation with Max that morning. His close-ness to Goebbels, and his complete lack of criticism of the regime, disturbed her. But what could she do about it?

'Come on,' she said to Clara eventually. 'You've played long enough. Time to get dressed.'

Clara obediently held her arms up to her mother, who lifted her out of the bath, wrapping her in a towel.

'I love you Mutti,' said Clara, nestling into her mother's neck.

'And I love you too.' The intensity of her feelings for her

daughter sometimes caught her off guard. As a young woman she could never have imagined loving someone so completely. But since giving up work, and spending most of her time with Clara, the bond between them had grown stronger by the day. There were times when she physically ached with love.

Clara toddled into her bedroom and pulled open the wardrobe door, pointing to a pink party dress.

'No dress today, darling, something more practical, I think.'

Minki took out a pair of corduroy trousers and jumper from the child's wardrobe and, once Clara was dressed, picked her up and carried her to her own room.

'You play here for a while, darling. I've got a letter to write.' Minki sat down at her desk in the window, overlooking the garden.

It had been months since she had written to Leila. She had never received a reply to her earlier letter, and now she feared Leila had not forgiven her for abandoning Viktor. Perhaps she never would, and that thought – that their friendship might be over – brought tears to her eyes. She picked up her pen, but didn't know where to start. She had already apologised, and what more could she do... what more could she say?

Clara stood up and nestled against her mother's side. 'Why you crying, Mutti?'

'Because my best friend and I don't speak to each other any more.'

'What's a best friend?'

'Someone you love, whatever happens.'

'Like me?'

Minki pulled Clara up onto her lap. 'Yes – exactly like that.'

While Clara ate lunch in the kitchen with Ida, Minki laid out the engraved place cards on the dining table. Most of the guests were industrialists who had donated substantial sums to the

Party. Minki had met most of them once or twice, and found them to be self-satisfied bores, with dull wives. But as she placed Goebbels' card next to her own, she shuddered at the thought of making polite conversation to him all evening. Checking Max's table plan for a last time, she noted his instructions:

> *Professor Staemmler to be seated opposite Goebbels – orders of JG'.*

The name Staemmler seemed familiar, but Minki couldn't recall where she'd come across it before.

As she finished laying the place cards, Clara toddled into the dining room. She gazed at the silver and crystal gleaming on the table, and clapped her hands delightedly. 'Party, Mama... I want dress for party.'

'Now, Clara, I've already explained. The party is just for grown-ups. You'll be in bed when the guests arrive.'

Clara's face fell. 'But I like parties.'

'I know, darling.' Seeing the distress on her daughter's face, Minki made a suggestion. 'Why don't you go and put on your best dress and then you can decorate the Christmas tree with me?'

Clara beamed excitedly and scampered out of the room. Reaching the stairs, she climbed them rapidly, as she always did, on her hands and knees. Minki followed her up to the nursery, opened the wardrobe and took out a new dress she had bought the child for Christmas. It was red velvet with a white lace collar, and Clara clapped her hands delightedly as her mother helped her into it.

Suitably pacified, Clara and her mother went downstairs to the drawing room, where Lena had laid out a basket of decorations in front of the Christmas tree. Clara rushed delightedly towards the basket and minutely examined the multicoloured ornaments.

'These first, Mutti,' she said, handing her mother a pair of dark-red pearlised metal baubles.

'They're very pretty,' agreed Minki, arranging the ornaments on the lower branches. Within half an hour, the tree had been festooned with sparkling decorations and tinsel, with brass candle holders clipped onto the branches.

Finally, Minki climbed a stepladder, clutching an angel to place on top of the tree. 'This evening, Clara,' she explained over her shoulder, 'we'll put candles in the holders and light them. The whole thing will come alive.'

Suddenly, Minki heard an odd guttural sound behind her – an animal-like growl, followed by a thud. She turned her head and saw Clara lying on her back on the floor. The girl looked as if she had passed out but, oddly, her eyes were wide open, the eyeballs rolled up into their sockets. Her rosebud mouth was flecked with white froth.

'Clara, Clara!' screamed Minki, nearly falling off the stepladder.

Lena ran in from the dining room. 'What's the matter, madam?'

'It's Clara,' Minki shouted. 'Look, I think she's having a heart attack.'

'I'll call the doctor,' said Lena, running to the telephone in the hall.

Minki dropped to her knees, stroking Clara's hair, smoothing her forehead and listening to her heart, which, to her relief, was beating soundly, if a little fast. 'Baby girl, wake up,' she whispered. The child lay stiff, her fists clenched, her teeth grinding. All Minki could do was watch with a sense of utter helplessness.

Finally, Clara began to relax. Her eyes rolled back into position, her fists unclenched and the strange guttural sounds

subsided. She looked up at her mother and smiled beatifically.
'Mama... the angel.'

'Yes, darling... the angel's on top of the tree. I'll show you in
a minute.'

The doctor arrived quickly, and found Minki still hunched over
Clara beneath the Christmas tree. Minki did her best to explain
what she had seen. The doctor nodded sagely, and stroked his
beard thoughtfully, before kneeling at Clara's side. He rested a
cushion beneath her head and gently examined her body.
Opening his instrument bag, he measured her heart rate, blood
pressure and temperature.

He turned to Minki and smiled. 'Well, Frau von Zeller,
you'll be glad to hear that your daughter's vital signs are normal,
and no bones are broken.' He picked Clara up and laid her
gently on the sofa. 'Let me tell you what I think has happened
to her. I believe your daughter has suffered a minor epileptic
seizure. It's not uncommon in small children. She may have had
a slight temperature, and when they're young children cannot
regulate these things properly. Occasionally, it causes these
temporary problems. I've seen it many times in my career. It
will probably never happen again. My advice is to get her to
bed. She'll sleep well tonight. The brain has experienced an
overload of activity.' The doctor smiled encouragingly.

Minki nodded, trying hard to concentrate on what he was
saying.

'Do try not to worry,' said the doctor, patting her shoulder.
'And call me again if you have any concerns.'

'Even over Christmas?'

'Of course – that's not a problem. Call me any time.'

· · ·

Minki carried Clara up to bed. But rather than feeling sleepy, the little girl was animated and wide awake.

'Look Mutti... giraffe,' she said, pointing at the wallpaper in her nursery, which was decorated with animals. 'Tiger, Mama, lion... big brown bear...'

'How clever of you,' said Minki, stroking the child's hair. Interestingly, although Clara had often made the sound of a roaring lion or a squeaking mouse, she had never identified them by name before.

'Lions roar like this,' said Clara, bellowing so loudly it reminded Minki of the guttural moaning she had heard earlier.

'You must go to sleep now, darling. I'm sure you're tired.'

But Clara's blue eyes were wide open and glinting. 'Clara not tired. Clara want story.'

While Ida tidied the nursery, Minki picked out Clara's favourite storybook from the bookshelf and began to read. Soon, she heard the sound of Max's car crunching over the gravel outside, and then his low voice as he spoke to Lena in the hall below.

Minki heard him climb the stairs. He stopped outside the nursery door, as if he were preparing himself. Finally, he opened the door with a flourish.

'Hello there,' he said cheerfully. 'How are my two best girls? I hear this little one wasn't so well today.'

'No, but the doctor says she should be fine now. Just a temperature, he thought.'

'Oh, good.' Max kissed his wife's head, before leaning over Clara's bed and kissing her cheek. 'Now you must go to sleep. Mummy and Daddy have important friends coming for supper, and Mummy has to go and make herself beautiful.'

'Mummy beautiful,' echoed Clara.

Minki burst into tears – of relief, despair and exhaustion.

'Oh, now,' said Max, 'don't cry, darling. Come on, it's all right... Ida, can you take over here?'

'Of course, sir.'

Minki didn't argue. 'All right, Max. I'll go and get ready.' She kissed her daughter again, stroking her forehead. 'Goodnight, darling.'

An hour later, the guests arrived and were shown into the drawing room. Minki, now bathed and coiffed, looked stunning in a dark-red bias-cut velvet dress. No one would have guessed the trauma she had just gone through.

When Goebbels and his wife arrived, Minki kissed them both on the cheek. 'Joseph, Magda, how lovely to see you.'

'You look wonderful, as always,' said Joseph.

'How kind. You must both have some champagne.' She beckoned Lena, who was holding a tray of filled glasses nearby. 'Now, if you'll excuse me I must circulate, but I know Max is dying to see you... he's over there in the far corner.'

Minki chatted gaily to everyone – as ever, the perfect hostess. The guests were all associated with either the Party or Max, so no-one showed any particular interest in her. If they knew anything about her, it was as an attractive but inconsequential wife and mother who had once written a column about knitting. In other words, she was a nobody, which suited her.

Dinner was announced, and the guests filed into the dining room. Max and Minki sat at either end of the long table. Goebbels took his seat on her right, with Professor Staemmler on her left.

During dinner, Minki was kept busy organising the staff. Both Goebbels and Staemmler seemed happy to make conversation with the other guests and largely ignored her.

But once the dessert had been cleared away, Goebbels turned his full attention on Staemmler. 'I'm so glad you were able to come, Professor,' he began. 'Your speech at Leipzig a couple of years ago in which you suggested putting an end to the cycle of reproduction between Jews and Aryans, but also the sterilisation of the disabled and mentally infirm, was inspirational to us all.'

Minki's stomach lurched. Now she remembered how she knew the scientist's name. Staemmler had been mentioned in an article she had read in the *Munich Post* a couple of years earlier, warning of the introduction of such measures.

'Thank you, Dr Goebbels,' Staemmler was saying, 'Without sterilisation, we will end up with a population dominated by the feeble and infirm.'

'Quite.' Goebbels smiled wryly. 'You know what Adolf calls them?'

The professor shook his head.

'The undesirables.' Goebbels laughed.

'An accurate description,' agreed Staemmler. 'There is no point in allowing people with serious genetic diseases to reproduce.'

'Exactly, which is why we are introducing a new law about genetics in the new year.'

'I'd heard about that. What have you decided to call it?'

'The Law for the Prevention of Genetically Diseased Offspring – long-winded but accurate, I think you'll agree.'

'Excellent,' replied the professor. 'I'm delighted we are finally making progress. But, if I may, I'd like to suggest something more, Herr Reichsminister.'

'Go on.'

'My university department estimates there are approximately four hundred thousand people with genetic defects in Germany – a staggering figure, as I'm sure you'll agree.'

Goebbels nodded. 'Quite so...'

'We need to identify these individuals and create a register of them – a special "stock–take", if you like, of people who are such a drain on society.'

'That sounds a splendid idea,' said Goebbels. 'I'll bring it up with Adolf when I see him tomorrow. I'm sure he'll approve. Would you like to run it?'

Staemmler nodded, beaming. 'I would be honoured, Herr Reichsminister.'

'No, Professor. The honour belongs to us, and the German people. Your vision and expertise will be invaluable.'

Minki felt sick. Leila's warning about the Nazis' policies was beginning to come true. But she ventured to enter the conversation, feigning a neutral interest: 'How interesting... what sort of genetic diseases are you talking about?'

'Oh... everything from schizophrenia to epilepsy,' Staemmler replied casually.

Minki's heart began to thump inside her chest.

'Really, anyone with any mental infirmity,' Goebbels added. 'Manic depression, for example, or alcoholism. The blind would be included, naturally, and the deaf. We need to purge our population of these undesirables, if we are ever to achieve our goal of a pure Aryan race.'

Minki struggled to sound dispassionate. 'How do you propose to go about it?'

'Compulsory sterilisation,' answered Staemmler, matter-of-factly. 'With women – a hysterectomy, ideally when they're young...aged ten or eleven. With men – castration. Quite simple really.'

Minki felt bile rising in her mouth, and began to choke. 'Will you excuse me, gentlemen,' she said, abruptly pushing her chair back from the table. 'I must just go and check on things in the kitchen.'

As her chair scraped across the oak floor, Max glanced up from his end of the table with a puzzled expression. Minki wiped her mouth on her napkin, almost threw it down on the table, and left the room.

She ran upstairs to Clara's nursery, where to her relief she found the child sleeping peacefully in her bed, her arms thrown up above her head, the covers kicked away. Minki touched her forehead, checked her temperature and pulled the covers back over her. Then, sitting beside her bed, she listened to her child's even breathing. Gradually, Minki began to calm down, aware of her own heartbeat slowing.

The thought that her child might be classed as an 'undesirable' seemed unimaginable. 'The wickedness...' she murmured.

Clara stirred in her sleep and opened her eyes. 'Mama...' she whispered.

'Mama's here, darling. Go back to sleep.'

Clara's eyelids closed and her breathing became slow and easy once again.

Minki leaned over the bed and stroked her child's forehead. 'No one will ever hurt you, my angel, I can promise that. I will protect you with every fibre of my being.'

27

MUNICH

Leila was sitting at her desk in the window of her parents' sitting room. Although Viktor was still in prison, and her job as a journalist was finished, the urge to write was as compelling as ever. She had embarked on a new project and had begun to assemble notes and ideas for a book about the plight of women in Germany, and how they were being manipulated by the National Socialist regime.

Although she was quite alone in the apartment, she was struggling to concentrate. Her mother had taken the children to school, and her father was at work. But this morning, even the ticking of the clock on the mantelpiece intruded on her thoughts.

She stood up to stretch and, looking out of the window, noticed the postboy running up the steps to the apartment building. Leila rarely left the apartment now, fearing for her safety, but she decided to go downstairs and collect the mail. Opening the postbox in the hall, she took out the bundle of letters. Most were for her parents, but near the bottom was a letter addressed to her with a Dachau postmark. Hoping it might be from Viktor, she ran back upstairs, laid her parents' mail on the hall table, and eagerly ripped open the envelope.

With regret, we have to inform you of the death of Viktor Labowski. Cause of death: Tuberculosis.

Leila let out a gasp and began to wail. She sank down onto the parquet flooring of the hall and wept, railing against the loss of the only man she had ever loved, and the wicked regime that had caused his untimely death. The anger she felt at the injustice of her beloved husband dying – alone – in that awful place was unbearable.

Her mother found her an hour later, still prostrate on the hall floor. 'Leila... whatever is the matter, darling?'

Leila pointed to the letter lying abandoned on the floor.

Hannah quickly skimmed it. 'Oh, my God,' she breathed. 'Let me help you up. Come into the sitting room and I'll make tea.'

Her mother settled Leila on the sofa but, as she turned to leave, Leila reached for her mother's hand and pulled her down next to her. 'Don't go... stay with me.'

Hannah sat down, holding Leila's hand.

'I just keep thinking of that last time I saw him – last winter – you remember?'

Hannah nodded.

'I wonder if he knew then that he was ill?'

'Possibly.'

'He begged me to leave Germany, you know.'

'I know... you told me. Let me make tea.'

Listening to the familiar sounds of the wheezing kettle and the clink of china as her mother made tea in the kitchen, Leila felt numb. All she saw was a blank future filled with uncertainty. The only thing she knew with absolute clarity was that she now must take her children out of Germany; away from everything they knew, everything that was comforting and familiar, and forge a new life. She was now in sole charge of the children's destiny, and it was her duty to protect them.

Telling Sofia and Axel that evening that their father had died was the hardest thing Leila had ever done.

Sofia listened quietly and intently, hugging her mother, kissing away her tears. 'I'm so sorry, Mutti, but I'm glad his pain is over,' she murmured. Leila was taken aback by such a grown-up response. Perhaps, Leila thought, the fact that Sofia hadn't seen her father for a year had prepared her for his loss.

But Axel, who at seven was far less mature, reacted in the only way he knew – with anger. He hurled his toy train across his grandmother's living room, shattering a glass figurine on the windowsill.

The ensuing argument between mother and son about 'care-lessness', and 'thoughtlessness', somehow eased the pain of facing Viktor's death. But when the broken glass had been cleared away, the little boy ran into the bedroom and slammed the door. Leila could hear him sobbing.

'We should go to him,' suggested Sofia.

'In a moment,' Leila replied. 'Let him cry a little first.'

The following day, Leila received a parcel wrapped in brown paper. Opening it, she found a pile of clothes, and on top a neatly typed list of the contents. Carefully folded was Viktor's white shirt, the collar still stained slightly where his neck had rubbed. Underneath was the dark suit he had been wearing on the day of his arrest. In a separate envelope were his 'valuables': a gold watch – her present to him on their wedding day – and his gold wedding ring. It surprised her that these had been returned. There was a bizarre meticulousness about it – as if his jailors had been more interested in taking care of his belongings than of the man himself. Also in the envelope was his wallet – empty of money, she noticed, but still containing a photograph he had taken of her many years before when they first met. She had looked so happy then, so innocent, so full of hope and dreams.

A few days later, Leila had a visitor. It was Charlotte Zerfass.

'I've only just heard about Viktor. I'm so sorry – and so is Julius, obviously.'

'Thank you. Please, come in,' replied Leila, ushering her into the sitting room.

Charlotte sat down uncertainly on the sofa, looking uncomfortable and nervous.

'Charlotte... what's the matter? '

Suddenly, Charlotte burst into tears. 'I just feel so guilty.'

'Why?'

'Because I had a letter today saying that Julius will be released next week. I'm just so sorry he survived and Viktor didn't.'

Leila sat down next to her, gently taking her hand. 'Please don't feel that way. It's no one's fault. I'm really pleased Julius is getting out... so pleased for you both.'

The pair sat for a while in silence, each contemplating the other's situation – one on the brink of happiness, the other in despair.

'What prompted them to release Julius now?' Leila asked at last.

'Adler, the lawyer, had been negotiating on behalf of them both.'

'Yes, I was aware of that...'

'Just in the last few days, he received word that if Julius

agreed to leave Germany, the authorities would release him.' Charlotte paused, uncertain how to proceed. She looked into Leila's eyes and shook her head. 'I'm sure they would have done a deal for Viktor too... it's just so unfair.'

'It is...' muttered Leila. 'If they had offered him that deal sooner, he probably would have survived. I could have taken him to a sanatorium in Switzerland for treatment. I knew he had a weak chest, and the conditions in that place were so harsh, he was bound to fall seriously ill. In some ways, his death isn't a complete surprise. But still... the injustice of it. To think how close he was to being released. It breaks my heart.'

'What will you do now?' asked Charlotte tearfully, wiping her eyes with the back of her hand.

'I don't know. When I last saw Viktor, he begged me to leave Germany, and take the children away somewhere... anywhere.'

'I think he was right. We hope to leave as soon as Julius is released. Why don't you come with us?'

Leila gasped. 'That's so kind, Charlotte... and believe me, I'd like to leave. But I worry about my parents – how can I abandon them?'

'Bring them with you.'

'My father would never leave his business – it's his life's work.'

'Well, try to persuade them. You can't stay in Germany, not now. I know Julius would be much happier knowing you were coming with us.'

That evening, Leila sat her parents down and explained her reasons for wanting to leave Germany. 'Now that Viktor has gone, I feel I must make a life for myself and children else-where... Switzerland maybe, or even London.'

Hannah's eyes filled with tears.

'Mutti, I'm so sorry – but you have to understand... I can't get a job here, and without work how can I support the children?'

'You mustn't worry about money – your father and I will help you out,' Hannah ventured. 'Or maybe you could find a job here doing something else?'

'What am I good for but writing? And while it's kind of you to offer to help, it's more than just money. We have to accept that, as Jews, we are considered "undesirable". Things will only get worse for people like us.'

'What do you mean –"people like us"?' interrupted her father defensively. 'I'm a respected member of the community.'

'I know, Papa... but for how much longer?'

'Don't be ridiculous. There have been Jews in Munich for hundreds of years – since medieval times. We're not outsiders. Besides, I'm too old to leave Germany now.'

'No, you're not. And if you come with us, we can all be together.'

'But *I* still have to earn *my* living – I can't live off my daughter.'

'Papa—'

'No, Leila,' he interjected. 'You say that you must work. Well, so must I. I've spent a lifetime building up a successful business. I can't leave it all behind.'

'But you must see the way things are going. Hitler and his Party are so determined to revolutionise society... and people like us are not part of the plan.'

Leila glanced across at her mother, who nodded her head encouragingly.

'That's nonsense,' replied her father. 'They have no argument with jewellers. Some of my best customers are members of the Party.'

'Maybe they are now, but things will change.'

'Anyway, no government lasts forever, Leila. They'll be voted out if the people don't like the way they behave.'

The old man stood up, indicating that the conversation was over. 'I'm going to bed – I've got an early start tomorrow. You must do as you see fit, Leila. And once you're settled, your mother and I can visit you for holidays.'

He went out into the hall, and the two women heard Levi closing his bedroom door. Hannah shook her head sorrowfully. 'There's no arguing with your father sometimes. He doesn't want to see what's in front of his eyes.'

'I know,' said Leila sadly.

'You know that I'd come with you like a shot, don't you? But I can't leave your father.'

'Try to persuade him, Mutti – please?'

Two weeks later, Leila and the children were standing on the crowded platform of Munich station, surrounded by suitcases. Steam belched from the waiting locomotive onto the platform, which throbbed with people, all saying tearful farewells, Hannah and Levi among them.

The train was bound for Zurich in Switzerland. Julius and Charlotte had already boarded, but Sofia and Axel were still hugging their sobbing grandmother. 'Look after yourselves, darlings,' she cried. 'And write to us when you get there.'

Leila kissed her father's stubbly cheek, tasting salty tears. 'Take care of yourself, and especially Mutti.'

'Of course I will take care of her. I've spent the last forty years looking after your mother. Why would I stop now?'

'And, Papa, do think about coming to join us... please? I'll let you know when I'm settled.'

'Yes, yes...' Levi said impatiently, flapping his hand. 'You'd better get on, or the train will leave without you.'

The stationmaster blew his whistle and the family scrambled up the steep steps into the carriage. Julius was waiting for them and led them to the compartment they were sharing. He opened the window for Leila to lean out.

The train slowly began to move, chased by Hannah, who ran along the platform waving a white handkerchief.

'I love you, Mutti,' Leila shouted.

'I love you too... and I'll miss you... Goodbye my darlings... good bye.'

The journey to Switzerland took them through the Bavarian Alps and on to Austria. At the border, German guards boarded the train and sullenly worked their way through the carriages, examining everyone's passports. Leila was worried that they might find some spurious reason to prevent her leaving – or worse, arrest her. They took their time examining the family's papers but, to her immense relief, finally stamped the family's passports and moved on.

A couple of hours later, Leila was woken from a dreamless sleep as the train chugged slowly across no-man's-land and into Switzerland. Once again, she braced herself as the border guards entered the carriage. But this was a very different experience. 'Welcome to Switzerland, Frau Labowski,' said the border guard, smiling broadly.

Leila, Julius and Charlotte embraced and began to laugh. The children, who had slept through the whole experience, suddenly woke up. 'Where are we, Mutti?' asked Sofia sleepily, peering out of the window.

'We're in Switzerland, darling,' said Leila. 'And we're free.'

Julius and Charlotte had rented a small chalet high up in the hills overlooking Zurich. The taxi driver drove them as far as he could, but finally ground to a halt when the road petered out and became a farm track. 'You'll have to walk the rest of the way, I'm afraid.'

They all set off up the track carrying their suitcases, just as a small herd of cows ambled contentedly towards them, the bells round their necks clanging melodically, led by a young man carrying a staff.

'Hello,' said Julius. 'I'm looking for Herr Keller, the farmer.'

'I'm his son, Klaus,' replied the boy. His accent was strong, and he spoke in the local Swiss-German dialect.

'I've rented a chalet from your father – my name is Julius Zerfass.'

'Yes, he told me to expect you. The chalet is at the end of the track. Just let me get the cows into the field, and I'll show you inside.'

The chalet was painted black, with red shutters which glowed in the evening light. The young man led the family onto the covered porch and opened the front door. It led straight into a modest sitting room warmed with a woodstove; there was an old sheepskin-covered sofa and two battered armchairs. A further door led to a small kitchen with a stone sink, a dresser and another wood-fired oven.

'There's wood stacked on the porch, and you get water from the well out the back,' said the boy. 'The toilet's in a hut down the stone path. My father will be down later. He's taken some goats' cheese to the market. If you're all right, I'll be off.'

Left alone in their new house, Leila and Charlotte looked at one another quizzically, and suddenly burst out laughing. 'My God,' said Charlotte. 'I'm not quite sure this is what we were expecting... is it, Julius?'

'No... perhaps not. But it will do for a while.'

While the adults looked around the house, the children ran outside and began to race around the fields, laughing and shrieking.

'Well, they appear to like it,' said Leila, smiling. 'Shall we inspect the accommodation?'

There was one small bedroom downstairs, with a double bed and a chest of drawers. Upstairs was a large and airy attic. Although it contained only one single bed, there was enough room to add two mattresses for the children. Peering out of the attic window, Leila looked down over forests and fields to the Zurichsee – a long meandering lake named after the city. Surrounded by hills, with snow-capped mountains in the distance, it created a spectacular view.

'You must have this room, Leila,' said Charlotte magnanimously. 'Julius and I will be quite happy downstairs.'

Late in the afternoon, they had a visitor – a middle-aged man driving a pony and cart containing two straw mattresses.

'Welcome!' he called out. 'I'm Fritz Keller – my son told me there were two little ones, so I've brought these for them to sleep on.'

Keller was fair-haired, with a round face and ruddy complexion – clearly a man who spent his life outdoors. He hauled the mattresses up into the attic, and then clattered back downstairs to introduce himself properly.

'I've brought you a welcome gift,' he said, taking a wicker basket from the cart. 'Come and sit on the porch, and I'll show you.'

Inside the basket were bread, eggs, a dish of butter, a can of milk and a bottle of dark-red liquid.

'It's cherry brandy,' said Keller, pouring out four glasses. As Leila, Charlotte and Julius clinked glasses with their new landlord, they felt instantly relaxed.

'It's good, eh? My wife makes it. We have a small orchard near the house. It's a simple life up here, but a good one.'

Gazing down at the lake, with the surrounding hills glowing purple in the sunset, Leila had to agree.

Herr Keller's tenants soon settled into a routine. Leila took to rising early. Pushing open the shutters of her attic window, she relished the cool, clean mountain air that rushed in. As the morning mist rose over the lake, it revealed the teal surface beneath. Leila was struck by how the hills gradually changed colour with the rising sun – from grey, to purple, through to green.

Every morning, the farmer's son delivered a can of milk, along with half a dozen eggs. Once a week one of the adults accompanied Herr Keller to the local market town on his pony and cart to buy meat and groceries. Life was simple and care-free. The two families hiked in the hillsides, paddled in the streams, and occasionally the whole group would hitch a lift with the farmer down to the shores of the lake, where Julius would hire a small rowing boat and fish for trout. It was a golden time in many ways, and yet tinged with such sadness. Leila grieved for Viktor and often wondered how much he would have enjoyed this bucolic life. The light and colours of the Zurichsee reminded her of their honeymoon on Lake Maggiore.

In her darker moments – usually in the middle of the night – Leila would torment herself. Why had they not heeded the warning signs and left Germany earlier? Perhaps if they had, Viktor would still be alive – a thought that ate away at her constantly. It also spurred her on to urge her parents to join them. How could she live with herself if they met the same fate as Viktor? She wrote to her mother each week, begging her to leave Germany as soon as possible. But her mother repeatedly replied that her father was still clinging stubbornly to his view that Germany was perfectly safe.

Over the course of the summer, the beautiful surroundings

and the friendly welcome of the local people began to restore Leila's spirits. But she knew this idyllic life could not last. For one thing, she was running out of money, and needed an income. And although the children loved country life, there was no future for them on a Swiss hillside. Leila decided to write to friends and contacts looking for work.

Frances McFadden was the picture editor of *Harper's Bazaar*. Although she was based in New York, she and Leila had met occasionally in Munich when Frances came over to cover a story, and Leila had been impressed by her determined nature. There was something about her that reminded Leila of Minki in the old days, before she became embroiled with the Party.

Leila had corresponded with Frances ever since, and although their professional lives could not have been more different – one working in the glamorous world of photojournalism, the other motivated by politics – their friendship had grown stronger over the years.

When she first arrived in Switzerland, Leila had written to Frances giving her the good news that she and the children had escaped Germany. Over the following weeks, she regaled her friend with tales of their life on the mountain.

> *It's like a dream here, Frances. A cosy and delightful dream... We get water from a well, cook on open fires, hike in the hills and fish for trout. The sanitary arrangements leave something to be desired – but compared with Hitler's Germany, we are in heaven.*

By the end of the summer, having made the decision to leave Switzerland, Leila wrote again to Frances, this time with more urgency.

For once, I won't regale you with 'tales from a mountain'!
Although we have enjoyed our time here, I know it can't last.
At some point I must face reality again, and find a job. I
realise it's a lot to ask, but might you know anyone who could
help?

Frances wrote back.

My dear Leila,

I have so loved hearing about your adventures – you are like a
real-life Swiss Family Robinson! Your chalet life does indeed
sound cosy and delightful, but as you say, there's no future for
you there and I agree, you need to get back to work. Personally,
I'd love you to come to New York, but I realise it's a long way,
and with two children in tow perhaps too daunting a prospect.
Instinctively, I feel you'd do better in London, where I have
one or two contacts in publishing; I'd be happy to put you in
touch. Your book about women in Germany would, I'm sure,
find an eager audience there.

That evening, once the children were in bed, Leila sat out
on the deck with Charlotte and Julius. The sun was slipping
behind the hills, and the moon was rising, glinting on the lake
below.

Sipping cherry brandy, Leila sighed. 'It's so beautiful
here... and part of me never wants to leave. But I know I must go
some time. A friend has suggested we move to London. What
are your plans, Julius... will you stay here?'

'No. Like you, we must move on. I think we'll try for
Geneva. I've been liaising with a couple of newspapers there.
Why don't you come with us? There's always work for a good
journalist like you.'

'That's kind, and it's a tempting offer. I've loved spending time with you both – you've been like a family to me and the children – but it's time to stand on our own feet now. The holiday is over...'

A couple of weeks later, Frances wrote again.

> *My dear Leila,*
>
> *Good news!*
>
> *I took the liberty of speaking to a publisher on your behalf and they're interested in your book on women in Germany. I also happened to be liaising with a couple of academic publishers I know, and they mentioned they are looking for German–English translators. I convinced them you would be the perfect choice!*
>
> *I feel sure you can put together a nice little career once you get to London. And I'll be coming over myself in the fall – I have a couple of photo stories lined up there. So we can actually meet!*

There seemed little reason to delay, and the following morning Leila began packing up the family's belongings. She was up in the attic searching for missing socks and shoes when she spotted Herr Keller's son arriving with their usual order of milk and half a dozen eggs.

Noticing Leila at the attic window, he called up to her. 'Hi – I've got a letter for you.'

'I'll come down,' she called back. The letter was postmarked Berlin and from the handwriting she knew instantly who had sent it. Minki had written twice over the last year, but Leila had felt unable to reply.

Her refusal to help Viktor had been such a blow that Leila had felt utterly betrayed. Even Minki's apology in her last letter had not quite thawed Leila's feelings towards her old friend. Nevertheless, she sat down on the deck in front of the chalet, and opened the envelope.

My darling Leila,

I have only just heard the awful news about Viktor. I rang your mother a few days ago, and she told me everything. I'm so, so sorry darling. I can't imagine your pain – and that of the children. I think your decision to leave Germany was both brave and sensible. And Switzerland, I know, is a place with such fond memories. You were last there with Viktor, weren't you?

I have some painful news of my own. I hardly know where to begin. My darling Clara has developed an illness – epilepsy. She had one fit just before her second birthday. We had hoped it would be an isolated incident, but in the last few months the fits have increased in frequency and severity.

You will know – because you wrote about it so bravely in the Munich Post *– that the government is intolerant of such people. There is a strong movement to sterilise those with hereditary diseases. Max, who is also devastated of course, has recently told me that his aunt suffered with the same condition. She spent much of her life in an institution, poor thing. I have already told him that I will not contemplate such a life for my beautiful girl. But I worry, Leila. I worry all the time. What will become of her – of us?*

One other piece of news – I am pregnant again – but can take no joy in it. I will say goodbye now. Please write and tell me how you're getting on.

I miss you always.

With love,

Minki

To her surprise, Leila found herself weeping. In spite of her feelings of betrayal, there was a deep well of affection for her oldest friend, and she was particularly concerned for Clara. Of all people, Leila understood the danger the child was now in. The new regime was not kindly disposed to children with disabilities. It would take all Minki's strength and guile to keep her daughter safe.

She glanced up from the letter to see Sofia and Axel running across the fields towards the chalet. They had been gathering mushrooms for breakfast, and as they clattered onto the deck, their faces wreathed in smiles, she felt grateful to have two such healthy, happy children. Together, they stood on the brink of a new adventure – and with luck would make a success of their lives in London.

Minki, on the other hand, was trapped in a darkening world, with a child who faced a frightening and uncertain future.

PART THREE

1941–1945

Our starting point is not the individual:
We do not subscribe to the view that one should feed the
hungry, give drink to the thirsty, or clothe the
naked... Our objectives are different: we must have a
healthy people in order to prevail in the world.

JOSEPH GOEBBELS, 1938

28

LONDON

August 1941

Leila Labowski darted between the buses careering down the Aldwych, arriving slightly breathless at the grandiose pillared façade of Bush House. As she walked into reception of the BBC's European Service, the uniformed doorman tipped his hat. 'Morning, Mrs Labowski.'

Leila was constantly surprised at 'Nipper' Williams' ability to remember the names of every member of BBC staff – even freelancers like her.

'Good morning to you, Mr Williams. It's a bit chilly out there this morning.'

'Yes... but it's bound to warm up later,' he replied cheerfully.

With a heave, Leila parted the stout metal gates of the lift, closed them behind her and pressed the button for her floor; the lift plunged downwards into the basement. Walking along the airless corridor, she passed trays of half-finished food and drink, presumably left by the night staff for the cleaners to remove. Outside the brown door that led to the offices of the BBC German Service was a plate of congealed beans on toast and something that may have once been shepherd's pie, but was now a beige mush smeared across a chipped canteen plate.

Yvonne, the English secretary, was already hard at work. 'Morning, Leila,' she said, scarcely looking up from her typewriter.

'Morning... Someone didn't like their supper last night,' said Leila, gesturing towards the corridor.

Yvonne looked bemused.

'The food... left outside.'

'Oh that,' said Yvonne. 'It was Heinrich – he did the night shift. When I came in this morning he was having one of his hissy fits about it. "Bloody English food. Why can't you people learn to cook?"'

Leila smiled at Yvonne's uncanny impersonation of her German colleague, and raised her eyebrows knowingly. 'I apologise for my countryman,' she said, laughing. 'Anything interesting today?'

'Just the usual... Alec left the bulletin in your in-tray. He asked if you could get it translated by nine thirty – he wants to run through it with you before your meeting with the new chief at ten.'

'Oh yes... Hugh Carleton Green. I heard he was taking over as Head of Service this week. Have you met him yet?' asked Leila, hanging up her coat.

'Yes... he popped down here last night. Took Alec and me for a drink in the bar. I liked him. He's quite young and rather good-looking.'

'Yvonne!'

'Well, a girl's got to dream,' replied Yvonne, laughing. 'He mentioned that he lived in Munich back in the early thirties –

working for the *New Statesman*, I think he said. That's your
hometown, isn't it?'

Leila smiled and nodded. These days, any thoughts of
Munich brought mixed emotions. She missed the elegant architecture, the river curving gently through the city, the green
lungs of the parks. But it also brought back memories of Hitler's
supporters marching through the streets, of attacks on Jews and
the constant danger facing her parents.

Glancing up at the clock on the office wall, she noticed it
was already quarter to nine. 'Well, if I'm going to get this
bulletin into shape before my meeting with Alec, I'd better get
to work.'

When Leila had first arrived in England in the mid-nineteen-
thirties, she had managed to scrape together a modest income –
translating academic works, and writing for magazines. Frances
McFadden's contacts had proved invaluable and on Leila's list
of credits was the translation of the works of a famous Austrian
playwright, and the compiling of a modern German textbook
for English schoolchildren. She had also found a publisher for
her book on the women of Nazi Germany.

In 1939, when war was declared, most German nationals
living in Britain were automatically interned, and Leila and the
children were initially on the internment list. But fortunately,
her talent had been spotted by a Foreign Office mandarin, who
asked her to join the newly created BBC German Service.

'You'd be far more use working for us, Mrs Labowski, than
languishing in some prison camp in the middle of Oxfordshire.'

Relieved, Leila had taken British citizenship and signed the
Official Secrets Act. Now, she was one of several German-
speaking newsreaders who worked in shifts broadcasting news
bulletins to their home country.

The remit of the German Service was to transmit accurate,

unbiased news to the German people about the progress of the war – even if accuracy meant sometimes having to broadcast negative stories about British military progress. Bulletins were transmitted on the hour throughout the day. Written by BBC staff news journalists, they were then translated and read by native German speakers – mostly freelancers like Leila. There was concern that these freelancers might not be trustworthy, possibly sending secret messages to people back home, so a British 'switch censor' sat with them during bulletins to check they did not deviate from the script. In his hand, the censor held a 'switch', which was connected to the microphone. If he detected any deviation, he could 'switch' the newsreader off in an instant.

Each bulletin was followed by expert analysis by British political commentators. From time to time the service produced talks given by well-known German emigrés. Thomas Mann, the Nobel Prize-winning novelist, who had fled his home city of Munich for sanctuary in New York, was a frequent contributor, as was his daughter, Erika. An actress and writer living in England, Erika approached these talks with an almost messianic zeal, urging her countrymen to abandon Nazi Germany. At the start of the war these talks were subjected to considerable scrutiny to ensure that they did not break BBC and government guidelines of objectivity, but slowly the shackles had loosened and people like Erika were able to speak with real passion. The Service also commissioned satirical comedy skits about Hitler and other leading Nazis, using actors and writers who were refugees from Germany.

At ten o'clock, Leila and Alec, the news editor, filed into Hugh Carleton Greene's office. Leila's translation of the bulletin already lay on his desk. He stood up as they entered. 'It's Leila, isn't it?'

'Yes... it's good to meet you, sir.'

'Oh, Hugh please, and I'm pleased to meet you too. Alec has nothing but good things to say about you. I know you worked at the *Munich Post* – an excellent newspaper.'

Leila blushed. 'I was only their deputy political editor – under Edmund Goldschagg. He was a good teacher.'

'I met him once, before I moved to Berlin in '34. He was a fine man. Well, we must have lunch or something and chew the cud. I loved Munich.'

'Me too,' replied Leila sadly.

'I'm sorry,' said Hugh. 'That was crass of me. It must be terrible to be separated from the city you love. And I'm sorry about your husband too. I hope you don't mind, but Alec filled me in on what happened to him.'

'No, I don't mind. It's better to be open about these things.'

'Good,' said Hugh, sitting down at his desk. 'Well... to work. Do sit down, both of you.' He pointed at the two chairs opposite his desk. 'I see we're leading the bulletin with the RAF bombing raid on southern Germany last night. It's only the second or third time the bombers have got that far, isn't it?'

'Yes... They had Karlsruhe, Stuttgart and Nuremberg in their sights,' replied Alec. 'But the topography's a bit tricky round there and, in the end, they missed Stuttgart completely.'

'Quite so... I understand it's part of a new strategy by Bomber Command. Up till now they've been concentrating their firepower on the industrial cities on the Ruhr and northern oil terminals. But it's now thought that bombing civilian targets might break the Germans' morale. I suspect this raid on the south is just the start.'

For Leila, this was not welcome news. Nuremberg was only a hundred and fifty kilometres from Munich, meaning her hometown could well be next. Her parents' apartment in the centre of the city would be very vulnerable.

Hugh sucked thoughtfully on his empty pipe. 'How do you think the people will react to this new RAF tactic, Leila?'

Leila was flattered to be asked – it was rare for newsreaders to be asked for their opinion, and she sensed that Hugh might be sizing her up. 'Funnily enough, I was just wondering the same thing. If the RAF manage to get as far as Munich it could hit Hitler personally quite hard. After all, the city is his emotional as well as his political home. As you know, it's the place where the Nazi Party was born, and the citizens had been promised they would be safe from attack.'

Hugh nodded. 'Interesting to see how it plays out.'

They ran through the rest of the running order – the German 6th Army had made its first assault on the city of Kiev, and the British submarine HMS *Cachalot* had been sunk in the Mediterranean by an Italian torpedo boat.

'Pretty depressing all round,' said Hugh, knocking his pipe out into an ashtray. 'Well... if there's nothing else?'

A couple of hours later, Leila was facing the microphone in the newsreaders' booth, with Alec acting as the switch censor. As the second hand on the studio clock ticked round to midday, the sound engineer on the other side of the glass flashed the red 'on air' light, and Leila began:

'*Nun folgt eine nachrichtensendung der BBC...*'

After the bulletin, Leila's job was to be continuity announcer for the German programmes that followed – an analysis of the day's news, a talk from an émigré philosopher, and a comic sketch featuring the actor Herbert Lom doing a passable imitation of Hitler.

Leila watched the sound engineer barely containing his

laughter on the other side of the glass. But she couldn't laugh. To her mind, nothing about Nazi Germany was at all amusing.

Her shift finished at five, when she was replaced by her colleague Heinrich. '*Guten abend, gnädige Frau.* Looking lovely as always...'

'Thank you, Heinrich,' she replied, trying to disguise her irritation. Heinrich had been flirting with her for months, and it was beginning to grate.

'Fancy a drink after work? I clock off at ten...'

'Sorry, Heinrich, not tonight. Got to get back home – the kids will be waiting.'

She smiled and quickly slipped out of the studio, sensing him watching her leave.

Since starting her job for the BBC, Leila had observed an atmosphere of lust among the staff. Perhaps it was the war, and the ever-present threat of death; maybe it was people working long hours and yearning for companionship; or perhaps they just wanted a bit of plain old-fashioned sex. As one of the few women working at Bush House, she was frequently the target of sexual advances. She was neither offended nor flattered. It wasn't that she didn't feel the need for affection, or even sex, but in the five the years since Viktor's death she hadn't once felt tempted. The truth was she still loved him.

Debating whether to take the tube or the bus home, the decision was made for her when she saw a bus heading north up Holborn. She jumped on board, settled herself in one of the front seats, put her large leather bag on her lap and retrieved the manuscript she was working on. She spent the journey to north London editing, marking the typed pages with a red pencil, until the bus conductor called her stop.

When she had first arrived in the capital, Leila and her two children had lived in a succession of down-at-heel boarding houses. The rooms were always cramped and lacked a kitchen. Instead, meals were taken in a communal dining room, mainly filled with a strange mix of refugees and travelling salesmen. It was a depressing way to live – especially for the children – and Leila had found herself pining for the chalet in the Swiss mountains.

But within two months, her old friend Frances McFadden once again came to the rescue. She travelled to London for a story she was covering for the magazine, and the two friends arranged to meet at a restaurant in Soho. Over lunch, Leila explained her housing crisis, and Frances was shocked.

'My dear girl, that boarding house sounds positively uncivilised. You can't stay there another minute. I tell you what, I have a great friend who might need a tenant. He has just inherited a huge pile in Hampstead, and his old house – a charming little cottage overlooking the Heath – is now empty. Let me talk to him and see if he'll rent it to you.'

'It sounds very glamorous, but I can't afford much, Frances. My income can be rather erratic.'

'Don't worry. Along with the house, he inherited a small fortune. He'll probably just be happy knowing that the house is being looked after. Leave it to me.'

Built between the wars, the cottage stood on the edge of Hampstead Heath. Every time Leila approached the white-painted house, with its tiny front garden dominated by a pair of apple trees, she thanked God for the intervention of Frances and her rich friend. The cottage was the perfect home for her little family.

Walking up the garden path, she noticed there were still a few apples clinging to the branches of the trees. Enough to make apple fritters for supper – a traditional German dessert much loved by the children.

She hung up her hat, coat and gas mask on the wooden coat-rack in the hall, and flicked through the mail on the highly polished side table. She had been hoping for a letter from Minki. It had been months since they'd last communicated and Leila was anxious for news about Clara. Not for the first time, Leila found herself grateful to be safely in England with her two healthy children.

'I'm home,' she called out.

'Hi, Mutti,' Sofia replied. 'We're in the kitchen.'

Sofia and Axel were doing their homework sitting at the kitchen table. 'What a lovely sight,' said Leila, kissing each one on the top of their head. 'Good day at school?'

'Yes, it was all right,' replied Sofia. Now sixteen, she was studying for her school certificate.

'You writing an essay?' asked Leila, peering over her shoulder. Sofia's neat handwriting spread elegantly across the page.

'Yes... it's about the schism in the church under Henry VIII.'

'Impressive,' replied Leila, turning her attention to Axel. He was attempting a page of maths, but his exercise book was filled with crossings-out and smudges from his pen. In contrast to Sofia, he struggled with school, preferring to work with his hands, and had turned a small shed in the back garden into a workshop.

'Mutti... what's for supper?' His voice was beginning to break, a process Leila found both fascinating and rather touching.

She kissed the top of his head. 'Do you know, Axel, that is always the first thing you ask me when I get home. Let's see, shall we?' She opened the door to the larder – a tiny windowless room on the north side of the kitchen – and reappeared with a string of sausages and a bag of potatoes. 'Will this do?'

'Give those to me,' said Sofia. 'I'll make dinner. I've finished my essay and I suspect you have work to do.'

'You're such a good girl,' said Leila, kissing her on the cheek. 'I do have quite a lot to do, as it happens.'

The cottage was too small for Leila to have a separate office, so she had set up her desk in the window of the sitting room, overlooking the front garden and the Heath beyond. Although the view was totally different, the placement of the desk in the window reminded her of her parents' apartment in Munich. The great advantage was the quiet – the only sound was the ticking of the clock on the mantelpiece, and the distant barking of a neighbour's dog.

She laid the manuscript of *Women in Nazi Germany* on the desk; the first draft was nearly complete, but it was covered in her red pencil edit marks and would need to be retyped before being sent to the publisher. Most of the book focussed on the years leading up to the outbreak of war, and how Hitler had convinced the people – and women in particular – to support his totalitarian plans. But she had recently been sent more up-to-date information from contacts in Germany, outlining the latest strictures on women's lives, and was keen to include them.

Leila slipped two pieces of paper into the typewriter with a carbon between, gathered her thoughts and began to write.

In 1933, German women voted for Hitler in their millions, lured by the promise of 'marriage loans' and a better quality of life. But those financial incentives came with strings attached – not least the requirement to produce a minimum of four children, and concentrate their efforts on caring for their families. To encourage this behaviour, Germany's propaganda chief, Joseph Goebbels, masterminded a new women's exhibition in Berlin, in which mothers were held up as the ideal of womanhood. 'Men make history,' he said in his opening remarks, 'but women raise boys to manhood...'

For several years women were happy to play their part as mothers and homemakers. But all that changed when the

*regime took the country to war. With the men fighting at the
front, the Nazis now need women back in the workplace. As a
result, millions of women, already burdened with numerous
children, are also required to work exhausting twelve-hour
shifts in armament factories.*

*No allowance is made for the health and well-being of
either children or mothers. Women are treated as mere cogs in
a machine. Take the case of a 35-year-old woman I heard
about recently. Ill with consumption and pneumothorax, she
was pregnant for the fourth time. Her doctor was doubtful the
child would be born healthy, and suggested a termination. But
a group of Nazi 'experts' who examined the case forbade it,
declaring: 'The Third Reich demands from every married
couple – even those with tuberculosis – a minimum of four
children.'*

*Is it any wonder that women in Nazi Germany are
becoming disillusioned?*

'Dinner's ready, Mutti.' Sofia came into the sitting room,
breaking Leila's train of thought. She stood behind her mother,
her hands resting on her shoulders.

'Oh, Sofia – thank you. Have you done it already?'

'Yes… it wasn't difficult.'

'I'm sorry – I meant to help, but I must have lost track of the
time.'

Sofia kissed the top of her mother's head, and scanned the
page in the typewriter. 'Interesting stuff,' she said. 'Those poor
women… The Nazis are just using them as baby machines,
aren't they? How appalling.'

Leila turned to look at her daughter. 'You're absolutely
right, Sofia. I'm afraid the regime in Germany no longer sees
people as individuals with free will, but as a part of a totalitarian machine. People are just pawns, to be moved about and
controlled. What is extraordinary is that so many Germans

actually voted for this insanity. It's a warning to all of us. Governments should carry out the will of the people, and not the other way round.'

Sofia kissed the top of her mother's head. 'I'm so glad you're my mother.'

Leila hugged her. 'And I am fortunate to have you as a daughter. Now... let's go and eat and, if you're lucky, I'll make apple fritters for pudding.'

29

BERLIN

AUGUST 1941

Minki was kneeling on the floor of the nursery, watching Clara in the final stages of a grand mal seizure. Minki's initial horror and fear of her daughter's epilepsy had long since subsided. Now she merely had to make sure Clara did not choke on her own tongue, and wasn't near anything hard or sharp that could injure her.

Apart from the seizures once or twice a week, Clara's life was remarkably normal, with one important exception – she had never attended school. Fearing that the authorities might find out about her condition and insist on sterilising her child, Minki had taken the decision to educate her at home. She had converted an upstairs bedroom into a schoolroom, and Clara was now a proficient reader, a competent mathematician, and had a good understanding of history, geography and science. Minki was surprised at how much she enjoyed teaching her daughter. Clara was intelligent and attentive, and their lessons enabled Minki to revisit some of the books from her own child-hood. Clara was good with her hands too. Minki's own mother had taught her to sew when she was a little child, and now she passed that knowledge on to Clara. It gave her a huge sense of satisfaction that a childhood skill she had learned could be passed on to a third generation. The one talent Minki lacked was cookery, so one afternoon a week the housekeeper taught Clara how to make cakes, biscuits and simple supper dishes.

In many ways, Minki was proud of her daughter's achievements, but she also understood that however delightful their life was together, Clara needed more than mere learning. At the age of nine, she was a bright, sociable child who yearned for friendship with other children, which home-schooling could not provide.

This problem was alleviated to some extent by Clara's two younger brothers. The twins had been born a couple of years after their sister and fortunately showed no signs of epilepsy. Felix and Wilhelm, known affectionately as Willy, were happy, energetic, rumbustious boys, who occasionally joined in Clara's lessons, but spent most of the time playing noisy games in the nursery or the garden.

Now aged seven, the boys were about to start school. This presented Minki with a problem: what they might say about their sister.

On the eve of their first day, Minki sat the boys down for a chat. 'I'd rather you didn't mention you have a sister. But if someone finds out about her, and asks why she's not at school with you, just say she goes to another school away from here... all right?'

The boys looked puzzled. 'But why, Mutti?'

'Because there are nasty people in the world who might want to take Clara away from us if they knew she had epilepsy. So, please promise me, Willy... Felix... to say nothing about Clara and her illness.'

The boys nodded, but Minki feared they had not really understood.

Predictably, Clara was indignant that the boys were allowed to attend school and she was not. When asked why, Minki struggled to think of a plausible explanation.

'Because... your school might not understand your condition, darling,' Minki faltered. 'It's better to teach you at home, where I can look after you.'

Clara looked doubtful. 'But you can't look after me forever, Mutti.'

Minki smiled. 'No, but when you're a grown-up you won't need me so much. You'll have a husband and children of your own, and they'll look after you.'

Minki hoped that would be the end of the discussion, but that evening, over dinner, Max also raised the subject of Clara attending school. 'I understand why you like to teach her at home, but she needs to get out into the world and make friends.'

'Has she been talking to you?'

'Well, yes... she has. She feels so left out, and I can understand why. Obviously a normal school is out of the question – she would need to go somewhere that can cope with her epilepsy. But my aunt went to a specialist boarding school, and her life wasn't too bad.'

'What rubbish! Your aunt lived her entire life in a mental institution,' retorted Minki. 'She went away and never came home again. I can't believe you would want to condemn your own daughter to a similar fate.'

'Obviously, I'm not advocating that, but we should allow Clara to mix with other children. It would be no different to the boarding school you went to, surely.'

'For a start, there are no private boarding schools anymore, Max... Hitler has seen to that. So an institution would be the only option. And I won't condemn her to a life like that. She's better off at home with me. No one could possibly care for Clara as I do.'

'But it's you I'm thinking about,' Max reasoned. 'You've had to sacrifice so much to care for her – your career for a start, let alone spending time with the boys.'

'That's nonsense,' replied Minki. 'The boys are absolutely fine – I spend more than enough time with them. As for my career, Clara is far more important than any job, and besides, there's no point in being a journalist in Germany any more – Goebbels has seen to that.'

Max stared at his wife uncomprehendingly. 'I don't understand you sometimes... Joseph is your friend.'

'Joseph *was* my friend, but not now. You know as well as I do, that he is effectively in control of the press, and has become a tyrant. Look, Max, I know you mean well, but it's pointless discussing this. I won't allow Clara to go to school and that's an end to it.' She stood up from the table. 'I'm sorry, but I'm rather tired. If you don't mind, I'm going to bed.'

As she washed her face and brushed her teeth, Minki raged inwardly at the injustice of her daughter's situation. Of course she would have loved Clara to go to school, but the risks far outweighed the benefits.

She turned off the bathroom light, and climbed into bed. But she couldn't sleep. In the semi-darkness, she tossed and turned, wrestling with Clara's situation. She knew she couldn't really keep her daughter hidden away for the rest of her life, but what else could she do? Her secret hope – one that she kept from Max – was that Hitler's rash invasion of Russia would end in Germany's defeat, and bring about a new, more moral government. Then, her beloved girl could take her rightful place as an equal member of society. But for now, she simply had to hang on, educate Clara as best she could, and hope that no one revealed her daughter's secret.

When Max came up a couple of hours later, he lay down next to her and reached across to stroke her back. 'I'm sorry if I upset you, Minki. I do love you.'

She shrank from his touch. 'Please, Max, leave me alone. I'm not in the mood.'

One evening, a few days later, Minki was alone in the sitting room, preparing for Clara's German history lesson the following day. The children were all in bed, Max's supper was waiting for him in the kitchen, and she was enjoying a rare moment of peace.

As soon as he arrived home, he bounded into the sitting room, his face wreathed in smiles. 'Darling – I've got some wonderful news. You know I've been working on a new film...?'

She put down her book with a slight sigh.

'...Well, Joseph loves it and he's arranged for it be premiered next week. I've got a huge budget to organise a lavish party. Everyone will be there. Please say you'll come.'

The prospect of spending an evening in Goebbels' company was depressing, but it had been months since she and Max had been out together, and she felt compelled to support him. 'All right, but I might need a new dress...'

'Of course, darling – buy whatever you like.'

The premiere was held in a small cinema in central Berlin. Max had gone to the party straight from the office, so Minki, dressed in her new turquoise evening gown, arrived alone, and a little late. The champagne reception was already in full swing, with at least a hundred people crowded into the vestibule of the cinema. Searching for Max, she finally spotted him with

Goebbels, surrounded by a small group of beautiful young women – aspiring actresses, she presumed. To her surprise, Magda was not with him. Minki had heard rumours that all was not well between the couple. Joseph had apparently developed a passion for a young actress named Lída Baarová, inviting her to his weekend villa on the shores of a lake outside Berlin. Although a holiday home for his family, the gossip was that Goebbels had used it as somewhere to 'entertain' young actresses. Magda was apparently furious.

Minki took a glass of champagne from a waiter, and idly watched her ex-lover enjoying being the centre of attention. His young women admirers hung on his every word, laughing and smiling, desperate to impress the head of the German film industry.

Suddenly Minki heard a familiar voice behind her. 'Minki, how lovely to see you.'

She turned to see Magda Goebbels. 'Oh, there you are, Magda. I wasn't sure if you were coming.'

'Of course, where else would I be but by my husband's side? I'm glad to see you though. We've not seen you out and about for such a long time. Is all well?'

Minki had the feeling that she was being interrogated by Magda. 'Yes, thank you. I'm just busy with the children – you know how it is.'

'Oh, I do indeed. Our number six was born before Christmas. Another girl... we've called her Heidrun.'

Minki marvelled at Magda's ability to produce children – five girls and one boy had arrived in the previous eight years. But motherhood had taken its toll on her appearance – her brown hair was streaked with grey, and she had gained a little weight. The dark-haired, slender beauty who had first attracted Joseph Goebbels was no more.

'Gosh, Magda, I don't know how you do it. Six children! I can't cope with three.'

'But they must all be at school now, surely? And how is Clara – we don't hear much about her.'

'Oh... she's fine. She's a quiet child and prefers life at home.'

'You need to break her of that habit,' said Magda. 'One of our girls is shy too. Get her involved with the Young Girls League. After all, she needs to learn skills and make friends.'

Minki quickly changed the subject. 'How's Joseph?'

Magda's tight-lipped smile momentarily faltered. 'Oh, he's fine,' she replied tartly. 'Very busy, of course. Adolf can't do without him – he leans on him terribly and it's quite a strain on Joseph.'

Wearying of Magda's company, Minki was relieved to see Max weaving through the crowd towards them.

'Good evening, Magda,' he said, bowing politely and kissing her hand. 'Well, ladies, the film is about to begin... shall we go through?'

Max led the two women to the auditorium. Goebbels was already seated in the centre of the front row, and motioned to Magda and Minki to sit next to him. He then rose to his feet and addressed the audience. 'It's my great pleasure to announce the latest production from my excellent team at the Potsdam studios. It deals with a very important subject, as I'm sure you will agree after seeing it. So without further ado, roll the movie!'

Goebbels raised his arm to the projectionist, the cinema lights were dimmed and the film began:

ICH KLAGE AN – I ACCUSE

The film portrayed the tragedy of a beautiful woman, happily married to a research scientist. She soon develops multiple sclerosis, however, and the couple seek help from specialists as well as their family doctor. But her illness worsens, and it becomes clear that nothing can be done – the lovely woman will ultimately suffocate to death.

So she begs both her doctor and her husband to end her suffering with euthanasia. The doctor refuses, saying it's because he loves her. But her husband agrees to her request because 'he loves her more'.

After her sensitively handled death, in which she falls calmly to sleep, her husband is arrested, and put on trial for murder. In the final dramatic courtroom scene, the husband declares his own guilt. 'Yes, I killed my wife, at her request, because I love her.' He asks that the five judges of the court to acquit him – not just for his sake, but for all the people in the future who want to assist the suicide of their suffering relatives, free from criminal charges. Dramatically, the film ends before the verdict is given, inviting the audience to make up their own minds.

As soon as the credits had rolled, the audience burst into applause. The cinema lights went up, and Max, as producer, together with the director and stars, stood up and took a bow. But Minki felt unable to join in the approbation.

On one level, she could see that the film was simply exploring the awful dilemma of those with terminal conditions, but she also suspected Goebbels had another motive – to 'soften' public opinion, preparing them to accept state-controlled euthanasia for the congenitally ill. She knew that there was already a law encouraging the sterilisation of those considered 'unworthy' of procreation. How long would it be before this developed into ending the lives of anyone who was not considered perfect?

Her thoughts were interrupted by her husband addressing the audience. 'Thank you for showing your appreciation of this important film, and the many people behind it – cast, crew, director and scriptwriter. But there is one very special person here tonight, to whom we must all owe our deepest thanks – our esteemed benefactor, Minister for Propaganda, and the head of the German film industry, Reichsminister Joseph Goebbels.'

The audience applauded loudly, and Goebbels rose and bowed. Again, Minki didn't join in. Looking up at him, she felt nothing but hatred.

The guests had been invited to a grand dinner after the film, but Minki couldn't face the prospect of watching Goebbels preening himself for the rest of the evening. She just wanted to get home to the children.

Minki took Max by the arm and pulled him away from the crowd of enthusiastic well-wishers who had gathered around him. 'Max, well done for tonight – I'm sure the film will be a great success, but if you don't mind, I won't stay for dinner.'

'You can't go now,' he insisted. 'I know Joseph is keen to see you.'

'I doubt that. He's far more interested in foreign actresses these days.'

It was a casual, throwaway remark, but Max blanched and lowered his voice. 'What do you mean? How do you know about his affair?'

'Oh, so the rumours about Lída Baarová are true then?' Minki had not been deliberately trying to tease out the truth, but now that she had she felt rather smug. 'Quite honestly, Max, it doesn't surprise me. Joe's always been sexually incontinent. One woman has never been enough for him. I'm amazed he has stuck with Magda for so long.'

'Now listen to me,' replied Max, gripping her firmly by the arms and looking around to make sure he was not being overheard. 'You must keep quiet about Lída. Magda is really upset. She's already had a word with Adolf, who has told Joseph in no uncertain terms to end the affair. Joseph is furious, and I promised him you'd be here tonight. He thinks of you as an old friend he can rely on, and he wants you next to him at dinner – for moral support. But be careful what you say. You sometimes forget that he is now one of the most powerful men in the country. Treat him with respect... please.'

. . .

Reluctantly, Minki agreed, but bored by the other guests, took another glass of champagne and wandered into the dining room. Long tables had been arranged, creating three sides of a square. Covered with starched white tablecloths, they had been laid with sparkling glassware and flowers. Sauntering around the edge of the tables, looking for her place card, she soon found it at the top table, with Max on one side and Goebbels on the other. Although initially surprised to be placed in such a position of honour, it all made sense when she saw who was sitting on Goebbels' other side – the actress Lída Baarová. Minki realised she hadn't been placed next to Goebbels to console him, but to distract attention from his latest paramour.

Minki had seen Baarová in a couple of films. A delicate, dark-haired woman in her mid-twenties, she was not as glamorous as Marlene Dietrich, but an attractive 'girl next door' – the sort Goebbels had often fallen for.

Minki sat down in her place and finished her glass of champagne, waiting for the tables to fill up. The first guest to enter the dining room was none other than Lída Baarová herself. Being alone with the woman at the centre of the latest scandal was too good an opportunity for the journalist in Minki to pass up.

'Hello,' said Minki. 'Were you bored with the reception too?'

Lída smiled. 'Something like that. I find these events rather overwhelming. I just came in to check where I was sitting at dinner...'

'Me too,' replied Minki. 'I'm Minki von Zeller, by the way. I'm married to Max, the film's producer.'

'I'm Lída... Lída Baarová. It's nice to meet you.'

'I recognised you. Baarová... is that Czech?'

'Yes, I'm originally from Prague – do you know it?'

'No, I've never been. I've heard it's beautiful though. Your place is here, by the way, next to Joseph Goebbels. I'm on his other side.'

Lída looked momentarily alarmed. 'Oh, I see.'

'It's quite an honour to be seated next to the Reichsminister,' said Minki, pouring them both a glass of wine from the crystal decanter on the table. 'Have you met him before?'

'Yes... once or twice.' Lída blushed slightly, and lit a cigarette, her hand shaking slightly.

'I suspect he asked to sit next to you... he's always had an eye for a pretty girl.'

Lída sat down at the table, and inhaled deeply on her cigarette. Minki got the impression she was not happy to have been singled out.

'I went out with him myself years ago – when we were both in our twenties,' Minki went on. 'Even then he could be very charming – even witty.'

'Oh, I'm not going out with him,' replied Lída hurriedly. 'I already have a boyfriend – Gustav Fröhlich, the actor. Do you know him?'

'No, but I've seen him in films – he's very handsome. What does Gustav make of these rumours about you and Joseph?'

'What rumours?'

'Oh come on... everyone's talking about it. That you and Goebbels are having an affair.'

Lída's eyes filled with tears. 'That's absolutely not true! Obviously, Gustav is not at all happy about it.'

Minki was beginning to feel sorry for the girl, who had put out one cigarette and was nervously lighting another.

'I think you should know,' said Minki, leaning forward conspiratorially, 'that Joseph's wife is rather upset about your "relationship". Apparently she's mentioned it to Hitler, who is angry with Goebbels on her behalf. He adores Magda like a daughter... so take care.'

'It's not fair,' said Lída indignantly. 'Joseph and I are not having a relationship. We're certainly not lovers. The problem is he won't leave me alone. He finds any excuse to be with me, so I'm not surprised to find myself seated here. But the real problem comes at weekends. Gustav owns a house on the lake next to Goebbels' villa. Now, whenever I'm there, Goebbels invites me over, and I don't like to say no. We just chat, eat and drink a little, and sometimes he plays the piano – rather well, as is happens. If the weather is good, we go for moonlit walks by the lake. It's quite romantic, I suppose, but it can also be embarrassing. These evenings always end the same way – I make my excuses, and go back to Gustav, but I can sense Joseph's disappointment.' She stubbed out a cigarette and took a gulp of her drink. 'Oh, it's so difficult – I just don't know what to do about it.'

'Perhaps Gustav should have a word with Joseph?' suggested Minki.

'Oh, he'd like to, I can assure you. But I've persuaded him not to. Goebbels is so powerful he could destroy both our careers. It's a nightmare, really it is.'

Minki found herself rather liking Lída, and admired her for resisting Goebbels' seduction. She knew from experience how persuasive he could be. But the girl was in a precarious situation – caught in the middle of the Goebbels–Magda–Hitler love triangle. If she continued to refuse Joseph, he might turn against her; but if she accepted his advances, Hitler could have her removed from Germany in an instant. Either way, it would mean the end of her career.

Gradually, the room began to fill up with guests. Magda took her place next to Max, but she scowled furiously when she saw that Lída had been placed in the centre of the main table. Finally, Goebbels arrived, all smiles and easy charm, shaking hands and kissing cheeks. He pulled out his chair and sat down between Minki and Lída. 'Well, how lucky am I to be between the two most beautiful women in the room.'

'Oh really, Joseph,' said Minki wearily, 'surely you can do better than that...'

He smirked and kissed Minki's cheek. 'Still a little fire-brand, I see. Have you met Lída?'

'Yes, just now. We had a very interesting chat, didn't we, Lída?'

The young actress inhaled on yet another cigarette and smiled anxiously.

'Minki, you must be very proud of Max,' said Goebbels, pouring them all a glass of wine from the decanter on the table. 'I thought the film was stunning.'

'Yes... it was a very elegant piece of propaganda.' Minki took a cigarette from a silver case, and slipped it between her lips.

'I don't know what you mean by that,' said Goebbels, lighting her cigarette.

'Oh, come on Joe... it wasn't exactly subtle, was it?'

'It was a moving account of the sort of dilemma we all might face at some time or other. As a journalist, you of all people should think it important to air these issues, surely?'

'There is some moral justification for discussing such dilem-mas, I agree, but what worries me is that it's not a huge step from "let's forgive a man for taking pity on his terminally ill wife", to "let's end the lives of people the state thinks are worthy of termination".'

Max, sitting on her other side, coughed discreetly, and pressed his leg firmly against his wife's thigh, warning her to keep quiet. But she had drunk too many glasses of wine, and was ready for an argument. Taking another gulp from her glass, she was about to launch into another angry outburst when she was stopped in her tracks by Goebbels leaning over and whis-pering in her ear: 'My advice is to keep your opinions to your-self, Minki. Your own family is not without its own "moral dilemmas", I understand. I'd hate for that little girl of yours to come to any harm.'

With that, Goebbels turned away, and spent the rest of the evening flirting outrageously with Lída Baarová.

During the drive back home, Minki sat next to Max in silence, trying to work out how Goebbels could have found out about Clara. The answer was glaringly obvious.

'I had the oddest conversation with Joseph tonight,' Minki began calmly. 'He implied that he knew about Clara's epilepsy. How could that have happened? We've never mentioned it to anyone.'

In the darkness, Minki could sense Max stiffening with anxiety.

'Max... was it you? Did you tell him?'

'Yes... I may have mentioned it.'

'Why, in God's name?' Minki thundered. 'Since her first fit, I've done everything I could to protect her from the authorities, and now... for you to tell him, of all people. Do you understand what you've done?'

'He's my friend. I wanted to discuss it with someone. You have such strong views about Clara, I feel excluded sometimes. I love her too, and I want what's best for her. I was just trying to get a bit of perspective on the problem.'

'Perspective! From Goebbels! Good God, are you completely insane?' Minki screamed. 'The last person on the planet to provide perspective is Joseph Goebbels.'

She put her head in her hands. 'Oh Max,' she groaned, 'you have put our daughter in the most terrible danger.'

'Don't be ridiculous. Joseph wouldn't harm our child.'

'You think she's safe because we're old friends? Then you don't know Goebbels at all. That man has no loyalty to anyone other than himself. And you are doing his bidding by producing a film that makes the view of the Party perfectly clear. Your charming tale of "beautiful woman begs for mercy killing" is just a short step from "let's just terminate these people because they are valueless".'

'No, that's nonsense, Minki – that would be unthinkable.'

'Would it, Max? Don't you understand that your own daughter is considered "valueless", as far they are concerned? Do you realise what the Party think about people with hereditary diseases? They call them "useless eaters"'.

'No, no – that's not the same thing at all. The film was very clear – that we just want people to be able to discuss how their lives might come to an end with dignity. We're saying that people should have autonomy over their lives, that's all.'

Minki felt rage boiling up inside her. Part of her wanted to hit Max, to beat him about the head for his stupidity and naivety.

Arriving home, she leapt out of the car, slamming the door behind her. 'Please don't be so upset,' Max called after her.

As he joined her on the front doorstep, she turned and looked him straight in the eye and said in a low, quiet voice: 'Let me tell you something, Max... if it turns out that you have brought our daughter into danger, I will never forgive you – never.'

30

LONDON

Leila was on her way to an early-morning meeting at the Foreign Office. Her publisher had got in touch a few days before, with the news that her book about the women of Germany had attracted some attention in government circles.

'They're very interested in your perspective and would like to talk to you about how you might help them with the war effort.'

'Me? How could I possibly help them?'

'I don't know, but I can understand their interest. You're a valuable asset, as you have first-hand experience of how half the German population have fared under Nazism. Let me know how it goes. And needless to say, the meeting is top secret for now – so mum's the word.'

As she walked down King Charles Street towards the magnificent nineteenth-century Foreign Office building, Leila looked up to see a barrage balloon hanging over its roof, bobbing curiously in the breeze. She knew it was there to obstruct bombing raids, but it also struck her that it was rather odd to put a marker in the sky, inviting the German Luftwaffe to 'bomb here'.

A pretty young secretary was waiting for Leila in the impressive entrance hall. 'Good morning, Mrs Labowski, my name is Amanda. It's very nice to meet you.'

As they ascended the grandiose staircase, past murals depicting Britannia and the triumph of the British Empire, Amanda kept up a constant stream of idle chit-chat. 'Have you been here before? I've been working here for six months and I still get lost...'

Finally, at the end of a long corridor, they arrived at their destination.

'Here we are,' said Amanda brightly. She knocked smartly on a solid oak door, opened it and ushered Leila inside, then shut the door behind her.

Facing Leila was a wide walnut desk between two shuttered windows. In the gloom, the room appeared to be completely deserted.

'Ah, Mrs Labowski, welcome.'

The voice came from the other side of the room. Leila turned to see a tall middle-aged man rising from an armchair in front of a magnificent marble fireplace.

'I'm Michael Sullivan, Permanent Under-Secretary for Foreign Affairs,' he said, approaching her, hand outstretched. 'It's so good to finally meet you, I've heard such a lot about you.'

'Oh, really – I can't imagine what...'

'Oh, no false modesty, my dear lady... your reputation has gone before you. Can I offer you tea, or coffee? I fear I can recommend neither in these straitened times, but both are available.'

'Coffee please.'

Sullivan picked up the phone on his desk. 'Coffee for two,

Amanda, please.' He then led the way to the group of armchairs in front of the fireplace. 'Please – do sit down.'

Moments later, Amanda appeared carrying a silver tray with a pot of coffee, cups and saucers.

'Just put it there,' said Sullivan, pointing to the low table in front of him.

Leila took a sip of coffee, and tried to suppress a shudder. The man had been right – the coffee was dreadful. 'Mr Sullivan, I'm not quite sure why I'm here. I understand it has something to do with a manuscript I'm working on. It's not even finished yet, so I'm perplexed as to why it's attracted so much attention.'

Sullivan settled into the opposite armchair. 'Let me come straight to the point. We are interested in your clearly detailed knowledge of the female sex in Germany. They are, after all, half the population. Here at the FO, our job is to look ahead. We have high hopes our American friends will soon enter the conflict, after which we can be pretty certain of being victorious over Hitler. And when we are, we need to be ready.'

'Ready for what?'

'The German people, as you will know only too well, have been subjected to over fifteen years of propaganda. Their minds have been... how should I put it... warped by Hitler and his Minister for Propaganda, Dr Goebbels. People like your good self – journalists with a good reputation, who have lived under Hitler's regime – have a detailed understanding of the effects of this propaganda. Your publisher kindly sent me an advance copy of your manuscript, and I have to say your insights are remarkable. From what I've read so far, I believe that, when the time is right, you would be a fine resource for the British government, advising us as to how we might help the German people – and women in particular – towards a more liberal way of thinking after Nazism.'

'I see. I'm flattered of course, but I'm not quite sure how I could achieve that.'

'Neither am I just now, but I wanted to have this initial chat so that we could get to know each other and be ready... when the time comes.'

'Well, of course, I'd be pleased to help, but I do worry about what might happen if Germany is *not* defeated. Things are not looking too good at the moment...'

'I understand your pessimism, but I don't share it. We must keep victory firmly in our sights. As you may know, President Roosevelt and Churchill have recently signed the Atlantic Charter setting out their joint vision for the future of the world after Hitler's defeat. With the Americans on our side, I really don't see how we can fail.'

'I hope you're right but I still don't see how *I* can help?'

'I believe that, once we have peace, the Allies will need an army of people to help us win over hearts and minds in Germany. Hitler and his propaganda machine have managed to persuade seventy million people to abandon democracy and civilised values, and ignore the destruction of human rights in their midst. If I may put it crudely, Mrs Labowski, the German people will need to be re-educated. In order to do that we will need experts with a detailed knowledge of the German population, who have good communication skills. You would seem to fit the bill rather perfectly, wouldn't you say?'

'Well, put like that, I suppose I might be of value. But I'm struggling to grasp my actual role. Will you want me to write articles and so on?'

'That will be part of it, of course, but also perhaps you might be invited to go back to your country and work with your compatriots – on the ground – convincing them that liberal values, rights to life and a free press are the bedrock of democracy.'

'But I live here, in England,' protested Leila. 'I am a British citizen now, and am bringing up my two children here. I can't just up sticks and go back to Germany – however much I'd like to help.'

'Do you love your country, Mrs Labowski?'

'Do you mean Great Britain, or Germany?'

'Both, I suppose.'

'Well, yes, of course I do. I love this country because it has provided me with a refuge, a job and a home. I'm a British citizen now and proud to be so. But I also love Germany because it's my homeland. It broke my heart to leave, but who knows what state it will be in after the war?'

'Quite so,' replied Sullivan. 'A lot depends on the next couple of years. At this stage, I really just wanted to establish contact. If things go as we hope, I will be able to be more forthcoming about our plans when we next meet.'

As Leila walked back up Whitehall towards Bush House, she saw all around her evidence of a city in daily fear of attack. Anxious civilians scurried by, gas masks swinging from their shoulders; sandbags were piled high outside government buildings; barrage balloons swayed in the wind. Sometimes, it was hard to recall life before the war. Certainly few people could imagine a time when it might be over. But men like Sullivan were paid to look ahead, and were right to plan for it. There must, one day, be peace, and she was flattered that he had picked her out. She owed it to her adopted country and to her homeland to do whatever she could to help – to work to end the evil that had infected the people of Germany.

It was a few minutes to ten when Leila walked down the corridor towards her office. Alec was waiting for her, fidgeting impatiently, a clipboard in his hand.

'Oh, there you are,' he said, hurrying towards her. 'We've got to get a move on – we were supposed to have a meeting with Hugh quarter of an hour ago.'

'I'm so sorry,' she said, 'but I did mention to Yvonne that I wouldn't be in before ten.'

'Never mind,' said Alec, taking her arm and rushing her down the corridor. 'There's a big story brewing in Germany. Hugh wants to see us in his office urgently.'

'Oh dear, I hope it's not too serious,' said Leila, struggling to keep pace – she was always anxious about bad news from her home country.

Carleton Green stood up as the pair arrived. 'Hello both of you. Do please take a seat, and I'll come straight to the point. We've been sent the text of a sermon given by the Bishop of Munster. It seems that Herr Hitler is proposing to terminate the lives of those he considers unproductive – the elderly and disabled – even children with disabilities. The bishop is, quite rightly, incensed. I've got a copy of the sermon here – the key passage is marked. Have a look.'

'My God,' Leila gasped as she and Alec quickly scanned the text.

> Do you or I have the right to live only as long as we are productive? If so, then someone has only to order a secret decree that the measures tried out on the mentally ill be extended to other 'non-productive' people, that it can be used on those incurably ill with a lung disease, or weakened by aging, or disabled at work... even on severely wounded soldiers. Then not a one of us can be sure of his life any more.

'It's strong stuff, isn't it?' said Hugh. 'Can I ask, Leila... did you have any inkling of this?'

'Yes, to a degree... the concept of eugenics has been around as part of Nazi ideology since the early thirties, and my newspaper wrote several editorials about it. What has always surprised and horrified me is the widespread support it has among the scientific establishment. In fact, some physicians were already ahead of the politicians, particularly in the field of sterilising people with disabilities. But to proceed from sterilisation to murder is a giant step. I can't believe Hitler will be able to carry the public with him on that.'

'That's why we feel it's so important to tell the German people what's going on,' said Hugh. 'The British government have ordered the text of the bishop's sermon to be printed in leaflets and dropped by the RAF across Europe. They have also asked us to broadcast extracts from the bishop's sermon over the next few days. Highest priority, Alec... understood?'

Reading the words of the Bishop of Munster that day in the bulletin, Leila managed to maintain a professional detachment. But when she had finished and was alone in the studio, linking between a satirical comedy and a talk by Thomas Mann, she found anger building up inside her. The German people had been remorselessly encouraged to think that Aryan perfection was the basis of a sound society – first by dehumanising Jews, and culminating in this latest doctrine that all imperfect Germans were a drain on society and should be eliminated.

Mr Sullivan at the Foreign Office had been right: Hitler and Goebbels had persuaded the German people that the unthinkable was, in fact, the solution. And it was up to people like her to alert her countrymen to the horror that was about to engulf them.

31

BERLIN

AUGUST 1941

The air raid sirens started some time in the middle of the night, rousing Minki from her sleep. She shook Max awake. 'We have to get the children into the basement.'

As the planes rumbled overhead, the family and their two maids scurried down to the coal cellar. Air raids had become more frequent in recent months, so Minki had made the space habitable – with a couple of old mattresses and some blankets, along with books and playing cards for the children. While Clara lay snuggled up in an old eiderdown, reading, the boys were too excited to sleep. As the planes rumbled overhead, the house shook with each falling bomb.

'What planes are they?' asked Willy, standing by the cellar door. 'Can we go outside and have a look, Papa?'

'Of course you can't, Willy,' said Minki firmly. 'Sit down immediately. There's no way you're going outside in a raid.'

Reluctantly, Willy did as he was told, and he and his brother began to play a desultory game of cards.

The night passed slowly. The maids and children eventually slept, while Minki and Max spent a restless night anxiously listening to the waves of aircraft passing overhead.

'I think the explosions are getting farther away each time, don't you, Max?'

'Possibly. Hopefully we're past the worst.'

Finally the engine noise subsided. A glimmer of light shone through the tiny cellar window and the birds began to sing in the garden outside.

'Thank God that's over,' said Minki, standing and stretching.

Suddenly there was a choking noise from the floor.

'Oh no,' said Max, irritatedly. 'Not this... not now.'

'It's all right,' said Minki calmly, arranging Clara carefully on a mattress to ensure she was safe. 'You really have to get used to it, Max.'

'I can't,' he replied petulantly. 'It reminds of my aunt... I saw her fitting once as a child and it appalled me.'

'Well, thank God neither of our boys react in such a childish fashion.'

'Is it Clara?' asked Felix, rubbing the sleep from his eyes and shaking his brother awake. They took up positions on either side of their sister, one singing to her, the other stroking her hair.

The maids also began to wake up. But instead of coming to Clara's aid, they kept their distance, almost as if they disapproved of her illness. In fact, Ida had once suggested that Clara might be better off in a children's home. Minki had told her firmly that if she ever made such a comment again she would be dismissed instantly. Since then, the girl had kept her thoughts to herself but, as Clara slowly recovered and opened her eyes, Minki noticed Ida's familiar look of disapproval.

It was early morning when the family emerged from the basement. While Ida dressed the children, Max and Minki retreated to their room to prepare for the day.

'I'm getting really worried about these raids, Max,' said Minki, as she lay in the bath.

'It's war, darling,' replied Max, scraping his chin with a razor. 'But we've been all right so far, haven't we?' He turned and looked down at her. 'My God, you are beautiful,' he said wistfully.

'Still, I do wonder sometimes if we'd be better off outside of the city.'

Max wiped his face with a towel. 'We're fine as we are, Minki. Now, I'd better get going – got a busy day.' He leaned over and gave her a brief kiss.

After he'd gone, Minki sat at her dressing table, brooding on their conversation. Max seemed oblivious to the danger they were all in. She sometimes wondered if his closeness to Goebbels had infected him with the regime's arrogant sense of invincibility. If so, he was a fool.

Her father had written a few days before and mentioned that raids over southern Germany were almost unknown – the city of Augsburg being beyond the range of RAF bombers. It suddenly occurred to her that his house would be an ideal sanctuary for herself and the children.

She suspected that Max would hate the idea, and if she was going to persuade him to let her leave Berlin she would need facts. She turned on the radio in her bedroom. The national news service led on the bombing of Berlin. In hyperbolic terms, they raged against the RAF, complaining that the British were targeting innocent women and children. She sensed the heavy hand of the propagandist, and decided to try tuning in to the BBC.

It was illegal to listen to foreign news broadcasts, so Minki first locked the bedroom door, and turned down the volume of radio to prevent the maids from overhearing.

She placed her ear close to the speaker and fiddled with the wavelength control knob until she found the BBC frequency. Out of the ether came a familiar voice. Within an Instant, Minki knew who it was. 'My God, it's Leila,' she whispered to herself. Her eyes filled with tears, as she listened to her friend's strong, clear intonation. After all these years apart, hearing her voice was like a miracle.

The BBC bulletin also led on the bombing of Berlin; but it was the second story about the Bishop of Munster that grabbed her attention. Hitler's proposal to end the lives of the 'undesirables' with genetic handicaps made her blood run cold. Even children were to be targeted. Minki instantly thought of Clara, now playing innocently in the nursery, and how easy it would be for the authorities to classify her epilepsy as a disability. For a German bishop to be so outspoken was both brave and remarkable.

It crystallised Minki's decision to leave Berlin. It would surely be safer for Clara to be hidden away deep in the countryside than to live in the capital, under the noses of the Nazi authorities. She hurried downstairs to the hall and put a call through to her father's number.

'Papa?'

'Yes... Minki. How nice to hear from you. There was bombing last night in Berlin, I hear. Are you all right?'

'Yes, the raid flew overhead, but dropped its bombs nearer the city centre. Papa, I have a favour to ask... I'm worried about the children and their safety. I wondered if we might come and stay with you.'

'Of course.'

'Are you sure? It would mean some disruption. Three children would be quite noisy, and I would have to organise schools for the boys, and so on.'

'Minki my dear, I would be delighted.'

'I'm so grateful – thank you. I'll make the arrangements at my end and let you know when we're coming.'

That evening, after the children were in bed, Minki poured Max a drink and calmly set out her arguments for leaving the capital city.

Max's reaction was predictable. 'It's madness to move to Augsburg... it's too far away.'

'That's the point, Max. The further away, the safer for the children.'

'But for how long? It won't be long before the RAF can reach those cities in the south. They've already hit Stuttgart.'

'Well, if Augsburg did become a target they would aim for the factories, not houses like my father's which are way out in the country.'

'What about the boys' education?'

'I can find them a school down there.'

'And Clara?'

'Well, I'll continue to educate her as I do here.'

Max suddenly flushed with anger. 'Oh I see,' he shouted. 'So you intend to move down there as well, do you? And leave me here all alone? No, Minki, I won't allow it.'

'You won't allow it? Well, I'm sorry, Max, but my first priority must be the children. I'm moving to Augsburg, whether you'll allow it or not. As soon as I find a school for the boys, I'll be leaving.'

Minki stood up and swept out of the room. She retreated to their bedroom, hoping Max would calm down, so they could discuss it calmly over dinner. But within a few minutes she heard the front door slam. Peering out of the bedroom window, she saw Max climbing into his Mercedes, revving the engine hard and screeching out of the drive and out onto the road, heading towards the city centre.

Some time in the middle of the night Minki was woken by the sound of Max falling into bed next to her, reeking of drink.

The next morning, she woke with a renewed sense of determination, and began to make preparations for the move to her father's. She sent off letters to several schools in Augsburg, and within days received word that one had two places for the boys that autumn term – now just a few weeks away. With no time to lose, the children's trunks were brought down from the attic and packed with their favourite toys and clothes. Having lived in the city for their whole lives, they had nothing suitable to wear for country life, so Minki drew up a list of items they would need – hiking boots, corduroy trousers and warm jackets.

Max continued to insist that she was overreacting. Over dinner one evening, he pleaded with her to change her mind, but Minki refused to budge.

'Nothing you say will change my mind, Max. I won't stay. If you don't want the family to be split up, come with us. It's not you I'm leaving, but Berlin. I just want us all to be safe – surely you can understand.'

'How can I leave Berlin? Joseph depends on me. We have too many projects in the pipeline.'

'Well, then come to Augsburg at weekends and see us. Or I could come up to you. I'm sure we can make it work.'

'We have something called petrol rationing, Minki – or haven't you noticed?'

'Take the train, then.'

Max threw down his napkin in exasperation and stormed out.

That night, he reached out for her in bed. 'I'm sorry,

Minki... it's just that I can't bear the thought of being parted from you.'

'I understand, Max, but if you love me you'll want what's best for me and the children.'

'I do love you.' Max nuzzled her neck, running his hand down her back erotically.

When they'd first met, his mere touch would have excited her. But now, even the thought of making love to him left her cold. 'I'm sorry, Max... I've got too much on my mind.'

He sighed, rolled away from her and was soon snoring.

But Minki couldn't sleep. Lying awake that night, she tried to analyse what had gone wrong in their relationship. When she and Max had first met he had been a brilliant man at the top of his profession. Her pride in his success was the foundation of her love for him. But since he had become part of Goebbels' propaganda empire, she had lost respect for him. And without respect, love couldn't survive. Was it possible, she wondered, that her desire to move away and live with her father was about something more than keeping the children safe? It would also put a physical distance between her and Max, effectively severing their relationship. Was that what she wanted? To leave Max behind... perhaps forever?

As August turned to September, there was an autumnal chill in the air. Minki ordered the staff to bring the family's trunks down to the hall.

'Are you planning on leaving today?' asked Max over breakfast. 'I noticed the trunks...'

'Tomorrow, I think – first thing. I just need to buy Clara a new winter coat – she's grown so much. And the boys each need a pair of boots for the winter.'

Max nodded, and sipped his coffee silently. 'I do see the logic of what you're doing, darling,' he said at last, 'so I won't try to stop you. In fact, I mentioned it to Joseph yesterday and he agreed it would be better for you all to be out of the city. He also has concerns for his own family's safety and is thinking about moving them to his country house outside Berlin.'

'His love nest, do you mean?' she asked acidly. 'Why do you have to tell Joseph everything about our lives? He's nothing but trouble, Max – don't you understand that?'

'Don't be ridiculous. I work for him... he's a friend.'

'You're so naive, Max. If you believe that, you're a fool.'

Max smiled weakly. 'I'm sorry you feel that way.' He stood up, and briskly pulled on his jacket. 'I might be a bit late home tonight. I've got a viewing with Joseph this afternoon at the studios, and it might run on. I've arranged for a car to pick me up this morning and take me to work, so you can use my car for your shopping.' He came round the table and kissed her forehead.

'That's kind, Max – thank you. I'll see you later, then.'

At the doorway, Max stopped and turned to look at her. 'I do love you, Minki... I want you to know that.'

After breakfast Minki went upstairs to get her coat. As she passed the nursery, she could hear Clara speaking clearly to the boys. 'You've got ten minutes to finish those sums.'

Smiling, she opened the door. Clara was standing next to a small blackboard with a piece of chalk in her hand. She had written up some multiplication sums on the board and the boys were sitting at little desks, with notebooks and pencils.

'Hello, you three,' said Minki, 'you look busy.'

The boys looked up at their mother and frowned. 'Clara's making us do sums, and they're too hard.'

Clara shrugged. 'Well, I don't find them difficult... besides, they need to be ready for their new school, don't they, Mutti?'

Minki hugged her daughter. 'They do, darling. And well

done... I'm very impressed. Now, I'm just going out shopping for the last few bits and pieces for our trip. I won't be long.'

'When are we leaving for Grandpa's house?' asked Clara.

'Early tomorrow morning... it will take most of the day to get there by train.'

'I can't wait,' said Willie eagerly. 'I love Grandpa's house. It's full of great stuff – lots of old toys, and secret places in the attic.'

'Will I be there for my birthday?' asked Clara.

'Yes... I expect so. We're going to stay with Grandpa until the bombing stops.'

'Can I have a party at Grandpa's house? I'm going to be ten, after all.'

'Of course you can have a party – with cake and presents and everything. But it's not for another couple of months... we've got Christmas first, remember.'

'Will Dad come down and see us at Christmas?' asked Felix.

'Yes, of course – if he can get away from work. Now, you three, I'd better be going. Be good boys, and do what Clara tells you.'

As she pulled the nursery door closed, Minki heard a chorus of groans as Clara announced they were going to do long division.

Minki returned home a few hours later, to find the drive to her house blocked by a large grey single-decker bus. Its windows had been blacked out so it was impossible to see inside, but it looked like a modified postal bus. She stopped the car and waited for the bus to drive off.

Suddenly, to her horror, she saw Ida hauling Clara out of the house towards the bus. The child was screaming and trying to pull away, but Ida had a firm grip on her arm with one hand;

in her other was a small suitcase. Minki leapt out of the car, but before she could reach Clara the child had already been pushed inside. Minki rushed to the bus doors, but they closed in her face. She could still see Clara, standing on tiptoe, peering out through the windscreen. As soon as she saw her mother, Clara banged her fists on the glass, screaming: 'Mutti, Mutti...'

'Clara... Get out... get out!' screamed Minki.

But before the child could even get near the doors, a tall burly man rose from his seat next to the driver, grabbed hold of Clara and bundled her away inside the bus. The driver put the engine into gear and, with a cloud of exhaust smoke, drove off.

In a state of shock, Minki was temporarily rooted to the spot, unable to move, watching helplessly as the bus disappeared down the road towards Berlin. But within seconds she raced back to her car and sped down the road, determined to catch up with the bus. She managed to reach it, but had to stop to allow a long tram to snake its way between them. By the time the tram had finally passed by, the bus had disappeared. Minki drove on frantically searching the city, but after a couple of hours finally had to accept that the bus had gone – and with it, her daughter.

Minki arrived home in utter despair, only to find Ida crumpled on the hall floor, weeping in the arms of the housemaid. Incensed, Minki hauled Ida to her feet and slapped her face. 'What have you done, you wicked girl? Why did you put her on that bus? Where are they taking her?'

'I'm sorry, madam, but the master told me to do it,' replied Ida, rubbing her cheek. 'After you'd left this morning he telephoned saying Clara had to go away to a special school. He asked me to pack a small bag with clothes for her. He said it had all been arranged and he promised you knew all about it.'

'Of course I didn't know about it!' screamed Minki. 'I've

just spent the morning buying her a new coat. Our bags are all packed for our trip tomorrow – they're right there in front of you.'

Ida, fresh tears now spilling down her cheeks, mumbled repeatedly: 'I'm sorry... I'm sorry.'

Minki realised that if she was to get any sense out of Ida, she should change tack. She took a deep breath, lowered her voice and took the girl gently by the shoulders. 'Look, Ida, I'm not saying it was your fault, but where is this school, do you know?'

Ida shook her head. 'I'm sorry... I just did as I was told. I packed her favourite toys, though...'

Realising she needed some answers – and fast – Minki stormed out of the house, got back into the car and drove off to Max's office at the Potsdam studios.

'Where's my husband?' she demanded of the receptionist.

'He's in the viewing theatre, Frau von Zeller, but he's very busy. He left instructions not to be disturbed.'

Minki stormed out of the reception area, ran down a long corridor, and flung open the doors of the viewing room. There were Max and Goebbels sitting together in the front row, their faces lit up by the screen in front of them. 'What have you done with my daughter?' she screamed. 'Where has she been taken?'

Max stood up, signalling to the projectionist to stop the film. As the theatre lights went on, Max held his arms out to her, and tried to embrace her. 'Minki, darling...'

But Minki angrily shook herself free. 'You bastard... what have you done?'

She then turned to Goebbels: 'This is all your fault – yours and Hitler's and those evil scientists you listen to,' she shouted. 'Where have you sent my baby girl?'

'Calm down, Minki. Your daughter will be quite safe,' replied Goebbels calmly. 'Clara is going to an institution which will care for her. These are the new rules. This is how it will be from now on. I explained to Max that there can be no exceptions. Just because you are my friends does not give you special rights. Anyone over the age of ten, with a disability, must be dealt with – that is the law.'

'But she's not ten!' Minki shouted. 'She won't be ten till January. Max, tell him – they've made a mistake.'

'A couple of months here or there... it makes no difference,' replied Goebbels firmly. 'Max, I'll leave you to deal with your wife, but well done on the new film. Oh, by the way, I hear *I Accuse* has been very well received. It's being distributed all over the country, and even abroad. I sincerely believe it will turn the tide of public opinion.' He shook Max's hand. 'I'll see myself out, and perhaps we can continue this viewing later.'

Alone with Max, Minki hurled herself at him, beating his chest with her fists. 'Why, why... you bastard, why?'

'I had to,' he said quietly, as the blows rained down on him. 'Joseph made it clear that Clara had to go, or our lives would be made intolerable. "We must all make sacrifices," he told me. Goebbels is lashing out. Hitler has banned him from seeing that actress – Lída Baarová. Apparently, Hitler threatened to deport her. The last I heard, she had escaped in the middle of the night and has gone back to Prague. Goebbels is heartbroken.'

'I don't care about Baarová, or Joseph and his broken heart,' said Minki, sinking down onto one of the red velvet cinema seats. 'He still has all of his children.'

Max sat down next to her and reached out for her hand, but she snatched it away. 'Don't touch me.'

'Minki, I'm so sorry.' He sighed. 'Take the boys to your father. You're right, they'll be safer there, and while you're away I'll do all I can to find out where Clara is. I was promised she would be sent to a children's home where she would have friends and be looked after. But, if you're so unhappy, perhaps we can persuade them to let us have her back?'

Minki looked at him, her eyes filled with hate. 'If you believe that, you're a bigger fool than I thought. We won't get her back unless we fight for her.'

She stood up to leave the viewing room, but turned at the door. 'I told you once that if Clara came to any harm I would never forgive you, Max, and I meant it. If anything happens to her, I will do everything I can to destroy you.'

Max didn't return home that night – through either shame or fear, Minki presumed. Lying alone in her bed, she kept reliving those last moments when Clara was forced onto the bus. The memory of her daughter screaming in terror was torture. Where had they taken her? Clara had never been away from home before and would be terrified, wretched and hungry.

She must try to stay calm, Minki told herself. As soon as the boys were settled with her father, she would begin the process of finding Clara. For if she was sure of one thing it was that Max would never be able to get their daughter back. Only she had the determination and guile for the task.

At first light, she woke the boys. 'Get dressed quickly, and wait for me in the hall.'

She went to Ida's room and shook her awake. 'Pack your things and get out of my house now. And don't come back.'

Downstairs, Minki rang for a taxi. As soon as it arrived, she bundled the youngsters inside together with the luggage.

'The main railway station, please driver,' she said, wrapping her arms around the boys.

The taxi crunched away down the gravel drive and headed out into the road, but Minki didn't once look back. Her marriage to Max was over. All that mattered now was Clara's survival.

32

LONDON

SEPTEMBER 1941

Leila walked home from the bus stop one evening, admiring the autumnal shades of trees on the Heath. Turning in to the cottage's front garden, she noted the wasps humming angrily around the rotting apples littering the lawn.

Letting herself into the hall, Leila noticed a letter written in a familiar hand, with a Munich postmark, which had been left on the hall table. She had the familiar sense of relief and anxiety that always accompanied her mother's letters. Rather than opening it immediately, she went first to the kitchen to check on the children. Sofia was sitting at the table doing her homework.

Leila kissed the top of her head. 'Hello darling... Good day at school?'

'Yes, it was all right. Oh, and did you notice you had a letter from Grandma today. I put it on the table in the hall.'

'Yes, thank you. I'll read it later. I wanted to get dinner ready first. By the way, there are lots of fallen apples outside – could you and Axel pick them up? If you choose the ones that aren't bruised and wrap them in old newspaper, we should be able to store them in the shed for a few weeks. Where is Axel, by the way?'

'He's in the shed, "making something", he said.'

As Leila approached the old hut at the bottom of the garden, she could hear laughter. Axel had installed a radio in his workshop so he could listen to Home Service comedy programmes, and had improved its reception by trailing a long copper wire aerial from the window and attaching it to the washing line. As Leila approached the door of the shed, she realised it was not *ITMA* that Axel was listening to, but the nasal intonation of someone else entirely. It sounded alarmingly like the German propagandist William Joyce, popularly known as Lord Haw-Haw.

Leila abruptly opened the shed door, startling Axel, who instantly switched off the radio.

'Axel, what are you doing? You shouldn't be listening to that awful man and his lies.'

'I only listen because I think he's funny.'

'Nothing about Germany, or that man, is funny, Axel. You of all people should know that.' Furious, Leila stormed out, slamming the door behind her, and returned to the kitchen, where Sofia was still doing her homework.

'Mutti... are you all right?'

'Not really – I just found Axel listening to that awful man William Joyce. Has he done it before?'

'Maybe,' replied Sofia nervously. 'But lots of people I know at school listen to Lord Haw-Haw.'

Leila looked shocked. 'Really? And their parents allow it?'

'They listen too... the whole family do. People say he gives them a different perspective on the war.' Sofia shrugged her shoulders.

Leila sighed and took some meat from a plate in the larder.

She began to fry it with a little lard in a pan, where it sizzled invitingly. 'Lord Haw-Haw is not giving people perspective, Sofia. He is belittling the British people and undermining their bravery. What you need to understand is that these programmes put out by Goebbels' propaganda team are not "entertainment" – they are intended to weaken the resolve of the British people.'

'But isn't that what some of the programmes you make are intended to do? You told me you have actors pretending to be Hitler, portraying him as an idiot... aren't they intended to shatter his image in the eyes of the people?'

Leila was startled by her daughter's analysis. 'On the surface, it might appear to be the same thing, but there are differences. Most importantly, the BBC news broadcasts are as accurate as possible – we even run stories that are negative about Britain's progress in the war. The Germans would never be so honest. Admittedly, some of the talks on the BBC try to open the minds of the German people to the evil that Hitler represents. But that's because he *is* evil, Sofia. In Germany anyone who steps out of line is liable to be imprisoned, tortured or murdered. People like your father.'

Sofia's eyes filled with tears. 'I'm sorry, Mutti... I hadn't thought of it like that.'

Leila came over and hugged her daughter. 'It's all right. I'd just prefer that neither of you listened to that awful man.'

'I promise,' said Sofia. 'Shall I go collect the apples now?'

'Yes please, darling.'

Sofia took a basket from the shelf and went out into the yard, calling for her brother. As the children walked past Leila and out into the hall, she heard her daughter admonishing Axel. 'You mustn't listen to that man any more – Mutti doesn't like it.'

Leila put the browned meat into a casserole dish, added a little water and a few chopped vegetables and put the dish in the oven. Once it was cooking, she collected her mother's letter from the hall table, went into the sitting room and sat at her desk in the window.

The children were diligently picking up fallen apples, but Axel kept looking anxiously towards the window where his mother sat. He was obviously feeling guilty, she realised, so she smiled at him encouragingly, and opened the letter.

My darling Leila,

I hope you and the children are well.

I wanted to let you know that I have finally convinced your father that we must leave Germany. I mentioned in my last letter that his business had been shut down by the authorities, and money is getting tight. Did you also know that they have introduced a law insisting that we Jews must wear a yellow star on our clothes? They have turned our Star of David – a symbol of our religion – into something loathsome. You see awful things happening to anyone wearing the star. A couple of weeks ago, I was coming back from shopping and passed the cinema. There was a line of people waiting to get into the next film. Two SS officers were passing, and noticed two women in the queue wearing the star. The men hauled them out of the queue, handed them a bucket and brushes, and forced them to clean the pavement. These two ladies, in their best coats, were made to go on their hands and knees and start scrubbing – can you believe it? And no one stood up for them – no one!

Then, last week, a man who lives in the apartment upstairs was taken away by the authorities. He was such a nice man – Jewish of course. His wife has no idea where he's been taken, but she fears it might be to a camp – perhaps the same one Viktor was in. Oh darling Leila, it frightened me very much. I spoke to a friend about it. Do you remember Emilia Becker? She was the dressmaker who made your wedding dress. She is a widow now, you know, and could tell how frightened I was. She suggested that we move in with her. Wasn't that kind of her? She's a Catholic so I think it was doubly brave of her. Anyway, I packed some clothes and we set off one morning, terrified we would be arrested on our way there. Your father didn't want to go at all, and I had to pretend it was just for one night.

We have been here now for over a week, staying in her children's old bedroom at the back of the apartment. Your darling father finds it all very confusing. He keeps asking, 'Where are we, Hannah? Why can't we go home?' Emilia still sees clients in the sitting room, so when they visit we have to stay in our room. Last week, she had a visit from a woman married to a high-up in the Party. Your father wanted to make a cup of coffee, but he obviously couldn't go to the kitchen while the woman was there. He kept trying to get out of the bedroom, and in the end I was forced to lock the door. Now, every time there is a visitor, I'm so scared we will give ourselves away, and bring both us and Emilia into danger.

You were right all those years ago when you pleaded with us to leave Germany, and now I wish we had done as you suggested. I fear we've left it too late, but I so want to get away. The problem is I have no idea how to go about it. I understand that we will need something called an 'exit visa' to leave the country. But how can we get one, locked up here in Emilia's apartment?

Leila, darling, I feel so alone and frightened. Please help us and tell me what I should do.

All my love,

Mutti

Leila laid the letter down on the desk, gazed out at the garden and burst into tears.

'Mutti... what's the matter?' She turned to see Sofia standing at the door with a basket of apples.

'Read this,' she said, handing her the letter. Sofia read it quickly. 'Oh, I'm so sorry. Poor Grandma and Grandpa,' she said, holding her mother tightly. 'What can we do to help?'

'I don't know, darling. But we must do something. My mother's right – getting an exit visa will be almost impossible. While it's still technically legal for Jews to leave Germany, they are at serious risk of being imprisoned as soon as they show their faces. Like the poor man who lived across the hall from Grandma – taken from his apartment and imprisoned...

'And even if we managed to get them an exit visa, how do we get them physically out of the country? When the three of us left in '35, we took a train to Switzerland, but it's far more dangerous now. I met a young Hungarian woman in London recently who had managed to get out just before the war began. In spite of having all her papers in order, guards still tried to force her off the train as they approached the border. It was only the pleading of a kind German doctor that persuaded the guards to let her leave.'

'Oh, Mutti... I hadn't thought of that. Perhaps someone could get them out by car?'

'Maybe – but who? And there's one final problem that my mother hasn't even thought about.'

'What's that?'

'If they want to come to England, they will need an entry visa, and the British government stopped issuing those two and a half years ago.'

'Why?'

'To prevent enemy aliens entering the country. The Americans have done the same thing.'

Sofia, normally so calm and controlled, began to cry. 'They're going to die like Daddy, aren't they? Oh Mutti I hate Hitler and his awful government. I hate them all... they are evil,

evil people. How could they be so cruel? Granny and Grandpa have never done anyone any harm.'

Leila held her arms out to her daughter. 'Come here, *liebling*... oh Sofia, perhaps I shouldn't have told you. You seem so grown up these days, and I've come to rely on you too much. But it's not fair...you're still a child.'

'No!' said Sofia. 'I'd rather you told me the truth. And I'm sorry to be so pathetic. There must be a way we can help them. You'll think of something, Mutti – you always do.'

Suddenly, Axel called out from the kitchen: 'Mutti, the dinner's burning!'

Leila ran to the kitchen, grabbed a cloth, removed the casserole from the oven and put it into the sink, where it sizzled angrily. 'Damn – that was our meat ration for the week.'

Sofia, who had followed her into the kitchen, wrapped her arms round her mother. 'Don't worry about the supper. The casserole will be all right if we add a bit of water. And as for Grandma and Grandpa, we'll find a way to get them out of Germany.'

'I hope you're right, darling... I really hope you're right.'

33

AUGSBURG

Minki's train from Berlin to Augsburg had taken much longer than usual. Bomb damage to the track meant it had to divert several times en route, finally arriving at Augsburg station three hours late. She and the two boys climbed down onto the platform, and a porter wheeled their luggage into the station hall. There was Minki's father waiting to greet them. He was initially all smiles, but then suddenly looked perplexed. 'My dear Minki... I'm delighted to see you all, but where is Clara?'

Minki forced herself to hold back the tears. 'Let the boys get settled first, Papa, and then I'll explain.'

The moment they arrived at Gunther's house, Willie and Felix rushed out into the large garden, glad to be free after a day cooped up on the train. Minki joined her father in the drawing room, keeping an eye on the boisterous youngsters through the window.

'So tell me, Minki... what has happened to Clara?'

Minki related the awful story of Clara's kidnap, while her

father stared at her in growing horror. 'The authorities did this without your knowledge or permission?'

'Max gave his permission – behind my back.'

'I'm appalled. What did Max imagine they were going to do with her?'

'They convinced him that she was going to a special school and would be well looked after.'

'Well, that could be true?'

'No. I wish it were, but I know too much about their plans to believe them. In their eyes, as an epileptic she is a burden on society. They will probably sterilise her.'

Gunther gasped in shock. 'They do that to children?'

'I'm afraid they do, Papa.'

'Poor, dear little Clara.'

'I'm surprised. I thought you would take Max's side. You usually do.'

'Not about this – it's disgraceful.' Gunther stared sadly out of the window, shaking his head from side to side. 'To do it behind your back... that's not right. You are her mother, after all – that relationship is sacrosanct.' He turned round to face Minki. 'We need to act, Minki. What is the name of this school? Can we go there and visit her?'

'No Papa. As I told you, I have no idea where she is. But I'm determined to find her. I'll scour the country, if necessary. Will you look after the boys for me if I have to go away?'

'Of course.'

'I've found a school for them here in Augsburg. They'll be able to catch the bus from the village into town every day. It will do them good – give them independence. They're such delightful boys – funny, brave and strong. You'll love having them here.'

'Of course I will, my dear. But what about Max – surely he must take some responsibility and help you find Clara?'

'I doubt it. He's so weak, Papa. He's frightened of people in power – Goebbels and the others.'

'But Goebbels is your friend. He came to your wedding, after all.'

'I know, but he's changed. Everything's changed – and for the worse. Anyway, I'm leaving Max.'

'Oh, my dear girl... I don't approve of divorce, as you know. But perhaps – given what he's done – I can understand it. He must be devastated though.'

'I've not told him yet. Clara is all I can think about. Besides, what's a failed marriage in comparison to a child's suffering?'

Her father squeezed her hand and looked into her eyes. 'Minki dear, I realise I've not been the best father to you. You've been let down by both of the men in your life. You go and find that girl. The boys will be fine with me, I promise.'

'Thank you, Papa. I'll go to the library in Augsburg tomorrow. They will have records of every medical and educational institution in the country.'

Minki spent the next couple of days at the library compiling a list of residential children's homes and hospitals. There were literally hundreds of them, and Clara could have been in any one of them.

'I don't know where to even begin,' she told her father, laying out a map of Germany on the table in the drawing room.

'If I were you, I'd start at the top.'

'What do you mean? In the north?'

'No. Go to Goebbels. He is your friend, after all.'

'Papa, you don't understand... he won't help me. I suspect he is responsible for her abduction, after Max had told him about Clara's condition. It must have been Goebbels who informed the authorities. Why would he help me now? And in any case how could I trust him?'

'You must try, darling,' said her father. 'The journalist of your youth would have used every contact she had to get what she needed. She would have been ruthless in her determination. Find some of that courage now. Go to Berlin and confront Goebbels.'

Minki took the overnight train to Berlin station. Arriving first thing in the morning, she hurried to the taxi rank.

'The Ministry of Public Enlightenment and Propaganda,' she told the driver as she climbed into the back seat.

He looked at her askance in his rear-view mirror.

'It's in Wilhelmplatz,' she added.

'I know where it is, madam,' he said darkly, heading out of the station forecourt.

The ministry was housed in Leopold Palace – originally, a fine classical eighteenth-century building opposite the Reich Chancellery. The palace had been greatly extended since Goebbels had commandeered it for his HQ. As the taxi drew up outside, Minki noticed the addition of a new façade – plain and imposing in the modern National Socialist style.

Her shoes echoed as she crossed the expansive marble-floored reception area, and boldly approached the guard on duty behind the desk. 'I'd like to see the Reichsminister urgently.'

The guard looked up from his paperwork. 'Do you have an appointment?'

'No.'

'Then I'm afraid it won't be possible.' He returned to his work, implying that the conversation was over.

'Joseph Goebbels is a personal friend of mine,' Minki insisted imperiously. 'Please call his office immediately, and tell him Frau von Zeller is here... I can assure you that he will want to see me.'

Her firm manner had the desired effect. Reluctantly, the guard picked up the phone and briefly muttered into the mouthpiece, finally nodding. 'Dr Goebbels' secretary will come down in a moment, madam. Please take a seat.'

Minki chose a high-backed leather sofa and waited. Five minutes later, a young woman approached her. 'Frau von Zeller?'

'Yes.'

'Please come with me.'

Minki followed her up a grand staircase to the first floor, and along a parquet-floored corridor towards a pair of impressive double doors at the far end. Opening the doors, she motioned Minki inside. As Minki entered the plush wood-panelled office, two further secretaries looked up, scowling, as if annoyed by her interruption to their perfectly ordered day.

'Please, do sit down,' said the young secretary, indicating a sofa set against the wall. 'The Reichsminister asks if you could wait – he is very busy.'

Minki sat down nervously, mulling over how to approach Goebbels. In the old days she could have seduced him, or at least flirted a little, to get her way. But the last time they had met – at the premiere of *I Accuse* – they had argued, and afterwards, he had not even bothered to say goodbye. Now she regretted her behaviour, cursing her own frankness.

The young secretary interrupted Minki's thoughts. 'Frau von Zeller, would you like some coffee?'

'Yes please.'

The young woman left the office, and returned with a pot of coffee and, on the side of the tray, a folded copy of Goebbels' newly founded newspaper – *Das Reich*.

The headline was eye-catching and alarming:

ALL GERMAN JEWS TO BE DEPORTED

Minki read the article with growing disbelief. Hitler, it said, had demanded the Greater German Reich be cleansed of its Jewish population by 17 September. All remaining Jews were to be moved to ghettoes in eastern Europe.

Glancing up, Minki noted the date on the office calendar. Today was the twelfth. That meant there were just five days before all those people – like Leila's parents – were rounded up and banished. In disgust, she laid the paper aside.

Time passed, and Minki anxiously checked her watch. 'Will he be much longer?' she asked the young secretary.

'I'm not quite sure. He's very busy.'

From time to time, one or other of the secretaries disappeared through a second set of double doors, which Minki presumed led to Goebbels' private office. They would reappear some minutes later and start typing. She guessed the great man was busy with dictation.

An hour went by... then another. Minki's initial anxiety was replaced by irritation at being kept waiting so long.

Towards one o'clock, lunch was wheeled in on a trolley by a guard in SS uniform.

'Go through,' said the senior secretary. The guard pushed the trolley into Goebbels' private office and withdrew. Another hour passed. The same guard returned to collect the trolley.

Two visitors briefly came and went. Finally, after checking her watch, Minki realised she had been at the office for nearly five hours. 'Excuse me,' she said to the senior secretary, 'but has he forgotten about me? I really must see him. It's most important.'

The secretary sighed and gave Minki a tight-lipped smile. 'I'll just check, Frau von Zeller.'

She reappeared at the double doors a few minutes later.

'The Reichsminister will see you now.' Minki sensed the secretary's irritation as she walked past her and into Goebbels' office.

He was sitting behind a large desk at the far end of the room, head down, concentrating on something – a paper perhaps – when Minki entered the room. He seemed smaller than she remembered. When he spoke in public – at press conferences and rallies – his personality was so powerful and mesmeric that he appeared statuesque, almost majestic. Even at dinner or drinks parties, his charm and magnetism increased his stature. But now, seated behind his absurdly large desk, the great man appeared diminutive and insignificant.

Finally, he looked up. 'Minki, what an unexpected pleasure.' He briskly stood up, hurried round the desk and, to her astonishment, kissed her boldly on the mouth. It was something he had not done for years and was clearly designed to be both disarming and intimidating. 'Sorry about the wait but without an appointment it's hard to fit people in. How is Max?'

'I don't know... I haven't seen him for days. In fact, I've left him. Can I sit down?'

Goebbels indicated a visitor chair opposite his desk, and offered Minki a cigarette from a silver box.

'Thank you,' she said, as he lit it.

'Drink?'

'Please.'

He limped across the vast office to the drinks tray, which had been set on a table between two long windows, returning with two glasses of schnapps.

Resuming his place behind the desk, he studied her for a moment. 'So, you and Max... what's going on?'

'He let them take Clara away – I'll never forgive him for that.'

'I think it's rather unfair to blame Max,' he replied, lighting his own cigarette, and exhaling smoke out of his nostrils in two fine jets. It reminded Minki of a picture of a dragon in one of Clara's favourite picture books.

Minki felt her anger rising, and her resolve to remain calm – and even flirtatious – melted away. 'Unfair!' she shouted. 'What's unfair is taking a child away from her mother. What's unfair is the authorities refusing to tell me where she's being held and not allowing me to see her.'

'Keep your voice down,' said Goebbels quietly. 'You don't want everyone to know your business.'

'I don't care who knows!' she shouted, standing up and pacing the room. 'What your government has done in taking my child – and God knows how many others – is a disgrace. My daughter has a mild illness that hardly affects her life. And for that she is deemed "useless", surplus to requirements.' She stopped and turned to face him, softening her tone. 'Joseph... you must you tell me where she is. If you have any love left for me at all... please, please tell me, I beg you.'

Goebbels stood up and walked round the desk. His hands were shaking, she noticed, and his eyes were cold. He took Minki by the arms, gripping them tightly until they hurt. 'I want you to understand something, Minki. What has happened to Clara is nothing to do with me. I am not in charge of medical policy. These directives come straight from the Reich Chancellery. They are the work of physicians, not just politicians. Physicians who believe that it is right – no... it is our *duty* – to remove physically and mentally impaired people from our society.' He nodded towards Hitler's headquarters on the opposite side of the road. 'To be clear – this was not my decision.'

Tears of fear and frustration were now pouring down Minki's checks. 'But you've encouraged it, Joe... with your films and documentaries and articles. You've spent years softening the public up to accept eugenics. You know you have.'

'You're upset. I understand that, but nothing will be

achieved by you ranting in this way. I think you should leave now.' He released her arms suddenly, and returned to his desk, picking up his cigarette and inhaling deeply. He studied her for a moment. 'It's such a shame... you used to be an attractive woman. I did care for you once, but now...' he shook his head, 'you're just an embarrassment.'

He pressed an intercom buzzer and the youngest of the three secretaries materialised at the door. 'Ah, Helga, please take Frau von Zeller back to reception.'

Faced with such a harsh rejection, Minki felt a sudden visceral hatred for her old lover. With apparently nothing left to lose, she angrily stubbed out her cigarette on the top of his desk, leaving a small black hole in the tooled green leather. 'So that's it, is it? My little daughter, who has been stolen by the authorities, is to be sacrificed on the altar of your Party's belief that anyone with a disability, however slight, is to be removed from society. You'd better watch out, Joe, or someone might take you away in the middle of the night for having a club foot.'

'Don't make things worse for yourself,' he replied coldly. 'Just get out.'

The secretary nervously approached her. 'Frau von Zeller... please.' The girl's voice was calm and gentle; she took Minki's arm and guided her across the office. But at the door Minki turned round. 'I wish I had never met you, Joseph Goebbels – you are an unscrupulous, corrupt, evil man, who will do anything for power. And one day, I hope one of your children suffers the way Clara is suffering now.'

The secretary manoeuvred Minki into the outer office, and closed the door behind them. She then led Minki, sobbing, out of the office and down the corridor. In reception, she didn't leave Minki at the main entrance but took her arm and guided her out into the street. 'Come with me, please.'

'Where are you taking me?'

'Just away from here – please...'

She led Minki down a narrow passageway at the side of the building, stopping outside a service entrance. 'We must be quick... I can't be seen with you. But I couldn't help overhearing – your daughter, has she been taken?'

'Yes.' Minki was weeping. 'She has epilepsy and they took her away and won't tell me where she is. Clara's only nine years old. I had hoped Joseph might help... we were lovers once, you know.'

The young girl looked around her nervously, checking they were alone. 'I really shouldn't say anything, but have you heard of T4?'

'T4? No, what is T4?'

'Aktion T4. It stands for Tiergartenstrasse, the name of the road overlooking the park. Number four is the headquarters of where they decide who is taken and where they're sent.'

'You mean there's a whole department organising this?'

Suddenly the service doors swung open and an SS guard manoeuvred a metal trolley full of files out of the building. He stopped for a moment, looking suspiciously at the pair, before wheeling the trolley away up the passageway.

'I must get back,' said the girl. 'I can't say any more.'

She headed back towards the main entrance, but Minki followed her. 'This place in Tiergartenstrasse... can I go there? Will they tell me anything? Who's in charge?'

'I really don't know... it's top secret.' The girl quickened her pace, but when she reached the main road she turned round and called out, 'I hope you find her. Good luck.'

34

LONDON

Leila worried away at the problem of how to help her parents escape from Munich. She finally decided to tackle it piece by piece. The exit visa from Germany appeared intractable, and there was little help she could offer from the UK. But the other end of the journey involved acquiring an entry visa for her parents, and over that she might be able to use her connections at the Foreign Office.

She called Mr Sullivan's office one morning, and asked for a meeting.

'Of course, Mrs Labowski,' replied the secretary. 'Might I tell him what it's about?'

'It's complicated... but essentially I'm trying to get my Jewish parents, who live in Munich, an entry visa to the UK.'

There was a pause. 'I see. Well, I'll give Mr Sullivan your message, and see if he has any space in his diary. As you can imagine, things are very busy at the moment...'

'Yes, yes of course,' replied Leila, sensing the girl's reluctance. 'Well, if he could find time to see me, I'd be very grateful.'

. . .

At the BBC, Alec sensed all was not well. 'You seem distracted, Leila. Is there something wrong?'

'It's nothing you can help with, but thanks for asking.'

'I may not be able to help, but try me...'

'It's my parents – they're stuck in Munich and I need to get them out.'

'Mmm, that is tricky, I agree,' said Alec. 'It's getting an exit visa that's the problem...'

'Quite,' replied Leila.

'Perhaps an old colleague from your Munich days might help?'

Leila had long since lost touch with most of her old colleagues at the *Munich Post* – Martin Gruber and Edmund Goldschagg had both gone into hiding when the paper was closed down – but she had kept up a regular correspondence with Julius Zerfass.

Julius and his wife Charlotte had remained in Switzerland after Leila moved to England, and now lived in an apartment in Geneva. He worked as a freelance writer, and she taught at a local school. That evening Leila sat down at her desk in the window and wrote to him, asking for his advice.

Two weeks later she received a reply:

My dear Leila,

How wonderful to hear from you and thank you for your news. I'm glad to hear the children are doing well. Charlotte and I continue to thrive. I write a little and manage to scrape a living. Geneva is a most convivial city, if a little dull by Munich's standards. But I have discovered that 'dull' can be most comforting.

Now, my dear, you ask for my advice about how to help

your parents. I remember Hannah and Levi well. But at their age, I fear, leaving Germany will not be easy.

Acquiring exit papers will be the major difficulty. The legal route for Jews to leave Germany is about to be rescinded. Hitler has just set a deadline of 17 September by when all Jews still living in the Reich will be moved to ghettoes in the east.

So, we are left with the unorthodox route out. First, they will need forged papers, and here I have a suggestion. Do you recall a journalist named Ruth Andreas-Friedrich? She worked for a big publishing house in Berlin. She generally wrote about women's issues – so perhaps your paths never crossed. I only know her because of my time as the cultural correspondent for the Post. *She lives with a wonderful orchestral conductor called Leo Borchard, and through our shared love of music we became friends. When Charlotte and I left Germany, we tried to persuade them both to come with us. Although they are not Jewish, I worried that they would find the descent into totalitarianism too painful to witness. I believe both could have had very successful careers in America, for example. But neither would budge – they were determined not to abandon their homeland, and now they see their role as helping to protect as many Jews as they can. They run an organisation called Uncle Emil – so-called because anyone who rings them on the phone must first use the code, which is simply enquiring about Uncle Emil's health.*

They provide shelter for Jewish refugees and can also help with forged documents. I've already helped them from my end get a few of their people out through Switzerland, and I'm sure Ruth would have some valuable advice. The two routes refugees are currently using are through Switzerland and Spain. The latter would mean crossing the Pyrenees – clearly a problem for your elderly parents. But if you can get them out through Switzerland I will do all I can to help them get to

England. Alternatively, Charlotte and I would make them welcome here.

I am including Ruth's address and telephone number below. But needless to say, secrecy is vital. If you write to her, ensure that the letter contains nothing that could alert the authorities – letters are frequently intercepted, as I'm sure you understand. And if you manage to put through a phone call, please remember the code: 'how is Uncle Emil?'

Wishing you all the best.

Julius

PS: Charlotte sends her love.

Although she was keen to get in touch with the organisation, Leila feared that phoning or writing from England might put them in danger. A personal approach would surely be safer and the obvious person to help was her friend Minki, who lived in Berlin. There would be risks, of course, but Leila was certain she could rely on her friend's discretion.

She took out pen and paper to write to Minki but with no time to lose, decided to try to contact her by phone instead. Leila had no telephone at home. Although it was against the rules to make personal calls from work, particularly ones that involved the overseas operator, she decided to risk it.

The following day, when she came off shift, she went into an unused office next to her own and dialled the BBC operator. 'I'd like to put in a call to Berlin, please.'

'Berlin, madam?' The operator sounded surprised.

'Yes. I'm calling from the German service – it's urgent.' Her heart was beating fast, but to her relief the operator began the laborious process of putting the call through.

The line crackled as the phone was answered. 'The

von Zeller residence.'

'Can I speak to Minki, please?

'I'm afraid she's not here, madam.'

'Oh, when will she be back?'

'I'm not sure – you see... she's left, madam.'

'What do you mean, left?'

'I really shouldn't say – it's not my place. The master is here... would you like to speak to him?'

'Yes, please.'

'May I say who's calling?'

'Yes, just tell him it's Leila.'

When Max came on the line his voice sounded weak and dejected. 'Leila. What a surprise.'

'Hello Max. How are you?'

'Oh, you know...' His voice trailed off.

'Max, I need to talk to Minki urgently – I need her help. The maid said that she had left, but wouldn't say where or why.'

Suddenly, Max began to weep, his sobs ricocheting down the phone line. Leila had never been close to the man, and ever since he joined the Party, she had come to despise him. But now, hearing his voice crack with despair, she couldn't help but feel sympathetic. 'Oh, Max – what's the matter?'

He took a few deep breaths, and then launched into a brief account of Clara's kidnap. 'The thing I can't forgive myself for, Leila... is that it's all my fault,' he sobbed. 'I was so trusting and stupid, whereas Minki was right about everything, all along.'

'Max, don't be so harsh on yourself. No one could have envisaged them stealing your child away like that. Particularly when you had friends in such high places.'

'But I should have seen it coming. Minki told me to be careful and I didn't listen.'

'I can't imagine what you and Minki must be going through. What is your plan?'

'I don't know,' he muttered.

'Well surely you must ask for Goebbels' support. Minki could always wrap him round her little finger.'

'Perhaps...'

'Max, I'm so sorry for what you're going through. Sadly, I can't see any way I can help. In the meantime, I really need to speak to Minki urgently. My parents are in terrible danger and she's the only one who can help me. When do you expect her back?'

'I'm not sure. She took the boys to her father's in Augsburg. You might find her there.' Once again, Max sobbed. 'Oh Leila, I fear that if we don't find Clara I may never see Minki again...'

'Try not to think like that. If anyone can find Clara, it's Minki. And good luck.'

As she replaced the receiver, Leila rocked back in her chair. She tried to imagine Minki's anguish at the prospect of searching for a child abducted by Hitler's ruthless authorities. But Leila had meant what she had said: if anyone could find Clara, it would be Minki.

The world, it seemed, had just got a little darker. Now there was a lost child as well as her vulnerable parents to worry about. And to Leila's enormous frustration, there was little she could do about either problem. Minki was the one person on whom everything now rested.

35

BERLIN

Number 4 Tiergartenstrasse was a large nineteenth-century house, near the centre of Berlin. It overlooked a park that had been home to Berlin's zoo before the war.

Wide steps led up to the neatly painted front door. Curtains hung at the large windows. In every way it appeared to be an unremarkable building. Except that what went on inside was anything but innocuous. As Minki stood outside on the opposite pavement, she tried to imagine how people could work in such a place, organising the removal of children from their parents.

From time to time as staff emerged from the building, Minki had to fight the urge to run across the road and demand that they tell her where her child had been taken.

But Goebbels' secretary had said the operation was top secret, so Minki knew that a direct challenge was pointless – clearly no one would talk. If she wanted information, her only option was to wait until the staff had left for the day and then try to break in. She sat on a park bench opposite, watching people gradually drifting out of the building. By six o'clock, she estimated that most of the staff would have left for the day. Nervously she crossed the road, went up the steps and gingerly pushed against the front door. It was locked.

Frustrated, she decided to search for a back entrance. Behind the row of houses was a narrow alleyway, separated from the gardens of each house by a high brick wall. Each house had its own rear garden entrance – a wooden gate set into the brick wall. To Minki's frustration, the gate to Number 4 was also firmly locked. But placed on either side was a pair of dustbins. In the failing light, Minki had an idea. All offices produced waste paper that had to be disposed of. But waste paper may also contain scraps of information. Surely it was worth having a rummage in the dustbins. Looking around to check she was alone, she peered inside one of the bins; it was filled with general rubbish – some food waste, used typewriter ribbons, and what appeared to be an old moth-eaten curtain. But the second bin was more promising. It was filled with paper, which, frustratingly, had been shredded. Hitler, she recalled reading somewhere, had installed paper shredders in all his top government buildings.

Nevertheless, she reached inside the bin, pulling out handfuls of paper strips until they lay in a huge white heap on the ground. Towards the bottom of the bin were a few intact sheets that had somehow missed the shredder. Eagerly she retrieved them. The first few pieces of paper appeared to be irrelevant – memos of meetings, even someone's shopping list. But then she found a copy of a letter. Frustratingly, the first page was missing, but the second page had been signed by a name that was familiar: Karl Brandt. Racking her memory, Minki recalled that Brandt had been Hitler's personal physician for some years. Goebbels had told her that the policy of abducting the infirm and disabled was mainly administered by the medical profession. Might Brandt be involved somehow?

As she quickly scanned the remaining page of his letter, it became clear he was integral to the whole operation.

> ... *gassing and subsequent cremation is now out of the question, since the Bishop of M's intervention. But suffocation, injections, poisoning and starvation are all suitable alternatives, followed by burial in the hospital grounds. The Führer is concerned that nothing must leak out to the population about this programme. There has already been far too much public disquiet. Once a life is terminated, a suitable medical condition must be found to explain the subject's demise. Sepsis, meningitis and blood poisoning due to infections of the tonsils, and so on, have all proved acceptable in the past and we suggest their continuation.*
>
> *I look forward to our discussion later in the week.*

> *With best wishes,*

> *Etc etc.*

The letter had been scored through with a red pen, indicating that it was a rejected draft.

It took Minki a few moments to understand what she was reading. The letter was obviously discussing means of killing people – or 'subjects'. Her heart almost bounced in her chest. Was her child one of these 'subjects'?

She delved further into the bin and found another unshredded fragment of paper entitled 'T4 Transports to Hadamar, January to August 1941'.

Lined up neatly in columns beneath the headline were the year, month, date, number of patients – or 'subjects' – and the name of the 'interim' institution.

> *1941, January 13: 30 Subjects, via Eichberg*

January 15: 30 Subjects, via Weilmünster

January 17: 19 Subjects, via Kalmenhof

The rest of the sheet was missing but, reading these three short entries, Minki deduced that within a space of four days in January seventy-nine people had been transported to somewhere called Hadamar.

Rummaging among some soggy coffee grounds at the bottom of the bin, she found a final scrap of paper that had also escaped the shredder. At first glance it looked like a blank sheet, stained dark brown. She was about to throw it away when she noticed a few lines of indistinct type. At first sight they seemed innocuous enough – merely a list of German towns: Brandenburg, Grafeneck, Bernburg, Sonnenstein, Hartheim... and Hadamar.

Were these all destinations for T4 subjects? She put the coffee-stained list into her handbag along with the other two sheets of paper.

Then, in the fading light, she stuffed the pile of shredded paper back into the dustbin, and hurried to the main road, where she caught a tram to Potsdam.

She walked the fifteen minutes from the tram stop to her old house.

Lena opened the door. 'Madam! You're back.'

'Is my husband in?' Minki pushed past Lena and headed for the stairs.

'Yes, madam... he's in the drawing room.'

'Don't tell him I'm here. I'll see him in a minute.'

.   .   .

Upstairs in their bathroom, she washed her face and hands, desperate to rid herself of the filthy contents of the dustbin. Drying her hands, she caught sight of herself in the mirror – a white-faced, hollowed-out version of the pretty girl she had once been. She smoothed her blond hair, and went downstairs to the drawing room.

Max was sitting by the window staring out into the darkening garden.

'Hello, Max.'

Startled, he leapt to his feet. 'Minki... you're back. Oh, thank God.'

'No, I'm not really back... I just wanted to show you something. And I think I'll need to borrow the car.'

He rushed towards her, his arms outstretched. 'Of course you can borrow the car. Let me drive you. Where are we going?'

'I don't know yet.'

'What do you mean, darling? And you're white as a sheet... sit down. I'll get us both a drink...'

While he poured two glasses of brandy, Minki sat down on the sofa and opened up her handbag.

'Oh, Minki, I'm so glad to see you.' He laid the drink in front of her and sat opposite her, gazing at her lovingly.

'I know, Max, but I can't talk about "us" now. All I can think of is finding Clara.'

'Me too... I think of nothing else. I worry constantly what they're doing to her, what they might already have done. Oh, Minki, I was so naive, so stupid – can you ever forgive me?'

Minki didn't respond. She was sorting the sheets of paper she had retrieved from her handbag and laying them out on the table between them. 'I think I may have found something. Take a look – I don't know if it will help or not.'

'What am I looking at, exactly?' He picked up the piece of coffee-stained paper.

Minki lit a cigarette. 'Look at the words beneath the stain.'

He peered at it closely, holding it under the light of the table lamp. 'This is just a list of towns. What's their significance?'

'I think they might they be places where they take children – and adults – for sterilisation... or worse.'

'Where did you get it?'

'I found it.'

'Found it?'

'In a dustbin behind an office in Tiergartenstrasse where, apparently, they organise the murder of German people, including children.' Her tone was sardonic and cold.

Max's face went white. 'Oh God. Do you think that's what's happened to Clara?'

'Obviously, I pray not. But look at this.' She laid out the last page of the letter from Karl Brandt outlining the methods of killing.

Max gasped as he read it. 'No. Oh God, no.' He put his head in his hands. 'What have I done?'

'Stop saying that, Max. You mustn't go to pieces now. It's not about you. Please try to concentrate...'

She showed him the final sheet – the list of people transferred to Hadamar.

Max read it and then stared at Minki, his eyes spilling over with tears.

'What is it, Max... do you know something about this?'

'Maybe...' He walked over to the drinks tray, refilled his glass, and downed it in one gulp. 'I recall Goebbels mentioning that town – Hadamar – a while ago. There had been some sort of rumpus – a bishop complained that a mental home in his diocese was incinerating so many dead patients, the stench filled the air, and the people in the town were complaining about it. Children at the local schools used to taunt each other with threats: "If you're not careful, you'll end up in the ovens at Hadamar..."'

'Why would Goebbels tell you about this? I thought it was top secret.'

'It was in the context of a discussion about how we could minimise such negative information around eugenics. He was angry that the story had got out.'

Minki bristled. 'So you knew they were killing people, Max, and yet you still let them take our child.'

'I didn't know they were killing children! I was told it was only adults – people with awful deformities, mental disabilities, incurable schizophrenics... alcoholics. I had no idea about the children. I promise.'

'But even to kill adults, Max – surely you can see how wrong that was.'

Max was weeping again now, mumbling almost incoherently. 'Joseph said people would come round in the end – would be grateful to be free of the burden of caring for such people.'

Minki stubbed out her cigarette and lit another. 'Do we have a map of Germany?'

'Yes... somewhere.' Max went to the bookcase and brought out a large folded map, which he opened out on the table in front of her. Minki examined it, marking with a pen the locations of the towns on her coffee-stained list.

'I'm going to visit all the places on this list, as I have to assume they are all extermination centres. I'll start with Brandenburg, as it's the closest, and see if they have any record of Clara. After that, I'll work my way round the rest.'

'I'll come with you.'

'No, Max. I can only do this by keeping my emotions in check. You're too hysterical. I'll sleep here tonight and leave first thing tomorrow. And I'd like to be left alone...'

'Of course. I'll sleep in the spare room.'

She stood to go upstairs.

Max was still standing in front of the fire, glass in hand. 'Minki...'

'Yes, Max.'

'Do you hate me?'

'I'm too exhausted to hate you, Max.'

'I've let you down... let you all down.'

'Max... please – now is not the time.'

She turned to go, but he called after her. 'Oh... I nearly forgot... your friend Leila rang a couple of days ago.'

'Leila rang – here?'

'Yes. She needs your help apparently... something about her parents. But I explained we have our own problems.'

Upstairs in her old room, Minki packed a few clean clothes in a small suitcase, and then lay down on the bed she had shared with Max. Unable to sleep, she got up, sat at her desk and wrote a brief letter to Leila.

My darling Leila,

I write in haste, as I am about to embark on a traumatic journey, searching for Clara. My mind is filled with awful visions of what might be happening – or may already have happened – to my child.

Max tells me that you rang asking for my help with your parents. I presume you're trying to get them out of Germany. I promise I'll do what I can for them, but first I must try to find Clara. I have no idea if I'll be successful, or how long I'll be away, but pray for me darling. Pray hard...

Your friend,

Minki

At first light, Minki bathed and dressed, and went downstairs to the hall with her suitcase.

For a brief moment she recalled the first time she had seen this house, and the optimism she had felt at marrying a rich and important man who had promised to support and protect her. But Max had let her down, and now she was on her own, back to relying on the one person who had never yet failed her – herself. She laid Leila's letter on the table with instructions to the maid to post it immediately, and walked out of Max's house... forever.

36

HADAMAR

An opalescent full moon hung over the horizon as Minki drove into the outskirts of Hadamar. A small town, nestling in a steep valley, it was a tranquil semi-rural place – a mixture of small terraced cottages and fine detached houses. Realising it was too late in the day to either locate or visit the institution, she checked into a small hotel. A middle-aged man stood behind the reception desk, which doubled as a bar.

'Just the one night, is it?' he asked, laying the register in front of her.

'Yes.'

'Sign here, please.'

He took Minki up to her room on the first floor. When he unlocked the door, it smelt musty and unused.

'Do you serve dinner?' she asked.

'I'm afraid our kitchen is closed, but the inn across the road should still be serving.'

.   .   .

The inn was almost empty, apart from one customer – a man drinking beer at a corner table, his belly spilling out over his trousers. As Minki settled at a table by the window, he glanced furtively over at her. Fearing he might try to pick her up, she pointedly averted her gaze and studied the menu.

The waitress arrived and took her order – schnitzel and potatoes, and a carafe of local red wine.

'I've not seen you here before,' the waitress said when she returned with the wine. 'We don't get many visitors in Hadamar.'

'I've not been here before.'

'What brings you here now?'

Minki paused, unsure how much she should reveal. 'Family.'

'Oh... you got family here?'

'Possibly.'

The waitress looked at her quizzically and went off to get her order.

Minki was in two minds as to how much she should reveal about the purpose of her visit. But she needed local information, and the woman seemed friendly enough. So, when the waitress returned with the schnitzel, Minki broached the subject of the institution.

'What do local people here in Hadamar think about the home?'

'What home's that?'

'The mental institution...'

'Oh that...' The woman shrugged. 'Awful place – we don't have much to do with it. Can I get you anything else?'

Minki shook her head.

The following morning she woke just before dawn. She washed, packed up her suitcase and came downstairs. A young girl was manning reception.

'Good morning. I'm leaving today – I'd like to pay my bill.'

The girl smiled – an open, friendly smile. 'Of course, Frau von Zeller. Did you enjoy your visit?' She began to write out the bill.

'Yes, thank you. There's a medical institution here in Hadamar. What is it exactly – a mental hospital?'

'Sort of,' said the girl.

'What do you mean – sort of?'

'Well...' The girl leaned forward conspiratorially. 'People say they do terrible things there. There have been complaints, you know,' before adding in a whisper, 'about the smell.'

'What smell?'

'Burning bodies – that's what they say.'

Minki blanched, and the girl reached over and touched her hand. 'I'm sorry, I didn't mean to upset you.'

'No, it's fine.' Minki laid some banknotes on the counter. 'Can people visit this place?'

'Why would anyone want to? There are all sorts of strange people in there.'

'I'm looking for someone – a relative.'

'Oh, I see.' The girl dropped her eyes and blushed, clearly embarrassed. She looked relieved when the owner appeared from his private office behind the reception desk.

'Heidi, I'll take over here. Please go and help Monika serve the breakfasts.'

The girl scurried off, and he turned to Minki. 'So, you're leaving us, Frau von Zeller?'

'Yes. I've paid my bill – thank you.'

'I couldn't help overhearing... You're interested in the hospital?'

'Yes. I'm looking for someone who might be there... my young daughter.'

'Well, I hope and pray your daughter is not a resident...It's an evil place,' he said quietly. 'It used to be an asylum. That was bad enough, but now... you hear such wicked things are going on there. It's a disgrace.'

'Is it far?' asked Minki.

'No, madam. It's a large grey building on the northern hillside above the town – you really can't miss it.'

Driving along the main road, Minki quickly spotted the hospital on the side of a hill overlooking the town and surrounding countryside. She followed the winding drive uphill, finally parking at the side of the long two-storey building. It was gloomy and forbidding, and her heart was racing as she walked towards the main entrance. She was about to ring the bell when something gave her pause. Surely, if everything she had heard about the place was true, they would not welcome a casual visitor. So, instead, she walked its whole length – a hundred metres or more – peering through windows. Curiously, there was no sign of life – she could see neither staff, nor patients. Walking round the side of the building, she found another entrance. She pushed at the door, but it was locked. Walking on another forty metres or so, she found a large black barn, with doors wide enough to accommodate farm machinery or tractors – an incongruous structure in a hospital setting.

She sat for a while in the sunshine on a stone bench opposite the barn. The peace and quiet seemed at odds with all the nasty rumours she had heard from the townspeople. Interested to see the rest of the site, she stood up and continued walking along a tarmacked road, past a couple of insignificant buildings, and noticed a set of steps leading further up the hill. As she climbed them she turned round from time to time, admiring the view across the valley. It was a scene of bucolic charm – rolling fields, a distant vineyard, and little farm buildings dotted on the skyline. Birds sang in the trees above her head. At the top of the steps was what looked like a cemetery, with serried ranks of simple wooden posts set in the ground. Her heart beating fast, she walked among the simple wooden markers. Would Clara's name be among them? But the graves were marked only with numbers. A high wall made of stone surrounded the graveyard, and set into the wall was a wooden gate. Minki pushed it and to her surprise it gave way. All around was countryside as far as the eye could see – fields of wheat, surrounded by woodland.

Retracing her steps, she was approaching the hospital when she saw a long single-decker bus coming round the corner. It was painted grey, with its windows blacked out – just like the one that had taken Clara away. Her heart beating fast, she stood in the shadows of a large conifer, watching the bus swing round and stop outside the black barn she had seen earlier. A man leapt out and unlocked the padlock. The doors swung open, and the bus drove inside. Once again the barns doors were firmly shut.

Minki crept closer, expecting the passengers to emerge from the barn. Perhaps, by some miracle, Clara would be among them. She could hardly breathe with the anticipation. But as the minutes went by, no one came out through the barn doors. She heard the distant sound of voices chattering. Were these the passengers? And if so, where had they gone? Eventually the chattering subsided, the barn doors were reopened, and the bus reversed out and drove away.

The barn doors had been left ajar and Minki crept closer. She could hear two voices coming from inside.

'Are they all in?' asked a man.

'Yes, yes,' a woman replied impatiently. 'I know how to do my job – I don't need you telling me what to do.'

'We just don't want any mistakes.'

'There won't be any,' snapped the woman. 'Mind you – it was so much easier before.'

'Before?'

'With the gas... we'd get them inside, and it was all over in minutes – much more efficient. Now we have to think of all sorts of tricks to deal with them. It's a nightmare. Anyway, I'd better get on.'

Minki felt as if she was going to be sick, and her legs gave way beneath her. She sat down heavily on the bench just as the man emerged from the barn.

'Hey, you there, who are you? What are you doing here?'

'I'm sorry,' said Minki, getting to her feet. 'I'm not feeling very well. I just had to sit down for a moment.'

'No one's allowed round here. You'd better come with me.'

'No, no, it's all right. My car's just parked at the front. I'll be leaving soon.'

But the man had already taken her by the arm and was frog-marching her towards the side entrance. Unhooking a bunch of keys from his belt, he unlocked the door and pushed Minki inside. It smelt of carbolic and bleach, just like a hospital.

'Where are you taking me?' she protested. 'You have no right... I'd like to leave, please.'

'You're not going anywhere till I've sorted out what you're doing here.'

The man propelled her down a corridor. She passed a ward filled with iron beds. There were no patients apart from one painfully thin man who was stumbling about, wailing. A nurse hurried towards him. 'Back into bed with you,' she said, pushing him down onto the bed and tucking the rough blanket into the mattress so that he couldn't move.

Minki finally found herself outside an office door marked MATRON. The man knocked.

There was a cough, then, 'Come in,' came the croaking reply.

The man opened the door and pushed Minki inside. A middle-aged woman in a starched uniform was sitting at her desk, smoking a cigarette.

'Excuse me, Matron, but I found this person outside, near the barn,' said the man.

'Did you indeed?' The matron looked Minki up and down. 'And what exactly were you doing there?'

Minki could have lied. She could have made something up on the spot – she was good at lying – but she felt compelled, now she was inside the hospital, to tell the truth.

'My name is Minki von Zeller and I'm looking for my daughter. My husband Max and I are close personal friends of the Reichsminister, Dr Joseph Goebbels. He suggested we came here. We believe a terrible mistake has been made.'

It was a white lie, of course, but Minki hoped it would be enough to frighten the woman.

The matron raised her eyebrows. 'Joseph Goebbels? I don't believe you.'

'My husband works as a film producer for Dr Goebbels at his ministry. You can call his office, if you like, and check.'

Minki paused, letting the information sink in. She was gambling that the woman wouldn't bother to make the call. The matron studied Minki's face, and exhaled cigarette smoke.

'We have been told that our daughter might have been brought here in error,' Minki went on. 'You see... she's not yet ten years old. If she's here we have permission to take her home.'

It was a bold move, but Minki was on fire, adrenalin coursing through her veins, sharpening her wits. Experience had taught her that if you tell a lie, tell it with confidence.

'I see,' said the matron, stubbing out her cigarette. 'And what is the name of your daughter?'

'Clara von Zeller...'

'If you wouldn't mind waiting for a moment, I'll make some enquiries.'

The matron left the office, and returned a few minutes later with a man in a white coat with a stethoscope round his neck.

'Good morning, Frau von Zeller. My name is Doctor Wahlmann.' He held out his hand. Reluctantly, Minki shook it; it felt clammy to the touch. The doctor sat down in the Matron's chair.

'Please, do sit down. Now... I understand that you think your daughter might be here?'

'Yes... possibly.'

'I think that's most unlikely. We are a mental institution – you may have seen one or two of our patients – they are most unwell... up here.' He tapped his head. 'They are challenging to care for. We keep the doors locked in order to protect the patients, but also to protect the people of Hadamar. We have very few children here – only patients with severe mental difficulties.'

The doctor's manner was smooth, but his face was hard and lined. His eyes were too close together and his mouth set in a firm line. He looked as if he never smiled.

'I believe my daughter may have been brought here in error. I'm a friend of Dr Joseph Goebbels.'

'Yes, so the matron informed me. You can be assured that if your daughter was here, we would certainly tell you. I am sure you're mistaken, but to set your mind at rest we will check our records. Many people pass through here, you understand, and we pride ourselves on our meticulous record-keeping.'

The matron, as if on cue, laid four large leather tomes down on the desk in front of the doctor.

'Excellent, Matron. Well, let's see, shall we?' He opened the top ledger, glancing at Minki. 'When do you think your daughter was brought here?'

'I'm not quite sure. She was taken from us a month ago.'

'As recently as that... And how old is she?'

'She'll be ten in the new year.'

The doctor raised his eyebrows slightly, and began to examine the pages one by one. From her position sitting opposite him, Minki could make out neat columns written in copperplate script.

'You see, Frau von Zeller... we are most meticulous,' said the doctor. 'Every patient is listed – with their name, the illness that brought them here, their arrival and departure dates.'

He smiled at Minki encouragingly, before returning to the ledger and running his finger along the lines. 'No, I can't see her there... nor there, not there either.'

He turned the pages laboriously, checking each line, and when one book had been thoroughly investigated he laid it down and picked up another.

Suddenly, he sat up. 'Ah, yes. Here it is... Clara von Zeller.' His tone was clipped and efficient.

Minki leapt to her feet and leaned over the desk, trying to read the entry herself, but the doctor put his hand over the page. 'I'm sorry, but this is confidential. Now, please sit down. You should prepare yourself for a shock.'

'No... no, no,' said Minki, tears welling up.

'Your daughter's condition was epilepsy – is that right?'

Minki nodded.

'I'm sorry to say that she had a very bad fit soon after her arrival, and died.'

'No, no... please that can't be right,' Minki gasped. 'You must have made a mistake...'

'No. I'm afraid there's no mistake. And I must apologise – I should have recognised the name sooner. Now I remember... she was such a pretty child. I'm so very sorry.'

He turned towards the matron. 'I can't understand why the parents were not informed immediately. It's most unsatisfactory.'

The matron looked chastised. 'I'm very sorry, Doctor. It must have been an unfortunate oversight.'

'I should say so... now, do we have the young lady's effects?'

The matron blushed. 'I'll go and get them.'

Minki felt sick, her head spinning. She was in a state of shock – disbelieving – and stared at the doctor. 'You're actually saying that my daughter is... dead? But surely people don't die of epilepsy, do they?'

'I'm afraid on occasion they do, Frau von Zeller. I will have the death certificate drawn up for you immediately. Everything will be in order.'

Minki felt numb, her mind a void. She sat, weeping, struggling to comprehend what had happened. 'But surely... this is a hospital – how could you let her die?'

'I agree, it's most regrettable, but these things do happen on occasion.' He smiled grimly, and stood up, as if the meeting was over. 'Well... Frau von Zeller – if there's nothing else?'

'Where is she, Doctor? I mean... where is her body.'

'In our cemetery, of course. But her remains can be returned to you, if you wish. Parents often prefer to have their loved ones' remains close to home.'

'Her remains...' Minki murmured, staring up at the doctor.

'When Matron comes back with your daughter's effects, we will arrange for you to visit her grave,' said the doctor. 'There is no headstone, you understand, but we have a map of the plot, marking every burial.'

The matron returned with a brown paper parcel, tied with string. Minki laid it on her lap and carefully opened it. Inside was the little blue dress Clara had been wearing when she was taken – washed and ironed. There was her hairslide, her favourite doll, a pair of socks and her new little shiny black shoes, still barely worn – Minki had bought them for her only shortly before she was taken. As she touched each item, she recalled Clara wearing the dress – the colour matching her eyes – and sobbed. Finally she folded the dress up again and returned it to its brown paper wrapping along with the rest of her child's belongings.

'Is this everything?' she asked.

The matron nodded.

'I'm sure you'd like to see the grave,' said the doctor. 'Matron, can you arrange for someone to accompany Frau von Zeller? Plot eighty-seven, I believe...' He closed the ledger with a slam.

The man who had first brought Minki to the matron's office was selected for the task. Still carrying Clara's parcel of clothes, Minki followed him blindly down the corridor, past the barn and up the steps to the cemetery. Her whole being felt empty. It was the shock, she supposed. That, and grief – an unendurable grief.

Plot 87 was situated next to the wooden gate in the wall. Minki knelt next to the pile of earth, just beginning to grow weeds on its surface, and stroked the soil, desperate to feel her child beneath it. It seemed somehow strangely ironic – that her daughter's grave was just a few feet away from open country-side... if only Clara could have found her way up these steps, perhaps she might have escaped.

'I want her brought back home,' Minki said to the man hovering next to her.

'Of course.' The man's tone had changed since their first encounter. Now, he was sympathetic, almost gentle. 'If you leave your address at reception, we'll make the arrangements. I'll leave you, shall I? I expect you'd like to be alone for a moment. And, I'm so sorry,' he added.

As Minki knelt on the damp earth, she tried to come to terms with what had happened. Her child's body was lying beneath the ground, and yet it seemed impossible that Clara was there in this hostile place. That her happy, vivacious, smiling child was no longer breathing, no longer exuding her boundless energy.

Minki finally stood up to go. Her mind was full of questions, but she had no strength left to challenge the people in charge. She wanted nothing more than to leave this place and get back to the boys and her father. She would stop in Berlin, of course, and tell Max what had happened. And one day, someone would have to atone for her child's life. Someone would be made to suffer the agony she felt now. But first, she needed to sleep.

Minki stood for a while staring at her child's grave, as if imprinting every detail on her memory. This unmarked grave was not where her daughter was supposed to end her life. She stumbled back down the stone steps, and round the side of the hospital. In reception, fighting back the tears, she left her name and her father's address. 'Please let me know when my daughter's remains will be transferred.'

'Of course, madam,' said the nurse on reception, smiling sympathetically. She handed Minki an envelope. 'The death certificate.'

Minki backed away, down the steps, clutching the envelope and the parcel of clothes. She laid them on the car's passenger seat.

Eventually, she started the engine, and listened to the low rumble as she put the car in first gear. Driving towards the exit, she had to pass the front of the hospital. It was odd that, apart from that one distressed man in a ward, she had seen no patients at all. Where were they all? Puzzled, she stopped the car, climbed out and stood looking up for one final time at the gloomy brick façade. Suddenly, a young man ran down the steps of the hospital towards her. He looked agitated and tearful. A nurse in uniform was racing after him. 'Come back,' she shouted. The young man reached Minki, and fell into her arms. 'Take me away, I beg you. They've already killed my brother...'

The nurse arrived and grabbed hold of the young man. 'Heini, you're very naughty. You're to come back with me.'

'Hang on,' shouted Minki. 'He says you've killed his brother.'

'Oh, Heini,' said the nurse, 'that's a terrible thing to say...' She had her arm tightly wrapped round the boy's waist. He was painfully thin and weak, Minki noticed – like the poor man she had seen earlier on the ward.

'They tell some awful stories,' said the nurse, 'please don't let it bother you. Come on, Heini,' she said sweetly. 'Back inside now...'

Minki watched as the sobbing boy was led back up the stairs to the front door and inside. At any other time she might have tried to defend him, but her grief suddenly enveloped her and she fell, howling, to the ground.

A little blond girl peered out of a top floor window and saw the woman crying. She held her hand up to the glass and silently mouthed the word: 'Mutti'.

But Minki didn't see her. She stumbled to her feet, climbed back into her car and drove away.

37

LONDON

CHRISTMAS 1941

The relentless bombing of London had left its mark. Yawning gaps opened up between buildings; jagged wooden beams, torn curtains and smashed sanitary units lay abandoned, like reminders of past lives. Every time Leila passed one of these bomb sites, she wondered what had happened to the inhabitants. Occasionally she spotted personal possessions among the debris – photographs still in their frames, frayed items of clothing. Their owners had obviously not survived.

She frequently thanked the God she did not believe in that Hampstead had so far largely been spared. It was one of her greatest fears – that one day she might walk back home to find her house and her beloved children had been destroyed.

As she walked to the bus stop one morning on the way to work, a dark yellowing fog descended on the city. People struggled to see their hands in front of their faces and, once she was on the bus, it crawled forward achingly slowly, preceded by a man carrying a lantern. It took over an hour to get to the

Aldwych, and Leila had to run to Bush House, arriving over half an hour late.

Rushing into reception, she was surprised to see a tall Christmas tree dominating one corner of the entrance hall. She had been so been preoccupied with her parents' predicament, coupled with concern about Clara and Minki, that she had almost forgotten it was Christmas. A couple of secretaries were taking it in turns to stand on a stepladder to decorate the tree with baubles and tinsel. They were being watched over by an anxious commissionaire. 'You take care up there, miss, we don't want any accidents before Christmas.'

Leila smiled at the friendly commissionaire and got into the lift, which descended with its familiar lurch into the basement. She hurried along the corridor towards the German section.

'Sorry I'm late,' she said to Yvonne, hanging up her coat and gas mask on the hooks by the door. 'It's a pea-souper out there.'

'I know, don't worry – everyone's late. Hugh only arrived ten minutes ago.'

That day's bulletins were dominated by the news that the Americans were finally joining with the British against Germany, following the Japanese bombing of Pearl Harbour on 7 December.

As Leila translated the bulletin, she remembered her last conversation with Michael Sullivan at the Foreign Office. He had assured her that the Americans would have joined in the war effort by Christmas, and he had been right. It was almost eerie to think that he had such foresight. It gave her a small sense of optimism that the tide might finally be turning.

Leila left the office soon after five. The fog had descended once again, and her bus crawled slowly back up Haverstock Hill towards Hampstead. When she finally arrived home, the house was in darkness. The children were normally home by this time and, for a moment, she panicked. She let herself into the hall, calling their names. 'Sofia... Axel, are you there?'

The sound of sniggering reassured her that all was well. 'Where are you?'

The children burst out of the sitting room, laughing. 'Come in here, Mutti... we've got a surprise.'

Sofia turned on the light, revealing a Christmas tree in the corner next to the fireplace. 'Da-dah!' she exclaimed.

'We bought it on the way home,' said Axel excitedly. 'We didn't have enough money, but the man at the stall said you could pay him tomorrow. Isn't it lovely?'

'Yes, darlings, it's beautiful.'

'Can we decorate it now?' asked Axel.

'I suppose so, although I'm not sure how many decorations we've actually got...'

'We made some at school, look,' said Sofia, revealing a handful of papier mâché balls, painted in garish colours. 'Oh, and there's a letter for you on the hall table.'

'Thanks, darling. I'll read it in the kitchen while I make supper.'

Leila rarely drank alcohol these days but, noting that the letter had an Augsburg postmark, she felt the need to prepare herself for bad news. She tipped the remains of a bottle of sherry into a glass and took a large gulp.

Nervously, she slipped a knife through the envelope and opened Minki's letter.

My dearest Leila,

I hardly know where to begin.

Firstly, I must tell you that my angel child Clara, who was taken from me so cruelly, has died. As I write those words, it seems quite incredible and I can scarcely believe it. What makes my grief even more unbearable is that I found the hospital where she had been taken – in a town called Hadamar in Hesse. Here the mentally disturbed are incarcerated, and to think that my little child – who was full of so joy and happiness – spent the last weeks of her life in that awful place is unendurable. What she must have seen and suffered there. They told me she died after an epileptic fit. But how could a child die of epilepsy, particularly in a hospital? It makes no sense.

I stopped briefly in Berlin to give Max the news, before returning to my father's house in Augsburg. I had arranged for Clara's remains to be returned to us – to be buried next to my mother in the family plot. On the day of her funeral, I received another piece of terrible news. Max had shot himself.

It was an awful shock, of course, and the boys are devastated. To them, their father was a talented, powerful man, and they adored him. But as far as I was concerned, Max was no longer the man I had once loved. He had become weak and ineffectual – the 'creature' of Goebbels – and ultimately he represented all that is wrong with Germany. I have asked myself why he took this way out. Ultimately, I believe it was the guilt. After all, if he had kept Clara's secret, she might still be with us. I know it must sound harsh, but in many ways I feel it was the only decent thing he could have done. I will never forgive him for his betrayal, and so I cannot mourn his passing. I play the part of grieving widow for the boys' sake, but inside I feel nothing.

The loss of Clara is so profound that I too briefly considered ending it all myself. But who then would be here for Willie and Felix? So I must go on, my dear.

This tragedy has focussed my mind, and I have decided I must take a stand against the regime. I have made contact with people locally who are doing what they can to fight back. What

I reproach myself for is that it has taken the death of my own
precious child to give me the courage to act. I feel such guilt for
all the years when I ignored what was in front of my own eyes;
when I refused to see the evil that was growing in our country.
You saw it from the first – can you ever forgive me?

I have not forgotten your concern for your parents. You are
right to be anxious. Are they still living at the same apartment?
If so, I shall visit soon and see what I can do.

Write, if you can, my darling friend,

Minki

The sound of Leila's sobs brought Sofia and Axel running
through from the sitting room.

'Mutti... what's the matter? Is it Grandma, or Grandpa?'

Leila shook her head, and pushed the letter across the
kitchen table towards Sofia. She too had tears in her eyes when
she had read it.

'Oh, Mutti. How awful. Poor Minki – and poor Felix and
Willie.'

'What will you do?'

'What can I do?' said Leila, wiping her eyes. 'We are a thousand miles apart. I feel utterly helpless. But my God, Minki's
bravery is amazing. I worry though... it sounds like she has
joined some sort of resistance group. I hope she doesn't take too
many risks – the boys don't deserve to lose their mother as well
as their father and sister. I'll write back after supper.'

That evening, once the children were in bed, Leila took a
spare Christmas card from her desk drawer and wrote a brief
note to Minki. It was vital that she didn't say anything that
might attract the interest of the authorities, so she couched her
message carefully.

I cannot tell you how sad I am at your news. I am broken-hearted for you. Your strength and bravery shine through.

As for my parents... They are now living with the seam-stress who made my wedding dress. Do you remember her? They would enjoy a visit over Christmas.

I would be grateful if you could also pass on my best wishes to Uncle Emil in Berlin. Julius Zerfass mentioned that Emil's health is poor and he would appreciate a visit. Julius's contact details are below. Do please ring him or write and he will pass on Emil's address.

I will leave it there... and wish you, the boys and Gunther a peaceful Christmas.

My love to you all,

Leila

There was a risk, of course, that the card might be inter-cepted before it was delivered. It was also possible that Minki would not understand its significance. But Leila hoped that her friend's keen mind and journalistic instincts would kick in.

A few weeks later, she received a card in reply.

Dearest Leila,

Thank you for your kind words. They give me comfort. Christmas was hard – as I'm sure you appreciate – but I did my best to be cheerful for the boys.

I'd be pleased to visit Uncle Emil. I've already been in touch with Julius and he's given me an update on our poor uncle's state of health.

I'm going to visit your parents next week and will pass on your love. Be assured that I have everyone's best interests at heart.

With love,

Minki

Leila breathed a sigh of relief. Her friend had understood her message about her parents, and how to help them. Leila just hoped it wasn't too late.

38

MUNICH

Emilia Becker's apartment was in a block overlooking the Englischer Garten. As she mounted the stairs, Minki recalled the last time she had visited the seamstress – for Leila's wedding. She gently knocked on the door.

'Yes?' The voice was tentative.

'It's Minki Sommer, Frau Becker. I've come with news from Leila Hoffman in London.'

She heard the sound of several locks being unbolted, and the door finally opened.

The seamstress's appearance had changed little over the years. She still had the same slim, neat figure, shown off to perfection in a well-tailored navy-blue dress, decorated with meticulous cream topstitching. The only signs of the passing years were the grey streaks through her blond hair. 'Do come in, Minki. It's good to see you again.'

Minki was shown into the sitting room. It was all very familiar. Bolts of cloth lay on the walnut table, and mannequins dressed in half-finished outfits stood around the room, like a silent audience.

'It's so good to see you too, Frau Becker.'

'Oh, call me Emilia – please. I'll go and get the Hoffmans.' She disappeared into the back of the apartment.

The old couple came tentatively into the room. Leila's father Levi had greatly aged. His hair was completely white, and he seemed to have a curvature of the spine, presumably from years of hunching over his jewellery workbench. But it was the look of fear and confusion in his eyes that concerned Minki most.

Hannah, by contrast, was relatively unchanged. She still had the same dark hair, and kind eyes, but had lost weight. She rushed towards Minki, her words tumbling out with excitement. 'Oh, my dear girl, how wonderful to see you, and how clever of you to find us. Emilia has been so kind giving us sanctuary in her beautiful apartment. What is your news? Have you heard from Leila?'

The two women embraced. 'Yes. Leila and I have been writing to each other. And I know she wants to try and get you out of Germany. How are you both?'

'Oh, fine, fine,' said Hannah, joining her husband on the sofa.

Minki knelt at his side. 'Hello there, Mr Hoffman. It's Minki – do you remember me?' He looked intently into her eyes, but shook his head.

'Never mind,' said Minki kindly. 'It's been a long time, and so much has happened. But I'm really pleased to see you.' She leaned over and kissed his cheek, and, as she stood up, he ran his fingers over the place where her lips had grazed, and smiled.

Turning to Emilia, Minki's tone was calm and workmanlike. 'You've been very kind to the Hoffmans, but their presence in your apartment is putting you all in danger. I've heard what happens to good people like you who shelter Jews. I'm going to try and make arrangements to get them out of Germany through a contact in Berlin.'

'Berlin!' gasped Hannah. 'But how could we travel to Berlin? As soon as we got on the train, we'd be arrested.'

'You're right, the train would be impossible – there are too many police checking papers everywhere,' replied Minki. 'But I'm in touch with a resistance group which may be able to help. Please try not to worry. I'll be back with more news as soon as I can, but in the meantime stay hidden here.'

'Oh, don't worry, we never go out,' said Hannah firmly. 'But dear Emilia has to share her rations with us. You see, we can't use our own ration books, as it would give us away.'

'I do see, yes. I'm afraid there's nothing I can do about the ration books at this stage. But hopefully you won't need them much longer. I wonder... could you let me have your existing identity papers – we'll need the photographs in order to create new ones.'

'Yes of course,' said Hannah. 'I'll go and get them now.'

She returned with their identity booklets and handed them to Minki.

'Thank you. Well...if there's nothing else, I'd better go.'

'I've not even asked how you are, dear?' said Hannah kindly. 'Your children – are they well?'

Minki's firm resolve to stay calm and professional weakened. 'The boys are well – yes. But my daughter...' She began to sob.

'Oh my dear... what has happened?'

'She was taken from me, and now she's dead.'

'Oh, Minki, I'm so sorry. I can't imagine the pain you must be in. It makes what you're doing for us even more remarkable. Thank you for sparing the time to come to see us. I fear I have misjudged you in the past. Forgive me.'

'There's nothing to forgive, Frau Hoffman. Leila is like a sister to me. I want to help...' She kissed Hannah's cheek.

'Losing my daughter has been the worst thing imaginable. At first, I feared I would die myself, but now I'm just determined to do what I can to help others. I'll try to come back soon. I'm not sure when. But please have a bag packed and ready – only essentials, you understand. We may need to act quickly when the time comes.'

Hannah nodded. 'We'll be ready.'

The following day Minki took the train to Berlin. As soon as she arrived, she hurried to a phone box and flicked through the fat Berlin telephone directory. To her relief Ruth Andreas-Friedrich was listed. She dialled the number.

A woman answered: 'Hello.'

'Hello – I'm a friend of Uncle Emil. I understand he's not been well...'

'That's kind... he's on the mend, but is too frail to get to the phone. Can I ask who's calling?'

'My name is Minki Sommer. Perhaps I could speak to Ruth?'

'Ruth speaking.'

'Ah, good. Ruth – I believe we may have met a few years ago, when I was working as a journalist, editing the women's pages of the *Deutsche Allemagne Zeitung*. I wondered if we could meet.'

'Oh, yes, I think I remember you... You're a tall blonde, yes?'

'That's right.'

'Where are you?'

'At the railway station – Ostbahnhof.'

'Meet me at Café Berlin in half an hour – it's just outside the station.'

The line went dead.

·   ·   ·

The café was bustling with passengers when Minki arrived. She squeezed into a corner table and waited. A dark-haired woman wearing a grey suit strode into the café and walked straight towards her.

'Minki?'

'Yes... hello, Ruth – how good to see you again.'

They ordered coffee.

'So who gave you my name?'

'Julius Zerfass – he's a friend of Leila Labowksi – Leila Hoffman was her maiden name.'

'Ah yes, Leila. I recall a few of her articles. She was good – and very brave. But I've not read anything by her for a while.'

'No, she left Germany after her husband died, and went to London.'

'So many good people have left.'

'Not you, though.'

Ruth smiled. 'No. My partner Leo and I... we cannot abandon our country. So, you mentioned you need some help?'

'Yes, for Leila's parents. They're in Munich at the moment. I want to help them get out of Germany, but first we need... certain things.'

'Don't say any more,' said Ruth, throwing a few coins into a saucer to pay the bill. 'Come with me.'

They took the tram to the south-west of the city. Ruth led the way to a tall apartment building overlooking the Botanical Gardens. Inside they walked up to the first floor.

'It's all right,' Ruth called out, as she unlocked the apartment door. 'It's only me. I'm with a friend.'

Minki was led into a large sitting room crammed with people. Men and women of all ages sat at the dining table playing cards, or were squeezed together on the sofa and any available chair. It had the feel of a sociable get-together, but without the usual merriment.

'Goodness – do they all live with you?'

'They do now,' said Ruth, smiling. 'We take in anyone who needs our help.'

'But how do you feed them all?'

'We receive many gifts from friends – people are generous. And we have a wonderful forger who creates fake ration books. We manage. Come with me.'

She led Minki to her bedroom, and closed the door. 'We can talk alone here. It's the one room I won't give up to others. There have to be limits.' She smiled.

'What will happen to all those people?' asked Minki.

'Some we'll get out – if they're young and fit. The older ones... it's not so easy. The journeys are hard and dangerous. Leila's parents... I presume they are old, yes?'

'Yes. And her father is rather confused.'

Ruth nodded. 'Then don't bring them here. I have no room – and besides the route out of Berlin is too difficult. They are in Munich, you say?'

'Yes. They're hiding in a Catholic friend's apartment.'

'So many brave people are helping out,' Ruth murmured. 'Now to business. From Munich, the best route is through Switzerland. But the trains are difficult to negotiate – escapees need to avoid the guards and have their wits about them. Could someone drive the couple to the Swiss border instead?'

'Drive them? I suppose I could.'

'They'll need papers – false exit visas in case you're stopped. Do you have their photographs?'

'Yes, I brought their old identity cards with me,' said Minki, reaching into her handbag. 'I hope the photographs are all right?'

'They're perfect,' said Ruth, examining the documents. 'If they make it as far as Switzerland, Julius will be able to help them. I presume Leila will try to get them entry visas for Britain?'

'I suspect so.'

'I'll get our forger to work on their documents. It will take a few weeks, and I'll send them to you, all right? They'll be hidden inside another document or perhaps a magazine – anything to put the authorities off the scent. Then it's up to you to get them across the border and liaise with Julius. Is that clear?'

'Very clear. I don't know how to thank you... you've been wonderful.'

Leaving the apartment that day, Minki felt a profound admiration for the work Ruth was doing. Like her, she was an Aryan, and was risking her life every day to stand up to tyranny – something that Minki was now determined to do.

39

LONDON

MAY 1942

During the cold winter months and into the following spring, reports filtered out from Germany that Jews were being rounded up and murdered. For Leila, waiting for news of her parents, it was an agonising time. She had heard nothing from Minki, nor from her mother, and worried constantly that her efforts to save her parents had come too late.

At work her frustration boiled over. The British authorities refused to accept that the growing slaughter of Jews was in any way state-sponsored, so the BBC were unable to report it.

'The world needs to know, Hugh. We should be covering this,' Leila insisted at one of their morning editorial meetings.

'We can't... the FO simply forbid it – they say the reports are too unreliable. The evidence is just too flimsy.'

'But we know it's going on, Hugh.'

'I'm sorry, Leila, we can't go against government policy. I fear we are just going to have to wait for more evidence.'

'You know as well as I do, Hugh, that "The Final Solution"

has always been Hitler's plan. If any German Jews survive this war it will be a miracle.'

Towards the end of May, the BBC reported that Jews in Nazi-occupied Paris were being ordered to wear the yellow star. Reading the news bulletin, Leila felt a sense of growing despair – for her country and her parents.

As she travelled home that evening, she was overwhelmed by a sense of hopelessness that both surprised and depressed her. She had always managed to maintain some sort of optimism, but now she could feel it ebbing away day by day.

Even the warm spring air, and the sound of birdsong in the apple trees as she opened the garden gate to the cottage, failed to lift her spirits.

The children were lying on the grass, and leapt up when they saw her. 'We've been waiting for you. Oh, Mutti... something wonderful has happened.' Sofia was brandishing a letter. 'I opened it... I hope you don't mind. It was in Grandma's writing. Here...'

Leila looked into Sofia's eyes. 'Is it good news?' Her voice was tentative and nervous; she could barely dare to hope.

Sofia nodded enthusiastically. 'The best. I'll get started on supper while you read it.'

Leila sat down on the grass, and read her mother's letter.

Dearest Leila,

We are in Geneva! Can you believe it? I still can't. Your father, of course, is most confused, but quite frankly, I don't care. He'll recover. The point is – we are alive and safe.

Julius and Charlotte are so kind and have taken great care of us. But our thanks must really go to your friend Minki, without whom we would simply not be here.

She showed such bravery, Leila, such ingenuity and strength that I am still in awe of her. It took several weeks for our papers to be ready. Then we had heavy snowfall all through March and April. Minki suggested we should wait until the roads were clearer. Finally, in May, she collected us late one night from the apartment, armed with the appropriate papers, in case we were challenged. Her plan was to use small back roads in order to avoid roadblocks. In the back of her father's Mercedes, we drove through the night. Once, in spite of the devious route, we encountered police. Minki was cool as a cucumber. She told us to pretend to be asleep, and showed our false identity papers. She said we were Frau and Herr Schwab visiting relatives. Minki was magnificent and showed no fear. I think that's how she got away with it.

Anyway, we finally arrived at the meeting place near Lake Constance. Julius was waiting in a wood on the edge of the lake in his own car. We had to drive down a small track and, when we saw him signalling with his headlights, my heart was in my mouth. What if it was a trick, and it was actually the Gestapo waiting for us? When I saw Julius, I was so relieved that my legs just gave way. I literally fell into his arms, and he had to carry me to his car. Within minutes, your father and I were bundled into the back, and we were off, driving through the Swiss forests. It was all over so fast, I didn't really have a chance to thank dear Minki.

Julius has spoken with the authorities and we have temporary leave to stay. How long they will allow I don't know, but he says you might be in a position to help with our onward journey.

Darling, you have helped so much already – I am speechless with admiration for you and your friends.

Write soon sweetheart,

Your loving mother

Leila lay back on the lawn and gazed up into the sky. The sun had disappeared behind the line of trees, and the moon was just rising. Doves cooed gently in the eaves of the cottage and the leaves of the apple trees rustled in the breeze. For the first time in years, she felt calm and peaceful, at one with the world.

Sofia emerged from the house and lay down next to her. 'Are you happy?'

'Oh yes, darling, very happy.' Her eyes welled up with tears.

'Oh, don't cry, Mutti. It's going to be all right.'

'I know... I'm not sad – just relieved.' She gave Sofia a big hug. 'Come on, let's get inside.'

Axel was sitting at the kitchen table, doing his homework. He leapt up excitedly when his mother and sister came into the room. 'Do we have to go to school tomorrow, Mutti?'

'Of course you do,' said Leila, hugging him. 'But nice try. I have to go to work tomorrow too, so it's life as normal for us, I'm afraid. Now let's see what your sister has prepared for supper, and maybe tomorrow I'll try to get an extra meat ration and we can have a very special celebration dinner.'

That evening, when the children were in bed, Leila wrote two letters – one to her mother and the other to Minki. As usual when writing to Minki, she had to guard against being too explicit.

My darling friend,

I have had wonderful news from Geneva. What you have done for us is beyond brave.

I will write again soon, but I wanted you to know that I will never forget your kindness to me and my parents.

Your loving friend,

Leila

. . .

Over the summer, Leila corresponded regularly with Julius, trying to make arrangements to get Hannah and Levi out of Switzerland and into England. But frustratingly nothing could be finalised without an entry visa.

She rang Michael Sullivan's office on several occasions, but was fobbed off. Then, one morning in early October, Sullivan's secretary rang Leila at the BBC and invited her to a meeting the following morning.

Praying her request for visas would finally be resolved, she rushed to the meeting and was shown into Sullivan's office.

'Ah, dear lady,' he said, 'so good of you to come. I have someone I'd like you to meet.'

Sitting on a sofa near the fireplace was a sandy-haired man dressed in the khaki uniform of the American army. He stood up and held out his hand. 'Hi, my name is Brewster Morgan. It's great to meet you.'

Over the following hour Major Morgan outlined a plan that was being hatched as a joint initiative between the British Foreign Office and the United States Office of War Information, the OWI. The Americans intended to establish a European broadcasting station based in London, to be known as ABSIE.

'It will be part of a tactical approach,' said Brewster, 'in preparation for our joint invasion of Europe – preparing the people over there for life after the war.'

'I was under the impression that the OWI was more focussed on propaganda than news,' said Leila.

'No no... real propaganda, by which I mean black ops, is the job of the OSS. We're more about gentle persuasion. But ultimately the Department's primary objective is to achieve the defeat and unconditional surrender of the enemy, and to win understanding and approval of the American story among the peoples of Europe.'

'That sounds like a speech you've given before,' said Leila, smiling.

'You're right. It *is* something I've said before, but that doesn't make it any less true. We're not interested in teaching people about America, or even boasting about America. We don't care if people *like* the United States; what we want is that they *understand* the United States, on the assumption that the more the truth about America is known, the more the nature of American democracy, as opposed to Nazi totalitarianism, will be understood. It's soft power, soft propaganda.'

'We see it,' interjected Sullivan, 'as an opportunity to attack enemy morale on the home front, but also to spread accurate and dispassionate information about America and her allies and thus to build confidence among occupied and liberated countries.'

'Isn't that what the BBC is doing already?' asked Leila.

'Of course,' said Brewster, 'the BBC is doing a great job – and we intend to work closely with our BBC colleagues. Indeed we'll depend on them for many things – not least, their transmitters, their personnel and even their programmes sometimes. But the emphasis of this radio station will be to put over a greater understanding of America.'

'I see. Well, it all sounds very interesting, Major Brewster, but how can I help?'

'Ah... well,' began Sullivan, 'this is the exciting part...'

Brewster raised his hand. 'If I may, Michael... I'm a radio man, Leila – can I call you Leila? This uniform I'm wearing is simply a means of protecting me in the unlikely event that I'm captured by the enemy. In fact, I've spent the last twenty years at CBS as station chief. So I know broadcasting and I know talent – and you have it in spades.'

Leila smiled modestly.

'I've listened to your broadcasts – you have a great voice. I've gotten hold of sections of the newspaper you edited back in Germany – where you did a great job, may I say. You're a skilled writer – and you have vision. I understand you're writing a book about the women of Germany, is that right?'

'Yes, it's due to be published this summer.' Leila hesitated. 'Major Brewster, I'm flattered by your generous opinions of my talents, but I am still not sure what you're asking me to do.'

'I'm offering you a full-time job, Leila – a permanent contract working for us, right here in London.'

Leila was taken aback. A full-time job would certainly help with the bills. 'Well, I'm flattered, obviously, but what would this job involve?'

'Much as you're doing now. By next year London will be filled with people working for the OWI. Our ambition is to promulgate positive information about the United States – in radio programmes, magazines, newspapers, books, films, leaflets – in a variety of languages – German, Polish, French. If you agree to take the job, you'll be broadcasting to the German people – just as you're doing now for the BBC. But, unlike your current position, we also want to harness your journalistic talents. You'll be sourcing stories, writing bulletins as well as reading them. Ultimately, your responsibility will be to bring some truth and perspective to the citizens of Germany, to show them that after the war the Americans are people they can trust. How does that sound?'

Leila had to admit that the range of Brewster's ambition was exciting.

'It's a very tempting offer, Major, but there is just one issue. Some time ago now, Mr Sullivan here also made me a professional offer.'

'Ah well, Mrs Labowski,' said Sullivan quickly, 'this new initiative from our American partners changes things somewhat. You would now be working *de facto* for both governments. Then, once the war is over, we would still be keen to include you in our post-war planning in Germany. It's all part of the same journey, if you understand me?'

'I see. Well, if I am to do this for you, Mr Sullivan, I have a small favour to ask.'

'Name it, dear lady.'

'That you kindly arrange for my parents to be given an entry visa into England. They are both Jews, and have managed to escape to Switzerland, where they are now safe, but I need them here – especially if I am to work full time for our allies.'

She smiled at Brewster Morgan, who locked eyes with Michael Sullivan and nodded.

'I'll certainly see what we can do,' said Sullivan.

Leila looked him straight in the eye. 'No, Mr Sullivan, I'm afraid vague promises are not good enough. I need a cast-iron undertaking – here and now.'

Michael Sullivan rocked thoughtfully on his heels, and Leila wondered if she had gone too far. But finally, he smiled at her.

'Mrs Labowski, you have my word that I will obtain entry visas for your parents. Please let my secretary have the details, and the British government will set the wheels in motion.'

PART FOUR

1945

We are faced with either death or victory.

JOSEPH GOEBBELS, FEBRUARY 28TH 1945

40

AUGSBURG

The sky was threatening snow as Minki arrived at the cemetery, carrying a little bunch of white heather and blue hyacinths to put on Clara's grave. She had read somewhere that white heather symbolised purity, and hyacinths stood for sorrow and regret. That summed up her feelings about Clara perfectly. She placed the flowers in a small vase in front of the grey head stone.

CLARA VON ZELLER
MUCH BELOVED DAUGHTER AND SISTER
HER STAR SPARKLED BRIGHT AND WAS
EXTINGUISHED TOO SOON
1932–1941

Clara's grave lay next to the Sommer family tomb. An austere granite sarcophagus, the tomb had long ago been placed in a prominent position in the cemetery, between a pair of ancient yew trees. Generations of Minki's family had been buried there, including her mother, but Minki didn't want her child hidden away inside the tomb. She had insisted that her grave be placed outside – 'where she can breathe' – and had planted wild cyclamen on the surface of the grass all around. Her hope was that these tiny pink flowers would spring to life in the winter months in celebration of Clara's birthday. As she looked around now, Minki's heart lifted slightly to see the pale-pink flowers spreading across the surface of the grass like a blush.

'I'm glad to see you visiting the cemetery each week,' Gunther had said that morning as Minki stood at the kitchen sink, preparing flowers for the grave. 'I'm sure it gives you great comfort. Don't forget to say a prayer.'

'No, Papa... I won't forget.'

But the truth was, Minki didn't find comfort at Clara's graveside. Instead, she felt only fury – a white hot anger that burned inside her – that a child with such promise could be cut off in her prime, destroyed by the evil policies of her own government. As she stood alone in the wintry cemetery, she wept salty tears of regret. 'Forgive me, darling... I should have stopped them, I should have kept you safe...'

Back home, she tidied the house and prepared dinner. Her father's old housekeeper had died at the start of the war, and since then domestic staff had been thin on the ground – most had been sent to work in the armaments factories. And so Minki had finally taught herself to cook. 'If little Clara could master it, I'm sure I could,' she told herself. Now, she actually enjoyed it.

Late in the afternoon the boys, now aged eleven, arrived back from school, bringing energy and joy into the house. Minki hugged them tightly, reluctant to let them go, enjoying the life force they emanated – such a contrast to the silent, cold grave she had visited earlier.

'Ow, Mutti,' said Willie, 'you're hurting.'

'Sorry, *liebling*.' Minki handed them a plate of home-made biscuits. 'Take these upstairs. Supper won't be long.'

She heard them running noisily up to their nursery, eager to play with their model railway. Her father had unearthed it from his attic soon after the boys arrived.

'My parents bought this for me,' Gunther had told them. 'It was one of the first model railways to be built – and was invented by a German – so take good care of it.'

Now the railway covered more than half the floor area of their nursery. No one was allowed entry except 'Grandpa' – not even for cleaning – so drifts of dust had gathered in the corners of the room. The train itself was a miniature, fully working steam train, which chugged round the track, pulling half a dozen carriages. The boys had made model buildings out of card – with painted-on bricks, windows and doors – creating entire villages complete with stations and signals, and had peopled them with tiny tin men and women. They had even acquired miniature dogs, sheep and cows. As she listened to the boys' happy chatter in the room above, Minki felt comforted by their presence. Peeling potatoes, she repeated a daily prayer: 'Please God, let the war be over before they're old enough to fight. Spare them, I beg of you.'

When dinner was nearly ready, she put the various dishes in the bottom of the range to keep warm and sat down at her desk, which had been placed in an alcove overlooking the garden. Unlocking the top drawer with a key she kept on a string round her neck, she removed a letter she had received that day from Ruth Andreas-Friedrich of Uncle Emil. Since joining Ruth's team, Minki had helped to coordinate the escape of many Jewish families from the south of the country. She never again personally drove people across the border – the risks of capture and death, she told Ruth, were too great, and the thought of abandoning her boys too distressing – but she made the arrangements, acted as a go-between, and liaised with Berlin to get hold of false papers.

The letter she had received that morning was a request for help for a family trapped in Munich. She made a note of what would be required – false papers, planning a route, before pinning the letter and the note to a fat sheaf of papers and once again locking them away in her secret drawer. She sometimes wondered if she should destroy these records. Hidden away in her drawer were the names of over thirty people she had helped to survive. But something made her hang on to them – a need to confirm the difference she had made to so many people's lives, written down in black and white.

She had been helped in her work by her old friend, the countess. Franziska, like Minki, was disillusioned with the regime, and keen to help. 'I'm too old for sex, Minki darling, but I need some excitement in my life. Working against the government gives me a thrill, and makes me feel young again.'

But a few months earlier, tragedy had struck. The bar in Schwabing where Franziska lived took a direct hit during a bombing raid. Sadly, the countess and Gerhard, the owner, were killed instantly. A few weeks later, Minki received a letter from a solicitor, explaining that the countess had left her the family tiara. Along with the letter was the key to a safety deposit box in a bank in the centre of Munich. On presenting herself at the bank, Minki was shown to the basement and the box was removed from the vault. When she opened it, there lay the tiara on a blue velvet cushion. With it was a note from the countess.

Minki, darling.

I took your advice and moved my tiara to the bank. It is yours now... I hope it brings you luck. Just remember – a lady never sells her jewels.

Somehow, Minki managed to keep the two parts of her life – the domestic, and her work for the resistance – in completely separate compartments, so her father knew nothing of her double life. And although the work was risky, it gave her satisfaction that she was fighting against the regime that had murdered her child.

Her notes once again safely locked away, Minki went to check on her father before supper. He often worked late in his study. She knocked on the door.

'Come in,' he called out.

'Can I get you anything, Papa? Dinner will be ready in half an hour or so.'

'No, I'm fine, my dear.'

'In that case, I'll just listen to the radio for a while in the sitting room.'

'Very good,' he said, smiling at her.

It struck Minki as ironic that she had finally become the domestic creature her father had always hoped she would be. She often reflected on how angry she had been at him in her youth. Now, they got on well. In many ways, she, her father and the boys had become a happy family. The old man still ran his steel manufacturing business, and still went to work each morning in his big Mercedes. He had even bought Minki a small car to get around, and there were times when she felt something akin to contentment – running the house, caring for the boys and her father, doing what she could to help those in need. Her anger at what had happened to Clara would be with her forever, but she tried to leave those negative feelings at the graveside. It was important for the boys' sake to try to remain positive and cheerful.

It had become a daily habit to pour herself a small brandy or glass of schnapps before dinner, smoke a cigarette and listen in peace to the radio in the sitting room. She rarely listened to German news stations – they were still filled with ridiculous propaganda, insisting that victory was within sight. Everyone knew it was nonsense.

She preferred to listen to the foreign news stations, and had often tuned into the BBC in order to hear Leila reading the bulletins. Then, in 1944, she had discovered her on a new station – the American Broadcasting Station in Europe – and just to be able to hear Leila's voice, in spite of the poor reception, raised her spirits.

The fire she had laid a couple of hours earlier was dying down, and the room was chilly. Minki threw a couple of logs onto the glowing embers, poured herself a glass of schnapps, and turned on the radio. As she twiddled the dial, the calming music of Beethoven filled the room. It would make a pleasant change to listen to a concert. Settling herself on the sofa, she closed her eyes, and tried to lose herself in the music. But to her surprise, the broadcast was suddenly interrupted.

'*We now bring you a special announcement from the Reichsminister, Dr Goebbels.*'

At first, Minki's hand instinctively reached for the off button – for she now loathed the sound of Goebbels' voice – but something made her stop and listen.

In a relatively short speech, Goebbels expressed his loyalty to the Führer. His voice, as ever, was forceful and strong, but his final remarks came as a shock. '*In the event of defeat, I would put an end to my life and that of my close family. If the enemy is victorious I would no longer consider life worth living, neither for me nor for my children.*'

It was an extraordinary statement. For Goebbels to take his own life would be an understandable and almost predictable event. He had allied himself so totally with Hitler and the success of Nazism that defeat would be intolerable. Besides, if the Allies won and he was captured, he would certainly be executed. Better by far to die by one's own hand. For Magda, too, who had aligned herself so closely with Hitler – even her life would seem unbearable in the face of his defeat. But to take the lives of their children was unimaginable. How could any mother agree to such a monstrous act?

She had never met the Goebbels' children but had seen many photographs of them. Now, as she imagined their trusting faces gazing up at their parents at the moment of death, tears came to her eyes.

Surely, Joseph and Magda were not just corrupted by Hitler's warped view of the world, they had descended into madness. It was the only way to explain it.

From that point on, Minki became obsessed with following the final days of the war. The Russians were closing in on Berlin from the east – and stories of rape and pillage by Russian soldiers swirled wildly among the population. The Americans, meanwhile, were moving inexorably in from the west and she was grateful that Munich and Augsburg would find themselves ultimately taken over by a more civilised army than the Russians.

In April, while searching for the few things their ration books would buy in Augsburg, Minki passed a newsstand. A headline jumped out at her from *Das Reich*, Goebbels' propaganda paper.

COMMITTING ONE'S OWN LIFE

Intrigued, she bought a copy and read the article feverishly while walking down the street. It had been penned by Goebbels himself, who once again suggested that after defeat, *'no one could imagine wanting to continue to live in such a situation.'*

From that day, Minki bought Goebbels' paper daily and

monitored the radio for his broadcasts. It gave her an insight into the feverish workings of the man's increasingly deranged mind.

On 15 April, Goebbels rejoiced at the news of the death of the American president, Theodore Roosevelt, believing that the Allied coalition would now collapse. It seemed absurdly optimistic, Minki thought – and so it proved to be when the following the day the Russians attacked Berlin.

On 19 April, Goebbels addressed the nation once again, this time in advance of Hitler's fifty-sixth birthday the following day. *'For over twenty years I've been at the Führer's side. I've participated in his rise and that of his movement from the smallest and most obscure beginnings until the seizure of power, and I've done my best to give it my support... Hitler is the man of this century... the heart of the resistance against world decline... He is Germany's bravest son and the one among us with the strongest will... He will follow his path to the end, and lead his people into a period in which ethnic Germans will blossom as never before... Never will history be able to report of this time that a people abandoned their Führer or a Führer abandoned his people.'*

Minki was astonished. It was a speech so full of lies and bravado that it must have been written for posterity – a gift for the Führer from his devoted disciple.

A couple of days later, Goebbels wrote another article in *Das Reich*.

RESISTANCE AT ALL COSTS

The war will be decided in the very last minute.

He ended by calling for a *'people's war even if it resulted in heavy casualties'*.

This call to arms, demanding the German people should lay

down their own lives in a pointless attempt at victory, made it clear that the German High Command had finally lost all sense of its reason.

The following day Goebbels announced on the radio that he and his family would remain in Berlin, along with Hitler.

After that, there were no more pronouncements from Goebbels. Huge swathes of Germany were now under Allied control and it was obvious that the end was in sight.

Finally, on the first day of May, German radio was interrupted by a piece of solemn music, followed by a grave announcement: '*Adolf Hitler is fallen. He died fighting Bolshevism until his last breath.*'

'Fallen'. It was an odd word to use, Minki thought. It implied the Führer had died in combat, which was absurd, as everyone knew he had retreated to his underground bunker. But either way, he was dead. For Minki, sitting alone in the drawing room, it seemed extraordinary to think that the man who had dominated all their lives for over twenty years was finally gone.

Over the following days, Minki listened to the foreign broadcasts almost continuously. The BBC confirmed Hitler's death, but there was no mention of Goebbels. Had he kept his promise and taken his own life, she wondered? She switched to the Americans' new network, and one evening in the first week of May she heard Leila introducing a reporter who was embedded with the American troops in Germany. His report contained the news she was expecting: Joseph Goebbels and his wife Magda had murdered their children before taking their own lives in Hitler's bunker.

Minki tried to imagine what those last hours must have been like for the couple. Joseph, she thought, would have been unemotional and determined. But Magda was a different matter. For any mother to murder her own children – whatever the justification – would be torture. Had Magda begged Joseph for reprieve, she wondered. Had she tried to hide them, or get them out of the bunker? However loyal Magda had been to the Party and the Führer, Minki felt she would have tried to protect her children, for she was nothing if not a devoted mother. But ultimately she had agreed to her husband's wicked plan and ended the lives of her six beautiful children.

To her surprise, Minki found herself in tears at the news – not for the deaths of either Joseph or Magda, but for their innocent son and daughters, sacrificed on the altar of their parents' insane beliefs. 'What an awful waste,' she murmured, as the tears flowed.

Suddenly her father rushed in. 'I was just listening to the news... it's over. The war is over. Hitler and your friend Goebbels are dead.'

Minki wiped her eyes. 'I know... I was listening too. But Goebbels was no friend of mine, Papa. I can't believe they were prepared to kill their own children – they must have been mad, don't you think?'

'Probably.' Her father poured them both a glass of schnapps. 'Looking back, the whole war was mad. Have a drink, darling. You're in shock. I'm pretty shocked myself.'

He sat down next to her and wrapped her in his arms, kissing the top of her head. 'But I'm also very relieved. At least the boys won't have to go to war...'

'Oh, so am I, Papa.' She sipped her drink. 'But oddly, alongside the relief, I feel a sense of despair.'

'Why, darling?'

'For Clara, I suppose. The truth is, I can never forgive myself for her death.'

'But you had no part in it – you must not blame yourself.'

'Maybe not, but I should have recognised what was being planned, and acted sooner.'

'And done what?'

'I could have resisted the regime earlier, and taken the children out of Germany. Instead I stood on the sidelines.'

'I think you're being too hard on yourself. Clara's death was the result of an evil policy created by madmen. It was not the fault of people like you.'

'I disagree. By standing back and doing nothing, I allowed that evil policy to take root. While Hitler and the others were the perpetrators, I, we, the German people, allowed it to happen. For that, I can never forgive myself.'

41

LONDON

Leila was standing by the window on the first floor of the ABSIE headquarters in Soho, watching crowds of excited Londoners hugging, laughing and kissing in the street below. A few minutes earlier, Winston Churchill had made an important announcement on the radio, declaring that war in Europe had come to an end. *'We may allow ourselves a brief period of rejoicing, but let us not forget for a moment the toils and efforts that lie ahead.'*

Clearly the crowds in the street below were taking the prime minister's injunction to rejoice quite literally.

Leila had listened to the speech, along with fifty or so others in the newsroom. The moment Churchill finished, even seasoned journalists whooped with delight, hugging one another and punching the air. Oddly, Leila struggled to feel any elation. Of course, she was glad the worst was over; was relieved that she and her children had survived and that her parents had been saved. But so much – and so many – had been lost that happiness seemed the wrong emotion.

'Aren't you coming outside to join the fun?' One of the secretaries was putting on her hat and gloves. 'We're going to walk down the Mall towards Buckingham Palace. Churchill and the royal family are due on the balcony any time now.'

'Maybe, in a little while,' said Leila. 'I've got a few things to finish first.'

'OK, well don't work too hard. Today's a day for celebration, after all. We're all going for a quick drink first – we'll be in the Coach and Horses if you want to join us.'

Leila couldn't quite work out why the idea of joining in the fun seemed so wrong. Instead of joy, she felt simply exhaustion. For it was not just the war that was over – for her it was also the twenty years of National Socialist rule that she and others had fought so hard against. On a personal level, there was also the loss of people she loved – Viktor, of course, was uppermost in her mind at that moment. He was just one of millions of other innocent men, women and children who had been murdered in concentration camps. Millions more had starved to death in ghettoes, or been killed in battle.

And while the fighting in Europe was over, in many ways the work was just beginning. There was so much to do, so much to rebuild – in both England and Germany.

Leila had recently been recruited to the American Army by a man named Colonel Potter. 'I need you return to Germany,' he told her. 'We're starting a magazine aimed at the women of Europe. It's all part of our process of re-education. And I'd like to put you in charge of the German edition.'

'Me?' Leila had been surprised and rather flattered. 'But it's years since I've edited anything.'

'Your work here at ABSIE has been greatly admired. I do hope you will consider this offer. We need you, Mrs Labowski... the women of Germany need you.'

This speech had convinced Leila that her duty lay in her homeland – at least for the next year or two. But as the date of her departure drew closer, her worries at leaving her family behind grew stronger.

At sixteen, Axel was approaching his school certificate, and hoped to become an engineer. But in so many ways he was still just a boy, and Leila was grateful that her parents were now safely installed in the cottage in London, and could look after him. Sofia was now eighteen, and had joined the ATS for the last year of the war, but was due to be released soon to become an undergraduate at Cambridge. Leila tried to reassure herself that in many ways it was the perfect time to take on a new role. The children were moving on with their lives and would survive without her – but would she cope without them? They had been her constant companions since Viktor's death, and the thought of daily life without the comforting love of her family was more intimidating than she cared to admit.

Now, as the office gradually emptied out, Leila sat at her desk, enjoying the peace and quiet. She was absorbed in her work, assembling some ideas for the new magazine, when, to her surprise, she heard her name being called out. 'Leila?'

She looked up. 'Yes?'

The man was wearing American army uniform – which was unsurprising, as many of the journalists and broadcasters at ABSIE were part of the army. He wore the insignia of a major and was tall, silver-haired, and rather good-looking.

'I'm afraid everyone has gone to the pub up the road,' she said. 'The Coach and Horses – do you know it?'

'Actually, it's you I came to see.'

'Me?' She studied the man's face intently and suddenly it came to her where she'd seen him before – twenty years before, in fact. 'Peter... Peter Fischer?'

'The same.' He grinned broadly and came over and kissed her cheek.

'What on earth are you doing here, Peter?'

'I've been in a meeting with some people upstairs. I got

talking about my past life before the war. We were discussing
Hitler's trial, and I mentioned your name. One of them leapt up
and said: "She's here... working downstairs in the German
section". I nearly fell off my chair.'

'Well, I'm delighted to see you.'

'And I, you... shall we go for a drink? There's so much I'd
like to talk to you about.'

'Well, I was trying to do some work, but presented with
such an offer how can I refuse?'

Outside in the street, Peter put his arm round her shoulders to
protect her from the excitable crowds. He began to lead her
down Wardour Street towards Piccadilly Circus.

'The Coach and Horses is the other way, Peter,' she said,
half-resisting.

'Let's not go there... too many people, and I want you all to
myself... do you mind?'

'No, not at all.'

He hailed a taxi. 'The Savoy, please driver.'

The two climbed in.

'I thought we'd go to the American Bar... my treat.'

'How lovely,' said Leila. 'I've never been before – it's a bit
out of my league.'

'Well, then it's time you did – and I'm glad it's me that's
taking you.'

Walking into the grand lobby of the hotel, Leila felt uncomfortable. Elegantly dressed people stood chatting in little groups
in front of the fire, or drinking cocktails on plump sofas. They
looked so at ease, whereas she felt shabby in her old woollen
coat and battered leather shoes.

'Peter,' she whispered, 'I'm not wearing the right clothes.'

'Don't be absurd,' he said, hooking his arm through hers.
'You look wonderful. Follow me.'

He led her up a narrow flight of stairs and into the American Bar. A waiter showed them to a small table in the corner, and Peter ordered two martinis.

'I've not had one of these before,' said Leila nervously.

'You'll love it, and if not I'll get you something else.'

The waiter set their drinks on the table with a flourish. Peter clinked his glass with hers. 'Cheers, Leila – here's to the end of the war, and to old friends.'

'I'll second that.' She sipped the martini, and felt it coursing through her body. 'Gosh, that's better than schnapps.'

He grinned. 'I'm glad you like it. You know, it's extraordinary, seeing you again after all this time, but it's like the years have just melted away.'

For a moment they sat gazing at one another, both recalling a past time when they had been so young, united in opposition to Nazism.

'Those days of the trial... feels like another world, doesn't it?' she said at last. 'Can I ask... what were you discussing with the people upstairs – are you joining us in broadcasting?'

'No.' He laughed. 'I was upstairs with the Office of War guys talking about another project. I joined the army at the start of the war, and I've been all over Europe. My foreign languages made me quite useful for the OSS,' he added in a whisper.

'Ah, black ops. I never got involved in that. It was just plain old-fashioned British and American propaganda for me.' She smiled. 'But I wish I'd known you were in England – we could have met up before.'

'Well, to be honest, this is the first time I've been back here in quite a while. And how about you? How did you end up here, working for the Yanks?'

'It's a long story...'

'We have time.'

'Well, I left Germany in '34 after my husband died.'

'Viktor... is dead?'

'You remember him, then.'

'Of course I remember him. He was a delightful man – so wise and intelligent. I'm so sorry, Leila, that must have been terrible. What happened?'

Slowly Leila explained how Viktor had been imprisoned, died in captivity, and how she had got to England with her children. Peter took her hand. 'I always admired you, Leila, but what you've been through... you're incredible. I'm so glad you made it.'

'I've been lucky, I suppose... apart from losing Viktor, of course. But I've got two marvellous children – and both my parents survived, which was a sort of miracle.'

'And what are your plans now war is over?' Peter asked. 'Back to writing books?'

'Sadly, no, but I will remain in journalism. In fact, I'll be joining the army too. The Americans have asked me to go back to Germany.'

'Doing what?'

'De-Nazification. In other words, changing hearts and minds – soft propaganda, they call it. I'm heading up a new magazine aimed at Germans. I need to go over there to find out what the last few years have been like for women – the poverty, the rationing, how the propaganda affected them. It will involve a lot of travelling in the first instance. I must confess, it's all a bit overwhelming.'

He smiled at her. 'Well, if anyone can do it, you can. Oh, Leila, there's so much to talk about. I hardly know where to start.'

'How about what you're up to, Peter – if that's not top secret?'

'Well, it's not for public consumption, you understand, but as we seem to be working for the same outfit, I'll tell you. I'm going back to Germany too – working with a group of interpreters and journalists who are investigating war crimes.'

'That sounds interesting, if distressing.'

'Yes, in fact, we're already getting reports of the most awful things our troops have uncovered.'

'In the concentration camps, you mean?'

'Yes, that of course... but also in hospitals and other institutions, where mass murder appears to have been a routine event.'

Leila's heart missed a beat. 'What sort of institutions?'

'Well, I shouldn't really discuss it, but it seems there's been an organised process of eugenics involving children's homes, hospitals and mental institutions. When the American army arrived in Hesse back in February, they found evidence of the most appalling crimes... that's all I can say right now. It's one of the first projects I'll be involved with – gathering information on the ground, and preparing a case for the lawyers.'

Leila paused, wondering if she should mention Minki. 'In Hesse, you say. Do you recall the name of the hospital?'

'I'm not sure, but I can find out – why?'

'It's a long story. You remember Minki, I suppose?'

At the mention of her name, Peter blushed. 'Minki... how could I forget her? I adored her. Is she... alive?'

'Yes, thank God. But she's had a terrible time.'

'Tell me.'

Over the next half hour, Leila related Minki's story, ending with Clara's death.

'Clara died at this hospital in Hadamar. Hadamar is in Hesse. Now, it might just be a coincidence, but if you're investigating crimes in that area, perhaps you could look into it? After what you've told me, she may not have died of fit, but actually been murdered. If there's any evidence, perhaps you could find it.'

Peter shook his head in disbelief. 'That's awful. You know – we approach these things in such an intellectual fashion, but when it might have affected someone you know, suddenly it becomes... so tangible.'

'Minki has shown such strength, Peter. Her husband Max committed suicide and she spent the rest of the war in Augsburg with her father.' Leila leaned forward conspiratorially. 'Between you and me, she also worked for the resistance. She was the person who got my parents out of Germany, in fact. I owe her so much.'

'She did that? Wow... so she finally got off the sidelines.'

'Oh yes, she got off the sidelines all right. In fact, she's shown amazing courage.'

'She was an incredible woman,' said Peter thoughtfully.

'She *is* incredible... and she loved you very much, Peter – you must know that. Minki was devastated when you left.'

'I don't think I really understood what she felt, until it was too late.'

'Well, you were engaged to someone else, so I suppose it was inevitable that you'd break up with Minki.'

'The crazy thing is that when I got back to the US, I couldn't get Minki out of my mind. Mary and I split up. I never married.'

'Oh, Peter! Why didn't you write to Minki? She was broken-hearted. I always felt she only married Max on the rebound.'

Peter sighed. 'Oh no, that makes me feel even more guilty.'

'Peter, you can't blame yourself. I didn't tell you about Max and Clara to make you feel guilty. I was just explaining what had happened. But it was a shame... you were so good for her. Her life would have been quite different if you and she...' Leila paused, suddenly recalling her own wedding day, and how Minki had lost Peter's baby. She wondered if she should mention it, but decided against it. What use would it be? And besides, it wasn't her secret to tell.

'I understand what you're trying to say,' said Peter. 'I guess at the time, I wasn't sure of her – do you understand? I always felt nothing really mattered to Minki... as if she lived life on the surface.'

'I think that was true of her when she was young. Her beauty and her brilliance made her thoughtless at times, and she sometimes treated people very badly – men in particular. But she changed. Even before she lost Clara, she began to realise that she couldn't stand on the sidelines forever. Her husband working for Goebbels created a lot of problems. She had so many fights with him about the terrible things the regime was doing. In the end, she made an enemy of Goebbels. I often suspect he had something to do with Clara's kidnapping.'

'Leila... I'd love to see Minki again. Do you think she'd meet me?'

'I don't know, Peter. From her letters, she seems utterly absorbed in her family these days. I'm not sure she'd want to be reminded of the past – but I might be wrong.'

'I understand. But, perhaps you could ask her if she'd see me? There are things I ought to say, things I meant to say at the time.'

Leila was slightly taken aback by Peter's earnestness. 'Yes, Peter. Of course I'll ask her if she'll see you.'

The pair sat for a while, each lost in their own thoughts. Finally Peter clinked his glass with Leila's. 'Well, I think we should drink up, don't you, and go and see what all the fuss is about at Buckingham Palace.'

'I suppose we should. As good journalists, we really should not miss the spectacle.'

Peter took her arm, and guided her out onto the Strand, joining the crowds surging towards the palace.

42

AIRBORNE OVER EUROPE

SEPTEMBER 1945

Leila felt queasy. The waistband of her new American army uniform pencil skirt – made of scratchy olive drab – was pressing uncomfortably against her stomach. Sitting in the bucket seat of a military transport plane, which rocked and bounced as it headed for Frankfurt, she began to have second thoughts about her new venture. She could be at home now, in the cosy sitting room of her Hampstead cottage, with her parents and children. Instead, she was nauseous and uncomfortable in a draughty, rattling military plane, sitting next to an American army colonel who had ignored her ever since she sat down.

She eased her fingers beneath the waistband, and put the other hand over her mouth; she swallowed hard, praying she would not throw up.

'You OK?' asked the colonel, glancing over in her direction.

'I think so,' she replied uncertainly.

'You look a little green, that's all.' He had a southern drawl, which reminded her of Rhett Butler in *Gone With The Wind*.

'I'll be fine, thank you, sir.'

The plane settled a little and she looked out of the window onto the patchwork of green below.

'If you were reincarnated,' asked the colonel suddenly, 'what would you rather come back as – a man or a woman?'

It was such an odd question that Leila temporarily forgot her sickness. She presumed he was attempting to make conversation. Perhaps he had never met a woman in uniform before.

'Assuming that's a purely hypothetical question, I suppose I can answer in the same spirit. Preferably, I'd rather be a dormouse or a sunflower.'

He looked at her wide-eyed, and then reverted to ignoring her. She smiled quietly to herself, and another hour went by.

'I can't pretend I wasn't a little surprised to find you on board, Major,' he said suddenly. 'What does headquarters want you to do exactly?'

'Re-education, Colonel. Or, at least, that's the way Colonel Potter put it to me in London when he recruited me. I'd been working for ABSIE – with Brewster Morgan... Major Morgan?'

The Colonel shook his head. 'Don't know either of them.'

Suddenly the plane went into a dive, causing her stomach to lurch violently. The colonel pressed a packet of chewing gum into her hand. 'Chew this,' he advised. 'It works.'

Leila unwrapped the gum and put it into her mouth. As she closed her eyes, she felt the waves of nausea gradually subsiding.

It was only when they had landed at the Frankfurt military airport that she reopened her eyes. 'Thank you for the gum, Colonel – it really worked.'

'I'm glad,' said the colonel, unstrapping himself from his seat belt. 'Well, good luck, Major – I'm sure I'll see you around.'

·　·　·

Climbing down the steps of the plane that afternoon, Leila stood for a few moments, enjoying the last rays of the evening sun. It was momentous. She was back on German soil for the first time in a decade.

'Excuse me, Major – but are you heading for HQ?' The voice came from a young woman in uniform – the only other female on board.

Leila nodded.

'They told me there would be a jeep to pick us up,' said the girl, looking around.

Within minutes a fleet of cars drew up next to the plane, and the generals and colonels were driven off, leaving the two women to fend for themselves.

'Let's ask over there,' said the girl, heading for the makeshift reception building. 'I'm Penelope, by the way,' she said, holding out her hand. 'Lieutenant Penelope McMasters.'

'How do you do, Penelope. I'm Leila Labowski. Major Labowski, I suppose I should say. I've not really got used to all the army titles, yet.'

The young woman smiled. 'You new to the army, then?'

'You could say that, Lieutenant. What's your job here?'

'Secretarial work, mostly. Don't worry, Major – I'll sort out our transport.'

Inside the reception building, an attractive young German woman was chatting animatedly with a group of American GIs. She had blond permed hair and spoke surprisingly good English with an American accent.

'Major Labowski is expecting a car to take her to headquarters,' said Penelope briskly. 'Can you help?'

'Sure, I'll sort that out,' said the girl.

She made a couple of phone calls while giggling and flirting with the GIs, flashing her nylon-clad legs.

'Clearly, being friendly with GIs is the only way to get on round here,' muttered Penelope, laughing.

A few minutes later a large staff car arrived, and the two women sank gratefully into the back seat.

'This is the sort of car they normally send for three-star generals,' exclaimed Penelope. 'You obviously have friends in high places, Major.' She smiled at Leila. 'Still, I'm not complaining. It's probably the last luxury we'll experience for some time!'

It was dusk as they drove through the streets of Frankfurt. Leila was horrified. London after the Blitz had been bad enough, but this once-magnificent city had been reduced to rubble. Debris had been piled by the sides of the roads, and now almost the only traffic was US tanks, troop carriers and jeeps.

A grey fog lay over the city, which Leila at first presumed was mere condensation but soon realised was actually dust rising up from the decimated buildings. Through the gloom she spotted the odd person, walking hurriedly through the devastated streets. Men and women – it was hard to tell them apart – were busy collecting firewood from the ruins, or trundling belongings on makeshift carts. On the stairway of a bombed-out house sat a child with a flower in her hand. She waved at Leila as the car drove past, and Leila – not for the first time – thought of Clara.

It was well after dark when the car finally arrived at the American headquarters in Bad Homburg. The driver stopped at the guardhouse, set into the barbed wire perimeter. Leila and her companion passed their identity papers through the car window, and were waved through. Once inside the compound, it was like a different world. Light streamed from every building, and music blared from loudspeakers. In the well-lit streets, uniformed men and women strolled about happily, laughing and joking.

'This is the quartermaster's office,' said the driver. 'They'll assign you to your rooms. Good luck.'

Inside, Leila handed her papers and military orders to the quartermaster.

Frowning, he grabbed a telephone. 'Colonel, I have a female here with the rank of major. Where do you suggest I put her, sir?'

He listened for a moment, then put down the phone and dragged a couple of brown woollen blankets from the shelf behind him, which he handed to Leila. 'House number seven, Major – it's the first room on the right.'

The room was bare except for a light bulb hanging from the ceiling. There wasn't even a bed. Leila dropped the blankets on the floor and sat down on her suitcase, musing on the wisdom of her decision to come back to Germany.

There was a knock on the door. 'Major, it's me – Penelope.'

Leila opened the door. Penelope burst out laughing. 'I'm sorry, Major, I shouldn't laugh, but I told you it would be grim. Mine's just as bad. I suggest we go and get something to eat and hopefully to drink. The world always looks better when your stomach's full and you're a little tipsy.'

They joined a queue of people outside the dining hall, located in a brightly lit building at the end of the street. Leila had to shade her eyes as she walked in, so blinding were the lights.

'Can I buy you girls dinner?' A handsome lieutenant colonel took both women by their arms.

Penelope winked at Leila. 'Sure,' she said. He guided them to a table and poured them each a glass of red wine.

'French,' he said seductively.

'Nice,' said Penelope.

As Leila sipped the wine, she felt the tension of the

previous twelve hours seep away. After dinner they made their excuses and retreated to their barren rooms, where Leila wrapped herself in her blankets, lay down on the floor and slept.

She was woken by a banging on the door. 'Major, Major Labowski... it's Penelope. You must get up, or you'll miss breakfast.'

Leila dragged herself awake. It was barely light outside, but at least she had slept – surprisingly well, in fact. 'All right,' she called back sleepily.

'The bathroom's down the hall,' Penelope told her. 'You have to share – so don't be shy. One person bathes while the others use the basins. You'll get used to it. And we need to be in the dining hall by seven – the doors are locked after that.'

'Gosh,' said Leila, checking her watch. It was just before six. 'I'll get up now – thank you. I'll see you in there.'

'And don't forget your tokens,' Penelope called back to her.

'What tokens?'

'The quartermaster gave them to us last night – they're in an envelope. You have to hand them over for any food and goods you want. See you.'

Leila finally arrived in the dining room at ten minutes to seven, dressed in her army uniform, her tokens tucked into her uniform.

To her relief, she spotted a familiar face. It was Colonel Potter, the man who had recruited her in London. 'Major Labowski,' he said, taking her arm, 'good to see you've arrived safely. Come and sit with us.'

He led to her a table filled with officers of every rank from generals down. The officers' plates were piled high with food.

'You can have anything you like,' explained the colonel, pulling out a chair for Leila. 'Oatmeal, cereal, fruit, pancakes, ham and eggs, grapefruit, rolls, croissant – and coffee of course.'

'Gosh, what a huge choice.' Faced with such indulgence, Leila was almost overwhelmed. After the restricted diet everyone in London had endured for years, she suddenly lost her appetite.

'Just coffee and toast for me,' she said to the waitress – a pretty girl who spoke with a foreign accent.

'That waitress, where is she from, Colonel?'

'Could be anywhere,' he replied. 'We have all sorts here – Ukrainians, Czechs, Poles – all of them displaced persons. With us, they have good jobs, enough to eat and they're learning English – well, American English, at least.'

Leila laughed. She liked this man – he was open, friendly and honest.

'When you've finished breakfast, please come to my office. You'll find it next to the quartermaster's. I'd like to introduce you to my team.'

Twenty minutes later, Leila found herself in the colonel's office with a handful of Potter's senior staff.

'Our job,' the colonel began, 'is to carry out a programme of cultural reconstruction, throughout the American occupation zone. To that end, I'm delighted to introduce you all to Major Labowksi, who has vast experience of advising governments about the lives of women and children. She's been recruited by the American army to investigate the predicament of women and children in post-war Germany, and present a report on what form that programme of reconstruction should take. Would you like to say a few words, Major?'

Leila blushed to hear herself described as having 'vast experience of advising governments.' Her occasional meetings at the Foreign Office had always felt rather inconsequential.

'You're very kind, Colonel,' she began hesitantly, 'and I appreciate your faith in me. It is true to say that I have made a particular study of the issues affecting women in Germany. But I've been away from my country for over a decade and, in order to really find out what's going on, I'm going to need to meet people – in particular, the women and children you speak about. Before I write my report, I need to go on a fact-finding mission all over the country. How else can I work out how best we can help them?'

Colonel Potter studied her for a few moments. 'All right, Major. But I'll need to clear it with the general. If he approves it, I'm on board.'

43

AUGSBURG

Minki was sewing buttons onto one of Willie's shirts in the sitting room one evening when the phone rang. She picked up the receiver in the hall, but the line was poor. 'I'm sorry,' she shouted, 'but I can't really hear you.'

Eventually, a voice came through the static. 'Minki... it's Leila.'

'Who?'

'It's LEILA!'

'Leila! Oh, my goodness. How are you?'

'I'm all right... and I'm in Augsburg.'

'In Augsburg? How, why?'

'It's a long story. I'm in the American army.'

'What?'

'I'm in the ARMY! Working for the Americans. Can I come over... now? I'll be there in about half an hour. Or is it too late?'

'No, no of course not. Come now.'

'Thanks, and I've got a driver – can you put him and me up for the night?'

'A driver? Leila, I don't really understand, but yes, of course we can.'

Minki put down the phone, and ran to her father's study. 'Papa, you won't believe this, but my old friend, Leila... you remember her? Well, she's in Augsburg and is coming to stay the night.'

'How delightful,' replied Gunther. 'I'll get some wine from the cellar.'

They had recently found a new housekeeper – an older woman who had been widowed in the war, and needed a job and a place to stay. Rushing to the kitchen, Minki found her cleaning the range. 'Heidi, Heidi, can you can stop what you're doing, please. I've got two guests arriving any minute. Can you run upstairs and make up two beds – two different rooms?'

Minki quickly prepared a simple meal for her guests – some cold meat, bread and beer – and then busied herself in the sitting room, stoking up the fire and plumping the cushions. Finally, she heard the whine of an engine. She went outside to see an open-topped jeep roaring up the drive, scattering gravel. Minki ran towards it, arms outstretched. 'Leila, Leila...'

Leila was so thrilled at seeing her friend that she didn't even bother to open the door of the jeep, but instead hitched up her tight army skirt and jumped out. 'Minki, Minki!'

The two women fell into each other's arms, while the jeep driver carried their bags inside the grand entrance hall, where Leila made the introductions. 'Minki, this is Corporal Harding, my driver – otherwise known as Joe. Joe, this is my friend Minki von Zeller.'

Harding, who had been looking around, wide-eyed, held out his hand. 'How do, ma'am... It's a great house – like something out of the movies.'

Minki smiled. 'Joe, let me take you to the kitchen, where you can get something to eat, and then our housekeeper, Heidi, will show you your room.'

.   .   .

When Minki brought Leila through to the sitting room, Gunther was waiting by the mantelpiece, a fire glowing merrily in the grate. 'Leila, my dear girl – how wonderful. I couldn't believe it when Minki told me you were on your way. I don't think we've met since Minki's wedding.'

They embraced.

'I've opened a bottle of champagne,' said Gunther. 'I've been keeping it for a special occasion.'

'Oh, I'm honoured,' said Leila, raising her glass. 'Here's to us... and to old friends...'

After a brief dinner, the two women settled in front of the fire.

'There's so much to discuss,' said Leila. 'I hardly know where to begin.'

'How long can you stay?'

'Sadly, only tonight. I have to go back to work tomorrow morning. Joe is taking me north to start a proper tour of the country.'

'It sounds very important,' said Minki.

'I'm not sure about that, but it's going to be hard work – that's for sure. But I don't want to talk about my job, I want to hear about you. So much has happened in the last few years... Tell me everything.'

'I'm not sure there's any point, is there?' said Minki. 'You already know the bare bones, and I try not to dwell on the past. I have to keep going forward – for the sake of the boys and my father.'

Leila nodded. 'That's very sensible.'

'But it doesn't stop me thinking about Clara all the time. We buried her here, you know – next to the family tomb.'

'Really? They sent back her body?'

Minki nodded. 'About a month after I'd visited Hadamar, the coffin arrived in a hearse. It was a nice coffin too, made of solid oak, with a brass plate. I was surprised that they had taken so much trouble. Maybe it was because I mentioned I was a friend of Goebbels.'

Leila nodded. 'Probably... I never got Viktor's body back. I just received a letter telling me he'd died of TB, along with a few of his things, including his watch – isn't that odd? You'd have thought it would have been stolen, but there it was with his suit and shirt and shoes... all rather meticulous.'

'I'm so sorry about Viktor,' said Minki. 'You must miss him very much. And it must be dreadful not knowing where he's buried.'

'Oh, I doubt he's buried anywhere,' said Leila darkly. 'I suspect he was incinerated. If he was buried, it would have been in a mass grave somewhere.' She bit her lip, her eyes filling with tears.

Minki wrapped her arm round her. 'I'm so sorry... at least I can visit Clara's grave each week. My father thinks I've finally found religion, but I haven't. It's just that the graveside is the only place I can talk to her in peace. I'll take you to see her, if you like. I've made it as beautiful as possible.'

'I'd like that.'

'The thing is, Leila, I still don't really understand how it happened – her death, I mean. How can you die from a fit – and in a hospital of all places? Sometimes I worry that something else happened, something they wouldn't tell me at the time... a dark secret that has been kept from me all these years.'

'Like what?'

'I don't know... they were sterilising girls in there, weren't they? Maybe she died during the operation, and they covered it up... or perhaps she was murdered by another inmate? When I went to Hadamar looking for her, a young man ran towards me when I was getting into my car, begging me to help him. He told me they'd killed his brother. The nurse chased after him, and made light of it, but what if it was true? What if they did kill that boy's brother... what if they killed my little girl?'

Leila reached over and grasped Minki's hand in hers. 'Oh, darling. These are all agonising scenarios which must torture you. But would you really want to know if she'd been murdered? Isn't it easier to think of her dying of an illness?'

'Curiously enough, no. I realise it sounds strange, but it's the not knowing that torments me. At night, I start imagining all sorts of frightening things – and I think I'm going to go out of my mind. If I just knew for certain what happened, there's a chance I could find peace – however painful the journey might be.'

'I understand, I really do. Like you, I worried for a long time about how Viktor died. Was it really TB, or something much worse? But at some point you have to let it go... to move on, do what you can for the people still living. For me that means the children, my parents... and my work, of course. But I can't pretend I'm not angry at the destruction of his life. There was still so much for him to do.'

'That's it, Leila,' replied Minki. 'I'm so angry that Clara was taken when she was just starting out on life. She was so bright, Leila – so clever and funny and beautiful.'

Suddenly, Minki began to weep. Leila wrapped her in her arms, rocking her.

After a while, Minki was able to wipe away her tears. 'I'm sorry... it just comes over me sometimes, like a wave.'

'I understand.'

'You know, Leila, I don't think you can ever prepare yourself as a mother – for the intensity of your feelings. A mother's love is so intense, it's almost unbearable. I dream about Clara, sometimes, and she's so *present*. I wake up and think I could reach out and touch her – almost as if she's still alive...'

'You must be careful – at a certain point one must accept

that someone is dead, in order to grieve properly. I still dream of Viktor and have the same sensation as you – that he's alive – but I know in reality that he's not.'

'You're right, of course, Leila. I suppose the truth is that a mother's love doesn't end with the physical loss of a person. It lasts forever.'

Minki reached over and took a cigarette from a silver box. She lit it, inhaling deeply.

Leila sipped her wine. 'Minki... I wasn't sure if I should mention this, but I met Peter in London.'

'Peter?'

'Peter Fischer.'

'Good Lord. I've not thought about him for years. Why was he in London?'

'He joined the American Army, and was stationed there briefly. In fact, he's in Germany now...' Leila paused, wondering whether to continue. 'Oh Minki, I don't think he ever really got over you.'

'Oh, don't be ridiculous,' said Minki, pouring them both another glass of wine. 'All that was over twenty years ago. It was young love – the sort that can never last. He was probably right to go back to America, and almost certainly right to leave me – I was a much more complicated person then. Besides, he got married, didn't he?'

'No. He never married.'

Minki's eyes widened. 'Really? Why not?'

'He said it was because he still loved you.'

'Well, well... Did he actually say that when you met in London?'

'Yes... and I think he meant it.'

'That's quite sad, isn't it?' Minki paused, adding wistfully, 'I really did love him, you know. Will you see him, here in Germany?'

'Yes. In fact, I'm going to accompany him on some of his work as part of my fact-finding mission.'

'Well, give him my love, won't you? Maybe we'll meet again some day.'

'I know he'd like that,' said Leila.

The pair sat for a moment, watching the flickering flames of the fire.

'Now,' said Minki, 'enough of the past... you must tell me more about your work – and what you're doing here.'

'Oh that... well, one of my tasks is to start a new women's magazine. It will attempt to show the women of Germany a different ideology – a different way to live.' Leila paused, and then leaned forward. 'There's a job for you, if you want it?'

'For me?'

'Of course, you'd be perfect for it – all those years editing women's pages, plus your natural instincts as a journalist – I can't think of anyone better to be my deputy editor.'

'Me... your deputy? But I've not worked for years.'

'I know that. But it's like riding a bike – you never forget. Look, Minki, I came to see you today because I love you and you're my best friend, but also because you're one of the best journalists I've ever met. Promise me you'll think about it?'

Minki smiled. 'Well, I'm very flattered, obviously. Where will the magazine be based? I can't leave the boys, you see.'

'In Munich, I hope. I'm even exploring using the old *Munich Post* printing presses, if they're still intact.'

'Well, I'll certainly think about it, all right?'

'Good. I have to go up north tomorrow, but I'll be back in a month or so. We can talk about it more then.'

As the pair stood on the landing, hugging each other goodnight, Leila wondered if she should have been more open with Minki about her plans for the next few days. For the truth was that, as part of her tour of the country, she intended to travel to Hadamar and try to solve the mystery of Clara's death. By chance, Peter Fischer was now based at the hospital, and had begun the gruesome task of investigating exactly what had gone on there in the previous decade. Leila hoped he might unearth some vital information that would clarify how Clara had died. Had she really had an epileptic fit, as Minki had been told? Or had she died during a sterilisation operation, or even been murdered – another victim of the Nazis' ruthless policy of extermination? Until this evening, she had presumed Minki would be unable to handle the truth, but after their conversation she now felt sure that whatever she might discover, knowing how Clara died was the only way Minki could ever lay her child to rest.

44

HADAMAR

It was mid-morning, and the sky was a cloudless bright blue, as Corporal Harding drove his jeep down the steep road that led to Hadamar.

'We're looking for a psychiatric hospital, Joe,' Leila shouted over the roar of the engine. 'I was told it's a grim-looking grey building on a hillside overlooking the town.'

'Is that it up there, Major?'

'Yes, that looks like it.'

At the end of the road leading up to the hospital, Joe stopped the jeep at a US army checkpoint. 'Major Labowski to see Major Fischer of the war crimes investigations team.'

'Go through, ma'am,' said the guard, saluting.

Joe parked the jeep in front of the hospital. Leila climbed out and looked around. The hospital itself was a long two-storey brick building, surrounded by well-tended gardens. An unkempt young man was raking fallen leaves from the drive and placing them in a wheelbarrow.

'There must be an army canteen somewhere, Joe. Why don't you go and have something to eat. I could be some time.'

The main hospital entrance was in the centre of the building. Leila pressed the bell-push and waited. The door was finally opened by a young soldier, who saluted.

'Major Labowski to see Major Fischer,' Leila said firmly.

'Yes, ma'am. I'll get word to him immediately. Please take a seat.'

The entrance hall was impressive, with a stone-flagged floor and high ceiling. Leila sat on a high-backed chair in one corner, observing the bustling activity. Men and women in uniform came in and out through the front door, chatting and laughing. In many ways its atmosphere resembled the Bad Homburg headquarters. The army, Leila had observed, had a way of taking a space over completely – of making it their own.

Peter Fischer arrived shortly afterwards. 'Leila! I'm so glad to see you. Let's go to my office.'

He led her along the corridor and, for the first time since she had arrived, Leila saw civilians – emaciated, sad-looking individuals who were sweeping and mopping floors. At the end of the corridor, Peter stopped outside an office marked MATRON.

'This is my office – ignore the sign! They haven't got around to changing it yet.' He smiled. 'It's the cause of a few jokes around here.'

He held the door open for her. 'Please come in.'

The room was cramped, and Peter had to take a pile of files off the visitor's chair to make room for her to sit down. 'I'm sorry about the mess, we're a bit short of space.'

'It's fine, Peter. Those people I saw just now – mopping the floors – are they residents here?'

Peter nodded. 'When we first arrived, there were still a few people living here – patients who had somehow become domestic servants – well, they were more like slaves really, because they received no wages.

'We're trying to contact their families, but some of them have been so traumatised they don't even remember their names. Until we can get them settled, it seemed kinder to keep them on, pay them a wage and give them a roof over their heads. Coffee?'

'Thank you, yes. So, how's it going?'

He sighed as he laid the coffee cup in front of her. 'You know, Leila, there are times in life when the sheer brutality of one's fellow man seems impossible to believe. The things we've uncovered here are just appalling. To be honest, no adjective that I can think of is up to the task.'

'Tell me...'

'If I may, I'll start at the beginning – and forgive me if you already know some of the background. This place was originally set up as a psychiatric hospital. But back in the mid-thirties they turned it into a sterilisation centre for people they deemed "unworthy to breed".' He held up his fingers, making quotation marks in the air.

'I knew about that,' said Leila. 'Before I left Germany, I wrote a piece for the *Post* about the new law. After that, sterilisation quickly became widespread – it was a disgrace.'

'Well in 1939 they went a step further and the whole hospital became... how should I put it... a centre for extermination.'

Leila felt her heart thump; had Clara been 'exterminated'?

'Did you have any foreknowledge of that?' Peter asked.

'Before I left Germany, we feared it might happen. Doctors at the time were enthusiastic about ridding society of people they considered useless.'

Peter shook his head sadly.

'Tell me Peter, the extermination you've uncovered, was it sanctioned officially, or was it overreach by the local physicians?

'Oh, it was sanctioned, all right – from the top. And it was incredibly well organised. We've uncovered an organisation called Aktion T4, which was run out of Berlin by Hitler's chief medical officer. He and his team made the decisions about who would be sterilised, and who exterminated. They selected people who were considered useless to society – the disabled, or children with congenital illnesses, the mentally ill and so on. They scoured mental hospitals and children's homes all over the country, and transported people to six centres, one of which was Hadamar. The man who ran the killing operation here was Dr Wahlmann. We have him in custody already, along with some of his staff. We're interrogating them, of course, but they maintain they were simply following orders.'

'I suspect that will be a common excuse,' said Leila sadly. 'As I mentioned when we arranged this meeting, one of the reasons I'm here is to see if we can find out what happened to Clara von Zeller – Minki's daughter. Did you find any records relating to her death?'

Peter nodded, and picked up a fat leather tome from the floor and placed it on his desk. 'When you rang and said you were coming, I dug this out.' He flipped the tome open and swung it round to face Leila. 'There', he said pointing to her name. 'It shows the date of her arrival, the date she died, her grave number – eighty-seven – and finally the date she was exhumed and sent back to Augsburg. It's all there...'

'Cause of death,' Leila read out loud, 'epileptic fit.' She glanced up at Peter. 'So that would seem fairly conclusive then?'

'Perhaps... but remember, that's just the word of the doctor – and if I'm honest, so many lies have been told here it's hard to evaluate how truthful those records really are.'

Leila sipped her coffee.

'I wonder, Leila, would you like to see around the place? It would enable you to understand what went on here.'

Leila nodded. 'Yes – I should see it all.'

Peter rose from his desk. 'OK, but I warn you, what I'm about to show you will come as a shock.'

Peter steered her down a series of dark corridors, past empty wards, until they reached a side entrance. Opening the door, he led her round to the back of the hospital, and stopped in a clearing dominated by a large black barn.

'What's this?' asked Leila, puzzled. 'How odd to have a wooden agricultural building outside a hospital.'

'Oh, it's not any old agricultural building,' said Peter, pulling apart the wide barn doors and leading her inside. 'This place was integral to the whole operation. Let me explain. The victims were transported from other hospitals around the country in old school or postal buses. As soon as they arrived, the buses were driven inside, and the barn doors locked behind them. The only way out was through this side door.'

Peter pushed open a door in the side of the building. 'Follow me.'

The path led to the hospital building itself, inside which was an empty reception hall.

'This is where the horror really began,' Peter explained. 'The staff who had accompanied the victims would get them undressed, pretending they were just going to be examined by the doctor. The women were allowed to wear old army coats to protect their modesty. They were then funnelled through this room here.' He led Leila to a smaller room off the main hall. 'Here, they checked their personal data – names, ages, medical history and so on. So far, the victims might have thought it was all above board. But as one physician examined them, another was sitting at an adjacent desk assigning a false cause of death to each patient. Effectively, their death certificate was written before they even left the room.'

'Surely not?' gasped Leila.

'I'm afraid so... come this way.' Peter held open a door leading to a second room. 'This is where the victims were weighed, measured and photographed.' He paused, and turned to Leila. 'I mean... why would they do that? They were going to kill them. It's just so absurdly meticulous.'

Leila felt barely able to breathe. It brought back memories of the parcel of clothes she had been sent after Viktor's death – once again meticulously folded and labelled.

'OK,' Peter continued, 'so now we come to the end stage. The victims were led down this staircase here – watch your step, Leila, it's quite steep. At this point other personnel took over.'

Leila found herself standing in a basement room; it had no windows and the ceiling was covered with pipework.

'Is this...?' She couldn't finish her sentence.

Peter nodded. 'This was "the death shower", so called because the victims believed they were going to have a shower. Up to sixty people at a time were forced in here. Some of them became suspicious at this point and fought back. We've been told that violence occurred – you can just imagine, can't you, the sense of terror and helplessness. Anyway, the doors were locked – they're air-raid doors, so totally airtight – gas was pumped through the pipes and, within minutes, everybody was dead. We now realise they were using these hospitals to test the whole gas chamber concept, which was later used so widely in the concentration camps like Auschwitz.'

Leila felt her legs give way. To actually be standing in the space where thousands of innocent people had been exterminated was almost unbearable.

'I'm sorry,' said Peter, taking her arm. 'Perhaps we should leave now?'

'No, carry on, Peter. I need to see and understand everything. Is there more?'

'All right, if you're sure. So, once the people were dead, the "disinfectors" – that's what they called the staff who disposed of the bodies – turned on a ventilator to extinguish the poisoned air, entered the chamber and extracted any gold teeth. At that point, any corpses the physicians had earlier identified as suitable for dissection were moved to the pathology lab, and the rest were burned in the crematorium. For a while the ovens were running twenty-four hours a day. It's said that the black smoke from the chimneys could be seen for miles around. The stench must have been appalling.'

Leila again felt her legs giving way beneath her.

'Hey... I think it's time I got you out of here and into the fresh air.' Peter helped her back up the staircase, down a corridor and outside. He guided her to a wooden bench overlooking a lawn, where they both sat, and Leila breathed deeply, grateful for the fresh smell of newly mown grass.

'I'm sorry,' said Peter, 'but I did warn you it would be shocking. I've spent so much time here trying to understand the process that I've become inured to it. I fear I may also have lost a little empathy on the way.'

'I do understand, Peter. But, God... the inhumanity of it...' She looked over at him, tears streaming down her face. She fumbled in her pocket and retrieved a handkerchief. 'When I worked at the BBC, we ran a news story about the burnings – the bishop of this area had spoken out about it.'

'I heard about that. It was back in '41, I think.'

Leila nodded.

'As I understand it,' Peter went on, 'the authorities stopped the gassing and the cremation at that point. But sadly, the killing didn't stop – they just used more conventional means. And instead of burning them, the bodies were buried.'

'What do you mean by conventional means?'

'Lethal overdoses, starvation – the sorts of things that could go on in any hospital and not raise suspicion. When we broke into the pharmacy here we found over ten kilos of barbiturates – the sort used to sedate patients. But they can easily kill if the dose is high enough.'

'How many people were killed in this way?'

'More than you can imagine – thousands.'

'Did anyone survive?'

'A few, yes. We interviewed one nurse who explained they sometimes allowed inmates to live if they could be put to work. Those were the people you saw working in the garden or around the building.'

'I know it's a long shot... but might Clara have been one of those people?'

Peter shook his head. 'I checked the staff list and there's no one working here called Clara von Zeller.'

'I see,' said Leila. 'That's disappointing. I wonder, could I see the cemetery?'

Peter led her through the hospital grounds, until they reached a set of steep stone steps winding upwards. They finally arrived at the top of the hill, where the cemetery was laid out before them, with grassy mounds marking the graves.

'There are no headstones,' Peter explained. 'Instead they wrote numbers on little wooden crosses that correspond to the numbers in the ledgers.'

'It looks so orderly...'

'It does on the surface, yes. But I have to tell you that we've already begun to examine the graves, and all is not what it seems.'

'What do you mean?'

'When you think of a cemetery you imagine neat coffins, one in each hole in the ground, don't you?'

Leila nodded.

'That's not what we have here. We found evidence of multiple bodies simply... tossed into holes in the ground. As we've exhumed them, we can see how painfully thin they were. Some were missing their heads – they'd been sliced clean off. So what we have here is evidence of a war crime. It's certainly not a graveyard as any normal person would understand it.'

Leila felt her heart racing again. 'Leila told me that she got Clara's body back in a coffin...'

'If they sent her back in a coffin, they would have acquired one specially, and placed the body in it. To be honest, Leila, from the evidence I've seen so far, I would doubt they even chose the right body. It's really hard to identify anyone when they've been in a pit for a while. And when there are ten or twenty corpses in each grave – some with their heads missing, some so rotten their faces have been destroyed, or eaten by animals – it's hard to tell who is who.'

Leila shuddered. 'How awful. Have you examined Clara's grave yet... you said it was number eighty-seven.'

Peter shook his head. 'The team are working as carefully as they can through the cemetery. I'm afraid they started with the lower numbers. Inevitably, it's a slow process, as we're gathering criminal evidence for a court of law. We do also try to identify bodies – although, as I say, that's obviously not easy...'

'I understand,' said Leila. She walked up and down the lines of crosses until she found number eighty-seven. The soil seemed firm, grass still growing on the surface. 'Minki came here, you know, and said she couldn't believe her daughter was buried here... and I think I understand that. It seems so impersonal. But after everything you've told me, is it possible that her body is, in fact, still here?'

Peter nodded.

'God, what a mess.'

'Once all the graves have been examined, I suppose we might find the evidence you're looking for, but it's been, what, four years since she died. It will be nigh on impossible to identify her.'

Leila took a handkerchief from her pocket, and wiped her eyes. She looked out across the valley, admiring the vineyards in the distance, the neat fields, the animals dotted across the landscape. She turned back to Peter. 'You just can't imagine something so dreadful happening in a place that is so beautiful.'

Back in the hospital, Leila took Peter's arm. 'Would you object if I spoke to some of the civilian staff here? It would be helpful for my research about women and children – and I might find someone who remembers Clara, or knows something about her death.'

'All right. I'll set you up with an office.'

'Thanks... an office would be useful, but first, I might just walk around a little. Is that allowed?'

'You're in uniform, so... yes. If anyone objects, refer them to me.'

Leila spent an hour or two wandering around. All the wards were empty. From time to time she came upon a few domestic staff – washing windows, or mopping floors. Most seemed too frightened or nervous to talk, and she realised it was going to be hard to get them to open up. On her way back to Peter's office, she stopped at the entrance to a small anteroom where a young woman, dressed in an apron and a cap, was scrubbing skirting boards on her hands and knees. As soon as the girl noticed her, she leapt to her feet and backed away.

'It's all right,' said Leila, sensing the woman's fear. 'I won't hurt you. I just wanted to talk.'

The woman didn't reply. Instead she knelt back down, and continued her cleaning.

'You're doing a great job,' said Leila. 'Do you like your work?'

The woman shrugged.

'I'd love to talk to you, if you have time.'

The woman glanced up, and studied Leila for a moment. Eventually she stood up, stretching her back as if it ached, and dropped her rag in her bucket of water.

'Come and sit down next to me,' Leila suggested, patting the chair beside her.

But the woman still hung back, so Leila took a bar of army-issue chocolate from her jacket pocket and held it out. 'Do you want some chocolate?'

The woman approached timidly. As she drew closer, it was obvious she was not a woman at all, but a mere girl – maybe no more than fourteen or fifteen. Thin and pale-faced, her brown eyes gleamed for a moment, and she grabbed the chocolate. Putting a piece into her mouth, she closed her eyes as if in ecstasy.

'Is it good?' asked Leila. 'I have more. Please come and sit down.'

The girl sat gingerly on the edge of the seat, and ate another square of chocolate.

'Have you worked here long?'

The girl shrugged.

'How old are you?'

Another shrug. 'I don't know.'

'What's your name?'

The girl frowned, as if struggling to remember. Leila wondered if she'd been drugged – she seemed so silent and repressed.

'Margarethe,' she said, finally.

'Good... Margarethe – that's a pretty name. Were you a patient here?'

The girl nodded.

'Do you have family?'

The girl's eyes filled with tears and she nodded again.

'Perhaps I could contact them for you?'

Again, the girl gave a little nod.

'Can you write? You could write down their names for me?'

She handed the girl a notebook and a pen, but Margarethe stared at them blankly. It occurred to Leila that she might never have learned to read or write. 'Tell me their names, and I'll write them down.'

The girl gave Leila her family name, and slowly her story unfolded. She had been born in the east of Germany, she said, and had struggled at school.

'They said I was... not normal. A doctor came and took me away. I had an operation – it hurt.' She clutched at her abdomen, and tears came into her eyes.

Leila reached over and clasped her hands. 'I'm so sorry, but no one will hurt you any more, I promise. I'll write to your parents and we'll take you home, all right?'

The girl nodded. 'Thank you.'

As Leila stood up to leave, a thought occurred to her. 'I wonder... do you remember a girl who was here – about your age? She was called Clara.'

The girl shook her head.

'Are there any other women here... women who work here, I mean? I'd like to meet them.'

The girl nodded.

'Can you take me to them?'

The girl stood up and held out her hand.

'Do you want more chocolate?' asked Leila.

Margarethe shook her head. 'No. Follow me.'

Leila followed her along the corridor and downstairs to the bowels of the building. There was a smell of carbolic, and steam filled the air. Leila realised they must be near the hospital laundry.

Margarethe led Leila down a narrow corridor, past a series of pipes and finally into a small room. Through the steam, Leila could just make out the slim shape of a woman, standing with her back turned, pushing a sheet through an iron wringer.

'Irma,' said the girl, pointing at the woman's back.

Hearing her name, the girl turned round. Leila gasped. She was looking into the face of her friend Minki, when they had first met at university. This girl had the same golden hair, the same bright-blue eyes and almost ethereal beauty.

'You say this is Irma?'

Margarethe nodded.

'No,' said Leila, 'this is not Irma... this is Clara von Zeller.'

The blond girl stared wide-eyed at Leila. 'Clara...' she repeated. 'My name is Clara.'

'Yes, I know, my darling. And my name is Leila. I'm a very good friend of your mother's. Oh, Clara – I've come to take you home.'

45

THE JOURNEY HOME

That night, Leila checked them both into a hotel. Here, Clara had a bath and something to eat. Finally, a little colour returned to her cheeks.

'Would you like me to telephone your mother?'

Clara nodded.

Leila dialled Minki's number. 'Minki, darling. I have some news. I'm in Hadamar, and I need you to sit down.'

'Why are you in Hadamar? What news? What are you talking about?'

'Darling, you don't understand – it's good news, the best news you can imagine. Clara is alive, and she's all right. She's standing next to me now. I'll put her on.'

Leila handed Clara the phone. 'Say something, Clara.'

Clara, still disoriented and frightened, seemed unable to speak. She merely listened to her mother weeping. Finally she spoke – softly, almost in a whisper. 'Mutti, it's me, I'm here....' But could say no more

Leila gently retrieved the phone. 'Minki, I'll drive Clara

home tomorrow morning. We're in a hotel for the night. I'll try and get as much out of her as I can tonight, and then put her to bed.'

Leila sat with Clara and gradually the girl began to open up a little.

'Soon after I arrived, I had a fit, and the nurse came and sat with me. Afterwards we talked, and she was nice to me. She said it was wrong what they were doing and that she would look after me. When I next had a fit, she hid me from the other staff. And she gave me extra food. After a while, my fits stopped... I don't know why.'

'People grow out of them sometimes,' said Leila sympathetically.

'That's what the nurse said. One day, she told me that she had arranged for me to work in the laundry, but I should call myself Irma, not Clara. I was to say I was an orphan. She said if I worked hard they might let me stay. So I worked really hard. I didn't mind it in the laundry... it was warm in the winter. I did the washing and put things through the wringer. I caught my fingers sometimes.' She held out her hand to Leila. A couple of her fingers were badly bruised. 'Then I had to dry everything on big airers up in the ceiling. After that, I had to iron, and fold and store. Storing was the best bit.'

'Why?'

'Because I was allowed to leave the laundry for a while and walk round the hospital with a trolley while I put the sheets away.'

Leila squeezed Clara's hand. Her description of life in the hospital was heartbreaking. Suddenly, the child yawned and rubbed her eyes.

'You must be tired,' Leila said kindly. 'Let's get you to bed – we've got a long drive home tomorrow.'

. . .

The following morning Leila found a clothes shop and used her dollars to buy Clara a new dress, coat and shoes. The girl joined Leila in the back of the jeep, in a smart navy dress and coat, with Joe's army coat over her knees, holding tightly onto Leila's hand.

Late in the afternoon, they arrived at the outskirts of Augsburg. To Leila's surprise, Clara began to weep.

'What is it, darling?'

'I'm just happy,' replied Clara. 'I remember this place. I came here when I was little to see Grandpa.'

'That's right, darling... that's where we're going. Mutti lives with Grandpa now.'

As the jeep roared up the drive, Minki rushed out of the house, followed by her sons and father. She ran towards it, screaming: 'Clara, Clara...'

'She's here, Minki. She's alive!' Leila shouted, jumping down onto the drive.

Minki stood by the jeep gazing at her child sitting quietly on the back seat, as if she couldn't believe what she was seeing. Clara, who seemed equally confused, tentatively climbed out and stood for a second, staring at her mother. But as soon as Minki opened her arms to her daughter, Clara fell into them. Soon Gunther and the boys gathered round.

'Mutti, can we cuddle her?' the two boys chorused. They covered her with kisses and hugged her tightly.

'Don't squeeze her too hard,' said Minki, 'you'll frighten her.'

Gunther took control, wrapped an arm round Clara's shoulder, and steered her into the house.

'Don't get too excited, boys,' he said as the family gathered in the sitting room. 'Let her get her bearings and relax a little. She's had a long journey.'

As Clara sat down on the sofa, Willie and Felix knelt on either side of her, kissing her hands and stroking her face – just as they had done as little children when she had a fit.

Minki stood watching her three children, clinging tightly to Leila's arm.

'I can't believe it, Leila – am I dreaming?'

'No... it's real. She's really here – safe and well.'

Minki turned to her friend. 'I simply don't have the words to thank you, Leila. But... thank you.' Tears streamed down her face.

'You don't need to thank me,' replied Leila, hugging her. 'I'm just so relieved she made it.'

Eventually Leila pulled away. 'Minki, I really should go. You and Clara must both be exhausted, and you need some private time together.'

She kissed her friend on the cheek and went out into the hall to get her coat.

Minki followed her. 'Please, Leila... don't go yet. I'm frightened... what if I don't know how to be a mother to her? We've been apart for so long.'

'Do you remember when she was born?' asked Leila.

Minki nodded. 'I was frightened then too, wasn't I?'

'You were, but you went to that hospital and you took care of her. Now, you have to do it again. One day at a time... all right?'

Minki nodded. 'Thank you.'

'And if you need anything, leave a message for me at army headquarters.' She took a business card out of her jacket pocket and laid it on the hall table. 'I'll do anything to help.'

Over the following weeks, Leila continued her journey around the country, researching for her magazine. She gathered an initial picture of the horrors of war and the difficulties of life in post-war Germany.

There was bomb damage, of course, and poverty. But what distressed her more than anything were the thousands of children living on the streets, who had been forced into a life of petty crime. They formed themselves into gangs, and were forced to steal just to survive.

In December, she relocated to Munich to begin work on the magazine. Her offices were in Beethovenplatz. Once a government building, it had now been taken over by the Americans and rebranded as the Amerikahaus. Here, the citizens of Munich were encouraged to visit the library, where they could read all about America in books and magazines.

She was billeted in a fine old house in the centre of the city. Her housemates were seven other journalists embedded with the American army. Leila's bedroom was the original sitting room of the house. With its high ceilings and marble fireplace, it reminded her of the sitting room at the apartment she had once shared with Viktor.

As Christmas approached, she found herself thinking wistfully of their life together. One evening after work, she couldn't resist the temptation to go and look at their old apartment. In the fading light, she walked along the riverbank until she found herself standing outside the building that had once been her home.

The lights were just coming on all over the city, and as she looked up at the first floor she noticed the apartment was in darkness. For a moment, Leila wondered if it might be uninhabited. Perhaps, she thought, she could track down the landlord and take over the lease? But suddenly the lights went on in the sitting room, and a young woman appeared at the window and slowly closed the curtains. The sense of disappointment took Leila by surprise, and she burst into tears. It seemed so unjust that someone else was sleeping in her and Viktor's bedroom, eating in their kitchen, closing their curtains.

She had been forced to leave many of her possessions behind when Viktor was imprisoned, and now she wondered if these interlopers were using her china, sitting on her sofa, or writing at Viktor's desk. She walked up the steps to the main front door and considered ringing the bell, demanding admittance. Perhaps the new inhabitants would take pity on her, and let her in; perhaps they might even allow her to take some of her things away. But then she thought better of it. What was the point? It was not the apartment she missed but her husband. Without him, the apartment was just a collection of inanimate objects.

She turned away and began to walk back along the river, towards her lodgings. It came to her then that all that really mattered in life were the people she loved: Sofia, Axel and her parents – all now safely in England. She tried to imagine what each would be doing now. Sofia had started at university a few weeks before Leila had left for Germany. She had since written, excitedly telling her mother that she had bought a bike and was now cycling everywhere. Perhaps she would now be in a pub with friends, or studying at her little desk in her attic room. Axel was still living at home with her parents in the cottage on the Heath, studying for his school certificate. Leila could imagine her mother cajoling him to do his homework at the kitchen table. Perhaps her father would be in the shed at the bottom of the garden, making something. He had set up a workbench soon after he arrived in England, and had settled to a sort of routine, mending people's jewellery.

Arriving back at her lodgings, she found a letter from Peter Fischer.

Dearest Leila,

I hope you're well. With Christmas approaching I wondered if I might invite myself to spend it with you? I'll find a hotel to stay in but I'd love to take you out for a swanky meal or two. If you agree, I'll aim to arrive on Christmas Eve. Do you think there's a chance we might visit Minki while I'm with you?

That evening, Leila wrote back saying she'd be delighted to spend Christmas with him, and then rang Minki from the communal phone in the hall.

'How are you getting on?' she asked. 'How's Clara?'

'Oh, pretty well – Clara is still very quiet. She's in shock, I suppose. But the doctor is pleased with her. Incredibly, it turns out she was never sterilised – so there's no physical damage. But mentally and emotionally...' Her voice trailed off.

'It'll take time, but I'm so relieved that physically she's still... intact. How are the boys?'

'I think they're in shock too. They keep wanting to hold her hand. It's sweet. But eventually, I suppose, they'll get used to having her at home. Of course, she's missed so much education and normal life – but I have to hope she'll get there.'

'With you as her mother, I'm sure she will... Look, changing the subject completely, Peter Fischer has been in touch. He's coming down to spend Christmas with me in Munich, and we wondered if we could come and see you?'

'Of course. I'd love to see both of you. Look, I've got an idea – why don't you come and spend Christmas with us? We've got plenty of room, and it would be wonderful for us all to be together.'

'Are you really sure? That would be lovely – my digs are not exactly festive.'

'Of course I'm sure. But we've still got rationing, so there won't be a huge amount to eat.'

'Oh, don't worry about food or drink – the Americans have an endless supply of both! I'll ask Peter to bring a contribution – it's the least he can do.'

Peter arrived in Munich on Christmas Eve, driving his own army jeep. As they loaded Leila's bag into the back seat, she noticed a large ham, a turkey and several bottles of wine hidden under a tarpaulin.

'Oh good, you managed to find some supplies. I won't ask where they came from.'

'Best not,' he replied, smiling. 'Suffice it to say, I dropped in on the PX at Bad Homburg headquarters, and they will be having a slightly less generous Christmas meal than they might have done!'

As they drove the few miles to Augsburg, Peter admitted to feeling nervous. 'It's ridiculous, Leila,' he shouted over the roar of the jeep's engine. 'But I feel like a teenager on a first date.'

'But Peter – you're not on a date,' she shouted back. 'You're just visiting an old friend who's been through a very hard time.'

'I understand. But I can't help thinking... perhaps Minki doesn't really want me there – maybe she was just being polite.'

'Oh, Peter, don't be so silly. To be honest, I don't suppose she's thought about you at all. I'm sorry if that wounds your male pride. But all that matters to her now is having Clara back. A big romantic reunion is not high on her list of priorities.'

'No, of course, you're right.'

Coming up the drive, Leila noticed a large wreath made of winter greenery hanging on the grand front door. It looked so cheerful and full of life – a symbol somehow of a brighter future. Minki welcomed them into the hall, where a fire blazed in the old oak fireplace, and ivy and greenery were draped on the banisters.

'How wonderful to see you both,' she said, taking their coats. 'And Peter – it's marvellous to see you after all this time.'

'You too,' said Peter, blushing. 'You haven't changed at all, Minki.'

'The house looks lovely,' said Leila. 'I love all the greenery.'

Minki laughed. 'Clara and I got a bit carried away.'

'How is Clara?' asked Leila anxiously.

'Come and see...'

Minki led them into the drawing room. The three children were playing a game of cards with Gunther. He stood up when the visitors arrived. 'Leila, how lovely. And this must Peter?' He held out his hand to the younger man.

'It's good to finally meet you, sir,' said Peter. 'I've heard a lot about you.'

'All good, I hope. Now, Champagne I think...'

As Gunther handed round the glasses, Leila took Minki to one side. 'Peter's rather nervous. He's worried you two won't get on.'

Minki smiled. 'How sweet,' she whispered. 'I'll have a word... So, Peter, it really is wonderful to see you. It must be what... twenty years?'

'Twenty-one,' replied Peter, blushing.

'Peter has brought a jeep filled with food and drink,' said Leila, sensing his embarrassment. 'Peter, why don't you go and bring it inside and take it to the kitchen.'

'I'll come and help you,' said Gunther, and the pair went off together, leaving Minki and Leila in the sitting room.

'Minki, I can't get over the difference in Clara,' Leila murmured.

'I know,' Minki replied. 'Isn't she marvellous?'

Clara was wearing a dark-green velvet dress. She had put on a little weight, Leila thought, and her skin was glowing.

When Gunther and Peter returned, the children demanded their grandfather return to the card game. To Leila's amazement, Clara was not the timid, nervous child she had found in Hadamar. Instead, she held her own against her brothers as they played a noisy, competitive game of rummy.

'I think she's slowly coming back to us,' said Minki. 'And it's you I have to thank.' She kissed Leila's cheek, and hugged her tightly.

Later that evening, after their meal of ham and turkey, washed down by American wine, they all gathered in the sitting room. While the children decided what games to play, Peter sat down next to Minki on the sofa. 'It's been a wonderful day. I'm so happy to see you,' he whispered.

'And I you, Peter. Not least, because... if it wasn't for you, I might not have found my child.'

'Well it was Leila who actually found her, but eventually I guess I would have discovered that Irma was Clara.'

'Why don't we do the washing-up?' Minki suggested. 'Our housekeeper has taken Christmas off, so there's no one to do it but me.'

'Sure,' said Peter, 'happy to help.'

Leila looked over as the pair stood up to leave the room.

'Peter and I are just going to tidy up,' said Minki. 'You stay here in the warm, and keep my father company.'

In the kitchen, the plates were piled high on the draining board.

'I'll wash, and you dry,' said Minki. 'Here's a towel.'

They chatted easily. The twenty-year gap between their first love and now seemed to disappear.

'I don't want to dwell on the past,' Minki ventured at one point, 'but there are one or two things I still don't understand about what Clara went through and how she survived.'

'Go on,' said Peter.

'Well, for a start – why wasn't she killed with the others?'

'I think perhaps it was luck. She arrived after they had stopped exterminating people on arrival. Then I gather that a member of staff chose to keep her alive – either to protect her or because she was more useful as a slave.'

Minki shuddered slightly. 'I hate that word... slave.'

'I'm sorry,' said Peter, putting his arm round her. 'That was clumsy. Forgive me.'

'What I still can't work out,' she went on, 'is that when I went to Hadamar they insisted she was dead. Why not admit she was alive and let me take her, there and then?'

'There could be many reasons. But perhaps they were scared of recriminations – you had mentioned you were a friend of Goebbels', after all. What you have to remember is that these people had a sense of their own omnipotence. No one ever questioned them. They had free rein to do what they liked.'

'It just makes me so angry to think of all the years she was trapped there – years of unimaginable suffering and loneliness – years she should have spent at home with us.' She looked up into Peter's eyes. 'I'll never forgive myself. I should have searched that place from top to bottom. Instead of which, I believed them when they said she was dead. I was completely taken in. At the most important time in my life, when I should have used all my critical faculties, I behaved like a stupid, foolish woman.'

Peter reached out to her and she fell, sobbing, into his arms. 'No one could ever describe you as either stupid or foolish, Minki darling.' He held her close and kissed her hair. 'Don't punish yourself. This wasn't your fault. Hundreds, thousands of children were in the same position. Many parents came looking for their kids and were sent away empty-handed. Most of their children were murdered within moments of arriving. Clara, if you like, had a lucky break. She survived. I know you can't see it like that yet, but that's how you have to think of it. And don't forget – you were up against a powerful organisation which held all the cards.'

'I suppose so.' She took a handkerchief from her sleeve, blew her nose and wiped her eyes.

'I'm curious about something,' said Peter, 'and please tell me to mind my own business if it upsets you... but did you think of checking to see who was buried in the coffin – the coffin they sent to you?'

Minki nodded. 'Oh yes. A few days after Clara had been returned, and I had finally come down from my sense of elation, it suddenly struck me that we had buried someone else's relative. That another family were suffering as we had – not knowing what had happened to a person they loved.'

'What did you do?'

'I had the coffin exhumed, of course.'

'And?'

'My father was very upset about it – he thought it was sacrilegious. But I had to do it... I had to know who was in there. I'll never forget that day... the lid was finally heaved off, and I was braced... you know... for a terrible stench, or at least a poor shrivelled body. But there was nothing – it was just full of earth.'

'That's unbelievable. They obviously felt they had to send you something. But what a risk they took. I mean, what if you'd opened the coffin sooner, the whole scandal might have come out. I suppose it shows how invincible they felt.'

'It was a relief in some ways, of course. But then I thought of all the other families who had lost someone at Hadamar, and never found out what had happened. They all deserve justice, Peter.'

'I agree. I'm doing my best to give that justice to everyone who was killed there. We're digging up every grave, but it's a massive, painstaking task.'

Minki put down her scrubbing brush, leaned over and kissed Peter's cheek. 'I'm so glad you're working there. You're a man of honour and dignity, doing what you can to give honour and dignity back to all those unfortunate people.' She smiled briefly, and resumed the washing-up.

Peter blushed. 'That's a sweet thing to say...' He paused. 'Minki, there's something I've been wanting to say to you all day.'

'Go on.'

'I'm so sorry I left you back then before the war. I've never really forgiven myself for it. It was selfish of me, and cruel.'

'Oh, Peter, please don't worry about that. We were both so young and I was a bit wild – I can see that now. I suspect I frightened you off. I was so in love with you though.'

'I loved you too and yet I abandoned you. And that's what I can't forgive myself for. If I'd taken you with me... things would have been so different. I could have saved you all this grief.'

'You know, Peter – I don't do "what if". I never have. We play the hand we're dealt in life, not the hand we want. Besides, if I'd married you, I wouldn't have had my children. And however much sadness there has been, Clara and the boys have been my greatest joy.'

She put her arms round his neck and kissed his cheek. 'Don't regret anything, Peter. Let's just enjoy what we have now.'

'Do you think one day... we might...?'

She held up her finger and put it to his mouth. 'Sssh... don't say it. We don't know what the future holds, let's just wait and see, all right?'

'All right,' he replied, kissing her fleetingly on the mouth.

The washing up completed, the pair returned to the sitting room. 'Mutti, Mutti, there you are,' Felix shouted excitedly. 'Come and play with us.'

Minki laughed. 'All right – what are we playing?'

'Knock-out whist,' shouted Willie. 'We can all play.'

Minki sat down next to Clara, with Peter on her other side.

The game went on for some time, with players gradually being knocked out. Finally, there were just two left – Clara and her brother Felix. When Felix lost the final hand, Clara leapt to her feet. 'I won, Mutti... I won.'

'You did darling,' said Minki, her eyes filling with tears.

Leila turned to Minki and whispered in her ear: 'I think you have both won, don't you?'

'I do, Leila. I really do.'

A LETTER FROM DEBBIE

Thank you for choosing to read *The German Mother*. I hope you enjoyed it; if you would like to keep up with all my latest releases, just sign up at the following link. Your email address will never be shared, and you can unsubscribe at any time.

www.bookouture.com/debbie-rix

I stood in a cemetery at the top of a hill in a small town in central Germany called Hadamar, and wept. As a mother, I tried to understand how it would have felt to discover your child was buried here; a child who had been wrenched away from you by the government, and put to death – for no other reason than they had a slight learning difficulty, a disability, or an inherited illness like epilepsy. In Hitler's Germany many thousands of children were murdered in this way, leaving their families heartbroken and bereft.

Having visited this graveyard, and the hospital in whose grounds it stood, I knew this was a story I had to tell. What intrigued me, apart from the obvious human tragedy, was how a government had been able to convince the population of Germany that the state had the right to remove these children from their families – in the first instance to sterilise them, but ultimately to exterminate them. In some cases the children were removed by force, but many families permitted their children to be taken, somehow persuaded by government propaganda that their own children needed specialist treatment. By the time they discovered their children were dead, protest was pointless.

The 'Mother' in the title encompasses not just the two mothers who feature in this story – Minki and Leila – but all the mothers in Germany who were persuaded to give up their children for the 'greater good of society.'

The German Mother might be an emotionally challenging read at times, but this relatively unknown story of Nazi atrocity needs to be told. We need to be reminded of the horrors that powerful political ideologues are capable of inflicting on their fellow human beings.

I hope you enjoy the novel, and if you do, please leave a review on Amazon so that others might be attracted to this story.

Best wishes,

Debbie Rix

www.debbierix.com

facebook.com/DebbieRixAuthor

twitter.com/debbierix

HISTORICAL NOTE

I was inspired to write this novel some years ago when I read about a German Jewish journalist called Jella Lepman. As the women's editor of a national newspaper, she was forced to flee Germany in the mid-1930s with her two young children and seek refuge in London. During the war years she worked as an announcer in the newly created BBC German Service. After the war she returned to her homeland, to assist the American authorities with the process of de-Nazification.

Taking Jella as the inspiration for my central character Leila, I decided to set the novel in Munich. The city was the political birthplace of Hitler's fascism, and I was keen to explore his trial through the eyes of Leila and her newspaper colleagues. By positioning her at the *Munich Post*, I was able to reflect the remarkable story of that newspaper and its fight for truth and justice. The paper was founded by the leader of the Social Democratic Party in Munich, Erhard Auer, and was a beacon of liberal truth, opposing the rise of Hitler's National Socialist Party. Their most memorable headline, 'We will not be intimidated', was printed just six days before they were finally closed down by the authorities on 9 March 1933.

Leila's newspaper colleagues in my novel are all 'real people'. In addition to Auer himself, Martin Gruber was the editor, Julius Zerfass was the arts correspondent and Edmund Goldschagg was the political editor. The incidents that I describe in the novel – the attacks on the newspaper, the imprisonment of Zerfass – are all factually based.

Of course, as this is a novel, I have had to imagine their personalities and conversations. But all the *Munich Post*'s headlines, and much of the copy in the book, are taken from the actual newspaper editions of the time.

I wanted to contrast Leila with a woman who might not be so straightforward, nor sympathetic. As I read about various female journalists working at the time in Nazi Germany, I came upon Ursula von Kardorff. Ursula's background was politically conflicted. Her father was an ardent critic of the regime, while her mother was a supporter. Ursula considered herself to be a simple German nationalist, not a Nazi. And although she started her journalistic career working for the Nazi Party paper, *Der Angriff*, she spent most of her career at the centrist *Deutsche Allgemeine Zeitung*, working in the features section. Ursula became the basis of my portrayal of Minki. I saw her as a woman who felt herself to be above politics, initially refusing to take sides, but who ultimately would be forced to choose between right and wrong. Minki's child Clara is entirely fictitious, although her fate is heavily based on historical fact.

Inevitably, you can't write a novel about journalism during the Second World War without exploring the role propaganda played during those years. Both sides in this conflict – the Germans and the Allies – used various techniques to control the flow of information, but none so well as the Germans' propagandist-in-chief, and 'master' of the dark arts, Dr Joseph Goebbels.

An academic and intellectual with a PhD in philosophy from Heidelberg University, Goebbels was a frustrated novelist and playwright. As a young man he was also something of a professional failure, having been fired from his only job as a bank clerk. A true socialist at heart, he had been radicalised, to some extent, by the fact that his home state of the Rhineland was handed over to French control in the early 1920s when the German government was unable to pay their reparations from the Great War. On a trip to Munich he saw the rising political star Adolf Hitler speaking at a rally. Hitler appeared to be offering men like Goebbels the chance to rescue their national pride, and soon Goebbels became enmeshed in the fledgling National Socialist Party – himself speaking at rallies, and running his local branch of the Party. Hitler clearly saw Goebbels' raw talent, and quickly promoted him through the National Socialist ranks. When Hitler came to power in 1933, he appointed the young Goebbels Reichsminister for Propaganda. Within weeks, Goebbels brought the press, film industry and radio under government control.

There is no doubting the man's brilliance – Goebbels almost literally wrote the playbook on how to totally control the media. But what particularly interested me about him was how someone could be prepared to use his talents to such evil ends. Was it simply the lure of power? Or did he truly espouse the policies and beliefs that Hitler embodied? I suspect it was the latter – demonstrated most profoundly when, in the final days of the war, Goebbels and his wife Magda murdered their six children and then committed suicide themselves, rather than submit to a world without the Führer.

By making Goebbels a character in my novel, I throw myself open to criticism – how could I possibly know how Goebbels might have reacted or behaved in certain situations? Of course, I can't, but I have been able to draw on his extensive diaries, and where possible I have based dialogue in the novel on his own diary entries.

Other characters in the novel are also based on real people:

Ruth Andreas-Friedrich ran the resistance group Uncle Emil. Its members were mostly writers, artists and professionals, who protected Jewish citizens from the Nazi regime by hiding them in Ruth's apartment. Through their network of forgers they obtained false ration books, papers and documents, which ultimately enabled many Jews to escape Germany.

REFERENCES

In the course of researching this story I have been helped by the following reference books:

Andreas-Friedrich, Ruth. *Berlin Underground 1938–1945*. St Paul, MN: Paragon House, 1989.

Lepman, Jella. *A Bridge of Children's Books*. Leicester: Brockhampton Press, 1969. Jella Lepman's own story of how she brought children's literature to post-war Germany.

Longerich, Peter. *Goebbels*. London: Vintage, 2016. A brilliantly written biography of Dr Goebbels.

Petty, Terrence. *The Enemy of the People*. New York: Associated Press, 2019. A fascinating account of the rise and fall of the *Munich Post*.

Thomas, Katherine (aka Jella Lepman). *Women in Nazi*

Germany. London: Victor Gollancz Ltd, 1944 (out of print).

I would also like to express my thanks to the museum at Hadamar, which documents the horrific crimes against young children and adults in the name of euthanasia.

ACKNOWLEDGEMENTS

As always, I am indebted to my publisher Bookouture, and in particular my editor Natasha Harding, for their unfailing support. My thanks also go to their social media and marketing team for the work they put in around the launch of every novel.

I would also like to thank my family for their unwavering support. My husband – himself a journalist – is always my first reader and I value his views and critical eye.

Finally, my sincere thanks go to all the readers who have supported my storytelling journey, and who have left reviews and sent me private messages of thanks and encouragement.